# Hot Berry Punch

Bradford Tatum

**Hot Berry Punch**



Soft Moon Press
Los Angeles, California
softmoonpress@gmail.com

ISBN: 979-8-9887423-0-2 (Trade Paperback)
ISBN: 979-8-9887423-1-9 (eBook)

Publisher's Cataloging-In-Publication Data
Names: Tatum, Bradford, 1965 March 29- author.
Title: Hot berry punch : a novel / Bradford Tatum.
Description: Los Angeles, California : Soft Moon Press, [2023]
Identifiers: ISBN: 979-8-9887423-0-2 (trade paperback) | 979-8-9887423-1-9 (ebook)
Subjects: LCSH: Women—West (U.S.)—History—19th century—Fiction. | Vampires—Fiction. | Man-woman relationships—Fiction. | Desire—Fiction. | Frontier and pioneer life—West (U.S.)—Fiction. | LCGFT: Paranormal fiction. | Bildungsromans. | BISAC: FICTION / Literary. | FICTION / Coming of Age. | FICTION / Fantasy / Paranormal.
Classification: LCC: PS3620.A893 H68 2023 | DDC: 813/.6—dc23

*"Oh, love isn't there to make us happy. I believe it exists to show us how much we can endure."*

Hermann Hesse

*"A creature in the shape of a woman. What it was God knows."*

The Bourgeois of Paris, 1492

*For Sophia Mikal-*
*who has beguiled me since the night she was born.*

# A Country So Still Even The Angels Had Lost Interest

# Chapter One

I was born ignorant.

Nothing augured my fate. No hellhounds bayed upon their misty moors, and no frantic bats fled their belfries like cracks through a twilight teacup when I first tasted the ethers of this world. There was nothing in my birth that would have ever suggested a prolonged association with despair, bloody death, or horror. Any more than there was evidence that my life would be dedicated toward a constant pursuit of love and being loved.

I dropped out of my momma in a hot month sometime in the 1820s, on an anonymous swath of prairie, in what was then still an unbroken and unallied parcel of the country. I was christened Emma May Shinnecock by a half-sober Calvinist preacher, whose family was making the same ill-conceived overland trek as my own. They, like my momma and Da, were faltering in their faith that they would discover a new life among the mum buffalo grass, and only my birth, up to that point in the journey, provided the empirical evidence that such a tenuous faith could actually endure. Being the sign of that faith was the first among my many unasked for burdens.

I always hated my name. Emma May. Emma *May*. The internal alliteration, the almost stutter of the thing, made me feel unfinished. Which I imagine was only proper as I came from parents who, in their own half-finished ways, were as psychologically tentative as myself.

My mother's name was Cora Mayfield Spotswood. She had black, serious eyes and hair of a similar hue that kinked at even the suggestion of inclement weather. And she was a large woman, in both her body and convictions. She was the youngest and tallest of three daughters, who could claim lineage to the first rebels of Concord. Her parents were educators, liberal bluenoses who made it a point to set a place for whatever Protestant-educated black was inclined to break bread each Christmas Eve at Cora's house. She credited the precepts of Olympe de Gouges for keeping her free from the leers of males. But in truth, her lack of partners in pants was really a function of the epic profundity of her hamlike hocks. A full figure may have been fashionable, but the citadel of flesh she sedulously constructed was not built to entice physical intimacy but rather repel it. Her perfect love would have been spiritual in passion and bloodless in nature, where the only fluids exchanged would have been ink and sealing wax and perhaps the occasional tear. At her parent's fêtes and fundraisers, she was never asked to dance. Thoroughly wallflowered, she would ride out the waltzes and quadrilles with a fork and a wedge of vanilla cake the size of a mason's trowel. It seemed the more she ate the more spectral she became. And as her generous invisibility made her unassailable, it was only logical to send her to the more dangerous quadrants of the city, where her parent's charitable work was its most effective. She found herself in brothels and barrooms, slums and billiard rooms, as conspicuous as fogged breath in a blizzard. It was only when she began spending her midnights distributing children's shoes at the docks of Long Wharf that anyone answering to even a loose description of a man took any notice of her.

Such a man was my father, Silas Leviticus Shinnecock. And by Christ, never was a man more ironically named. Or whomever had named him had never read that book of the Bible that matched his middle moniker with its thunderous forbidding of every physical pleasure. For Silas Shinnecock would fuck anything. "The son of any mother," as he was fond of calling himself, he was raised in the briny squalor of a Portsmouth brothel by four whores all of whom had the opportunity, if not the inclination, to claim kinship to him. He'd been rocked to sleep by the syncopated brass of their beds, their consummating howls, mostly counterfeit, his first lullabies. At thirteen he was hired as a cooper's mate on an American slaver and soon became as handy and adventurous with a chisel as he was with his own member. Knot holes in the yardarms were not safe from his seed. And stories abounded as to the true reasons behind the labored gaits and skittish glances of cabin boys who seemed to jump ship at every new port. Simply put, on the evening their eyes first met, my father was suspected of indecent congress with a Lebanese water boy, losing in the process his standing on his ship's log and in desperate need of legitimizing female ballast. And my mother, at twenty-eight, the only one of her sisters still unwed, understood better than most the obligatory nature of marriage for those women who resided outside of the pages of novels. So perhaps they were just life boats for one another. Or maybe they were much more than that. Maybe she was, as my father once confessed to me, "the lovely loom gale that blew (him) toward (his) new horizon." And I suspect my mother's feelings for him ran deeper than the mere corrective. She was a robust woman, after all, a whole head taller than he and at least twenty pounds heavier. But whatever her reasons were for marrying him, it was not coercion. Nor was it the sex. For my mother, who only understood the progenitorial burden of the act, never the allure, it was at first a trial (like some feverish intestinal disorder), then a tedium (like prayers before bedtime), but never a pleasure. I've always felt sorry for her for that.

Silas had seen too much of the civilized world and Cora was fed up with that world's constant contradictions, so it was decided they would do what few of the innocent and the jaded were doing in those days. They would swap the raw disappointments of their respective pasts for a shared terror of the future and go West. Da accepted his yoke as a landsman by trading the pickled eel skin that once kept his long hair from his face for a wideawake hat and a pair of mule-eared boots. He had a greasy copy of *Fanny Hill*, a pristine copy of the Bible, an axe, and several saws of various tooth and gap. His compact chest of woodworking tools. With his parting wages he bought a long-stocked Pennsylvania flintlock (with powder, lead, and a bullet mold), a cast iron stove, and secondhand bed. *Kill, Cook, and Copulate* could have been the credo tattooed across his sinewy chest.

My mother brought a little more. A camphor chest of primers, chapbooks, and stuffy tomes on history and philosophy. (For my education when I came to be.) A brush, button hook, and hand mirror set of stamped silver. (To keep her prettied up, even if her nearest neighbor was a prairie dog twitching on a hunk of buffalo shit.) And her party frock of champagne charmeuse. (Had this dress ever known a touch? A blush? Any real real joy? Why she brought it I could not possibly guess.) She also packed in straw various unguents and creams in pretty porcelain jars she took as a balm against her skin's proclivity toward ash. And as the sole concession to her future as help-meet, bed-mate, and all around drudge, a cast iron frying pan. The horse and buckboard had been a reluctant wedding present from her family.

I still cannot imagine why they did it. An eighteen-month overland trip traveling at an average speed of five miles per hour over terrain so pitted and rocky it would take hours for the nerves to stop stuttering once they had settled for the night. And how much worse for my mother with me sloshing around inside her like a malignant pickle in a jar as she was jerked and jostled all the daylit hours. When I first questioned her about the crossing (I must have been ten or eleven years old.) I remember her using words like "uneventful" and "arduous." But upon later tellings, years after the emptiness and open spaces had swallowed the last of her decorum, she would roar like a momma bear on a bad scent and confess to a paralyzing fear of the Indians, a nightly, almost stultifying regret, and hemorrhoids so adamant they made the hard bench of their buckboard as fiery as a gas ring.

"And it wasn't just the constant jostling or the squatting in the buffalo grass with your skirts up over your ears, planting your filth in all that gaping greenery," she would say. "Or the wind that would come up from a clear day and blow your limbs senseless. Or the rain or the heat. Or the limited culinary diversions. God no, child. It was the *silence.* Your father and I shared perhaps twenty words between us in those first seven months. So I suppose a frank report of the journey could never be made with words. It must be orchestrated, perhaps, compiled of *rhythms.* If one were asked to describe the crossing, I suppose one would have to hum it. Grunt it. Growl it out. Then *shush* it." She was sometimes given to these stark poetics, even when describing the simplest things. She was a dedicated reader of Montaigne, her favorite quote being, "Lend yourself to others—but *give* yourself to yourself." She never, in all my memories of her, spoke to me as if I were a child. She felt it was her duty to be inconvenienced by life's difficulties. Perhaps that was the only motive force she took from the feral liberalism of her upbringing, that one *owes* the future. And that future, as cumbersome as I might have been, was me. But my father was not seeking the future. That would take care of itself. Denied his true love, the sea, he sought the next best thing: a verdant, rippling landlessness that could only attempt to fill him.

*Memory, a reconstruction:* I am a child, bare-chested and sunburnt, big bellied as a butcher, with my homespun knickers ripe with a fresh dump. We are out at dawn, collecting dried buffalo turds for burning. My father had made a wheeled barrow for the purpose. He crouches in the high grass as my mother bends to lift another stiff patty.

"You see that, child," he whispers to me, pointing to nothing, to everything. "Look there, my girl. That horizon. Sweet cunny of dreaming Christ, child. (*Silas, language!)* So like the sea." But I have no reference for the sea. I think it is the grass itself that whispers. "Close your eyes, my duck." And I close them. The morning sun is soft upon my eyelids. "Listen. You hear that? The shushing of these tall green waves?"

"*Susurration,*" my mother says, shaking her hands from the surprise of a particularly wet patty.

"Wha?" my father says, squinting up at her.

"The sound. That shushing sound. It's called—"

"Ah, leave off, woman," he says, chuckling. "What use are your prissy words when the very *air* knows the truth of itself? Them wormy tomes yer packin' will know their real worth as the bright side of a fire once the weather turns, mark me."

And her eyes. My mother's eyes. So wide with dread I think her lids might rend should they stretch any farther to swallow the regret inside her.

Like any young sprout, I reckon I loved my folks apart much more than together. Visiting their separate poles was easy. It was venturing into the equatorial friction of their combined *terra incognito* that made me uneasy. I didn't know then that I would one day ingest a similar polarity into myself. And that attaining the far shore of any kind of reconciliation between my two selves would prove the effort of all my coming days.

Occasionally they met fellow pilgrims during their crossing. Men as weathered as dry gullies and women weathered to the dimensions of men. Slapped dumb by months of hard daylight, they might stop. Share a story or a warning. Trade with or dismiss one another. There was always some kind of exchange. My mother lost her real pearl button hook at such a meeting. Traded it for a stout needle and ten spools of thread after my father lost a fly button off his only pair of trousers. She would have traded her whole toilet for that slender shaft of metal if it meant delaying his annoying carnal attentions even a second more.

Then I came. It was an etiquette on the open plains to mock potential misfortune. And so my father japed that "death stood in the high grass whistlin' a cullin' tune." My mother may have smiled. The probability that I, or both my mother and I, would die during the endeavor was exceedingly high. Near everyone they crossed had mumbled a confusing good-bye to a being they had selflessly loved but had never met. But my mother was not worried about the statistics. "There was a Delphic luster in your coming, Emma," she told me once. "An unnamable necessity that you *be*." Her expectations were thus freighted upon me before we even shared the same air. If she must give birth, fine. She simply, emphatically, did not want to be observed while doing it. That her potential audience would be the blind sky or an improbably curious rabbit did not dissuade her. She was always a modest woman, which was problematic given how much of her there was. She initially wanted to hide herself under the wagon when the first contractions came. But she could not fit under the axels, not with her knees to heaven. So she stripped to her drawers and chemise and removed her corset, which did indeed possess the width and integrity of a music hall's safety curtain, and had my father string this between two pitiful cottonwoods.

"Over there, Silas."

"Wha?"

"Stand over there! Avert that glutted gaze! I can't—*My Redeemer!*"

"If ye're afreared I'll be put off ye feminine bits after yer trial, I can assure ye—"

"No! *God,* no, Silas. *That* I would catalogue as the purest of blessings!"

"Crippled Christ woman! 'Tis a father's *right* to see the little beauty crown."

"You *mind* me, Silas Shinnecock, and make yourself scarce!" she shrieked. "Or I *swear* by His holy tears, if I survive this, I shall stitch my knees together and damn you to the unnatural receptacles of your youth! Eeeyah!" In the end, he held her hand beneath the tails of her corset strings while she screamed and cursed and cried to the bald sky above her. When I came crackling into the world, my father howled in triumph, running for his jug in the back of our wagon, me dangling from the thin crook of his elbow like a rasher of side pork.

"Silas! Deliver her to me at *once*!" Weak from strain and loss of blood, my mother still had her claws where untoward inebriation was concerned. My father obliged, sinking to his knees and depositing me on her still prodigious if more flexible belly before assuming his place on the other side of the corset.

"Mind ye paps," my father said like a confessor through the screen of the corset's laces. "Ye milk willna flow till ye pass ye puddin'." He was referring to the placenta. Having witnessed as a boy countless bastard births, he had earned the stripes of any midwife. But Mother would not be told.

"We are perfectly content, Silas. Your instigations are no longer required. *Ow!* Sweet mercy! Lightly with the jaws there, my dove. Sing something appropriate, Silas, if you insist on being useful."

We met the preacher who baptized me and his wife twice. The first time, days after my birth over a neighborly crock of travel-heated applejack where he christened me *Emma*, a name Da composed by taking the first letter from the names of each of the whores who had raised him and *May* which was all of my mother's *Mayfield* that my father could abide. A week later we met again. We came upon the abandoned hull of their wagon one gray morning, still smoking translucently in the soft morning sun. It had been set aflame but had failed to burn in the previous evening's rain. His wife was in pieces. But the preacher's body was just beginning to stiffen beneath the wet shroud of flies that covered it in the tall grass where it lay. The top of his head was missing, the edges of his ravaged scalp a hard red. He had six arrows in his chest and the tops of his thighs, and the width of his belly had been opened. I know now why his attackers had done this. Holes in a man's fallen body would keep him from walking the good red road of the afterlife. And with no death songs to announce him, he would stay a captive of the soil, his soul a feast fit only for foxes.

"Silas, we must bury them."

"They'll be buried enough in a wolf or vulture's belly come sundown."

"Bury them *now* or I shan't travel another league!"

My father must have complied for he lost the nail of his left index finger in the ordeal. The nail never grew back properly.

# Chapter Two

My father built our house in the middle of the North Atlantic. Or in the antelope shit, grasshopper-hull, east of bumfuck equivalent. He had chosen the seemingly most remote spot he could find, a spot where the eye would never be encumbered by a tree or even a clump of cone flower. My mother's hopes of a prettily brambled homestead evaporated with her sweat as he pitched the dirty canvas tent that would be our only shelter for as long it would take him to build our cabin. Ours would be a view seen from the crow's nest, ten days out of port that spoke not of desolation and mind-numbing expanse, but one his salted heart recognized and loved. The site's only concession to our survival was a spring-melt creek hidden below the south bluff. Sod, wrestled into vague brick-like shapes, would be the building material of choice for estates like ours. But my father would put his faith in nothing but wood. He kicked the buckboard from the bow of our wagon. With the aide of his tools and not a single nail, he bored and pegged and honed that buckboard into an ingenious shovel in less than a full afternoon. My mother stood half swallowed by the swaying switch grass, acquainting herself, yet again, with disappointment. She felt as lost as a sole survivor while he plotted out what would be the perimeter of our home with the dragged heel of his boot. And upon my mother's approval of the dimensions—despite her horror, fear, and regret—he began digging. When he'd cut a square trench as deep as his knees, he began looking for rocks. These, once found and fumbled to the site, he crushed with his mallet and poured into the trench as aggregate.

"We'll have near two stories, my girls," he said. "A full floor for day and a sleeping loft for them *cozy* nights!" He then took his axe, a tool he respected like a fair but fruitful god, and, leading the horse by its jaw, disappeared over the low hills.

My mother did little but weep and eat the full four days he was gone. She rinsed my soiled knickers in the cold creek water, but there was no joy in my nakedness. She cooked her daily meals of beans and hard tack in glum silence, examining with mute amazement the intricacies of the flintlock my father had left us. She hadn't the least intention of using it should necessity arise. Under the relentless sun, we both tanned deeply. The oil she rubbed into my soft skin ran like hot frosting off my shoulders, diluted from her tears.

She did her best to entertain me.

She wove tiny teacups and saucers from buffalo grass. I sipped a "tea" of hot air while she gently attempted to curl the pinky of my cup hand. In the late afternoons, she blubbered through a chapter of Malory's *Le Morte d'Arthur* until I napped. We bathed in the creek only at night. And even then, she always had her back to me. Each morning she laced and buttoned herself into proper attire as if the stark prairie had enough eyes or wits to offer her even fleeting approval.

Da finally returned with a load of cottonwood, four teenaged trees felled and stripped and squared by his solitary zeal. And he did this twenty more times until the grass around our camp yellowed beneath a small forest of drying timbers. If my mother was not impressed by his efforts, she was at least grateful for them, for his exertions left him too limp to ravish her at day's end.

He built our cabin like the pyramids, rolling the logs into place on huge dowels of stripped trees and then pushing the notched logs into place off shallow ramps he built from wagon scrap. When the work progressed above his head, he cheated gravity with the cantilevers of da Vinci's day. I was fascinated by the contraption and wanted to spend my days watching the dead forests rise into the air. I loved the creak of the straining pulley. The feel of the rough hemp of the rope that reminded me of my Momma's wooly hair. My first full sentence was, "Belay that blasted beam!" This quickly led to my first lessons in letters. So with chalk in my small fist and a slate on my lap, I dreamed of my midday break, when I could watch Da work and maybe even be trusted to hoist him an augur, mallet, or deliciously sharp chisel.

It took the best part of a year for the walls to settle in place, another several months for the logs to properly season. My father's skill as a cooper had made him a killer of light. Nothing, not even wishes, could pass through his joins. I was past six by this time and had graduated to Da's journeyman. I quoted Shakespeare and bits of Marlowe while I deftly chiseled end notches and whittled pegs.

"How you do that, Da?" I asked, looking at the smooth circumference of a wash barrel he had just built.

"Your Da ran molasses and monkeys when he was a lad."

"Silas!" my mother would hiss reproachfully.

"For molasses ye need a barrel and for barrels ye need a cooper."

"What about monkeys?" I may have asked.

"Just the lash, my girl."

"Silas! That will do. I'll not have her hardened by your ignorance. They are people, Emma. Do you hear? *People.* Every atom equal to us. Our aspects and customs would seem just as barbarous to them had they the misfortune of meeting *us*, believe me. It is the injustice of this so called 'civilized' world that has trapped them between dire intertribal economics and an odious American agrarian tradition. But they demand our respect nonetheless."

"Those blasted savages? *Coo*, woman. Them poxy beaches wher'in they frolic would make this plain seem a regular Camelot."

"Need I remind you, Silas, that Africa has sired at least *two* of the greatest civilizations on God's green earth? Medicine, geometry, and astronomy are but a few of the intellectual debts we owe that continent. Not to mention the glory of Alexandria that was once the repository of all we value as human. What could the dreary shores of your beloved England attest to beyond serial buggery and rampant inebriation!"

"Caw! Was merely a jape, woman!"

"And just how many sins has joking succored? You're a fool, Silas Shinnecock, if you think she doesn't take what you say to heart!" She was right. I took all they said to heart. I knew even then there was woe in wonder and wonder in woe. Wrong and right were like two hungry wolves fighting over a rabbit's carcass. Each side showed its teeth, but neither side gave a thought to the poor rabbit.

Even after our cabin was finished, my father would still not allow its tenancy. After years of the sky's rude gaze, my mother was desperate for a roof. "She ain't quite seaworthy yet," my father answered to my mother's frustrated whine. He had found a tar pit not far from the head water of our creek and never was there a more glorious day for him. He came home, grinning like the cat with the prize canary, a bucket full of midnight-colored slop in his grip.

"Now what on earth do you intend to do with that filth, Silas?"

"Seal them chinks, woman. 'Twill have 'er runnin' yar in no time."

"Seal them from what?" my mother griped. "You can hardly think we'll face a nor'easter upon this rambling dunghill. You promised me a home, Silas, not a reeking pillow in the rectum of Eden. And look at poor Emma, scabby and thick with dirt. Running around like a scrub jay from dawn to dusk." But I had no complaints. My father looked at me and winked.

"Oy, now, Cora," my Da said with a slight tuck of his weak chin. "I promised ye love undying and adventure everlasting." He cackled. "I never said nothing 'bout no worldly comforts."

He cut small ricks of tallgrass and let them dry in the sun. These he minced and then stewed in the tar he heated over a small fire. He called it *oakum*, said there was nothing better to arrest a leak in weather fair or foul. My mother and I watched him in horror as he lathered the pungent glop along every join of our new home. When he had finished, our house resembled a demonic wedding cake. Not cured in seawater, the cabin bled black in the sun. It did keep out the rain and wind. But in the summer it was stifling. That was when my father built first a ladder of split logs and rails and then a kind of sleeping porch on our roof. He carpeted the roof with sod. Summer became my favorite time of year, when my father and I could sleep on a soft, elevated square of prairie flowers, away from the nettles and night crawlers, closer to the breeze, closer to the shock of summer stars. Away from my mother. But if my father thought he had won me squarely to his side, he was wrong. Many a summer night, while he snored to high heaven, I'd soothe myself to sleep with Caliban's pretty speech from *The Tempest*:

> *Be not afeard; the isle is full of noises,*
> *Sounds and sweet airs, that give delight, and hurt not.*
> *Sometimes a thousand twangling instruments*
> *Will hum about mine ears; and sometime voices,*
> *That, if I then had wak'd after long sleep,*
> *Will make me sleep again; and then, in dreaming,*
> *The clouds methought would open, and show riches*
> *Ready to drop upon me; that, when I wak'd*
> *I cried to dream again.*

We lived on animals no larger than a house cat. Rabbits and prairie dogs. Baby badgers and squirrels. If the animal was not dispatched with a clean head shot, it was left to the crows. Anything other left pitiful little meat. A few times, if my father was quick enough, he would bring home a prairie chicken, and my mother would make soup. I remember spitting out the tiny gray vertebrae like the teeth of a barroom brawler. My father would pick up the theme and, pinwheeling his backward-facing fists Tom Cribb style, would jog around the walls of our finished house, sparring with the evening air, taking imaginary hits with exaggerated jerks of his head, spitting bone and blinking.

I remember laughing.

My mother's indulgent smirks.

Racing back to the table, my Da and I would lift our bowls to our mouths, Mother holding up our unused spoons with exhausted indignation, while we scrambled to see who would get the heart. Whoever had the chicken heart at the bottom of their bowl would be blessed with luck for the week. My mother would chide my father for his "superstitious imposition." But he would only grin. Invariably the heart would be in the bottom of my bowl. Holding up the pink gibbous nugget, I would bite it in two, tossing him half.

"Luck can be as good as labor, my girl," he'd say chewing, "if ye have her favor."

A few days, late in the summer, I remember seeing black clouds of buffalo on the low rise of distant hills, moving synchronized as starlings, forever out of our reach and off our plates. My father began collecting arrowheads for me. Muted pinks of jade, the glossy black of obsidian, chipped to lethal tips with tiny mouse bites. My mother hated these artifacts. Especially the real prizes, which were the arrowheads we found still lodged in the dry neck bones of the beasts. I thought the earth spit up the bone this way. I had no thought about the hands that had fashioned them, the bodies the hands belonged to, and how they were a constant but invisible presence, like the distance that fed my mother's bleakness.

Summer also meant visits from distant busters, trade, and new accents. My father swapped barrels he'd made or wagon repairs for feed and jugs and flour. The women sat stiffly in their wagons, glaring or gossiping, but the men—oh, how free and natural they seemed in their loose britches and sun-pinked suspenders, spitting, laughing, telling stories with broad and rude gestures, making the women suck their teeth or blush. My mother could tell from my enraptured grin and conspicuous loitering that I wanted to be just like those gents when I grew up.

As an antidote, my lessons in comportment began early.

I recited from a *Pearson's Primer* moral tales of virtuous turtles and jealous foxes. My father sliced crow feathers into quills at my mother's insistence. We made ink from boiled fat and milkweed flowers. My mother plied a perfect copperplate from my clumsy hands.

But I still had time to myself. Time to wander. Time for my *real* lessons. And I learned the world was most beautiful at a distance. Up close there was always something eating or being eaten. What looked like fur or feathers or scales was really a kind of armor, barely resistant to the gore that was the product of appetite. I knew fur rotted, but feathers never lost their luster. I knew beetles by their stink. An animal by the shape of its spoor. I got puke-sick on wild blackberries, learned to catch king snakes with a lightning pinch behind their jaws. I learned the adage, "Life is rooted in death's republic," from my mother and how to fish with gunpowder from my Da. And no matter how many times my mother made me recite sentences with the words "proper" and "young" and "lady" in them, my feet did not learn to speak shoes. Mine was a world of speed and freshness. I could run for leagues and feel I never moved, so changeless were my surroundings. And when my heart heated up, I would stop, swallowing birdsong until it slowed. I sought out nests for their stuffs. The smaller birds could be trusted to collect the softest bits of down for their nests, and these I stole and stuffed into the chest of my chemise. I would clump triumphantly home with my full, featherlight breasts like a Valkyrie, quoting Goethe. Da howled at my low music hall gaffs, while Momma applauded my perfect high German.

# Chapter Three

The world changed in winter. Became closer. Stronger smelling. Much more confusing. My father did not curb his carnal appetite in spite of my proximity. My parents slept in the loft and I on a mattress of feed sacks and straw near the stove on the ground floor. But the space was one. The only barrier the dark. Their voices were as clear as a church choir. Not long after sundown, the familiar discordant polyphony would begin.

"Oh, heavens, Silas," I would hear my mother say. "Again? At least be quick about it."

"Bless ye!" my father would whisper. "Ye know how ye addle me, my dove."

Wet kissing and dry shifting as the mesh of ropes beneath their mattress began to complain.

"At least attempt to dampen your usual enthusiasm, Mr. Shinnecock," my mother would sigh. "Remember the child."

"'Tis a natural education she be gettin' from us. Bit wider there, woman. *There's* a snug harbor!" And my mother would answer with a selection from Psalms or, if needed, Revelation.

Many times her belly swelled. She was sick first, in mornings and late afternoons, stopping her pounding of the laundry to spill a slosh of still-whole beans onto the grass. And for a month or so she might show. But never did she come to term. The life was too hard. Her chores too constant. At least that's what I thought until I found her special garden.

I was looking to wash the blood off. I had begun to bleed so was in my thirteenth year. I refused the wadded precautions mother insisted upon. You couldn't run or climb a tree with a hunk of worn sack squirreling your gait. So when it was my time, and if it were summer, I'd go about in the nude, letting the blood flow down my scabby legs as it may, washing in the cold creek only when the stickiness began to tempt the flies. I lived somewhat alone for those several days during my monthly troubles. I couldn't be near my father. Not if he had a mind to hunt. And I definitely did not care to endure another lesson in sanitary propriety from my mother. Did the prairie pups care if I trickled like a red creek? And so there I was, tanned dark and bug-bitten, knees scraped and elbows torn, happy as hell, soaking my nethers in the cold water, squinting against the lowering sun. She didn't hide the site well. Perhaps she hadn't meant to. Perhaps here was the lesson my Da's nighttime liberties couldn't teach. On the bank, in a clearing just off the bend, were three small mounds showered in wilting petals. Someone had taken care here. Someone had said good-bye. One mound was open, and as I approached, I saw a fox start and run into the shallow growth, dropping what had been in his jaws. A tiny skull, the teeth beds unbroken. Its dirt-caked upper jaw resembled the beak of a bird more than a human. The four panels of its cranium were still thin enough to let in the light. But I knew what it was. *Who* it was. My brother. My sister. Even tended as it was, with tamped dirt and wildflowers, I knew this was a factory of sorts, one that produced uncomplicated ends. For what were those purple-headed flowers that swayed so frolicsome in the breeze among the tiny graves? Squaw mint. Pennyroyal. Chew the leaves and it brings on the monthly cramps, my mother had taught me. Eat a bit more and the creature you carry will come early. And come still. Why was my mother killing her own children? Did she hate me so much that she would deny me the playful company of my own kin? I was young, but I remember that day among the small and pilfered graves being the first time I doubted my mother's sanity. I did not know then that real madness comes far more suddenly.

"Reflect on what you have read, Emma."

We are bare shouldered, our ankles cold in the creek.

"Which part, Momma?" We have been studying Plato's *Republic.*

"Any part that has piqued your interest." But only the hidden quarrel of the whippoorwill has piqued my interest. I am silent. I think on the water beneath my feet, the numbing current that flows yet remains unchanged, much like my mother's words.

"The cave then," she says impatiently. "What do you think the cave represents?"

"There was a cave?"

"Yes, Emma. There was a cave. And shadows and conversation and other pillars of modern polemic."

"I'm sorry, Momma."

My mother breathes deep. Her face is red, her breasts huge under the thin cotton of her chemise. "The cave is . . ." She waves a dragonfly off his trajectory. "The cave is *you,* Emma. The hidden part of you. That place of secret solitude, deep in your hollows." And her voice begins to trail off as her eyes glaze distractedly. "The cave is your . . . *cunt.*" She says this distinctly with a quiet curl of disgust. "Guard it, my daughter. Oh, the rude liberties we women must endure while attempting our rest are . . ." She blinks and looks at me as if I had just arrived. "Have you ever seen a man? Have you ever seen the dreary insistence that springs from a such a creature?" I am chilled suddenly in the sunshine. I don't know what she's talking about. Surely not that silly chicken neck I've seen my father pinch back into his britches after a good frothy piss. But she is becoming incensed now. "Have you? It's a simple yes or no."

"No." My lie is convincing.

"Silas!" my mother suddenly screams. She stomps up the embankment, not bothering to raise her wet skirts from the dust. What has riled her so? My heart races in my chest as I am forced to follow. I can see my father, shirtless, near the wood pile, his ropey muscles poised to split another chunk of cottonwood. She arrests him in mid-swing before he can split the waiting log on his stump.

"I want you to show her, Silas. She must be cautioned." My father senses her mania and tries to soothe her down.

"Ye've too much sun, my duck."

"Show her! Afford her this rough courtesy I was never given!"

"Easy, now, my love. Show her *what*?"

"Da," I caution.

"*Blecha beck*!" my mother screams nonsensically to the sky. "*Whemma heka shittaoook*!" And through her wet fricatives, I can make out no recognizable words. She is a jabbering Savonarola, furious in damp skirts, correcting nothing more than our shared confusion. She has the axe from Da's fingers before he can resist. She points a damning finger at the crux of his legs.

"Now, Cora! *Please!* What you're asking isn't reasonable. Or seemly."

"*Seemly*?" she asks, thundering back to her senses.

"Have I ever harmed you in my ardor?" Da whispers, shooting an uneasy glance at me. "Have I ever done anything but shown you how much I—?"

"Harmed me? With *your* pitiful member? How could you possibly have harmed me? You've *annoyed* me, Silas

L. Shinne*cock*! Fractured my nightly repose with your repetitive attentions, and I'll not have Emma similarly ambushed by any japing Johnny that might one day steal her affections! Now, show her that offending *tuber*, you gloating satyr, or by God I'll cleave the offending serpent from you!" And the smile flees from my father's face as she brandishes the axe at his groin.

"Christ woman! Have ye flown free of ye riggin'?"

"Momma, stop!" I scream. "I've seen it!"

"You *what*? Liar!" she booms, her dark eyes flashing hotly at me. Then, a hiccup of despair as her fury stumbles. "Silas! In what depravity have you lathered this child?" she sobs. My father stammers his defense. Only my voice stops her.

"I got a gander at it, Ma. Once. By accident. And, trust me, it ain't news!"

My father chuckles. She raises the axe, and he flees, his head hidden instinctively in the tangle of his elbows. He stops suddenly and she stalls, then she squares herself and swings. He ducks as fifteen pounds of honed steel sweeps the air above his cowering head.

*Whack!*

His slap is without anger, purely medicinal, but still he manages to land it squarely on the fleshy expanse of her cheek. For a moment, she is a child again, that child who was never taken over a knee or privy to a harsh word. Her hand leaps to her face. The axe falls to the ground. Then all childishness is gone.

"Silas!"

"I'm sorry, my love. But you left me little choice."

"Choice? *Choice*?" My mother's words are hot with flying spittle. "So you *chose* to break your vow to me? You *swore* you'd never strike me!"

I see the glimmer of panic in my father's pale eyes. He is a tall man, lean muscle and no chaff. But my mother has thirty pounds on him. She tucks the dirty hem of her skirt into her waist and raises her fists.

"Now, Cora. Be reasonable." But all that comes out of her is a warning growl I can feel to my back teeth. For the first time in my life, I see her spit into the dirt.

Books burn.

The Pantheon falls.

All civilization leaves her eyes.

The punch she throws is like a sprinting ham; so sudden, so ripe with hurt, it sends my father spiraling to the ground.

"Consider all connubial rights forthwith *suspended*!" she says, rooted above him, breathing hard. She suddenly jellies to her knees, her rolling flesh quaking like an unbaked cake, tears and mucous streaming, and her mouth, stringy with saliva, wide open and unable to make further sounds. I step back in horror, but Da wastes no time running to her.

"Oh, my poor angel," he mews as he embraces her. "Forgive me, my love. Forgive me." He covers her wet cheeks with kisses. "There, my duck. Let it all out." He shakes with her sobs, the blood of his split mouth staining her face with what look like lip rouge traces. "It's all my poxy fault. Forgive me."

# Chapter Four

It had a proper name, what had happened to my mother. A condition, a common concern among folks like us. The New York druggist who thought he'd try his luck homesteading and one Wednesday fed his six kids and wife possum gravy laced with arsenic. The sodbuster's daughter who answered the call of a traveling dry goods salesman with the business end of a pig sticker. Cabin fever, they called it. A quiet dike that betrays scant testament to the pressure accruing behind it. Until one day it breaks. And now that it had broken, my mother became bedridden. She took only bone broth but still her girth resisted shrinkage. What filled her? Hate? Hopelessness? Or was her girth her body's last maternal stand? A soft and heavy anchor tethered adamantly to her hopes for my future?

"I want you to be accomplished, Emma," she would say drowsily to me whenever I came with her broth. "I want you to be a lady. Get me the Thornwell."

"Aw, momma. Not more etiquette learning, *please*!"

We never spoke of her buried children. I never said a word about them to Da. And I decided then the only hold she might have on her remaining sanity was if I listened to her lessons. My bargain was a steep one. The creeks missed my naked soles. The trees hungered for my hugs. The chance that I would ever meet a fellow who could appreciate the vagaries of drawing room decorum, let alone know what decorum meant, were slim to none. But she was insistent I should be become "realized."

"Emulation of the masculine mystique pays far too much tribute to men, Emma," she said. "This instruction is merely more ordnance in your arsenal. A social fulcrum to help you shift the more cumbersome attitudes of men. Never a cage." The Thornwell was a guide to a lady's perfect gentility, and in her recovery, my mother became obsessed with its prickly lessons.

The art of conversing with fluency and propriety. (*Never induce familiarity in a man or induce them to suppose you are soliciting their notice.*)

How to treat flattery. (*Extend no encouraging word or smile.*)

How to address young gentlemen. (*Do not be tempted to indulge in another proof of feminine indecorum, which may be countenanced but can never be sanctioned by example, that of addressing young gentlemen of your acquaintance, who are unconnected with you, by their Christian names.*)

In other words, be a cold little lock-kneed prig, with a tongue even frostier, and hope a man isn't put off his feed when it comes time to swap a little spit. My mother's debilitating rage had been terrifying but not cautionary to me. I had felt more for my father in his humiliating exposure than for my mother's connubial plight. But perhaps all daughters are a mother's second chance. I wasn't afraid of sex. Not that I knew it as such. But I knew the feeling. I knew what it meant to touch myself after a good thaw in the bath. Or rub up the barrel of a tree, pause there in mid-climb, and rotate the old hips a bit to feel all warm and tingly inside. I didn't know about the mechanics. I just heard the voices in my parents loft at night, the fervent whispered prayers, and then the rhythmic creak of the brass. But I sensed, even then, that the fruit plucked beneath their sheets was well worth the squeeze.

Momma finally shed her bed but remained still somehow diminished. She left the cabin infrequently, relishing the winter months when her increasing comfort in the confines of the house would go less noticed. She took to reading aloud, to herself, to us. To the corner mice and bedbugs. It didn't seem to matter the subject. It was the sounds that attracted her as far as I could tell. One day it would be the "J" sound, and all would be a gumbo of that generous consonant. She would crouch on the swept dirt floor of the cabin, a great brown cat, with sometimes five separate books open before her, small stones, hair pins, sucked bones laid on the pages to keep them open. Her eyes would scan the pages as the tumblers of her personal clockwork began to whir, and she would begin softly: "John jostles jaundice javelins jealously. Jesus join the jowl." And as the annunciations grew juicer, so they grew louder: "Justify! Juvenile! Jesting! Jab! Jab! Jab!" She ran through the alphabet at random, through all the letters, repeating some, avoiding others, but always the mania of words that had no purpose in mine and my father's world of action. If I had begun to miss her, the old wry, imperious her that never would have been content to mumble from the whumping rails of a porch rocker, my Da's loss was at times immeasurable. Each night, as the stove embers cooled and the smell of my father's crude cooking began to drift into the heavy night, he would go to my mother, taking her filthy head in his hands and bury his face in her hair. I'd watch him breathe deeply of her while her eyes combed a horizon behind our cabin walls. "Up we go now, Cora," he'd say when it was time for her bed, his lips muffled by her cheek. "Time for our kip." Slowly his lean arm would wrap around her, settling under the fold that hid her armpit. She'd turn toward the stairs, and one by one, waiting until both her prodigious feet were planted on the step before ascending the next one, they negotiated up to their loft. He'd sing in a low and soothing voice that belied the bawdiness of the songs he preferred. The man and his once-wife. The father with his now-child. They disappeared from my sight, swallowed by the upper dark. And then I'd hear the long complaint of the mattress ropes that now only moaned twice as their bodies settled for the night.

I was washing my mother's fouled sheets in the same creek where she had once freshened my knickers, ruminating on the cruelty of circles. I was thinking how life is nothing but curves, concentric or obtuse, but always leading us back to where we had begun, when I noticed the handkerchief. It was swaying in the shallows of the creek. Instantly my bleak philosophy took wing as I fetched it out of the water. What the hell was this? It was a thin, fine fabric with a fussy border of crenellated lace. I wrung it out and pressed my face to it. It still smelled of human salt and rose water. This was not among my mother's effects. This was a stranger's possession. I squinted up creek. Then I ran to the cabin.

"What you reckon on this?" I asked Da, handing him the damp cloth. I could feel a spark of excitement inside me.

"They sure as sold them parcels by the headwater," he said, fingering the limp square.

"You mean there are *folk* upstream?"

The headwater was little more than half a day's walk. That meant whoever had lost it was close. Closer than any other homesteader with whom we'd frequented. Da and me were not solitary folk like Momma. We shared the guilt of my discovery, the welcome distraction it might bring, by not looking at one another.

"Aye. Perhaps a town," he said, lowering his voice to hide his excitement. "Definitely ladies. Ladies with some distinction, I should think." I didn't like the look in his eye. But I could hardly blame him. Our lives had become a penance. I tried to hide my smile while Da shot a look to Momma. She was rocking on the porch, slapping at spots of sunshine on her sleeves. The door to the cabin was open. I could smell the unwashed pans and plates in the sink, see the tangle of dirty clothes that littered the earth floor. It would have cut us dearly to admit to one another how desperately we wanted to escape the evidence of our daily lives, but that didn't stop me saddling the horse while my father approached my mother.

"Cora, my love," he said, sneaking up. "Emma and me's got a small errand to attend to. Are you needin' anything for yer comfort?"

She looked at him with a sudden imperiousness, stood, and shouted "Avast arrested appendages!" So she was back to the A's. My father stroked her cheek. She didn't blink. He looked to me. I shrugged. She was a creature now, not only of bovine body but of mind as well. And she could chew the cud of her distracted thoughts as happily as any animal. That, I am ashamed to say, was how we reasoned our departure. And so my father and I made sure my mother was well provisioned, left out cups of water and jerked meat within her reach, and lit out to find the owner of that frilly scrap of cotton.

We rode the horse in tandem, me front, my father behind. It was pleasant riding like that. I could feel his soft whiskers rub the curve of my neck, and the air was fresh and charged as if a storm was coming. We followed the creek until it gave out at the boulders of the headwater.

But we didn't need a cobbled road to tell us we were at the edge of some new civilization. We could smell it. Any town, no matter how small, will be surrounded by dung pits. And as we rode past the murky pits, the stink was as refreshing as clean grass after a spring rain. We heard hammers falling and the splash of slop buckets as they were dumped from upper windows. We heard horses chuff, and we could smell them too. Our excitement grew. And before we knew it, we were sauntering down what was in the industrious throes of becoming a real main street.

# Chapter Five

I knew more about the strict streets of antiquity than I did about any American ditchwater town. But to my eyes, I was strolling through the hanging gardens of Babylon. In truth, it was little more than a series of tents and a few lean-tos. The only completed structures were two clapboard buildings, one with a steeple that my father told me was a church, the other a merchant's with a gilt sign that read *Hegemore's, Purveyors of Drygoods & Fertile Bramble For The Soul.* Our feigned reconnaissance soon bubbled up into a passion we could no longer deny. We jerked the horse over to a hitching post, dismounted in a flash, and looked around. But there were no people. Or not ones fit to be noticed anyway. We hadn't marked the hour. We were always up before the sun in our day-to-day and so did not realize civilized folk don't rise until the sun is at least an hour spent. There were a few rumpled men staggering at the mouth of a filthy tent labeled simply *Miss Brown's.* Their suspenders hung loosely at their thighs, and there were dark stains around the unbuttoned flies of their canvass britches. They swerved and made soft sucking sounds when they collided with the ground.

"What ails them, Da?" I asked.

My father's face looked truly sympathetic, even wistful. "Loveless congress and too cheap a spirit, I reckon."

"How can you tell it's too cheap?"

"Ye canna afford to drink enough of the good stuff to get *that* pissed." A high, womanly laughter wafted from the darkness of the tent. Da shivered, gooseflesh rising on his arms as his mouth went suddenly slack. "Sweet sack o' Christ, tell a sinner 'tain't so," he whispered.

"What is it, Da?"

"Emma, light of my loins," he said, racking his nervous fingers through his hair before placing his hands upon my shoulders. "You wouldn't begrudge yer Da a small refreshment now, would ye?"

"We brought the canteen," I said.

Da grinned. "Yes, my duck. But 'tis another kind of thirst what ails me."

"What do you mean? What is that place?" He fumbled in his pockets, found a penny, and pressed it fervently into my palm.

"You suss that fine shop across the way?" he said pointing to Hegemore's emporium. "I reckon such a shop coddles no *end* of wonders." His hand was shaking as he curled my fingers around the penny. "Find yerself a nice sweet or some pretty bauble. There's a good girl. Run along now." He turned his back to me and was well on his way toward the tent when he said, "I'll fetch ye before the sun is over the church's steeple."

"But the sun won't be high for hours yet."

"And say naught to ye mum, now. Promise?'

"Promise? Promise what?" I shouted after him. "I don't reckon you, Da." But he was gone, skipping toward the mouth of the tent as if lured by the fruity tune of a calliope.

I looked at my penny. Its coppery surface caught the sun, and for a moment I was blinded. I stood alone in the muddy main street. A few stray hammers pocked the silence. Stacks of pale lumber. Sheets of plate glass still swaddled in straw leaned against a bevy of nail barrels. A tinker's wagon stuffed with glittery gewgaws. The horse hitched up to the wagon was fat with worms, and as I stroked his muzzle he answered with a long grassy fart. This was not the Rome or Carthage of my mother's books, but promise shimmered on the sour air. I crossed the street and stood beneath the gold letters of Hegemore's store. I had never seen anything so beautiful. It was festooned with corbels and cornices and every other kind of twisted ornamentation, all neatly painted with pastel shades of lavender, pink, and pale yellow. The whole effect feinted toward the polychromed statues I'd seen on a color plate in one of Momma's books about ancient Rome. But to me the garish structure resembled nothing as much as some cockeyed

Easter egg. Curious what would qualify as "fertile bramble for the soul," I pressed my face up to one of the huge plate windows. Inside was a cave of wonders fit for any yokel Aladdin. Shiny hookahs and big brass serving plates were stacked on a zebra-skin rug. A dress dummy with a pretty wax face wore a flouncy harem girl get up. Her waist was as pinched as a hornet's and she seemed perfectly ignorant of all the rough shovels and rakes stacked around her. Most of the exotic junk I recognized, but that pinch waist doohickey had me stumped. Could a woman's middle really look like that? Why was her obviously uncomfortable distortion so enticing to behold? Squinting through the thin fabric of her costume, I could see she was wearing some sort of contraption. It was ribbed at the sides with shiny silver clasps all down the front. Sort of like Momma's reducer, which she swore she wore for therapeutic purposes. But the effect of this thing had nothing hygienic about it. It gave the dummy's silhouette a sensuous, dangerous authority. The way the thing stacked her top and bottom bits, with that slow, severe curve in-between. It made you just ache to slip your arms around her. I felt mesmerized by it.

"Well, I'll be pickle-dipped in horse shit," I whispered. "If that ain't the damnedest thing I ever seen."

"Yes," a deep, feminine voice answered, giving me a start. "It is quite lovely isn't it. All the rage in Paris of late. But sadly too *a la pointe de la mode* for this backwater burg."

I turned around to see a fat little man sweeping the porch of the store. He was short—no more than my height—balding, and smelling too sweet for a man, with a fine curled mustache and lavender garters holding up his shiny white sleeves. I had never seen a man not dressed for the weather or chores. His trousers were narrow and striped. His wide suspenders were embroidered with whole flowering gardens of multicolored silk thread. And his boots were pointed and tight, with what looked like lavender gaiters covering the laces. The soles were so thin they seemed to be begging to be ruined in the first heavy rain.

"You'd look charming in one of my corsets," he said, putting his broom away. "Though by the divine cut of your figure, you seem hardly in need of one." There was nothing dirty or even untoward in the way he said it. But still I felt his words stoke a tiny fire inside me.

"You Mr. Hegemore?"

He turned for a moment and took a brocaded waist coat from a hook and slipped it on, buttoning the vest with one hand as he extended the other. "The same," he said and smiled. I shook his hand. It was as soft as butter but firm as harness leather.

"Emma May," I said, returning his smile.

"Emma may you *what*?" He chortled. I grinned at his joke. I liked this little fat man. Trusted him right away, which is not common for prairie folk. He was rare, easy in his confidence, easy in his fancy clothes, which would have made me feel like a prize pig in pants had I been wearing them. I suspected he was nowhere near as soft as he seemed.

"Hey, Mr. Hegemore," I said. "You reckon you got anything in that fancy store a girl like me could suck on?"

His small eyes widened as he stifled a discrete cough. "I assume you mean some variety of pastille or sweet?"

"I got a whole penny."

"Well, technically I'm not open for several more hours. But with such a fiscal inducement, how can I refuse?" He wasn't joshing me. He said it as if I had just offered him a whole cache of rare doubloons. With a click of his heels and pert tip of his head, he led me inside.

The plank floors were covered with plush Persian carpets. Moroccan oil lamps hung from a ceiling completely draped in swags of embroidered silk and damask. Behind a sleek mahogany counter were jars of every kind. Pickled pig trotters and peaches in Malvasian brandy. Mushrooms and pimentos and peppers layered like wallpaper patterns in amber-colored oil. Loaves of sugar, sacks of flour and feed. Bolts of fabric. Shovels, picks, lanterns, and hand-painted bed pans. Near the back were two suits of armor, a gauntlet from each holding the open drape of a red velvet curtain that formed a slightly forbidding proscenium to pure mystery.

"Might I have the pleasure of escorting mademoiselle to the back parlor? All the *choice* merchandise is ensconced behind these curtains."

"Don't mind if I do," I said cheekily, dipping my shoulder.

He had the loot of the world tucked back there. It smelled of sweet tobacco and fresh linen. There were racks of crisp men's suits in everything from dark broadcloth to Lynchburg plaid. Women's attire fit for every occasion. Beaded ball gowns as heavy as chain mail and floor-length peignoirs so sheer they seemed to flutter just looking at them. Fish knives, samovars, fingerbowls, and sabers. A whole cabinet of Ming dynasty vases and jade teacups carved as thin as tulip petals. Saddles inlaid with silver and shotguns acid-etched with scenes from the Revolution.

"But you said you desired a penny sweet. For that we must *flâner* over to Candyland." He led me to a counter lined with crystal jars. Inside were the colors of every wildflower I had ever seen.

"Licorice laces from Australia, sugared ginger from Tibet, Moroccan mint chews," he said moving past the glowing jars. "I even have chocolate-dipped grasshoppers from Samarkand. But, alas they have proved to be far from popular." I lifted the lids of a few jars and took a whiff of what was inside. Each jar's essence was better than the last. I closed the final jar and grinned at him.

"An embarrassment of confectionary riches," I said. He smirked at my sudden eloquence. "I can't make up my mind. You choose."

"Never," he said with a glint in his eye. "A woman must always choose for herself."

I was so moved by hearing one of my mother's prime adages, I put a hand on his shoulder. "I like the cut of your jib, mister."

He nodded and then moved slightly backward. It was a subtle movement but just enough to free him from my hand. "And I like the shape of your sloop, my dear. Now that we've dispensed with the nautical metaphors, what'll it be?" I just stared at him, dumb as a newborn ass as his dark little eyes glittered expectantly. I'd been warned repeatedly that all a man wanted was a soft place to pound. But this man was different. It wasn't mere etiquette. It wasn't salesmanship. He seemed to see me. Was there something more to me? Something approaching grace? Even something akin to actual beauty?

"You really think I'm pretty, mister?" I blurted. Sensing my unwarranted solicitation, I blushed so hard my ears burned. Hegemore stopped his reflexive retort. A slick customer like him knew when a lady was fishing for a compliment. But somehow he knew that wasn't my racket.

"Are there no mirrors where you come from, my dear?" My silence spoke the truth of it. "Surely you've been told how exceptional you are, my dear. Perhaps your sweetheart?" *Sweetheart?* Now I knew he was full of beans. Only a horn-bone buck would moon over an ignorant chore hound like me. "Please don't take my word for it, my dear," he said, reaching for a gilt hand mirror. "Behold the proof of my conviction." He handed me the mirror, which was a damn sight heavier than it appeared.

"You could drive a sixteen-penny nail with this sucker," I said, waving it with a few hammerish strokes.

"Catherine de' Medici herself gazed into that glass," the shopkeeper said, grabbing it away before holding it gingerly before me. "Though to less striking effect, I'm sure." I'd caught my reflection in ponds and pools but always to poor advantage, peering down to look up my nostrils, the rest of me compressed and blurry. This was my first real opportunity to see myself head-on, as it were. My gray eyes were large and almandine in my deeply tanned face. A good jaw, high cheekbones. A pug nose slightly wide at the sides like my mother's with a mouth as full as a water-starved trout. The mass of black curls that framed my reflection was matted in places and seemed to me to look like the ass end of a coal hold. "In the trade, we call that a heart-shaped face, my dear. See how your gorgeous cheekbones soften into that cunning little chin? We call that precious mouth of yours a 'cupid's bow.' With a face like that, you could tread the boards in any theatre from Moscow to London. Or shatter a thousand hearts."

"Christ on crutches," I said as he lowered the mirror. "I'm as dark as possum shit from all this sun."

"Nonsense, my dear," he whispered. "Would Cleopatra assess herself as such? And she won not only the heart of her randy Marc Anthony, but all of Rome."

I couldn't help but crack a smile at that one. "I'll be hog jizzed, mister, if you don't talk a streak." Jesus, I sounded stupid, like a character in one my mother's more obvious morality plays. Why the hell did I persist in this ruse? For a moment, I thought I might slip into a few casual lines of Byron or quote a lofty bit of Cato. But nothing came but a spastic kind of dip and bow combination that I hoped passed as a curtsy.

"Look at me, Emma," he said, tipping my face to his with a single finger. "I have been accused of many things in my life. But never mendacity. Simply put, you are a vision, my dear. And if I may, you must always caution against seeming to be less than you are."

How long can you long to hear a thing and not even know you longed for it? I wanted to cry right there and then. Just let all my worry and doubt slosh all over his fancy vest. But before I could squeeze out a tear, my father stumbled into the back room, held up by a gruff-looking redheaded man in a stained apron. Hegemore bristled at the sight of him. Gratitude at Hegemore's compliments quickly cooled to shame.

"Now, Barney," Hegemore said acidly, pointing to Da, "march that besotted trash out of my store this instant! And tell that cantankerous Irish whore mistress you have the misfortune of calling *boss* to keep her johns away from my doorstep. I need a shot of mercury just looking at him." I couldn't look at Da either.

"Crippled Christ, child," Da said weakly. "Tell this bastard beadle who I—."

"This man yer Paw, missy?" the gruff redhead said. I stared at him. I looked at Hegemore. Slowly, sheepishly, I looked at Da.

"Yessir."

Hegemore blanched. "*Your* father, child?"

"Afraid so," I whispered.

"Well, he owes me for four shots of rye," Barney said. "So pay up." I looked on in silence. My father smiled, stumbled, was righted.

"You know I'm skint, Da," I said. "All you give me was a penny."

Da licked his lips before shoving his face to my ear. He smelled to high heaven, like a whole damn whiskey still. "I promised this man you'd show him ye teats if'n he'd let me have the drinks," Da said. He shot me that bad-little-boy face he used whenever he got in a jam with Momma.

"You *what*?"

"That's preposterous!" Hegemore said. "How could you impose such a vile exchange on this child?"

"Ach! 'Tis nothing. Ye sprint about like a naked nymph with no prodding most of the damned year, anyway." He had a point. But this was business and required the measured response of an actual transaction.

"Easy there, Mr. Hegemore," I said evenly. "Didn't you say a woman needs to choose for herself? I reckon that goes for her debts too. Even if they ain't her own." Hegemore moved to speak, but a look from me shot him down. I took a deep breath as I calculated my options.

"You settling up, missy? Or am I taking payment in lumps?" the barman asked.

"Naw," I said after another thoughtful pause. "You really think you can get a gander at *my* titties for four pitiful tilts of the bottle?" Barney didn't crack a smile. But his eyes were not so casual and could not seem to pry themselves from the worn cotton covering my chest.

"What's your price then, girly?"

I had him. But a gambler's instinct let the moment hang.

"The bottle, you sumbitch," I said quietly. "And none o' that pig piss either. The good stuff."

The gruff man took no time to tabulate. He nodded immediately to the shopkeeper. "I get a bottle of single malt on credit, Hegemore?"

"This is ridiculous," the fat little man said, dipping behind the candy counter and surfacing with a bottle.

"Make it two," I said to the gruff man. "Or are you so witless you ain't never counted a women's breasts before." After a grudging nod, a second bottle hit the counter. "Damn, you menfolk are crazy." I giggled. Up went my flimsy chemise and out popped the men's eyes, and down went my shirt and everyone looked discontented all the sudden. "Didn't you like 'em?" I asked, a little crestfallen.

"Y-yes, ma'am," the barkeep stammered.

"Most bounteous," Hegemore said a bit stiffly.

"Then show a little *enthusiasm*, gents, next time I treat ya."

In addition to the hooch, we left Hegemore's store with a loaf of sugar, five pounds of dry beans, ten pounds of flour, a side of salt pork, two tin lanterns, and a copy of *The Liberator* for Momma. All on credit, all in anticipation of my return to Hegemore's shop. I set Da up in the saddle and was strapping our bounty to the horse when what should saunter to my side but the most ornery looking redheaded woman I'd ever laid eyes on. Barrel built and plug ugly, her crooked smile was as grating as nails raked slowly over a school slate. "Silas," she said, nodding her fiery red locks toward Da.

"Capability," my father mumbled back.

"You know this woman, Da?" I asked. My father said nothing.

"Not a bad haul for liftin' yer blouse," she said in a sour Irish brogue and chuckled. She unfurled a mottled paw I didn't want to shake. "Don't bother denying it, girly. I seen yer little peep show as I come up." Instantly I didn't like her. And I pondered, could her hair's auburn tint really bring my world to autumn?

"Brown," she said as I reluctantly took her hand. "Capability Brown." Her grip was as snug as keg's iron strap. I thought at first she was wrapped in a rind of filth until closer inspection revealed the offending blotches to be swarms of tawny freckles. "As I said, I had the pleasure of catchin' yer show just now. And I must say, a girl what has so little compunction at flashin' her paps to anonymous gentlemen is just the sort of colly I'm lookin' for." Her tiny green eyes sparkled malignantly. "Yer a natural-born whore, my dear. Did you know that?"

I slapped her hard across her speckled face, but Miss Brown remained as composed as if I had just blown her a kiss.

"Ye've fair pepper in yer fist, me dear," she grinned as she checked her lip for blood. "Ever wrestle a woman?"

"You light out of here, you bog-trash whore, 'fore I show you what I *can* do to a woman."

Brown just made a sarcastic little clicking sound with her tongue as if to say the loss was mine. "If yer ever lookin' to weight yer purse, look me up," she said as I mounted our horse. "Or better yet, tag along with yer Da there next time he come ruttin'. He knows how to find me." She flashed her amber teeth and spat before she waddled away.

As we headed out of town, I mulled her words in silence over the horse's muscular walk. Had she insulted me? Complimented me? Clearly she had noticed me, and that assertion, compounded by Mr. Hegemore's attentions, was enough to set my mind veering. Da was still cradling his two precious bottles when I looked back at him.

"You think I'm pretty, Da?" I asked finally.

"Wha?"

"Pretty," I shouted out the side of my mouth.

"More'n fair I'd say."

"Just fair?"

"Too thin a waist and backside. Don't really ballast with yer top half, if you reckon me, my girl."

"I guess."

"Vessel like that capsize at the first stiff wind. Now ye mum. There's a stately craft what would weather a frothing gale, I'll be blessed." Say what you like about Da, he only ever had true love for Momma.

# Chapter Six

We went back to the town often enough. Always on the pretense that such patronage would improve our lot. Even though it was clear we had gotten along quite well without things like bar soap, butter molds, and scientific rug beaters. As the year wore on, the object of our barter slowly changed. There was a new class of woman drumming the new town's floorboards, and my burgeoning assets were replaced by my father's more marketable carpentry skills.

He raised walls, laid floors, patched roofs. He even "bartered" his considerable framing skills to a buxom blond with an overbite known locally as Squirrel Tooth Alice. She was bent on giving Miss Brown a run for her trade, erecting what she called "a real class knocker" with cut glass sconces and sturdy army-issue iron beds. My father couldn't shiver her timbers fast enough. The considerable moral conflict he felt in anticipation of her establishment's opening was tempered with the bounty he showered upon our home. By the time I was in my nineteenth year, our spread was a regular castle of comfort. We had a machine-meshed coop with twelve laying hens and one ornery cock, a small barn with a milking cow, and a pretty little goat that seemed to share an affectionate, if tenebrous, bond with my father.

We were coming back one afternoon with more guilt-assuaging gifts for my mother, a Catherine Sedgwick novel and a Moroccan bound set of Tocqueville, when Da suddenly let out a gut-curdling shout.

"Cora!" he bellowed, goading our horse into a run. I looked up. The door to the cabin was wide open. My father had cause to be afeared of an open door in the middle of the day. Ever since Jackson had signed the Indian Removal Act, my mother had a paranoia of uninvited guests. And it was true, it was an increasingly common sight to see their rickety silhouettes shamble across the bluffs at dusk or dawn. I was never sure if her hypocrisy about respecting indigenous populations was endemic of her mania. Or did she really think people different than us were only worth fighting for as long as they resided flatly in books? Regardless, my mother was terrified of them, and she always kept the front door bolted whenever we went to town. Da leapt off the back of the horse, breaking into a dead run as soon as he hit the dirt. I hobbled the horse at the chopping stump and followed him. My father was stopped from entering the house by the huge twin bullnoses of her protruding rear.

"Cora? What in high holy hell . . . ?" he said, breathless.

She rose from the threshold and threw her arms around him. He smiled bewilderedly. She had never seemed so happy to see him. She turned to me and embraced me warmly as well. But her eyes were feverish, beatific, as if they had just endured the blaze of a barbecued saint.

"It's finished," she whispered, in a voice two octaves lower than her usual tenor. "I'd so hoped to finish it before your return."

She swept a large and exhausted arm through our front door, and we stopped cold at what lay spread on the floor. It looked like a Persian rug. But when our eyes adjusted to the interior gloom, we realized, with a relative sinking sensation, that what seemed to be clever knots of dyed wool thread were really rows of sprinkled sugar and tinted flour, carefully raked ground spice, and arranged flower petals, the whole intricate expanse of which extended to every corner of the lower floor. In what must have taken breathless hours, she had sieved and sprinkled lines of digestible powder into neat geometries, filling the interiors of these shapes with bright organic stuffs, iridescent beetles wings, spherical rabbit turds, blades of grass, dandelion tufts, all herded into perfect impressions of orange trees, partridges, and what I later learned to be elephants. It was a wonder of ephemera, a tapestry as fine and detailed as anything that might have graced a pasha's palace. Yet the faintest sneeze could have destroyed it utterly.

"What have ye *done*, woman?"

"Are you not pleased, Silas? It does so disperse the gloom."

"That's a whole *month's* rations right there on the floor, my duck."

"And put to far better use than prolonging our stale tenure out here, I should think."

We were not allowed into the house. The "carpet" could not be disturbed. We were to sleep in the chicken coop, in the piss-reeking hay of the barn, anywhere we could find shelter. She would sleep alone on the roof. How the hell had the idea come into her head? Was this some edible ode to the fleeting nature of delight? Or did she think she was back in Boston, in the family home with a dance pending, with all its attendant shame and anxiety? She said nothing. She was only clear in her directive that Da and I avoid it. The next morning, Da quietly climbed the ladder to her perch and spooned her sleeping body until she roused.

"Aw, Cora. The taint is back, I fear," my father said to her when she finally turned to him.

I had been sent through the window to steal a pinch of sugar for his tea. And while I stole the white grains from the highlights on an elephant's trunk, I could hear them through the ceiling calmly discussing my mother's relapse. When I climbed up to the roof with Da's sweetened tea, she was in his arms, blubbering wetly. It was a beautiful day, with high-vaulted skies of robin's egg blue. But there were dark clouds on the horizon. It would rain by noon.

They had decided it would be best if she returned to Boston, to her kin, to wood polish and dust-free plates and a comfortable, if solitary, life where she could get the proper care she needed. My father left that morning to go to town and buy passage on the next coach east. After he left, my mother wanted immediately to see her "carpet." She insisted I go down the ladder first as a precaution toward breaking her fall should she lose her balance. How she thought I could break her fall without breaking myself, I didn't dare ask. I opened the door of our cabin and stood with her upon the threshold. I caught my breath at what we saw. The morning sun slanted through the windows, illuminating her handiwork like God's own light through the stained glass of Notre Dame. It felt holy. Immaculate. I was filled with such a deep love and pity for her, I didn't care if I ever cooked or slept in that damned cabin again.

"It sure is pretty, Momma," I said, pushing a hank of wiry hair from her face.

"Stop sounding so *common*, Emma!" she spat, her black eyes flashing. "Surely the lexical color with which I have endeavored to imbue you would have you reaching for an adjective more varied and particular than 'pretty.'" And just like that, the sturdy brick and mortar of my love for her was reduced to rubble with just two sentences. She saw my stricken face, the tears I was blinking back. "I'm sorry, my dear, but you must always guard against seeming less than what you truly are." She pulled me close with a heavy drape of her arm. "We had a carpet like that when I was a child," she said, not looking at me. "We used to roll it up into the corner for dress balls. I always wondered what became of the trees and elephants when they were so ungenerously compressed. Especially the fruit on the trees. Were the oranges bruised? Why did the juice never flow?" I nestled my face to her cheek. I kissed her. And she began to cry. Is the love between a mother and daughter really meant to be as changeable as the weather? Or is it, as the bard once said, a fault in our stars?

My father failed to return home that night. For two more consecutive days, he was successful in failing again. We were pricked by worry. At least I was. My mother spent most of her time gazing at her carpet of floury flowers and reciting Thornwell's rules of formal ball etiquette.

"That's right, Momma," I said as soothingly as I could. "You'll be home again soon."

On the morning of the fourth day, I decided to go after him. And as the fifteen-mile journey by foot would take me a fair portion of the day, I ate hearty and left early. My mother was curled on the threshold of our cabin's open door, guarding, I imagined, the only treasure she had left. I remembered thinking how we had once thought of her as a kind of grand house cat, and how cruel yet apt that image proved to be after all.

"I'm leaving now, Momma. I'll try to be back before morning." She said nothing, just shifted the wide range of her flank and sniffed. "Momma, I'm going."

"Emma," she said, turning and looking up at me. "Come with me." I stepped back, shocked by her sudden lucidity.

"Where?"

"Boston, my darling." Her eyes were clear and unburdened, if slightly conspiratorial. "Life has endeavored to shroud me from its greater gifts. But you, Emma. You are a *beguiler*, on the cusp of such promise. Your willful charms could be honed to such honorable effect in Boston. We could be so much more. We could be . . ." What? Happy? *Free*? Didn't she realize I was already well acquainted with those inalienable rights? "Oh, Emma. *Dear* Emma. That's not freedom you feel," she said, reading my thoughts. "You think a few visits to some feeble boomtown is worthy of you? Such base distractions might serve your father. But you? With your mind? Your spirit? You've confused fulfillment of instinct with actual liberty, no better than a base creature that refuses to know this wilderness by its true name."

"Which is?"

"A cage. This wasteland, despite all its seductive vistas, is no more than a rambling prison. Let me take you to a place where I could garland your mind with actual wings." She pulled me close and kissed me. "Oh, Emma. Come with me. This is the future I'd always hoped for you. Let's live a life worth recollecting. Shall we?" The idea stirred something in me, an excitement I hadn't felt since my girlhood.

"Do you mean it, Momma?" The resolve on her face was unclouded. She smiled at me and put her hands on my shoulders, looking steadily into my eyes.

"Do you think I'm not aware of my condition? That I don't have an intimate grasp upon what ails me? What ails us both? I am not sick in *spite* of this place. I am poisoned *because* of it. Diminished to pitiful distraction the same way you are prodded to constant displays of gross physicality and feigned ignorance. We will never heal as long as we keep ingesting all this redundant green toxin."

Had she faked her illness just to seed her escape? Our escape? A plan formed instantly in my head. I would track down Da and wrangle two tickets east from him. As long as he hadn't spent all his wages on cheap spirits and even cheaper tarts. If he refused, I would bargain with his drinking and debauchery. Threaten to tell Momma everything. Could I do that? To Da? If my resolve wavered at that moment, Momma was quick to pump me up.

"This is why you were born, Emma," she said with streaming eyes. "To *live* your life. Not *spend* it." That did it.

"Wait for me, Momma," I said, turning and hitching my gait into a run.

"There is nothing proper in what you are doing, soldier," she said. I heard her laugh at my back. "But do try to kill me properly." She was quoting Cato's last words. I would have to hurry.

"Wait for me," I called over my shoulder.

# Chapter Seven

Rain began to fall from a still clear sky. But I did not feel the wet. My thoughts were too well occupied by my new resolve. Momma had made an excellent case as to the reasons for our departure. She cited my intelligence, my curiosity, my tenacity. My love for life. But these things meant nothing when I didn't believe them about myself. My real rationale for leaving our homestead was a far more earthy one.

Boston, despite its concessions to cobble stones and proper spoons, also meant boys. A subject that was increasingly on my mind.You might ask yourself: "Wasn't there a steady stream of warm young bucks feeding the prairie? Why pull up stakes just to get noticed?" Well, there is your answer. It was the way I was noticed. Out here with the teamsters, shitkickers, and drovers, I'd be just another washed out helpmeet, happy to chain myself to the stove, the bed, and dirty nappies. I needed a new light to be seen by, a new arena where my rustic charms would be novel. So what if I would have to wear ankle boots and petticoats just to step outside. Hide my burps behind demure fingers. The urbane young men of the East would be utterly charmed by my ability to both quote the lineage of every Roman emperor and still have the paste to trap them in a headlock. Young Andover-educated hands and shoulders and lips would be so much more inflaming than my stultified trees. And Da wouldn't mind. He already practically lived in town anyway. He would take our departure as a boon, a relief that could more fully salt the stories he was so fond of telling strangers.

The rain enlivened the color of the grass, as if turning up a frequency that was almost unnatural, almost too vibrant. And this vibrancy spread like fire to the low, distant hills, so when the sky finally darkened, the whole of the land seemed to leap forward from it in contrast.

But the town was not enriched by the wet. It sagged morosely in the slosh. Dogs, drunks, and ducks were the only creatures braving the street. A light burned in the town's one church. The doors were open but the pews empty. The priest or pastor or whatever he was watched the rain, smoking a thin hand-rolled cigarette. Only one building could brag attendance, the one my Da had single-handedly brought into existence.

Squirrel Tooth Alice's.

The place was packed, ripe with that spectral stink only the rain can bring out. But there was no hoochy-cooch upright piano tinkling away like the first few times

I'd been in there to fetch Da. No lacy-drawered dancing girls flogging their beef on Alice's small stage.

The attention of the patrons was focused on something new. Something that kept them in their seats and practically sitting on their hands. Every face in there was lamp bright as it beheld a young man who stood before them. He was four, maybe five years my junior with a shock of white hair and intoxicating windowpane eyes. I could tell right off he was far better looking than any preacher had a right to be. In his hands he held two serpents, a cottonmouth and a common rattler, and they twined around his palms and wrists as languidly as trinkets pulled from a pharaoh's arms. There was bottomland in his voice, a command of swamps and cypress and the terrible hidden knowledge of the dark.

"Behold, I give unto you power to tread on serpents and scorpions!" he sang. "The spirit of the Lord is quick unto me. And so shall be your haste to the Redeemer's side!" It wasn't his God talk that kept the women in there rapt. It was his ripe chest. His hard little backside in those tight homespun trousers of his. "Awake! I give you power over the enemy of Eden, and nothing shall assail you!" He lifted the rattler to his face. The triangular head flicked its nervous tongue, and slowly the boy opened his mouth, and the snake reached his head inside it, and the boy's lips closed around the rough diamonds of its neck. The men gasped. The women groaned. A few stood. And when this happened, I got a clear shot of my father sitting in the front row, a short glass of milky amber in one hand, the other deep in the generous cleavage of huge, towheaded Squirrel Tooth Alice. The harlot had one teat out, and this my father would squeeze while the woman closed her painted eyes in pleasure. A trickle of bluish milk squirted from her rouged nipple, right into my father's whiskey glass. "Be unmoved by the sins of this world," the young preacher said, removing the snake from his mouth. "For in His name shall you cast out devils and speak in new tongues and take up serpents as harmless as babes." The hands of the mostly female congregation shot high on raised arms like fields of smitten wheat. But it was clear to me it was not the tartness of brimstone that made those wash-worn hands seek the air. Intrigued as I was, I didn't have time for this revelatory slap and tickle. I saw Da kiss the cheek of the tart next to him. Instantly, I was as mad as a blue-balled bull.

"Silas Shinnecock!" I boomed. "Git your profligate claws off them heifer's *tits* and *git* on home to Momma!"

A libidinous sermon was one thing. But no one could resist a whiff of publicly aired laundry. All eyes turned to me. Even Da's, though bloodshot and bleary. The room went silent.

"Emma, love," he purred, his voice coming calmly from the bottom of his glass.

"This bitch yer *wife*?" the blonde whistled through her two enormous front teeth.

"Me *kin,* darlin'. Me one and only *lonely* daughter. Have you come to claim me then?"

"I shouldn't have to come claimin' your sorry hump't all. It's been four goddamned days!"

I shot a look to the beautiful boy with the snakes. He smiled at me. His serpents were dazed at his side. And I knew right then he'd been drugging his snakes with cheap hooch or valerian. I smirked at his neat trick. And even though I had caught him, he winked back at me. Something funny happened to my knees then, and I almost lost my feet. But I regrouped enough to continue my tirade.

"Where the high holy hell is Momma's ticket back home?" The congregation cleared a circle around us, revealing no inclination toward discretion. Squirrel Tooth stayed planted by Da's side.

"Ach, 'tis dear, I can tell ye," he said, reaching out to Squirrel Tooth's tit for another squirt. "Perhaps next month when I'm flush again."

"Little less coin on spreading yer spunk and we wouldn't have to wait 't all." I was aware I had said "we" but was also sure Da was too deep in his cups to register the implication.

"My arrangement with Miss Alice is strictly bartered, ye scoldin' harpy. I ain't paid for a dram or a flop in months."

"Wonder who's gettin' the better end of *that* deal," I said, smirking. The whore's bulbous crest of piss-colored curls quaked, but she said nothing. Da began to weep, as he always did when his crappy old-world guilt snatched him hard by the short hairs.

"Don't be cross with me, child. I can't bear yer ire."

Damn me if his blubbering didn't work. I reached for his collar and pulled him through the crowd. "Show's over, folks," I mumbled as we pushed through the swinging doors.

"But Silas," Squirrel Tooth whined, "you promised me another tumble."

"Ah, so I did," Da said with a beery slur. "But how much stronger is a rope, my love, once frayed then newly spliced? Tis the same with promises, I'll wager." The confused look on Alice's face made her look even dumber than before.

The rain had stopped but not Da's tears, and he milked his soggy state and made me strain and huff to get him a-saddle. We said nothing for a few miles.

"Is yer mum still ailing?" he said thinly.

"Fat lot you care about Momma."

"Aw, don't carry on like that, my girl. She's been quite clear about how she's chafed under the connubial burden. 'Tis me love and respect fer yer Ma what leads me hence." He may have had a point. If she was faking her distraction, she had found the perfect ruse that let her sleep in peace.

It was then we smelled the smoke.

# Chapter Eight

I lifted my head and turned to face him. His gaze was hard on a thin stream of black smoke that teased the air on the horizon. I kicked the horse and off it went like a shot. As we came closer to home, the air was a confusion of melting tar and a smell I did not recognize. The cabin was an oozing cube of syrupy black when we finally got there and leapt from the horse. Though not in flames, some great heat from the inside had made the oakum run.

"*Momma!*" I screamed. Oh the lies that surface and try to soothe when the truth is bare-assed before you. Was she baking? Roasting a feast of homecoming and had forgotten the pot in the oven? Taken a sudden chill in the middle of the day? Then I looked up to the roof and noticed the rain damper on the stove pipe was shut. Black smoke trickled through its weak seal. Momma had indeed intended on leaving. Her ruse was that we would go together. When my father pulled open the front door, a huge plume of acrid smoke threatened to swallow us. He stepped back, his eyes tearing, then he forced himself inside.

"Cora!"

"Momma!" I cried again. But there was only grief in my call. We knew she was gone.

Da backed out of the cabin, coughing, stained with soot. He ripped a boot from his foot and hobbled to the trough before clambering to the roof. He poured his boot-full of water down the stove pipe. The recesses of the cabin hissed, and the smoke began to thin as he kept limping up the ladder, one foot in a sock, one hand around the heel of his boot. He poured and poured and poured. The procedure seemed to take breathless hours to accomplish.

Finally, the air was clear enough to see through. The walls were coated a sooty matte black, and so we lit a lamp and peered inside. She was powdered with downy flecks of creosote, her arms folded beneath her cheek, as in sleep, on the open door of the stove. There were trails of pink where her eyes had run from the sting of the smoke and two more trails down her lip where her nose had run before her last breaths. And even though her dress was as black as her skin I could tell from the sleeves and the bow at the back that she wore her champagne-colored party dress from her last quiet ball. The stove was stuffed with husks of her novels and primers. I noticed her carpet was only disturbed where Da and I had trampled it. Angular fruit trees lay unmolested all around her. How had she done it? With what unnamable caution had she placed each loving foot upon its nap only to lay herself down to her last rest?

"God*damn* ye, woman!" my father choked. "Goddamn ye!" He slowly collapsed on top of her with a sob, and I noticed her bulk hardly shifted as it received his weight. But I did not cry. Not then. The shock had made me flee the confines of my body. I was not able, was not ready, was not willing to feel what my racing heart and numbed mind wanted me to feel. It was oddly soothing to see all the colors of my indoor world reduced to one final shade. The golden curves of my parent's brass bed, the white of my sleeping sack, the skillet, the rug beater, the vegetables sliced for the pot, all loose in their function, all reduced to just shapes under their mantle of smoky black, shadows of what they once were. My mother, now, was such a shadow. I looked at her and tried to reconcile that sad thing protruding from the open stove with the woman who had fought sadness all her life. I noticed an incongruity among the shapes of what were once her fingers. Tucked there at the root of her thumb was a rectangle of black. It would take but a mere breath to bring it forward from this dark tableau. An envelope. I blew on it as Da continued to whimper. *Emma*, in a perfect, almost taunting, copperplate was written there. The emotion surged so quickly I felt sick. Snatching the envelope, I ran from the cabin and puked up what little I had inside, the envelope still clutched in my hand. Whatever it contained was too much. To bring her back and feel her again would be too soon.

*Boston! You will thrive in Boston!*

*Fetch your father! I'll wait for your return!*

*Boston!*

I tucked the envelope into my shirt and headed to the creek, beginning the loop in my mind that would let her go unexamined, let her final riddle idle in my heart until I had the courage to unravel it.

That night I lit a dung fire in the dirt of our front yard and boiled some beans. My father refused them. I fetched him his bottle and let its deep draughts bring him down to sleep. I watched the fire and realized the night had lost its music. The grass was mute. The night creatures ceased their crackling. Even the night stars had stopped humming. It was the first night I had ever spent truly alone.

The next morning, I woke him from a sludgy sleep and set him on the horse. I felt like some kind of windup doll, going through her movements all stiff and thoughtless. Things needed doing. Da needed whatever comfort he could find now more than ever. In town among his baser desires was where he belonged. I told him to let the horse have its head. The horse would know the way by now. And I needed to be alone to do what I had to do. I would settle our estate, toasted and tiny as it was. There were practical considerations. The foremost being how to dispose of the body. At nearly two hundred pounds of dead weight, my mother's body was as good as rooted. I might as well try shifting blocks of sandstone at Karnak. Burning the whole pile seemed the most expedient.

I would send her off like the Viking queen I suspected she had always been. The tar would act as a natural accelerant and the bones would be easier to bury. But I couldn't do it just yet. Our spread needed a proper accounting. The shithouse and the barn I would let stand, a boon to future pilgrims. But what about the livestock? I walked to the barn in a daze and went inside. The floor of the barn was green with fresh grass. Both the goat and cow were grazing from this bleak pasture that had grown there from piles of their own manure. And I thought it the cycle of life most of us encounter—no claws, no gnashing teeth. Just excrescence and opportunity. The cow I would sell. The chickens could scratch a living from the prairie. That just left the goat. That settled, I cut a three-foot fire break around the whole cabin with Da's spade. The wind was up and probably wouldn't die until evening. I didn't need the whole damn prairie to go up. I refreshed myself with a few deep pulls from the goat's teats, feeling the milk soothe my gut, the gamey stink of the beast settling behind my sinuses. Sitting myself on the open prairie grass, I waited for the sun to sink.

I looked at my mother's envelope by the fickle brightness of our burning cabin. Still too soon, I decided. The conflagration spat up sparks and wafting bits of flame-eaten cloth and, I hoped, my mother's madness, innocence, and anger. But my anger was not so easily consumed. She had lied. She had left me. My face felt hot and not from the fire. My breathing became frenzied. How could she have done it? *Why* had she done it? She had always kept her word. Unlike Da, she had been my rock, my tower of strength that had held, however grudgingly, the promise of my better self. Now she was gone. A few angry tears came. I watched them glisten on my fingertips by the light of the swirling embers that rivaled the early morning stars. It wasn't sadness. It was furious indignation. The unassailable allure of operatic hurt that teemed in my abandoned, teenaged brain. If I could, I would have made the smoke billowing above me blacker. Would have made the flames raging before me hotter. Would have chased the morning stars around me even further to the very edges of their remote nurseries. I was alone, as every young person on the edge of themselves is alone. Only I was an orphan. And she had made me that way. Now there would be no Boston. No boys. I would never blossom into my full potential. "Coward!" I shouted to the dawn. "You bastard *bitch* coward! Why did you go?"

I heard the cow low. It was that hard nasal bleat that meant a wolf was near. That sobered me. I slapped the tears from my eyes and grabbed for the gun at my side. I spat powder down the barrel, set the wad and ball, and rammed it down. I cocked it as I walked slowly toward the barn. The door was open. I was sure I had latched it. Either the wolves had become exceedingly dexterous, or I was in deep shit. Through the slats of the barn the burning cabin cast bars of undulating light on the drunkenly chewing goat and the whites of the cow's eyes. All I could hear was the snap and roar of our rapidly burning home. I kept the muzzle of the flintlock raised, both eyes open, sighting in the dark on the cow, on the far wall of the barn that was smeared with pale and dancing shadows. Slowly these shadows began to congeal. I blinked, my finger soft but ready upon the trigger.

The shadow hardened.

Widened.

And I smelled her. The floral rebellion of her milled soap.

"Momma? Is that you?"

A movement.

It was so swift, I tracked it blind before I fired. I heard a slight grunt and something fell to the ground. I kept the gun raised, impotent though it now was. Into the wavering light rose up a face. It was not my mother's face. It was a boy. A young, beautiful man, really. The most beautiful young man I had ever seen. Intelligent eyes. Deep set and huge. Welcoming eyes. He must have had other features, but all I saw at first were those eyes. His eyes promised what the trunks of climbing trees had only implied. I was smitten. But more than that, I was enflamed. My whole body tingled as I watched him gather himself to his feet. I wanted him in the worst, most wonderful way. He was dressed in a neat serge suit, which he dusted off with his elegant hands. His shoulders were broad and muscular, bested by the rise of his chest that tapered down to the promises his fine suit could not hide. This was not a body forged by labor alone. This glorious son of a bitch had sprung from the deepest, most lustful crevices of Aphrodite herself. I lowered the gun. He raised his hand to the wound in his chest.

"Pardon my sudden intrusion, miss," he said with a rich, educated bass that made me shiver. He was no up-creek gulch rat. He was a Boston boy. *My* Boston boy. I was struck dumb, wet as a spring rain, but ultimately confused, for my aim had always been true, and I knew I'd hit him with a kill shot. How the hell was he still vertical? There was blood on the starched cloth of his shirt. He was clearly bleeding from a hole just left of the center of his chest. This didn't add up. He held up both hands in a gesture of surrender, grinning apologetically. "May I? Please?" he purred. "With your indulgence?" I didn't know what the hell to say. Slowly he lowered a hand to his wound. Looking on in amazement, I watched as he stuck two fingers into his wound and pinched something out. He held it up for me to see. Even in the weak light, I could tell it was my ball, still hot, still covered in his blood. He approached me slowly as my heart began to beat faster. When he was close enough to me that I could feel the softness of his heat, he gently pried my trigger finger from the rifle. "I believe this is yours, miss. I know how dear is the cost of lead in these western climes." Then he dropped my musket ball into my open palm.

"What the high holy hell," passed my stunned lips. My knees turned to water as his eyes shifted from diffident fear to real concern. The warm loaves of his arms were around me before I had time to fall. Oh, his momma had raised him right, and he knew how to let a lady down gracefully. Who was this quick and captivating stranger? And why would I gladly give my all just to linger for eternity beneath him? William Lloyd Garrison's "Urge me *not* to use moderation in a cause like the present," seemed the perfect prefix to what was raging inside me.

"I fear I've caught you at an inopportune moment," he whispered as he held me over the hay on the barn floor.

"W-Why would you say that?" I stammered.

"Isn't that your house burning out there?"

"Is it?" I could not rescue my gaze from the strong tides of his eyes.

"You have a creek nearby. I could help you quench it."

"It just got going."

"But I fear all will be lost."

Why was he still talking? Why weren't his lips engaged to better purpose? I moved my hand up the side of his body until it came to rest at the back of his neck. "Ain't nothing on this whole spread worth keeping," I said huskily, closing my eyes. But his neck wouldn't budge. His face just hovered over mine like a lovely pump handle arrested with rust.

"Just answer one query first," he said. Lord on fire! More talk! I relaxed my grip. His lips brushed my cheek.

I couldn't swallow. "I'm afraid I've become lost," he whispered into my ear. His breath was summer lightning on my dry fields. "My horse spooked and threw me, and I've been wandering around for hours. I'm trying to meet my uncle, Mr. Hegemore. Is his shop in the near vicinity?" Could I fault him his poor geography in such a moment?

"It is tonight." I yanked him to the ground on top of me.

"Careful, miss!" he said, once we hit the hay. "Did I harm you?"

"Not yet," I said impatiently.

"No broken bones?" he whispered softly. I could feel one of his hands begin at my ankle and move languidly up my calf to my knee, to the quivering medium of my thigh as he checked for any damage.

"I'm fit as a damn fiddle. You?" I moaned.

"I'm in terrible repair, I fear. Feverish. Feel that?" He gently took one of my hands in his and moved it to his cheek. "I'm simply burning up." My heart was fit to bust as he brushed my fingers with his lips.

"You should definitely get that looked at," I whispered.

"I was told *you* are a physician of sorts. A beautiful, young woman of deep, edifying gifts." His tongue probed the pulse at my throat. My tinder exploded.

"I reckon I could make you right as rain," I whispered with what breath I had left.

"You won't be wanting this," he said as he slowly worked his lips along my jaw. "I'll give you bad dreams."

"Promise?"

# Nature Red In Tooth And Claw And Every Other Damn Thing

# CHAPTER NINE

I woke to a fox licking the stranger's blood from my lips. There was no mistaking the rough stabs of the creature's tongue for that of the luxurious aptitude of the previous night. But there my memory faded. What memory? I waved the fox away and sat up. I tested my mouth with my fingers. I was not cut. My tongue tasted of iron and cinnamon. I was alone in the barn. Surely I had dreamed the attentions of my phantom lover. I squinted into the day. The sun was high and bright. The ruins of our cabin smoked faintly in the quiet air. I was woozy and dry, as spent as Da the morning after a good belly-up with his jug. What the high holy hell had happened to me?

*I'll give you bad dreams.*

I shook my head to clear it, tried to stand, and toppled to my knees on the rumpled hay. I was sore between my legs. But the pain was sly there. My breasts ached. But the rawness had a grin of its own.

*A beautiful, young woman of deep, edifying gifts.*

Why did the dream feel so real? How could I have conjured such a splendid congress with a perfect stranger with no personal experience to inform it? *Because you're your Da's daughter, Emma. A dirty little dreamer whose fantastic passions are the closest you'll ever get to real love. You'll spend the rest of your days scratching out bawdy penny bed-burners for dry old spinsters and aging widows.* Maybe I was a victim of self-abuse and vivid dreams. I ran my fingers through my matted hair, spat. I stood up again, swooned again, fell to my knees and puked. My vomit was carnation pink. A mixture of blood and goat's milk. Maybe I hadn't dreamed him after all. The goat still chewed languidly, but the cow was missing. Had he taken it? If he had, he was welcome to it. It was the least I could do. I fell back to the hay. It was strong with his scent. I held my wrist to my nose and found traces of him there as well. I raced my nose to the crook of my elbow, following his high honey and reached a hand between my legs. He was heaviest upon me there, but the scent was not skin-bound and continued in shallow eddies of the heated air between the thatch of the hay and the floor of the barn. It was a trail as clear as footprints in paint, a map of his movements that was strongest on the ground but rose like afternoon heat away from me. He had stood at some late hour while I slept, bent back to me (A farewell kiss?), then stood again and headed out of the barn. Had my sense of smell always been this acute? There was a pull, an actual hooking of my senses that drew me, on shaking hands and knees, into the day. My hope faltered as his scent grew thin, crushed by the traffic of a thousand other scent trails, leading in a thousand different directions, all with detailed narratives of their own. Rabbit panic, the quick retreat of ground hogs, beetles bested in mating combat, the funk of every phylum lingering like a tapestry of vaporous threads in the bright air above me. The morning world was loud with scent. I became confused. Desperate to find him but hobbled by the stink-chorus of the waking day. Then I remembered.

Hegemore!

He had said he was Hegemore's nephew. That's where he was. Among the most fertile soul bramble of Hegemore's even now more wonderful shop. I needed to set out now if I was going to beat the real heat of the day. Da still had our horse. And the damn goat would butt me in the gut if I even thought of mounting her. Town was fifteen miles away. All I needed was a canteen full of water, and I could be on my way.

*I'll give you bad dreams.*

The wind was up at the edge of the creek as I filled my canteen. There was gossip on the breeze I had never heard before. Was it Momma's voice? Is that where she had gone? Into the tongues of the tall grass? And what was she whispering under the noon-high sun?

Harlot.

Demimondaine.

*Beast.*

The grass rustled *shame*. The sudden guilt I felt laid low all my plans of amorous pursuit.

"But I did nothing wrong, Momma!"

On the opposite side of the creek loomed a large gray figure. It had no face. It had no future. But I knew it was her. Was Momma weeping, or had the evening whippoorwill mistaken the hour?

"I did nothing wrong!"

My shout made the figure begin to fade. And as the canteen dropped from my hand I watched as the figure retreated slowly between sparks of hard light reflecting off the running creek and the soft shafts of filtered sunlight. She was gone before I could call to her again. My mother might have thought sex was innately a reductive act because it favored an animal sameness over the integrity of the individual, but she was wrong. I was more now. Not less. She needed to know. Needed to know that what I had done the previous night was just a tad north of whatever joy, truth, and beauty she had found in the pages of Hawthorne. I ran to the still smoldering remains of our home. I was so flooded with the need to tell her about the good I had done that I did not realize I had not stood to run away from the creek. I had four-footed it like a dog who missed her master.

Her bones were covered with thick flakes of soot that made a false flesh. Her layers of heavy fat had made her burn hotly and she was charred free of any familiar traces. Save the teeth. The teeth I recognized, but not at first. I was used to glimpses of them in life, a tease.

She had been parsimonious with her smiles, and so they were precious with her. Not this stripped, shameless grin of her skull. I would bury her deep. I collected of her what I could, stacking her charred ribs like wagon rims, gaining a grip on only the more substantial shafts of bone. The grave would have to be satisfied with an idea of her. I chose a spot near her babies to lay her. But I could not leave it at that. I needed a token, a piece of physical evidence that said yes, you have a house in me, Momma. Whatever realm you now inhabit, a place where the crows quote Byron and the bees buzz about the social injustices found in Socrates, you will remain precious to me. I rolled her skull to the cup of my palm and pinched a front tooth from its socket. It came out easily, with a hard tail of root. I closed the tooth in my hand. A promise. A proof. This would have to be enough.

And like a lover's misplaced promise ring or a favorite thimble rolled away, I lost all that remained of that day and coming night.

The next morning's sun found me ravenous with hunger and with a caul of gore dried to my face. And no memory of the previous evening's hours. Flies buzzed around me, settling on my cheeks, sipping from the corners of my eyes. I peeled the dried blood from my cheeks and nose, slipping it absently into my mouth. It broke glassily between my teeth but satisfied my hunger no more than a penny sweet. What was happening to me? What had I become?

*You won't be wanting this.*

*I'll give you bad dreams.*

I was not dreaming. This was real. I was me but not me. Enhanced. Transformed. Polluted. What had that Boston boy done to me? What had he given me beyond that one many splendored night? Was I slipping into some sort of congenital madness? To what was I now such a willing and absent-minded host? The buzzing of the flies bored into my brain with force. I could hear the fine thunder of their vibrating wings. Smell the clean metal of their tiny bodies. Why were there so many of them? What drew them so? I felt grass through my toes and slowly became aware of the curious distribution of my weight. I was crouching, my feet and bottom in contact with the earth. Where had the night gone? Had I spent it in this stupor? I heard the trickle of water. Saw a tree branch caught at the river's bank. It was a tan-colored branch, leafless and sharp looking, like a branch from a tree I had never seen before. All the trees and grass and earth seemed novel to me. But this branch seemed to end in something completely foreign. Slowly, my mind moved toward recognition.

Branches broken from trees became rooted by moving water into soggy soil.

This broken branch was rooted in a face.

A long, triangular face, with milky eyes and a black, blunt snout. A deer. A dead deer drowned at the river's edge. But not drowned. For to be drowned, this deer would have had to have been whole. And she was not whole. She was a tangle of parts and pieces, her head torn clean off where the neck had once met her shoulders. Her dainty hooves looked like they could still sprint. But not without the middle of her. And there was no middle of her. Something had hollowed her out. Devoured her. Someone. With a strange amusement, I realized I had eaten the deer the previous night. Ravaged it raw. I had the thought of being sick. But no nausea. Only a vague remorse. And that gnawing awful hunger not even a deer's innards could sate.

*You know what you are now, Emma. A monster. An abomination.*

*A geek.*

I remembered Da's tale of a Blackpool carnival he had attended as a boy. Sick on cheap treacle and too many penny sweets, the two whores that accompanied him thought it might be a laugh if the queasy lad got a gander at what resided in the tents of the freak show. He saw Fiji mermaids as parched as toast. Babies with two faces floating in pickle jars. Fat men. Bearded ladies. A girl whose knees bent the wrong way. But the geek tent drew the largest crowd. Only here could the suffering poor feel like kings. Little Da had been terrified when the filthy, mad-eyed geek had taken the stage. And when he saw the raving geek tear the head off a live chicken with his bare teeth, he was miles from mere terror. Here was a creature beyond the limits of despair. A poor pitiful thing too horrible to live. And now that lost but still-living nightmare was me. It was clear what I must do.

I uncoiled myself from my crouching position and squatted near the head of the deer. I was sobbing so hard I had trouble gripping a point of the deer's antler. I finally managed it. It broke off like chalk in my hand. "Oh happy dagger!" I cried. "*Here* is thy sheath!" I drew it to my chest and pressed the point to the soft place below my sternum. The deer was old. The antler was dull. I would need all the pressure I could muster to help it do its work. With a squint and a grunt, it entered me with a sudden chill. I felt my heart and all its attendant plumbing veer at the intrusion. My breathing stayed steady. I had to look down at my chest to see that I had done it. What the *hell*? Why wasn't I jawing my sin to Saint Peter? Should I push it all the way through like a clean gunshot wound? Or leave it lodged there? The prospect tickled. I laughed. I felt the muscles of my diaphragm grip the antler buried in me like a mother grips her baby's extended finger. The same trust. The same tenderness. "Come on, now!" I said, still giggling. "What's it going to take?" I jiggled the butt of the antler around a bit. My beating heart walked around in my chest, refusing to be pierced. Exasperated, I pulled it out. I chucked it into the drink and examined my wound. The smell of my own blood made me suddenly ravenous. This was new. And exciting and sickening in a way I was too confused to ponder. The mouth-like tear in me buttoned closed like a child suddenly shushed. What was I to do? I slouched forward and tumbled headfirst into the river. I stayed under, hoping the rushing wet and cold would suck me into oblivion. Ophelia had lost her senses, and a river was swift in ending her. I took a few deep quaffs of the rushing water, but I seemed to exhale the water in my lungs back out through my nose. All I felt under there was the throbbing of the little life all around me. I could smell the sweetness of the waving cress, could hear the fractured heartbeats of fish as they passed me at speed. I opened my mouth and let the gently moving water fill my lungs again. I sank to the river bottom and looked up into the undulating current that rippled the sun. The light sparkled and trilled above me. Music, if music could be seen. I watched the sun set from the bottom of that river, saw the light fracture from white to yellow to rich orange before I pulled myself to the shore.

Sitting on the bank of the river until it was full dark, I watched the drifting current dice the light of the high full moon on its flowing surface. So that was that. If I couldn't die, I'd better feed. The hunger was a deafening wail in me now. And what did I crave? That old red sticky.

Hot berry punch.

But not any common vintage. The idea of drinking human blood still thrilled and revolted me. "Oh, no!" I said aloud to whatever was coiled inside me. "I'll *starve* to death first!" Somehow I knew hunger would not kill me either. Fear of death was no longer a motivation. *Make me move*, I said in my head. Force me like a father with a willow switch in his hand. *Goad me. Break me.* The night was loud with hidden frogs and crickets. I felt right at home. Nothing stirred within me. "See?" I laughed. "You got nothing! I'll sit here till I'm green with mushrooms! I'll not budge even when I'm covered with muffling snow! You hear me! I'll set right here, not moving one tittle till field mice burrow into my belly and slugs play faro in my noggin!" Suddenly, the night was quiet. But it was not the night that made no sound. It was that I could no longer hear it. There was a close rumbling in my ears, broken only by the frantic prodding of my heartbeat. I looked around and sniffed the air. Nothing. I could smell nothing. The dullness came upon me instantly. A total dampening of my senses like a lamp suddenly blown out. I looked at the river. I looked up at the moon. They were just river and moon. All their enchantment was gone. I felt a sudden spark in my chest as if something precious had been lost. "Hold on! That ain't fair!" I heard laughter from a deep recess inside me. A deep, sinister cackle neither male nor female that turned me cold.

*I will take the beauty of your world from you,* the voice inside me said. *I will hold the magic of your starry nights hostage. Mute the rambling philosophy of your day. I will make a drudgery of your world. And you will become a shadow caged within it. Unless you feed.*

I stood up suddenly and giggled my ears with both pinky fingers. Silence. I rubbed my eyes then stared. Everything around me was but a ghost of its function. Trees were dull pillars. The rocks and water were lost in translation. The night had leaked all its wonder. I was bursting with life. Yet all that life around me was walled up, hidden from me. Even my memories of nature, the catalogue of all my girlhood frolics upon summer grass and under winter stars, was locked behind the frosty glass of my mind. Our Redeemer at Gethsemane had bet against the cross and lost. What chance had I?

"Hold on now," I bargained. "Ain't there another way?"

In answer, I was drawn to my feet. The harsh fear inside me made me walk.

"Wait! Where am I going? What will you have me do?"

My walk became a run.

"Wait, goddamn it!"

I somehow managed to hook the heel of one foot against the other and tumbled to the dirt. I dug my hands into the dear earth, anchoring myself there. But there was no earth beneath me, only a cold indifferent surface. I knew I could never spend an eternity like that. And yet I tried. How long I clung to that bland patch of ground, I cannot say. I rolled to my back and stared at the sky. The sun and moon raced over head in graceless arcs of but variant brightness. I was lost in a flurry of similar days, neither hot nor cold. Not happy. Not horrified. The only sense left to me was the aching memory of all I had lost.

"All right," I said one day. "You win."

*That conclusion was inevitable,* the voice in my head purred after its long silence. *You will go to town. And there you will be a wolf among the lambs.*

"A what?"

*You will become a mirror that reflects the desire of others. You are now a Beguiler. You will lure your prey by assuming the aspect of the longed-for dead.*

"Come again?"

*Or you will seem to be lost loves still living and every manner of coveted being. And you shall know your prey by those drawn to you like the weary to rest. You will consume the deceived without mercy. And you will not cease until your victims are but hollow dregs.*

"Hell, *no,* brother!" I hollered. "I won't take no *innocent* life!"

My skull rang with the laughter of my terrible guest.

*The lives you will take will not be innocent,* it said softly. *Now hurry.*

# Chapter Ten

It was a right slog to town, but I made the distance in no time. I moved in a stuttering of consciousness, like a chess piece across a massive board checkered with grass and gravel. It was as if something lit a lamp in my mind one moment and blew it out the next. First I was here. Then I was there. With no recollection of anything in between.

I was only slightly winded when I noticed the lights of the main street jogging before my eyes. I stopped at a fancy new sign that could have only been erected a day or two ago. The town suddenly had a name. I will never understand this mania for naming things. Labels square the curves of things. Boxing up what could do so much better without edges. But there it was. The town was now called *Hollywood.* I recognized Da's handiwork immediately. What a damn fool name for a town, I remember thinking. But maybe it was fitting. Who the high holy hell was Holly? And what *wouldn't* she do for a grab, a stab, or a dirty piece of silver? Boom towns do just that. And even in the short time I was away, the last tents and lean-tos were all gone, fully replaced by crisp clapboard heaps that stood defiantly against the open plain. All had false fronts making them seem more grand or alluring than the little cracker tins they really were. I could barely navigate the boardwalk as it was congested with beer barrels and crates of white and brown liquor. Red lights shined above several shingles, letting you know the cheap vices awaiting within. Two penny beer. Three handed stud. Tin cut-outs of racy women pocked with buckshot. Every other establishment seemed to be a gaming den, sporting house, or gin joint. It was a quiet night, and only a light tinkling of piano drifted through the shutters of a saloon. I seemed to have the run of the place. I could not smell the sweetness of the night air. Or the new pine of the buildings. My nose was allowed to smell only people. The scent of sleeping flesh made me feel like a beggar at the back door of a bakery. Sweet and warm and intoxicating. The doctors here are made of pork, I thought to myself. The lawyers made of veal. Mothers have their secrets here. Fathers have their crimes.

*No one here is innocent.*

It played like a loop in my mind as I strolled. An order disguised as an offer. But still I hesitated. Perhaps the late hour was a mercy, for there was no one about. Only a few dim lights glowed in the windows above the shops. Walking down the center of the lonely main street, I smelled whisky on hot breath. Lye on a spinster's sleeping shoulders. Sour cotton. Rose water on hands clasped in prayer. Nothing had ever smelled so delicious. Horses neighed from behind their locked stables, and I could feel their eye-white panic as I passed.

*And you shall know your prey by those drawn to you like the weary to rest.*

One, I thought. I just needed one. I just needed to loiter about, and my hunger would be quelled as if by a mother serving supper. I never anticipated how powerless I would feel in my peculiar predatory state. I found him in an alley behind Hegemore's store. Or rather, he was found for me. Average height, bowler on his head. He was whistling as he relieved himself upon an advertisement for tooth powder plastered to a wall. His plaid suit was pinched at the waist, clocking him as unfashionable and so fair game. A traveling drummer ready for plucking. He reeked of booze. I could see the tops of his ears raise ever so slightly as he smiled, sensing me behind him.

"Who we got back there?" He chuckled loosely. "You one of Miss Brown's girls?" I said nothing as I moved closer to him. "Oo-ee, dumpling, you want a lick a' my peppermint stick? Can't promise I can oblige." I watched, sickened as he shook himself. "Your confederates at Alice's already done drained my balls to the dregs." He was repulsive. And slow. Perfect. "But you better not be no heifer when I turn around. You Brown girls run a tad plump for my taste. I like my slash high and tight. Like my money!" This would be easier than I had imagined. But then all the tingle of anticipating my kill shunted like a sluice gate. The sweetness of hating him, the righteousness of ending him, were suddenly stalled in me and flushed through with a hideous feeling of longing. And not just longing but a deep and stale sense of being beholden to him. My God, for one brief horrible moment I felt I actually loved the son of a bitch. My rhythms were different. My internal pressures were not my own. My countenance rippled in me as he rolled his head on his thin neck before facing me.

"*Elvira?*" The shock on his face was heartbreaking. His bleary eyes went wide as he fumbled to stuff himself back into his trousers.

"Oh, Edmund!" I squawked in a voice I did not recognize. "How could you?"

"What you doing back from your mother's so—" It was my jaws on his throat that shut him up.

Bright noonday sunshine exploded behind my clenched eyes as I drank. My ears rang with a terrible chorus as I floundered in the confluence of the guilt of killing the man I loved and the deep satisfaction that flooded me while feeding on him. I could not stop. The frenzy was too strong. I forced my eyes to open and all was white before me. Then I saw her face. Elvira. The poor beleaguered wife I appeared to be to him. She emerged out of my flesh and marrow and memories like a ship from a northern fog. A girl no older than I. A pale, chinless face, no more than an excuse for her sad, accusing eyes.

*Stop! You'll kill him!* I thought.

Her hair was the color of trampled wheat.

*Stop!*

Her eyes just dirty gray panes. Filled with waiting and empty afternoons.

*Stop!*

I didn't know I had lifted him off the ground until his weight vanished under my pumping throat. I was shaking so hard I could not steady my hands nor my breathing. All my senses flooded back a thousand fold as his blood filled my gut. The stars exploded above me. The night air a burden of fresh and fragrant delights. And what a cruel reward for no longer resisting the thing inside me as my keen senses were useless except in their shared revulsion at what I had done. What had been once so full of corporal integrity was now but a vaguely human-shaped ash. Only his clothes remained, strewn about my feet like so many cold autumn leaves. So this is what it meant to be a Beguiler. A perfect killer. For with no corpus to habeas, no body to confirm my crime, there would never be any evidence of my transgression. And yet I was the lowest kind of predator. For in my hurry toward satisfaction, I would first have to traverse the bleak chasms of believing, if only for an instant, that I was killing the thing I most loved. Something glinted in the wreckage of his empty vest. His watch and chain. Horror wrestled with a growing sense of wellbeing, and it was only a last vestige of my guilt that made me draw the watch from its pocket. I saw her. There at the end of his watch chain, a tiny, gold, heart-shaped frame held

Elvira's face in chemical grays and blacks. Her big blank stare boring into me in judgment over a loss that could never be revenged. I threw the watch into the street and wept. The night was rapturous above me. The stars no longer just hummed; they *sang*. Everything around me, from the chipped paint of the alley to the sour dirt beneath me, seemed to pulse with a purity of new life. Everything was beautiful. Everything was kin to me. And I was wretched among it. I gathered up the drummer's clothes and tossed them into a nearby privy. Even the foul stench of the shit box was as heaven's own ether. I jogged out into the main street. No one had seen me. But still I ran from the town as if pursed by hell's own angels. I needed to get back to what I knew. Perhaps among the trees and grass and morning sky I might hear some counsel that could soothe my fallen state.

I preferred the wild places. The places where time moved gently if at all. There is complexity in nature but no duplicity. It is even more itself upon deeper examination, unlike folks who become less and less so under similar scrutiny. In the week I took to wrestle with my plight, that was what riled the most. All this open space, all these warm, fleshy, blood-filled critters, all mine for the taking but as worthless as trophies. The hunger beckoned. But again, it was the horrible dullness of my senses that made me go back. Even a cursory assessment of my new disposition would reveal I had but one use for people.

I reasoned it out thusly: On the one hand, I was a sinner. I had engaged in lustful congress with a perfect stranger. And so, as my mother had ceaselessly cautioned, I was being punished. And not just a little bottom swat. A real beating. For not only had my carnality been sired by a loveless yen, I had done so while my mother was crackling in the flames of a fire I, myself, had set. I would forever have to wrestle with the fact that her arrival at the pearly gates had been heralded not by Gabriel but by the poor trumpet of my ecstatic cries. But on the other hand, how could I be so sure there even was a God? The idea that the flow of human endeavor was portioned out by some ornery old codger ensconced on some celestial throne with an ass as wide as the universe did not quite add up. And proof of His absence was evidenced not in what I had become but in what had become of Momma. Her loving God had let her go insane, had done nothing to stay those noxious fumes she had enlivened for her own end. If He could caution and punish the wayward, why could He not prevent the unraveling of one of His most faithful? In the raptor's claw, in the wolf's fang, was precedent for my plight. My mother's faith had no such evidence.

Could I continue to steal my victims' lives? Could I invite other faces like Elvira's to haunt me? Could I stand another flavorless day? I had to be practical. I had to accept what I had become or be forever in limbo. Surely whatever was in nature could not be reviled by nature. Someone had even said that once. Some ancient fart in a toga. One of Momma's dead Greeks. Town was my only hunting ground. That may have been fitting, for what were towns? Were they an extension of nature? Or an attempt to pervert nature by man's hubris? Fretfully, reluctantly, at times even angrily, I reconciled myself to becoming a kind of new venom in the pants of the wicked. A social disease if ever there was one. I was loath to do it. I hated leaving the site of our cabin. I hated leaving Momma. Or rather I *would* have hated those things if my wits had not been dulled by the keenness of my new addiction. The question was who to approach? Should I track down Da, come clean, and hit him up for a pint or two? Wasn't that pulling a tad hard on the reins of fatherly charity? I could not relive that horrible first time in town, so I reasoned I could outrun the Beguiler by trusting someone, explaining my plight, and getting them to pony up the hot berry punch, without having to loiter around again and off some poor stranger. I needed someone in between. An acquaintance. Someone who knew me well enough to be alone with me and yet not a limb I'd have to lop off the old family tree.

Mr. Hegemore.

That rang it. He'd be perfect. As a shopkeeper, surely he had preyed long enough on the needs of the poor to deserve my attention. *Say Hegemore, you reckon you could reach me one of those fine jars of brandied peaches?* And he would turn to me and see me as what? Some strapping young Adonis? A feast for six with leftovers. I owed my father a goat. So I squared my drawers and, pulling the goat behind me, slouched back toward Hollywood to be "born" as the new beguiling me.

# Chapter Eleven

In the time I had taken to reason my plight, I could hardly return to town as a dull and ravenous monster. I needed a quick pick-me-up so I could make my case to Hegemore as my usual spunky bumpkin self. The damned aren't privy to many of Providence's good graces, but the one thing the damned have is luck. And luck was with me as I strolled to town.

He wasn't much to look at. Just a poor old sodbuster I came upon while he was taking a dump up creek. One look at me, he probably thought I was Queen Vicky cutting across the verge to knight him.

"Albert," I had said as I approached him with a smile. "Is that you, cousin? Give us a kiss."

Filled up on his berry punch, I was ready to face Hegemore.

I was lit up like a German Christmas tree when I finally made it back to town. The raised sidewalks were cluttered with stinky mule skinners and ladies of distinction who ignored them. I saw hats tipped, heads bowed, with nary an impertinent eye meeting mine. And I saw plenty of worse than impertinent eyes leering at me from daytime drunks and squirrelly young bank clerks. But among all that pedestrian flotsam, I didn't beguile a single citizen. I was hoping maybe I could spare Mr. Hegemore my rough intentions. I still had a warm memory of him, despite my thirst. But no one stopped me with a grateful or relieved smile, addressing me by some random name, welcoming me to their own demise. Perhaps this was how the Beguiler worked. Once sated, my charming lure lost all its teeth.

Sticking to my plan, I scanned the shop fronts on my way to Hegemore's emporium. An opera house was under construction. A ladies temperance league had a pretty little store front where religious chapbooks were sold for a penny apiece. Even Capability Brown had proved up. I was in no rush, so I stepped inside her establishment.

Her fiscal horse sense seemed to have spread as wide as the strained stays of her girdle. Collapsing her tent, she had set up a small sporting house in an abandoned stable behind the old smithy. She didn't even bother to change the bones of the place's previous incarnation. She simply swept out the hay and set up sturdy brass beds in the reeking stalls. She called her girls "her mares," her place of business "The Stable," and even took the equine parody to graphic extremes when she labeled her employees' efforts as "rides: trots, canters, or gallops" each of increasing price. It was a crass approach but damn profitable. Her girls were passably clean and reasonably game, all Irish refugees fleeing the troubles of their homeland. It was a fragrantly warm day, the air entirely composed, at least to my newly agile sinuses, of equal parts horseshit, mule piss, and expectorated chaw.

Moving on, I was disappointed to learn Hegemore's establishment was locked. The once enticing windows were empty. Not a soul inside it. What had happened to him? Had he pulled up stakes? Or been run off? I needed answers. But first I needed to unload the goat I was toting.

Even though it was not quite noon, I figured I would find Da warming a barstool at Squirrel Tooth Alice's, his old haunt. But not even Alice's was there anymore. It was now some kind of cock-eyed teahouse named the *Garden of Allah*. I couldn't believe my eyes. How had some enterprising soul, even an incredibly industrious one, erected this magnificent structure so damn quickly? Did the Beguiler do something sneaky with my sense of *time*? The teahouse was a scaled down version of a pasha's palace, complete with onion-shaped turrets and finicky minarets, the whole florid mess painted pink with gold trim. This joint had Hegemore written all over it. I dragged the goat inside. I was truly rendered dumb by what I beheld. There was no bar. No stools. The walls were tiled a peacock blue with a tracery of complex Moorish multifoil arches, a topiary of an orange tree in a hammered copper pot between each one. The floor was a roil of rugs and cushions in jewel-toned silk and gold-shot satin. And on these cushions were men. Men in Sunday frock coats and cravats. Men with aggressive side whiskers. Well-heeled gents. Bathed. Affluent. They sat around a fountain that softly trickled water scented with neroli oil. Not all were so well dressed. There were a few teamsters, a couple of tradesmen, and pig farmers. But even they seemed remarkably well-mannered. The placid gents were served by pretty girls dressed in harem get-ups, slit and gathered according to their best advantage. They smoked from floor-standing hookahs, while others sipped from red-tinted glasses. But all conversed as if the hymn singing was about to begin. Someone had taught these apes how to wipe their asses. Someone had made them respectable. But who? As if in deference to my question, a gong sounded, and from between the part in a pair of beaded curtains, Hegemore himself appeared, pushing a gold samovar on a wheeled cart. He had dyed his hair black and grown an unctuous little beard. He wore a cherry-red fez and a short, embroidered vest, and he looked for all the world like a plump, demented genie.

"Mr. Hegemore?"

"Ah, the prodigal prairie nymph returns," he said, wheeling the cart to a dark-skinned girl with a triangular face and large ears. "Thank you, Marie," Hegemore said as he handed the cart off to her. She sneered at him as she took it, not even looking at me. "My dear, you look exhausted," he said with a curled lip. "And this abattoir-inspired ensemble you're sporting feels a bit *je ne sais quoi.*

Are you quite well?" I forced a smile. I had completely forgotten my chemise was lathered with blood from my morning feed.

"You still hawking flub-dubs, or you running women now?" I grinned.

He wiggled his melon-shaped head proudly. "My emporium is in transition. Not sure what I'll do with it."

"So now you run a cathouse?"

"Not exactly. But it's still quite profitable. Who would have thought mere tea would have such an equalizing effect on the varying social strata of our little burg." I noticed a few of his customers had conked out on the floor. One snored loudly, facedown in his spilled tea.

"What you got these boys drinking?" I asked, turning back to him. "They all seem a tad dazed." Hegemore seemed uncomfortable at my question. But only for a moment.

"A concoction of my own. Just premium tea leaves and juice of a few flowers. But you didn't come all this way to ply my trade secrets from me. How can I serve?"

"You seen my Da? I owe him this goat."

"What goat, my dear?"

The goat was missing. I looked around until I spotted it at the table of the snoring gentleman. The goat was lapping up his spilled tea, rousing him in the process. He seemed delighted at the intrusion and began "baaa-ing" with a loopy grin on his face.

"I wouldn't recommend you let your little friend there imbibe—"

"Why not? The damn thing was weaned on applejack." The goat sat back on its haunches, its angular butt landing squarely on one of Hegemore's silk cushions.

"Oh, my," he said.

I watched as the goat swiveled its boney head before toppling to the floor.

"Marie," Hegemore called to the girl with the big ears, "tend to this animal. Make sure it sobers." She sighed as she headed toward the goat. "Marie's people are simply marvels of husbandry when it comes to livestock. Born somewhere in the Basse-Navarre. The Basque region."

"*Eskualdunak*," Marie shouted over her shoulder.

"Of course, my dear," Hegemore called over to her. He pulled me to him and whispered to me. "You must be very careful what you say about her. She has the aural capacity of a bloody vampire bat."

"What the hell is she?"

"*Eskualdunak*. Apparently that's what the Basques call themselves. She speaks perfectly decipherable English but is very touchy about her homeland."

*Vampire.*

I hadn't heard that term in a while. Not since I came across John Murray's *Mazzeppa* collection. It was a compendium of poems and the like we had bought Momma while she was at her worst. As far as I knew she had never read it. But I had perused it. Byron had a frightful story in there that told the strange tale of Augustus Darvell. Da had bought the book from

Hegemore. So perhaps he had answers for me about my condition. But all that would have to wait.

"You never answered me about Da," I said.

"Perhaps you'd like to continue this conversation in more commodious accommodations."

"Have you seen him, Hegemore?" He clearly did not relish speaking while still on his feet. But what choice did he have?

"Alas, your father no longer frequents such wayward dens as mine," he said, adjusting his weight from foot to foot. "He has shunned the garden for the narrow gate."

"You sayin' my Da's found religion?"

"Sadly, yes."

"Horseshit. You got the wrong man."

"Would it were so. I miss his coin as much as his company."

"Hells bells. That puts a crick in it, don't it?"

"Honestly, Emma," he said with slight exasperation. "I must insist. If we are going to continue this happy little reunion, at least let it progress where my eager hospitality can be more fully appreciated. Can I offer you a refreshment?"

"I ain't hungry," I lied, eying all three of his chins. Hegemore looked to me like he could use an apple in his mouth and a roasting spit up his bum. But to him, I appeared to be the same old Emma. The Beguiler had not chosen him. I hid my disappointment with a flat smile as he hooked his arm in mine and began leading me toward the stairs.

"A bath, then," he said with a playful wink. "A lovely, hot ablution with geranium and lavender oil? I wager you've never had a proper soak in your life."

"You got hot running water in this joint?"

"The Romans had indoor plumbing, my dear. Hardly a novel concept. If we spent half our American ingenuity on more creature comforts than land swindles and firearms, we'd be reposing in democratic splendor within a decade." The offer was welcome. I was greasy and tired from my day. And a shot of hot berry punch was exactly what I desperately needed, even if my Beguiler was on the fritz. He led me silently up the main stairs, his backside swaying deliciously with each hoist of his weight. It was cool and oddly contained on the upper landing. I had never ascended to these sinful climes, but they were not what I expected. There was no smell of women and their briny work, no tinkle of hitching britches, no sound of rinse water when the work was over. In fact, the place hardly felt like a cathouse at all. At the top of the landing were a row of four discreetly closed doors, each numbered with a brightly polished brass plaque.

"What you got going on in here, Mr. Hegemore?" I asked, moving so close to him I could smell his luscious salt beneath his cologne. "Don't this place run whores no more?"

He exhaled a half laugh. "I did toy with the idea. But no. Let's just say I found a rather unusual solution to the needs of some of my more particular clientele." He tried to move me past the doors, but my curiosity was piqued. I wouldn't budge.

"What you hiding, Hegemore? What gives?"

As if to answer for him, one of the doors opened, and out stepped a man, hair combed, his neat suit brushed free of lint. Hegemore blushed as I stepped back, smiling. The man tipped his hat to whomever was inside then nodded to us and descended the stairs as if heading to his seat at the next Bible meeting. I stared at Hegemore, waiting for an explanation.

"Oh, all right," Hegemore said quietly, removing his fez. "I've made some changes to the place, is all." He rummaged in the pocket of his loose harem pants and produced a key. "See for yourself," he said, unlocking the door. Inside the room, the walls were lined with split logs stacked to look like the interior of a homesteader's cabin. A rough table with an oil lamp and two crude benches were all I could make out in the gloom.

"What the hell is this supposed to be? You got no *bed*."

Just then, the door to the water closet opened, and out stepped a woman I thought I recognized. She wore a pretty calico dress buttoned to the throat and was smoothing the tight bun on her head when she noticed us.

"Hey there, Mr. Hegemore. You wanting me up here or—"

"No, Nellie," Hegemore said quietly. "You may change and join the others downstairs for the remainder of your shift." She smiled, then looked at me.

"Hey," she said, grinning, "ain't you Silas Shinnecock's girl?" She was Nellie Maplethorpe, one of Alice's old bumping crew. I barely recognized her without her usual pound of face paint. "I ain't laid eyes on you since you drug your papaw out this knocker that time. You remember that cool drink of a preacher boy? Plug my cunny, if I wouldn't of punched that boy's ticket for free."

Hegemore winced. "That will be all, Miss Maplethorpe."

"Well, I best skedaddle, Emma," she said, skittering past us. "Say, honey," she said from the door. "You don't mind my sayin', you looking a might frayed."

I smiled wearily. "Well, you know what they say, Nellie. It ain't the work. It's the *stairs*."

"Damned if that ain't the truth of it." She wiggled her fingers at us as she headed down to the tearoom. After she had gone, I looked at Hegemore expectantly.

"Perhaps I should explain," he said with a sigh. "Months ago, I was approached by a man in my store. He confessed to a rather unusual bent, a need he felt I could satisfy. He said he would gladly depart with a fee of fifty dollars in gold should I be able to procure for him a rather unique experience."

"Fifty in gold for a tumble? Hell, I heard'a gals would have a go for two bits and a kind word."

"Please. If he'd wanted a 'tumble', he'd have bared his loins to Miss Brown. He wanted to . . . well . . . He wanted to hold an infant."

"What?"

"He was lonely. He'd been prospecting in California and had finally struck a vein, or load, or whatever the proper nomenclature is, and missed his wife and new daughter. So—"

"So this poor bastard paid you fifty in dust to hoist someone *else's* baby? No funny stuff?"

"*Lord* no. He simply wanted to hold it."

"And so you built this whole spread up here so lonely prospectors could play *house*?"

"That's rather reductive, but yes. I have three other scenarios. A park scene, a middle class parlor, and a church. Or a chapel, really."

"What the hell folks do in a fake chapel?"

"Why, they pray."

"Men *pay* you to kneel down with an ex-tart and *pretend* to pray?"

"I'm sure their prayers are genuine. The rest, is, yes—a proxy."

"Damn. You sure went to strides to limit your appeal." I was the daughter of a whoremonger after all. I knew where the average man's bread was buttered.

"This venture is rather selective, I'll admit. But the girls seem to appreciate the change."

"I bet they do."

"The real profit is in the teahouse, downstairs."

"*Downstairs*? You got this all wrong, brother. Cathouse coin's like cistern water. It's meant to flow *downwards*."

"Not when one charges those dandified rubes a whole gold eagle for a single cup of tea."

"Damned if you ain't full of secrets and wonders."

Then the floorboards fell away. I found myself floating in a great white void. I staggered, blinked, reached out for something to hold. The great moon of Elvira's sorrowful face was huge before me. I was but a speck trapped by the gravity of her lunar despair. I moaned as my hunger surged. The Beguiler had come calling, yet my aspect in Hegemore's eyes remained frustratingly stable. What the hell was I going to do?

"My stars, child. You *are* ill," Hegemore said as he steadied me. I calmed my breathing, thinking as fast as my hungry mind would allow.

"Ever since my momma passed I've been having . . . *frights*," I lied. "You reckon I could set a spell?"

"Must be the exposure. You'll feel worlds better after your bath."

My sudden urge told me I needed to pop my friend and get that hot berry punch flowing, pronto. But how? There was nothing in my mother's Thornwell about the proper engagement of violence, especially of the culinary variety. One thing was certain. I couldn't rightly go jawing into his throat on a semipublic landing in the middle of a work day. I needed some place private. And I needed it now.

"I fear I won't make it to your tub," I said, feigning a swoon I'd hoped I hadn't hammed up too much. "You got someplace closer?"

His motherly arms were about me once more as he pushed me through another of the four doors. We found ourselves, ironically, in the chapel setting he had mentioned. Italianate, early Renaissance, a Lippi madonna on the wall, a silver crucifix centered on an aubergine altar cloth. He guided me to a single fumed oak pew and sat me down. My mind teemed with various modes of epidermal egress, both practical and fantastical. Should I stoke up the charm and lure him close for a kiss? Stun him with a slap and ramrod my face to his jugular? Ask politely? Beg demurely? Flip a coin with him for it? Then what would I possibly wager? Faking a chill, I settled for what I hoped might appear a friendly hug.

"Hold me?" I asked as innocently as I could muster. My face wedged snugly between his doughy shoulder and ample jowl. I had to drill through a veritable strata of floral unguents before settling upon his meaty smell. He cleared his throat, impatient for this intimacy to end. I closed my eyes and lifted my lips from my teeth. My tongue landed lamely on his neck, and he let out a shriek of high, fruity laughter.

"Ahh! Please! I'm terribly ticklish!" He pulled away and slapped me playfully on the cheek. But the sting of his slap, benign in its intention, stoked something dark in me. Before I could think, I balled my fist and landed a hefty uppercut to his padded chin. The blow knocked him from the pew, sending him sprawling to his back. He floundered dumbly like a badly built beetle.

"Please, Mr. Hegemore!" I cried. "I need a friend!" Before I knew what I was doing I was upon him. His mouth opened to scream. My hand capped his cry.

"Listen to me," I said as nicely as I could. "You can help me with this. I just need a little. Just a splash of your hot berry punch to calm me down." Panicked, he kneed me in the gut, sending me backward. He scrambled from beneath me and was on his feet in an instant.

"Emma, my God! What are you *doing*, child?" he shouted, righting his fez.

"Please, Mr. Hegemore. Don't spar with me. It'll only go south for you if you do."

We squared off like two fighters. I feinted left. He was quick as a cat when he moved right. I lunged for him as he scrambled for some object that might protect him. His small eyes flashed a terrified delight as I looked down to see him brandishing the silver crucifix. I ducked as he swiped the cross at me.

"Come on now," I said breathlessly. "Don't make this harder than it needs to be." I rushed him. He parried smartly with the edge of the cross and nicked my ear. That decided it. Whatever reasoning was residual in my faculties was instantly sidelined. All was a monochrome of reds and pink. I felt my chest expand with a furious intake of air, and what came out of me was a sound so feral, so searingly primitive, not even I, in all my myriad experience of wild fauna, had reference for it. Hegemore's eyes went wide, and the crotch of his harem pants darkened as the piss trickled down to his ridiculously curled-tip slippers. The cross fell heavily to the floor. Hegemore slumped to his knees, a slobbering mass.

"*Please*," he whimpered. "How have I offended you?"

A knock on the door froze us both. Hegemore gasped. I jerked my head toward the sound.

"Mister Hegemore?" It was the Basque girl, Marie. "You okey doke in there, mister?" Hegemore looked to me. I held a finger to my lips. In that moment, he lost his luster. The Beguiler had never wanted him. It wanted Marie. And it had been cunning enough not to lure her until it knew I could have my way with her with very little audience. "I thought I heard a scream," Marie prattled. "You hear that, mister? A wolf. Ain't that *tuntuna*? A *big* wolf. Like when I was a girl in Aldude at my *ita's* sheep farm," she said, rambling. "You sure you don't got no *houndia* wolf in there with you?" Her giggle was dark with a dry humor. Hegemore read the shift in my intention, registering it with a blanched panic as he heaved himself to his feet. The knob of the chapel door began to twist.

"Marie!" he shouted. "Stay away! Go downstairs immediately!" But the door creaked open, revealing the girl, with her serious face and silly harem costume.

"All them customers asleep downstairs now so I thought I'd—*hey!*" Her huge blue eyes took in her frazzled boss, my feral face, the fearful miasma that still lingered in the room.

"Marie, *gaishua*," I cooed in a voice not my own. The girl blinked, stunned.

*"Ita?"*

"Marie! Run!" Hegemore bellowed. She turned, confused.

"Marie, *hator hona!*" I shouted.

The girl froze at the threshold. The sudden Basque I was speaking had complicated my tongue. My timbre was deep and work-worn, not used to harshness. "*Neshka polita*," I said softly, lifting my arms in welcome.

"*Ita?*" There were tears in the girl's eyes as she crept toward me. Hegemore gaped. "Poppa? Is it you? You've come back?" she asked. She walked toward me, her face filled with hope. Her tears were hot on my knuckles as she raised them to her lips. I felt a new weight in my fingers, a weariness and warmth that was not mine. I pulled her to me, sinking to my knees, holding her as she sobbed. "Oh, *Ita*! Oh, sweet Mother of Mercy! Oh my blessed saints! I thought I'd lost you! I thought you'd never find me. This is a terrible place. You were right. I should never have come. *Oren guziek dude gizona kolpatzen,*" she said, weeping.

"*Azkenekoak du hobira igortzen,*" I answered back through my tears. (All the hours shower blows on man. The last sends him to the tomb.)

The love I felt for her was huge. She was my daughter. My only child. She had always been thus. And in the shared joy of our sudden reunion, I sank my teeth into her little throat. Hegemore tried to scream, but no sound came out of him. I could see her memories of her father's funeral as I drank from her.

*Parched hills dotted with broken gravestones, each carved with curious serpentine crosses.*

*A priest in threadbare vestments, funeral rites croaked over the sounds of shovels.*
*The box they lower into the grave is still scabbed with its pine bark.*
*The sorrow in my small body longs for poppa.*
*Hates the green hills all around me.*
*I am too alone.*
*I am nothing.*

"Emma!"

Hegemore's scream brought me back to the room. The girl was no longer heavy on my lap. What was once Marie was now a husk, a vague and hollow girl-shaped parchment. My tears were real. Just as my fatherly love for Marie had been real.

"Oh, Mr. Hegemore," I cried. "What have I become!" He was not horrified. He did not look at me with scorn. If he showed anything, it was fascination with what he had just witnessed.

"I have dreamed of meeting a creature like you my entire life," he said finally, drawing me slowly to my feet. "But I believe I promised you a bath first."

# CHAPTER TWELVE

Hegemore's rooms were not really rooms at all. I understood a home to be a construction *of* nature *against* nature—recognizable in its materials and at least somewhat rational in its response to weather. His suites seemed to scoff at nature altogether. From every polished, gilt, and upholstered surface, the wilderness outside was rapturously vanquished. An aria sung against a hurricane. There were oil paintings from Flanders and Florence, rendered in eras when oil itself was still a novel concept. Roman marble covered in its original polychrome lined the perimeter, huge effigies of slouching muscled athletes with the whorls of their head and body hair exquisitely executed in blond, brunet, and auburn. He had a huge licorice-colored bed with a fussy canopy made of carved oak he later told me had been owned by Anne of Cleves. And every anthropomorphic image in there, every saint suffering in ecstasy, every lumbering wrestler catching his breath under the sculpted flaps of his chest, every butterball cherub or smirking satyr, was male. I must have counted nearly three hundred peckers in there, either flopping, sprawling, pertly pissing, or in high salute. In my glutted state, all this loot glowed with an almost palpable decadence.

The silence between us had been more stunned than formal as he left me to my bath. He knew I had been surprised at his response to my killing of Marie. I was even more surprised at the kindness, the deference, he showed me. Had I finally found a friend? An ally that not only appreciated the Beguiler in me but could also help me understand it? I washed the girl's blood from my face in water that had come out of the wall perfectly heated and floral scented. I dressed in a thin peach silk robe he had left for me. The garment lay like hoarfrost on my hot skin. Hegemore was sitting at his desk when I entered his room, bent over one of several leather-bound books that formed a small bulwark around his blotter. He looked up, startled, still alert, as I draped myself upon his bed.

"My, God," he said, catching his breath. "You look *ravishing*." He tucked his chin as soon as he said this, his eyes drifting back to an open page. Was it safe to offer me a personal compliment? I knew he had questions. We both did.

"How'd you come by all this swag?" I asked him as I picked up a gob of sky blue faience from his night table. A Greek figure of a hermaphrodite from the cult of Dionysus. But it looked to me like a lady with a johnson the size of a hoe handle.

"Most of it is the accumulation of personal collecting. The rest has been in the family for years."

"Your folks dead?"

"Heavens, no. Merely guilty. I suppose I was becoming an increasing embarrassment to them. And disowning me with a few family baubles seemed to lessen the blow." I put the sculpture back. He cleared his throat. He seemed calm. But I could tell he was still uneasy in my company.

"What should I call you?" I asked.

"Pardon?"

"I figure after everything, you could at least tell me your Christian name."

"Call me Augustus," he said with a slight bow of his head.

"*Augustus* Hegemore?"

"Augustus *Hadrian Anthemius* Hegemore.

"Damn. You got the whole Roman rule in there, don't you?" I said. I hoped my knowledge of Gibbon might somehow make him trust me.

"A smattering of the Western Empire, at least. My father considered Constantine the first proto-Christian stooge."

"Hell, I'm callin' you plain ol' Hegey. You square?"

What was I doing? I'd been taught never to name the beasts of our convenience. The horse had no name. Same with the goat. All our chickens had hit our table with no familiarity. Why the hell was I suddenly coming up with a cute little sobriquet for what might one day be my supper?

"Hegey?" He looked vaguely disappointed but clearly in no position to negotiate. "Sounds like some kind of diminutive rodent."

"Listen, I'm sorry you had to see that," I said shyly. "Is there someone we should write to?"

"About what?"

"Marie."

"Ah, yes. Well, when she came into my employ, she informed me she was an orphan."

"Of course. Her father's dead."

"How did you know that?"

I was unsure how to explain it. I looked at him in silence.

He cleared his throat. "She called you '*Ita.*' I assume that means father."

"Poppa," I said softly. The memory of her small, warm body in my arms brought new tears to my eyes.

"I'm sorry. I don't mean to pry."

"Are you afraid of me, Mr. Hegemore?" My voice cracked as I spoke.

"Conditionally, no" he said, his face softening. "Intrigued. Perhaps awed is more accurate." I saw his hand grope toward a small dagger he might have used to open his letters. I'd seen rabbits in snares with worried faces like his. "Might I inquire if you are at present entirely sated?" He raised the dagger slightly. I wanted to put him at his ease. But how could I? This whole mess was as new to me as it was to him.

"I'd say you're safe, Hegey. For now." He coughed as his eyes went wide. "You were pretty good with that crucifix earlier."

"Years of boyhood saber instruction. My father insisted. Thought it might make me more of a man."

"You are very much a man, Mr. Hegemore," I said.

He gave me a courtly nod, but I could see tears forming in the creases of his eyes. "Indeed," he said, clearing his throat with a slight smile. "You may be the first to so recognize me. I think we might be great friends, Emma."

"I need a friend."

I told him my story, starting with the most recent events and working backward. He listened intently as I spoke, only occasionally referencing a page from one of the books on his desk.

"And you knew this salesman's wife to be Elvira *how* exactly?" he asked when I finished.

"I saw her face in my mind as I drank from him. Her picture was on the fob of his watch."

"Which you saw only *after* you attacked him?"

"I wasn't asking him for the time."

"Do you still have the watch?" I opened my mouth to answer, but he cut me off. "Of course not! Why would you covet evidence that would confirm your guilt?"

"Mr. Hegemore—"

"And a similar event occurred with Marie? I assume you spoke no Basque before today." He was pacing around his room now, speaking more to himself than me.

"My mother could barely get Latin to stick," I said from my position on the bed. He flitted back to his desk, smiling.

"Indeed." He drew a finger down the page of his open book and swallowed. "Well, I think we can safely dispense with the Serbian strain. You seem completely immune to the usual Christian iconography."

"What strain?" I asked.

He stood shakily and hurried to his dresser. "You wonder what you have become. I think I know." He removed a large gilt box, looking at me over his shoulder before coming to the bed and dumping a slurry of diadems, earrings, and queenly cameos onto the duvet.

"Forgive me, Emma, but I must take advantage of this lapse in your . . . appetite." He stepped back and peered at me.

"You want to play dress up now?"

"Is that *all* you feel looking at these objects?" I noted a string of black pearls. A pretty emerald brooch. "You have no overwhelming desire to count them?"

"Strain of what, Hegey?"

"That rules out arithmomania and hence any Asian variety of your condition."

"Variety of *what*?" But the fat little man was on a real tear now.

"This stranger you said you laid with. Did he ever mention the name *Sanboson* or any variation thereof?"

"Sansa-*what?*"

"Because in certain reports I've collected, *Sanboson* can be easily confused with the more accurate *Asanbosam*. Which would be truly exciting." He rushed to a glass-fronted bookcase and leafed through several cracked tomes and parchments, settling finally on what looked to be a fragile curl of ancient papyrus. "I can't be sure my Coptic is up to snuff," he said gently, opening the scroll, "but . . . Ah! Yes! *Asanbosam!*" His eyes scanned the contents, darkening by degrees as he read. "That would make you a child of the Father of All Panthers, Emma. Your strain could be of the Ashanti of West Africa. A real filth-sister to the *Obayifo*, spawn of the *Okomfo,* and the most pure of all the blood thieves."

"Blood thieves?"

"This scroll is over four thousand years old, Emma," he said, rolling it carefully. "Purported to be from the famed library of Alexandria before its untimely immolation."

He tucked it gently back on its shelf, then crossed to me and sat on the edge of his bed. "It says the *Asanbosam* is the most powerful of all blood thirsters. Rival to the *vrykolakas* of Greece, the *draugr* of the Norse. Even the *strigod* of Romania that Dr. Polidori thought such lurid and charming stuff. You can obviously travel by day, have no adverse effects from blood cleansers like silver. Therefore—"

"*Hegey!*"

He was startled by my outburst, his face as fresh as a child reliving Waterloo with his lead soldiers. I softened my tone as I put my hand on his sweaty paw.

"Hegey, what fool strain are you talking about!"

"Strain of *vampirism,* you tedious child," he said with half a smile. "A bloodborne virus imparted from one's sire to his victim that causes hematophagy in that victim. And hence your present culinary proclivity toward *sanguis luxuriae.*"

So there it was in medical gobbledygook and cockeyed Latin. I was a monster. I immediately began sobbing like a wretched babe in a soiled nappy. Hegemore looked at me with disgust.

"Stop that blubbering at once!" he said, wrapping me in his meaty arms. "Don't you know how unusual you are? How *rare*?" I wept onto his flabby chest until he gently took my shoulders in his hands and made me face him. He wiped my tears from my eyes with his thumbs and smiled at me. "There is no historical precedent for your particular manifestation of this condition," he said soothingly. "All the creatures I've mentioned rely on their animal prowess to ensnare their victims. But not you. In all my studies of the subject, I have never come across a reference to this *Beguiler* you speak of. The way you lure your victims by transforming your aspect into someone they trust and thereby remove all the crude and messy necessity of the hunt?" He had heard me speak Basque, but had he seen the other changes I had felt? The heaviness of my work-worn hands? My gut bloated with age and sorrow? Had he seen those things too? Or had only Marie been privy to those physical deceptions? "My books and scholarship are useless.

You are something evolved, Emma. Something elegant. Something *new*!"

I sniffled and tried to grin as I looked at him. "You think?"

"Believe me. I know what it means to be different. To be something that defies categorization. You should never, *ever* be ashamed of that." I felt six years old, looking into the caring eyes of a mother I had lost. "There is no 'why' of you, my dear," he said. "No 'how' or 'wherefore.' There is *only* you. The originality and wonder of *you*."

Night blackened the windows of his apartments. He had left me on his bed with a book of Napoleonic pornography, amphora etchings of randy Greeks, while he burned all of Marie's clothes in the fire grate. I could get used to this. But something still nagged at me. The question none of his occult erudition had addressed.

"Let me get you something that will ease your mind," Hegemore said, wiping the ashes from his hands. He returned to the bed with a pretty box in the shape of a heart pressed to his chest like a queen's favor, a conspiratorial glint in his eye. "Now there are some who prefer French. Others who swear by the Swiss. But for my money, there is really only *one* thing at which the Belgians truly excel. Prepare thyself for the nectar of the anointed." He removed a small brown square of waxy stuff that to my unschooled eyes looked like a boxy turd. Before I could properly form a sneer, he held the little brownish chunk under my nose, and I got my first whiff.

Chocolate.

And there was no turning back. Regret flooded me first. Why did our Creator bother with the sweet breath of flowers when he could have defaulted to this toasted and sugared aroma? And, on a more personal note, why had the human heart been made such a poor pump that its only grease was a ruddy slosh of hemoglobin and corpuscles when people would be so much happier circulating tributaries of rich, molten cocoa? The contents of Hegey's jugular paled in comparison with this new promise.

"That stuff's not half bad," I said, reaching for another piece. But he snatched the box away.

"Ah-ah. The waistline takes as a promise what is mere flirtation to the lips," he said in singsong.

"You think I need to worry on that?" I said, snatching the box from him. "Only one thing still vexes me."

"Only one? How novel."

"Why not *you?*" I said, biting into another chocolate.

"Why not me, what?"

"Hegey? Ain't it obvious? How come the Beguiler didn't choose you? It had ample opportunity. I even helped it out a little and, still, nothing. Now, how you figure on that?" He reached for a handful of chocolates and stuffed them into his weakly pumping jaws. I noticed his face sparkled. Was he wearing face powder?

"I believe it may have something to do with fear. I was shocked by your congress with Marie. But not fearful of it. Fear might trigger some mechanical flux in your victim's brain. Some scent or other tempting effect."

"You were afraid when I came at you."

He peered at me, swallowing his mouthful of chocolate. He took a deep breath. Then slowly let it out. He looked somehow defeated, resigned to what he was about to admit.

"Then the answer to that is simple, my dear. Sickeningly simple." He wiped his eyes and smiled. "I have never been loved. Nor have I *ever* loved."

"Aw, Hegey," I said, moving my arm around him. "I still don't get it. What about all the people I passed on my way to you? Not *one* of them had ever lost someone they cared about?"

He took the empty box and placed it on his night table. "Perhaps they hadn't. Or perhaps they were not ruminating upon their loss as you passed them. Timing might be everything, and people are far more callous than they appear." Or maybe it was more complicated than that. The Beguiler chose my victims for me. Though under what criteria I was not sure I would ever learn. He took my hand as he led me from the bed, returning to it to fluff a pillow. "Now that we have at least a passible hypothesis as to the workings of your Beguiler," he said, "our next task will be how to keep you consistently fed. The answer to me is pure economics. You need to advertise. Like toothpowder or washboards." He chuckled. "Though *how* we will safely parade you before as many people as possible, we'll determine later. First we must rest and recover from our stimulating day."

# Chapter Thirteen

There is a pureness to romantic gestures not motivated by the promise of a future grope, an elegance to the pairing of seductive lighting and perfumed linen when the prognosis of swapping corporal fluids is nil. And thus, Hegey prepared the bed we would share, without trespass, without fear. He moored himself on his soft sheets on one side of his bed, and I curled against him, snug as a squirrel in her knothole. We passed the night without incident and, in my case, dreamless.

Baths, bed, and books were my mother's self-reward, the holy trinity that redeemed the endless domestic slog of her days. How many times, high in the summer, had I seen her neck-deep in the horse's trough, squinting over her Pope or Racine, elbows cocked at the calcified rim, trying to keep the grass flecks and spit-slosh from her pages. Lighting up print seemed a tragic waste of sunlight to me then. But that first morning at Hegey's, I wasn't so sure. Perhaps it was seeing books in their natural setting, on proper shelves, sequestered behind clean glass. Or perhaps the Beguiler understood, like Goethe, that both the mind and the body must be equally attended if we are to become truly whole. Hegey seemed to have all his literate wickets covered. History, science, poetry, medicine. I leafed through several folios before being drawn to two mossy-green tomes flecked with filigreed gold. I'd been reading for about an hour, enjoying the story of a funny thin man with a barber's basin for a hat and his fat little friend, when Hegey crept into the room.

"You're awake." He craned his neck to the book's spine and looked at me, perplexed. "I didn't know you could read classical Spanish."

Neither did I. Was my sudden fluency preparing me for some future victim who could speak Spanish? Too many questions. I put down the book and saw a knife glint behind Hegey's back.

"Hey, look at that," I said as he brought into view a tarnished silver basin with a cutout half-moon at its rim. "That's like the barber's bowl this Quixote character wears for a helmet in my book."

"It's a bleeding bowl, actually," he said, sweeping it from my gaze. "Once owned by the famed Dr. James Craik."

"Never heard of him."

"He was the personal physician of General George Washington. Perhaps you've heard of *him*?"

"Didn't he die from being bled too aggressively?" I had read that earlier in the morning while scanning some of Hegey's tomes. My reading retention surprised even me. Hegey raised his eyebrows, impressed.

"My, we have been a busy little bookworm. But I hardly think that has any bearing on our present conundrum."

"What's the bowl for?"

"Breakfast."

"I see." I laid back on the headboard, confused. "Why don't you just use your straight razor?"

"Germ infection is still theoretical, but why take chances. May I continue?" I stayed silent. "You see, the problem of your kind, Emma, has always been detection. The *Lilitu* of Babylonia might still be queens of modern culture if they had hidden the procurement of their groceries from their Hebrew conquerors. And the seventeenth century's Countess Bathory? Who knows what a paramount of fashion she might be today if she had bathed in something less incriminating than the peasant blood of virgins. That's why I feel with a bit of finesse, some self-control on your part, and the usual cups and cutlery, you can live a reasonably undetected life. At least until we come upon a more salubrious solution." He had obviously been giving my predicament a hell of a lot more thought than I.

I looked at the knife in his hand. He resembled a wide-eyed kid about to tear into a berry pie way too big for him. "Hold on. You're going to bleed yourself? For me? *You*?"

"Why not me?"

"Are you kidding? I'm gonna watch you stick yourself with a pen knife—"

"I'll have you know, I have a surprisingly lofty pain tolerance."

"And dribble into a dish and then what? Sip it out of a *cup*?"

"I was thinking hand-chased silver. I have a simply superb chalice from the court of Isabella."

"I can't let you do it, Hegey. Probably the nicest offer I've ever had, but no."

"You sure?"

"Hells bells, mister. Be like a cunny full of piss on a house fire."

"Oh, I was *hoping* to hear you say that," he said, almost tumbling from his seat in a theatrical swoon. "Perhaps less crudely, but I am *so* relieved, my dear. You have no idea."

It wasn't simply Hegey's proposal that brought my refusal. Or the dark sorrows submerged in his berry punch I might have to endure. For all I knew, a cup a day might keep me in clover and Hegey just a little light-headed. No. What had torn it for me was the idea of the thing, the implication of a captive, domestic arrangement where I would have to rely on him for my very sustenance. The last thing I wanted was to end up like Momma.

"I have a better idea," I said.

"You have my attention."

"The way I figure it, you have a whole moveable feast coming through your doors every day. Why don't I just work for *you*? Some forlorn sucker is bound to take the bait."

My plan, though solid in theory, only lasted one day. It seemed to benefit Hegey's shaky reputation more than my gullet. Hegey wasn't stingy with his fancy duds, and I wouldn't have been mistaken if I had assumed he encouraged my circulation among his downstairs regulars. He seemed delighted when he heard me referred to as his "upstairs girl." The rumors about him seemed to evaporate whenever he'd wrap an insinuating arm around my waist. His customers would coo and tickle, and I'd scare up a good blush on Hegey at the attention. But I wasn't looking to be admired. I wanted to be mistook. I had promised Hegey I'd keep my hunting grounds within the walls of his teahouse. But as the hours dragged on, the Moorish splendor of his tea parlor seemed more and more like the losing end of a fishbowl. Bank clerks and seed peddlers. Husbands on the loose and gamey rail splitters. All looked at me with the same drowsy faces, the same unfocused smiles. They had come to lose themselves in whatever they were sipping from Hegey's cups. Not mistakenly find someone they'd lost. I was infuriatingly only myself among them. And if the sweet oblivion my smile offered went ignored, the Garden's all-male population cared even less about what had happened to poor Marie.

Desperate that night, I left Hegey burping in his dreams and snuck down to the street. The unique sorrows my Beguiler needed to do its wet work were sadly lost in the shared joy of Hegey's patrons. As much as it pained me, such a revelation necessitated I break my promise to him and expand my territory beyond his walls. The leopard had her spots. The viper, her dusty diamonds. Hegey's old emporium seemed the perfect spot where I could similarly attire myself. The back door to the shop was locked. But the skylight on the roof was open. Hegey must have done that to insure proper circulation for his inventory. I climbed the shop's clapboard with ease and poured myself onto the roof, the tar-stink of the shingles up there reminding me painfully of home. There was a fine mesh grate over the opening the skylight covered, and peering through it, I saw a faint glow from somewhere inside. Moth traps, I figured. Hegey must have lit lamps full of camphor oil to guard against the pests. I peeled off the grate and dropped inside, quiet as a cat. My guess about the moth traps proved valid as I saw several burning lamps on small pedestals casting an eerie glow upon the racks of clothes. Only, somewhere off in the gloom, one of the lights was moving. That gave me pause. Why was I frightened? The shop was locked tight as a nun's knees. The only way out was through me. Why was my heart beating so? I hid behind the rack of men's suits and positioned myself so I could see past the backroom curtains to the front of the shop. Nothing.

Then I caught site of it. A shadowy figure standing at the candy counter, not more than a yard from me. I froze. I watched as the figure slowly opened one of the jars and dropped a dusky claw inside it. I could hear the brittle sugar shatter under its teeth. Something told me to light out of there, but I stayed anchored to where I crouched, too scared to move or breathe.

"Who's there?" came a girlish voice. I felt compelled to answer, but the moment was sundered by a bout of harsh coughing. She cleared her throat while she casually replaced the lip of the candy jar. "I know you are there. I can feel you in the dark." Her voice was educated, alluring, the fine timbre of it reduced only by her discrete coughing. "Mater said proximity to death heightens one's senses. She would know. She could read my very thoughts before she passed." In the flickering gloom, I saw she was dressed from head to foot in widow's weeds, a fine black mourning dress complete with a veil. She licked the fingers of one hand and moved blindly toward me, seeking me by the weak light of a lamp she held in her other. "Please," she said huskily, "I know you're not the law, for you would have apprehended me. And you are clearly not the owner of this establishment, or you would be reprimanding me. Won't you reveal yourself to me, dear stranger? It is my birthday, after all. It's so lonely to celebrate my last alone." What type of young woman would be prattling to a potential maniac in a locked store in the dead of night? Her fearlessness moved me as much as it terrified me, and I desperately did not want her to see me. I burrowed beneath the shadowy suits as she came closer and closer, my heart thundering in my chest. "There you are," she said as the frail light of her lamp pinked my clenched eyelids. She gasped as huge black wings tore through my shoulders with a feathery thunder. The air was suddenly heavy with the scent of dead roses as I reluctantly stood to face her. There was more relief than terror in her awed gaze. I looked down to my hands. They had become slender and as pale as winter moonlight. "The midnight angel," she whispered. "You are more beautiful than I imagined." The moment should have ended there. She would have drifted into my arms and between my jaws, and the prosaic end of her life would have been sweetened by her beguiled expectations of our profound and final embrace. But I couldn't allow that. Not with her. I couldn't be party to the huge hoax the Beguiler commanded.

"Hey, there," I said softly. She furrowed her pale brow, her bright blue eyes clouding with confusion.

"You don't *sound* the way I imagined Death—"

"That's because I'm not," I said lamely, cutting her off. "Or rather I *am* but not the way—It's all higgledy-piggledy." I could feel the Beguiler lurch inside me, straining, like a prompter at play, to get an actor back on script. But I resisted its corrections.

"But your wings," she said with a wry smile. I tried to tuck them back into my shoulders, but they had become caught in the shelves of bric-a-brac on either side of me. With an embarrassed tug, I managed to free them, upsetting several of Hegey's more expensive jade cups and pistols in the process. She giggled as my fetters crashed loudly to the floor.

"I see," she said. "You thought I might fear you so have made yourself ridiculous to calm me."

"No. *Yes.*"

"It is how I hoped," she chirped. "I always wished Death would come as a friend." The thought of her dying was no longer a prize to me. I *would* have been friends with this girl under other circumstances. A real boon companion. The thought of her ending, either by my hand or fate's, broke my heart.

"Oh, don't look like that," she said sweetly. "I'm tired of people moping around me. Death's not to be mourned. No more than the setting sun. Or a daylit moon dissolving upon a new morning. I only dressed like this so I wouldn't be seen coming in here."

"How long you been ailing?" I asked.

"Long time. It took Mater first. We were on our way to Los Angeles. Do you know it? The city of angels. There's a cultured Mexican community there where I could continue my studies. The air is supposed to be sweet and dry. Of benefit to people like me. They have an opera house. Cafes. Streets lined with orange trees. I would have so loved to have seen the ocean."

"How old are you?" I asked.

She smiled. "I'm nineteen today."

"We should toast with something. Can you caution a drink?"

"Caution has loosened all hold on me." She moved briskly past me to the candy jars where Hegey kept the prime booze under the counter. "I think I saw some brandy here earlier. French cognac or the like. Good stuff." She produced the bottle and bit off the cork while I got two cut crystal glasses from Hegey's stash. She poured two shots and raised her glass.

"To nineteen very full years," she said as I raised my glass. "A toast with Death. How splendid." She barely wet her lips while I knocked back my whole glass in a single swallow. The spirit brought on another coughing jag from her. But she smiled through it as she regained her breath. I couldn't let her go.

"What were you studying?" I asked.

"Music. Beethoven. Do you know him? Very modern. But such passion in his progressive chords." I shot a glance around the room. Wouldn't you know it? All this fine loot and not a piano in sight. I would have given anything just to hear her play one last song. A thought formed in my head. Perhaps I could give her a birthday gift instead.

"Let me ask you something."

"Anything."

"How'd you get in here?"

"Same way you did. Through the skylight." In a veil and full-length skirt? Perhaps this girl had pluck after all.

"How'd you get the screen back in place?"

"I lifted it and slipped under it. It *fell* back into place." And damn clever too. "Why are you asking me this?"

"You don't want to die, do you?" I said. She raised her eyebrows and grinned.

"I wasn't aware I had a choice."

"What if you did?"

"What if I did *what?*"

"Had a choice. What if you could live nigh on forever?" Her eyelids drooped as she nodded.

"Oh, I see. You mean life everlasting. Well, I'm not a strict Protestant, but I feel I'm enough of a Christian to ensure—"

"*No*, sister. I'm not here to convert you. Just the opposite perhaps. Would you do it? Would you take the chance?" She hesitated before she stepped back from me, a stiff smile on her face.

"I really do appreciate making your acquaintance and am honored you shared my birthday with me. But this conversation has gone—"

"Listen," I said stepping to her. "I ain't offering no smooth road. No gentle garden path. But you would be able to finish your studies. Maybe meet a boy. Pop out a few impresarios of your own. Are you game?"

Her eyes cooled. Her smooth brow furrowed. "You're toying with me," she said. "Please. Just take me."

How could I show her I meant her no harm? How could I prove that my intentions, as dark as they fundamentally were, ultimately held some kind of light? Without thinking, which was quite a habit with me, I smashed the glass in my hand. She gasped. Quick as a flash, I drew the jagged edge over my throat as she screamed. My wound was deep but it barely bled. She watched with staring eyes as my wound immediately began to heal before her.

"What *are* you? Some kind of mesmerist? How is this possible?" She dropped to her knees. I joined her on the floor with the brandy bottle. She took it from me absently and swallowed a long pull.

"I'm not Death, miss," I said quietly. "I'm a Beguiler. I'm *me,* that is, like you but a different version of you. Of me, rather."

"I see. And is it your habit to have great, crow-like wings burst through your shoulders among random racks of men's coats? Is this some sport you play with all young consumptives you happen to meet?"

"The Beguiler shows you what you most long to see."

"And I long for the company of the midnight angel. But you are no angel."

"Not in the usual sense."

"You are as I always imagined Death. And yet you are not Death."

"Death would hardly offer you what I'm offering."

"What's your name, stranger?" she asked suddenly.

"Emma May Shinnecock."

"Alberta Cosgrove." She shook my hand weakly, almost automatically, before she took another swig and looked at me with sly but interested eyes. "You really are not the midnight angel?"

"No. Just a girl with a very unique gift to give you."

"What kind of gift?"

We hunkered down on the floor with what was left of the bottle and a jar of chocolates while I told her my whole story. When I had finished, she was far more relaxed but still cautious in her questions.

"But that is fantastic. Like something by Dr. Polidori."

"Only this ain't no penny dreadful, missy. It's the real deal. That's why you gotta be sure. *You* gotta make the choice." And a lady always makes her own choices.

"But all that killing. All those people. How do you live with it?"

"I didn't have a choice in the matter. You do." She got up from the floor, unsteady in equal parts from the brandy and the conversation, and walked around the store. I watched her as her fine mind reeled with the implications of my offer. She walked to the rack of women's gowns and let her fingers play among the dimly sparkling beads and fine fabrics.

"I always wanted a dress like this."

"It's yours."

"And I'll still be able to play my music?"

"You'll hear sounds in Beethoven not even he could have imagined." She giggled as she pulled a pure white satin frock from the rack and held it up to her. She stood in front of a full-length mirror, whispering intently to herself things I could not hear in my dimmed and hungry state.

"Will it hurt?" she asked, looking at me from her reflection in the mirror.

"Not a bit."

"I was dead anyway," she said solemnly. "This could be a kind of rebirth. A little renaissance of me."

"Put it on."

"What?"

"The dress. Put it on. It's your birthday." She playfully undid the buttons of her mournful frock and pushed it from her pale shoulders to the floor. She stood before me as pale as her white chemise and bloomers. Her body was tall and fine and slender. Perhaps it was the Beguiler on the cusp of gaining its sweet that made me feel the way I did. But to me, at that moment, she was the most desirable thing I had ever beheld. I longed to put my arms around her tapered waist. To have my lips play upon her swanlike neck. She caught my look, and something secret passed between us. Strong passions that defied everything but the simple truth that we were both just living humans who wanted one another. She held my eyes with hers as she slipped the white dress over first her legs, then her flat belly, then her snowy shoulders.

"The rich feed on the poor," she reasoned in a singsong voice. "The beautiful feed on the ugly. The talented feed on the uninspired. It's wrong. It's unfair. But is it any more unjust than my fate?"

I drifted from my place on the floor until I was standing behind her. Even with my senses dulled, the scent of her was as rain-washed air.

"Everything in my mind tells me this is wrong, Emma," she said turning to me. I wrapped my arms around her. "But my heart just wants to *live*."

# Chapter Fourteen

We awoke in each other's arms.

I did not turn her the way I had been turned. The passion was surpassing, but the secrets of our similar bodies brought new pleasures to our congress. Our lovemaking was softer, fiercer. And lasted one hell of a lot longer. Wave after ecstatic wave made a mockery of time as the Beguiler in us both consummated with our drinking of one another. I held her when she awoke to the shock of her new self. So unlike the unattended shock I had experienced on my first morning. We realized we could read one another's thoughts. So what would have seemed a silent morning toilet among two young ladies was lively with conversation. I told her what to expect, the new sights and sounds, and how to trust and allow them as they flooded her newly born sensibilities.

We did not bother with good-byes. After breakfasting at one another's throats, I watched her dress, then kissed her and watched as she ascended through the open skylight like a white dove worthy of Noah. As I sat in Hegey's shop alone, I knew I had released love into the world. Not love without price. But love nonetheless. A love that could do wondrous and beautiful things and perhaps atone for the sins of its existence by bringing just a little more good into the world.

But what about me? What good could I do? I was fed and brimming, but my problem was the same. Where the hell was I going to find my hot berry punch on continuous tap?

The good news, at least for me, was that Alberta's ailment had indeed been scarlet fever. Plague hit Hollywood like a runaway mule train. Walking the streets the morning Alberta left, I noticed our main hotel had been converted into a makeshift hospital. Plague fires of children's toys and bedclothes dotted the main street like bonfires gone rogue. All the usual businesses were closed. And those who dared risk the daylight wore handmade cotton masks or bandanas over their faces. Hegey was annoyed but provisioned to hell and back and so could wait out the quarantine with grace. Folks helped one another. Food drives. Clean water drives. Even Brown offered a rickety old brass bed for the sick.

A few of the townsfolk were immune. And they, along with me, volunteered to be nurses. But only I would brave the bedsides of the terminal cases, where the fever was believed to be the most infectious. In my white apron and bleached headscarf, I had a license to steal. And steal I did. Every one of my patients left this earth with a smile on their face, swearing with their last breath their gratitude that they had been cared for and soothed off to paradise by some familiar face. I'd sweep their dry husks into the dust bin and tell their families how awful sorry I was there was no body to bury. The official protocol, conveniently informed by Hegey's medical knowledge, was that all the bodies of the infected needed to be burned immediately upon death. But fortunate natural disasters like plagues don't last forever. After the last surge ended, about six months after I kissed Alberta good-bye, the businesses reopened, and a few intrepid souls breathed the outside air unmasked. I had a bad few days while the town celebrated their tenuous return to normalcy and might have ended up a haint in windblown charmeuse if some fool Whig in Washington hadn't floated the idea of statehood for our territory. With one hand firmly up the skirt of manifest destiny, the other tweaking the nipple of expanded free markets, every huckster in a plaid suit willing to rattle his tailbone on a westbound overland stage was sussing out the congressional logistics of our crummy little burg. Whether they were Second Awakening abolitionists or medicine show hucksters hawking cocaine cure-alls, within days after the plague ended, our hotel suites, cafes, and beer halls where saturated with the city stink of self-seeking emigrants. And we all responded in kind. Nothing quickens vice faster than the promise of respectability. Like frenzied fruit hurrying past flower to beat the first frost, new shops pullulated in every vacant lot. The sudden rise in population was a boon for me. I could discreetly dispatch some anonymous Jack or Joe, squinting past their tart memories like so much pickle juice before dragging their clothes and effects to the lip of the prairie where a rogue wolf might have done them in. But what was good for me was a cause of tears for ol' Hegey. With all his refinement and gentility, he was an assassin of the bottom line and couldn't abide competition from the new merchants.

When a plump and rather pleasant woman from Toulouse opened a small emporium of female unmentionables, Hegey was furious. By some fluke of economics, this woman seemed to have a lock on lace inset muslin drawers, selling the garments at less than half Hegey's price. He wasted no time in sowing rumors. All her wares, he intimated with feigned distress, had been procured secondhand, from either deceased or incarcerated Marseille street whores. And no boiling borax could purge them of their invisible and happily imbedded crotch crabs. Within the week, she was sailing back toward Bayonne. When other dry goods stores had the poor manners to open their doors, he bribed teamsters to conveniently "misplace" entire shipments of salted pork and lamp glass. He sawed through the axe handles of various profiteers in the blue dark of midnight and spiked kegs of whiskey with lye. He even set a small fire in the kitchen of a tea and cake house, risking an injunction from the British monarch herself as the proprietor was purported to make scones of a buttery lusciousness indispensable to the crown.

But Hegey wasn't the only greedy capitalist suckling at that burgeoning municipal tit. With the civic influx, Miss Brown had goaded her sturdy mares to spread their thighs with such a frothing regularity as to afford actual walls to screen her Spartan stalls. She blew out the roof of The Stable and threw up a second story. Laying in a tangle of copper pipe that fed off barrels of ammonia under her kegs, she created a kind of cooling system and had cold beer running from her taps before the summer ended.

"Cold beer!" Hegey thundered one blistering August morning. "That Celtic carbuncle is serving *cold* beer to her johns! She's ruining my parlor business." He was right. The last thing a man wanted after losing half his body weight in sweat was a cup of hot tea, no matter how good it made you feel.

"You could have Brown licked in a fortnight if you had any real mind to," I said, yawning. "That's what this joint was when you bought it."

"Yes. But only under Squirrel Tooth Alice's tutelage. I haven't the slimmest desire to understand the untoward economics of such a libidinous endeavor."

"Then it looks like yer bound to loose a bundle."

"Damn her! I'll hobble her yet. I'll douse her sheets with French plague!"

"There's an easier way, Hegey. You just have to give the word." He was still in his dressing gown, a Chinese-style smoking hat perched on his huge head. It looked like a tea cozy sideways on a stockpot. So I looked away. I couldn't let a smile dampen the gravity of my new scheme.

"Listen," I said, "old Miss Brown runs a crib house. Nothing more. Just a straight-up knockin' shop for any poor sucker lookin' for a warm hole and an excuse to lighten his wallet. Now you. *You* got class. Taste. Not to mention a far more decent location. You could turn these upstairs rooms into a first class bordello with just your leftover knickknacks."

"Oh, you would love that, wouldn't you? Don't think for one second I don't know what you're up to, Emma May." He'd tossed in my middle name just to rile me. But I was determined to stay calm. "You'd have me turn this magnificent oasis into your own personal hot buffet."

"Hell, yes!" I said getting close enough to his face to smell the mint on his breath. "Why *wouldn't* I take a pull of berry punch from any sucker fool enough to think he could bed me? You want me to keep culling from the streets? Listen, you're looking at this the wrong way. Folks in this town don't give two cold shits about the likes of us. Hell, if they knew what we really were, they'd run us out of here with pitchforks and torches."

"Worse."

"There you go! So why the high holy hell should we jump to *their* fiddle. Let them jump to ours." I saw my argument spark in his revengeful little eyes. "Of course, you'd have to drop that funny tea of yours and switch to straight spirits for this to work." The spark in his eyes was gone. Had I said something wrong?

"No, Emma," he said quietly, removing his dressing gown. "I have my own reasons for keeping The Garden in business. The discussion is closed."

"Like hell."

"Hear this, Emma. This place is precious to me. Just as it is." There was no anger in his voice. Just a small but strident plea. "If you really wanted to help me, you'd go and speak to your meddling father. Brown's new base of operations didn't spring from an egg, you know." I had purposely avoided seeing Da since my return. He was a man who had pitifully loved and lost. But Hegey had given me an idea. It was just a matter of time before Hegey's Garden would be totally eclipsed by the town's more familiar vices, and when that happened, I needed to be ready with a cost-effective solution Hegey could not refuse. And what loving father could deny his only daughter a hefty discount on his carpentry skills? It was a low and manipulative plan, well beneath my tender affection for him, but I was desperate. The rumor was he was a changed man after finding religion. Perhaps he had found a new love. Besides, I was flush with a recent feed. I figured I could weather the risk in seeing him.

The Five Wounds of the Redeemer Tabernacle seemed a misnomer to me. First of all, five seemed a rather low number to assign to a Savior who had undergone a hearty scouring with a Roman flagrum, not to mention a whole mess of pricks and tears from that thorny crown.

But there was very little of the lamb in the sweatbox of a church where I went looking for Da. There was a sour pungency particular to the bodies of reptiles in there, mingled with the odors of sweaty bodies and dirty hair. It was a surprise to see again the towheaded preacher who had made my knees weak the first time I saw him. Even more of a surprise to see he was still hamming it up with serpents. He wasn't holding the attention of this new congregation as firmly as before. Time had filled him out and made him even better looking, but he was still spitting brimstone when I stumbled onto his spiel. I took a pew in the back, hoping to scout the place without being seen. If Da were here, like Hegey had said, and if he were really belly down with these Godeaters, I figured he'd have only one hand on the Bible. The other on an empty bottle.

"And when the day of Pentecost was fully come, they were all with one accord in one place." On and on the young preacher blew as I scanned the scant congregation, screwing his face into comic portrayals of righteousness, stressing words so randomly it was impossible to make sense of him. After quoting some thundering bit of scripture, he'd freeze with his arms in bizarre gestures that I guess were meant to punctuate the seriousness of his invective. But he didn't look serious. He looked like he was having some kind of fit. He'd rave then go all palsy. Then rave on again. On and off. On and off. Until he stopped suddenly. The seconds ticked by with nary a sound but some poor soul snoring. This exceptional pause was the congregation's cue to stand up and start jerking around, mumbling nonsense as testament to an uncontainable spirit. But the majority of the congregation seemed as confused by this prompt as with the rest of his sermon. They coughed and shifted in their seats. A few, thinking the sermon was concluded, dropped their hymnals onto their pews and left. I felt sorry for the preacher. He was blessed with the Spirit, but his strength in the Lord was far more evident in how well he filled out his homespun trousers than how he shilled for the Almighty. I looked around the emptying church before my eyes landed on him again. No one noticed the forlorn look on his face but me. No one saw his shoulders rounded by defeat or heard him whisper, "Aw, heck. Service is over, I guess." I waited for the shambling congregation to file out of the building, then walked the empty church, following the sound of familiar snoring. I found Da sitting up across the aisle near the front, his head cocked back in sleep. He'd filled out some and had tamed the scrub grass of his hair. He looked like Da. And didn't look like Da. He smelled shamelessly of bay rum and closed spaces. His cheeks were more drawn without his whiskers. And in his box serge suit and clean collar, he looked damn near respectable. But that wasn't it. Something fundamental had changed in him. I didn't know what it was until he opened his eyes and looked at me. That was it. The rascals. The rascals in his eyes had been sadly roped.

"How that goat I had Hegey bring you holding up?" I asked, smiling. "You two still on a first name basis?"

His bleary eyes focused on me, and I watched as tears began to flood his pale irises. He worked his jaw, but no sound came forth. Tears streamed piteously down his cheeks. The worst thing in the world was about to happen.

"Hey, Da. Remember me?" I asked casually, my heart thumping in my chest.

"*Cora?*" he rasped. My blood ran suddenly cold. I wanted to run out of there like my drawers were on fire. I couldn't move. "Cora! My love! Oh, my precious duck, you've come back!" I had trouble catching a breath to speak.

"No, Da. It's me. Your daughter, Emma. *Emma!*"

He leered as he lunged for me. "Oh you've been naughty, my Cora. Kept me idle far too long." I slapped him hard across the cheek, stifling a cry as I did it. He grinned, sat back down, further enflamed by the blow. "Rough, is it now? Been a slow dray comin', that. But well worth the wait!" And he was up on his feet, arms flailing toward me.

"No, Da! It's me! It's *me!*"

"Yes! Crippled Christ, it's *you!*" He spread his arms like a lovelorn scarecrow, but I could look upon him no more. I pushed hard on his chest. The force of my blow made him gasp in my face. I smelled his small sour wind and sobbed. What the hell had I done? I turned without a word and fled, crying as I ran.

"Cora! *Wait!* Come back!"

It had been a mistake. Everything had been a mistake.

I galloped down the main street in a blur, veering through the doors of the Garden and up the stairs, past the stultified customers drooling in their teacups, and leapt onto the bed, burrowing into Hegey's big arms. He was at first startled but immediately wrapped me in his arms once I began blubbering about what I had just seen. "There, there, my dear," he said. "We will sort this thing. Together."

After I had calmed, he sat on the bed next to me. "The first lesson we must learn," he said with a comforting hand on my knee, "is resiliency. The second lesson is resourcefulness. Then industry, shameless cunning, fiscal revenge, and, finally, the utter vanquishing of one's woefully misinformed naysayers. But in your circumstance, I feel only the first three are apt. I'll take care of the rest. If your father's skills are denied us, we will find another way." Had my wet feminine wiles really been so effective? The idea sickened as much as heartened me.

"You mean it?" I asked, still sniffling.

"Of course. I had no *idea* how selfish I have been. Your continued comfort is paramount to me. There's no reason I can't serve a little crumpet with my tea."

"But your damn tea's the whole reason I can't—"

He stood up from the bed and began pacing, ignoring my last comment. "Brown has already shut down every other sporting house in town through means similar to what I just mentioned. What she lacks are my resources.

What we cannot offer in quantity we shall make up for in quality. 'A little powder, a little paint. And plain little Sally is no longer a saint.' Or however the adage goes."

But that damn fool, Beguiler-squirreling tea! How the hell was I going to get rid of that? What I needed was a miracle. And not all miracles are performed by saints.

# Chapter Fifteen

In the historical annals of Hollywood, what ensued between us and Miss Brown became known as the "Whore Wars." Hegey was quick to launch the first offensive. One dark morning, a fair portion of the roof of Miss Brown's Stable was propelled skyward when all three of her ammonia barrels mysteriously exploded. The night before the explosion, I'd seen an open Hindu tract on Hegey's desk that detailed the balancing agencies of something called "karma." Right next to the Indian tract was Charles Tennant's treatise on chemistry. I noticed the branched formula for calcium hypochlorite had been underlined. No one took responsibility for the disaster, which left two of Miss Brown's best earners with florid facial burns. Hegey feigned to be as shocked as the rest of the town when the damage was deemed an accident. Unstable chemical agencies. Or some swill-loving god's revenge on the blasphemy of refrigerated beer. The town was split as to the actual cause. Brown, never one to lay down in a fight, was quick to retaliate. She strained the bounds of hypocrisy when she joined the Lady's Temperance League. How she convinced them to let her muster among their ranks had far more to do with the dirt she had on their husbands than her quick conversion to a teetotaler.

A week after the blast, Hegey and I were coming back from our morning walk when, to our horror, we saw that the Garden of Allah had been condemned, sealed with a printed injunction that read: *Closed for Moral Indecency.* Capability Brown and two of her stoutest associates stood with arms linked before our shuttered doors. They wore wide sashes with slogans embroidered upon them. Miss Brown's read: *Death to Ardent Spirits!* Mercy O'Day on her left, with fresh pink puckers for eyebrows, wore: *Industry! Sobriety!* The one on her right with her hairline singed to the back of her head wore one that read: *Abstinence+Total=Total Abstinence!* The needlework was excellent, the stitches as tight as stingy kisses. But the implication was far beyond the competence of mere handicraft.

"But I don't even *sell* spirits," Hegey cried, stamping his rose-colored Balmoral boot on the street when he was denied entrance to his tea house. "This is intolerable!" The accuracy of his defense might have swayed the gathering crowd to our side had he just changed his tone. Even a haughty spank of sarcasm would have served him better than the petulant whine he'd assumed. Brown played to the onlookers, grinning while Hegey twisted on her well-timed hook.

"Hah! I ain't gawpin' about nothin' as wholesome as liquor," Miss Brown said above two stout legs planted like pillars. "We know all about the slant-eyed poison ye press on these weak and shamblin' souls." She pointed to a few of Hegey's patrons who wandered in the street, blinking and dazed. "I'm known to most of ye," she said, walking among the crowd. "Though the highest among ye wouldn't deign look me in the eye. But no matter. I know me place! And hold no body to rights fer settin' me there, 'cept meself and that damned emerald isle of want and misery what forced a wee God-fearing girl like me to scratch her survival from this thorny crust any way she could!" Her rambling cadence betrayed a rehearsed resonance. "'Tis not my habit, I assure you decent folk, to pluck the living from a man's purse any more'n I'd steal the victuals from another man's lips—though it be plain our friend here could do with a bit less o' the feed bag." The crowd tittered at the well-aimed jab.

"But curse my Christian heart if I could set here idle and see his decadent and unnatural pestilence flow a minute more into our fair town's streets." She had gauged the town's final intolerance to a tee. It didn't seem to matter that there was no legality in what she was doing. Cheap booze and skirt were legal for every white man in the state. And the stuff that spiked Hegey's calming teas was present in several available tinctures. It was not the crowd's intolerance to stimulants that riled them. It was their unspoken intolerance to Hegey, himself. All they needed to turn against him was someone low enough to show them the way. "Ye all know the evil of ardent drink." She shook a comically schoolmarmish finger at the crowd. "Some by heart, others, I'm sure, by yer ailin' noggins come the mornin' after a right spree." Another titter from the crowd. "And the Lord knows we should cap *that* fountain of iniquity as well. But what this man has been sellin' is no keg of American spirit that Samuel Adams might have brewed himself!" she suddenly boomed. "This man sells the tarry-dark toe jam of Satan! Aye! From slanty-eyed demons what squawk the most confounded gibberish ever to assault a Christian ear he procures it! And brews those sticky serpents for the soul-bait of every God-fearing white man among ye! Can we, as a Lord-loving flock, ignore this foreign scourge another second?"

Shouts of "No!" and "Never!" from the crowd.

"Shall another sightless slip o' the clock stand dumb while he taints our innocent souls with his dusky slosh?"

"*Never! No!*"

"Then stamp it out! Stamp it *out*, I say!" Cheers and more noxious shouting. She raised her freckled hands to quiet the crowd. "I only ask for one t'ing," she said with theatrical innocence. "A simple, straight and *honest* t'ing! To make this town decent once more. Let's make our simple, honest home worthy of hardworking folk like yerselves—aware of the strengths *and* vices that make us what we are. Let us be willin' to use those strengths with courage and meet those fair and common vices with mercy. But never, *never* should we stain this earth, where our patriots bled, with a black liquid sickness our fathers and our father's fathers would never have abused. And tens times never would have tolerated!"

The frothy crowd was so adamant in its reproach, Hegey and I were obliged to ascend the rear stairs to reach our apartments. Miss Brown did not stay to gloat. She was far too practical with her time to linger where no actual profit could be mined. I was secretly pleased, but Hegey was inconsolable. I hefted him up the steps like a leaky sack and, after a scalding bath and six even hotter toddies, his nerves were sufficiently soothed to reduce him to a simpering but wistful state. He was tightly packaged in his silk shawl-collared dressing gown, a smoking hat with its limp tassel fringing his face like a rogue cowlick. I lit a lamp. I hoped Brown had not won. I hoped she'd merely paved the stony path to her own competitive undoing. But Hegey's emotional reserves were not quite dry. Something deeper than the closing of his business was in play. When I turned to him, I saw the light from the lamp kick off the fresh tears on his face.

"Now I shall no longer be beautiful," he said with a whisper. He turned to me, his face reddening as if embarrassed that I had heard him.

"What do mean, Hegey?" He cleared his throat and swiped at the tears on his face.

"My father was a great man," he said. "Great in the commercial sense that he never chased after trends. He created them." Braiding my hair with nervous fingers as I listened, my heart drummed in my chest. "He called himself an 'importer of joy.' Isn't that lovely? A happy bee with pom-poms of diverting pollen dangling from his gouty legs. We were from a sleepy little burg in upstate New York. Miles from the urbane bustle of Manhattan. We lived in the largest house in town. But most of that town was farmland. Our neighbors were simple farmers, practical in their habits. Thrifty in their ways. My father changed all that. He was the first to anticipate the Asian mania, the first to sell real Chinese Ceylon, a white tea that up to then had only passed the teeth of emperors. Porcelain commodes painted with fluid summer dragons shined in the woodsy dark of Puritan outhouses thanks to him. Chow fun noodles replaced cheap corn bread.

"From Tibet he brought in a special cheese aged from the milk of high-altitude yaks, cured on pallets of wormwood that was said to give the consumer visions of the ten thousand paradises. When T.P. Cooke made such a splash as Frankenstein's creature in *Presumption* and that blue-green color of his fright makeup became *ne plus ultra* from Piccadilly to the Champs de Mars, who do you think had the fashion sense to import hundreds of shawls in authentic hues of *vert de monstre*? Did those tacky dray driver's wives in hand-stitched calico know they were so smartly ensconced in one of the greatest fashion frenzies of the decade? Rhetorical. But my father knew. He always knew.

"He wasn't a bad father. Merely an absent one. So I kept him with me when I was a boy. In effigy if not in the flesh. I had taken one of my most precious porcelain dolls and, though it nearly killed me, traced a mustache and mutton chops on its elegant lip and cheeks. I cut its locks and marcelled the coif of its little empty head with a purloined dollop of Poppa's actual pomade. This was my proxy poppa. At my nursery tea parties, he was always given the place of honor. He'd compliment me on my graceful left-handed pour. We discussed the difference in hand feel between the Shanxi Province silk and the cut-rate version woven in India. Would the current trend in tapered trousers finally give way to a roomier leg next year? Does triple milled really mean a gentler foam or could one sell single milled at the same price with more floral lithography on the wrapper? We'd take long promenades in the garden, where I dozed while he held forth on the vagaries of tariff law. We were close. As close as any befrocked poppet and lonely little boy could be.

"Of course, I never could discuss work with my real father. I was too ugly for that. I was paraded out only before bedtime in my starched nightshirt and curls awaiting his perfunctory pat. Even my remedial French afforded me enough to know what he meant when he called me his *petite grenouille.* I make it sound worse than it was. Perhaps." He paused. The lamp glowed brighter in the gathering dusk. I could hear the pounding of nails, lonely in the distance, as I tried to imagine a child Hegey, with his cultivated curls and amphibious face, decades away from his profit and taste. "Don't misunderstand," he said. "He was never cruel. But I knew I repulsed him. I believe I repulsed them both. My mother's sick headaches were the blessing, I suppose—the *deus ex machina* that allowed the beautifying gods to descend."

It seems hard noodles and piss pots weren't all his father had collected on his oriental buying sprees. As a kind of premium tendered to vigorous merchants, his father's Asian hosts showed him what few tourists in those days would ever see. He was led to the skunky bliss of the opium dens. And in the dark, amid the pallets and pipes, he saw the same smiles on the faces of both slave and master. Hegey's father immediately saw the upside to this self-induced oblivion and arranged for a few hundred pounds of the stuff to be smuggled in the cavities of the less valuable fu dogs he imported. It was quickly discerned that only this tonic could ease his mother's migraines. With a house full of servants, the Hegemores couldn't risk the gossip fumes would incite. So they took to brewing the stuff as tea.

"My father, chivalrous to the last, felt inclined to join her. Most days, precisely at the strike of four, I could rely on my parents mounting their magical lenses. For that's what I thought they did, although I never saw such apparatus in evidence. They would drink their tea and magically their eyelids would droop, and silly smiles would smear their faces, and I knew for those brief hours I would be all things to them: witty, charming, intelligent. *Beautiful.*"

So years and several hundred miles later, why *wouldn't* he seek to recreate such an illusion among his customers? It was never about profit, the Garden of Allah. It was a place of no apologies for Hegey. A haven where his drug was not what he sold but how he was regarded.

"And now that bilious, freckled whore mistress has gone and torn my world to tatters," he wailed. "I am beaten, Emma. Licked. We will pack in the morning." He rolled over without another word.

I sat there stunned as the bed rocked with his thunderous weeping. Was he serious? What about his first rule of self-acceptance? What about resiliency? Where the hell would we go? Where could *I* go? Our town had its divisions, but they were negotiable. Predictable. If we left Hollywood, it would mean weeks in some tight overland stage. How would I stay fed? And if the inevitable happened and I snacked on all our traveling companions, who would drive the coach? Who would navigate? And once we had arrived at God knows where, I'd have to resume my wretched old method of bait, hit, and run. I thought I was past all that. Or *could* be if he just found his sack and stuck to the plan. What the hell was Hegey saying? It was full dark when sleep finally roped him. But I couldn't rest. Little moans of despair and worry issued from me as I lay there, wrestling with my fate. How could I change his mind and get him to stay? How could I get him to stick to our plan of personal buffet for me and good old whorehouse coin for him? Damn him! I fumed in the dark. He was an unusual man. But still a man, never *really* sympathetic to a woman's needs. It had all been bluster. Maybe I didn't need him at all. I could light out of here this minute and take my chances on the open plains. Could I do that? After all this time growing soft with ease and convenience? Had I been tamed? Oh sweet, Christ! Had I become my *mother*? That night, I was too upset to go out and beguile. I stayed in bed tossing and turning while Hegey snored and snuffled till first light.

# Chapter Sixteen

I awoke to a curious leather case near my pillow. It looked like a leather cigar case, if a cigar was the size of a baby's leg. I was puffy and irritable, but Hegey beamed at me as I lay sullen on our sheets, as fresh as a damn daisy, still dewy from his morning bath.

"You were wailing, my dear. In your sleep," he said gently. "I anticipated our domestic arrangement, beautifully amiable as it is in most ways, might leave certain *needs,* shall we say, unexplored. I thought I might provide some . . . relief." Had he thought my moans were from carnal frustration? "I have it on the most respectable authority that this is unparalleled in relieving the effects of female hysteria." His face was indulgent, if slightly embarrassed. I opened the flap covering the object. Inside was a white shaft that looked like it could have been made from horn or bone.

"What in high hell is this?"

"I believe it's called a 'widow's companion.' At least this one was referred to as such when I acquired it. Made from the jawbone of a sperm whale. My understanding is such an object is perfectly indispensable in the comfort it provides to the lonely wives of whalers." I couldn't stifle my chuckle when I realized what the thing was for. I snatched the whale bone shaft from its case and made a few slicing motions with it.

"Damn thing would do better with a hatchet head on it." I tossed it back, still too shaken from my fitful night to smile.

"Careful with that!" he snapped. "That's a valuable piece of folk art."

"Is that really what you'd have me do? Lay about all day, pleasuring myself with a damn whale bone while Brown runs roughshod over the two of us?"

"I was only trying to help."

"Let me at her!" I said, sitting up. "I'll bleed her dry, and you can turn her sour ashes to fancy soap!"

He placed the bone into its case and snapped it shut. "Please, Emma, you'd have to stab her like a rabid boar," he said, waving his hand dismissively. "A rather inelegant solution to our problem." He snuggled next to me with a conspiratorial glint in his eye. Had I missed something? "In the eyes of the town, we will accept our defeat with grace. But we will *still* open our own bordello and out-class the bitch." I couldn't believe what I was hearing. Hadn't I already campaigned for this very plan of entrenchment? And here he was, cool as Brown's beer, carrying on like it had been his idea the whole time.

"When the hell did you decide this," I said.

"This morning. While you slept."

"I *didn't* sleep! You couldn't have told me this last night?"

"I hadn't decided last night."

"Oh, *you* hadn't decided," I said, popping out of the bed so I could confront him standing. "What about me? Why didn't I get a say?"

"I was emotionally indisposed yesterday evening, if you remember," he said calmly. Which only made me hotter.

"Oh, knock it off!" I shouted. "You're tough as saddle leather! That half-pint bitch hurt your pride, not your horse sense. You had me jumpy all night with your 'we'll pack in the morning' mule shit!"

"Emma?"

"What!"

"You do realize it has been decided. And decidedly in your favor. Yes?"

"I know. But I'm still upset."

"Even though you've gotten what you wanted?"

"Don't make me sound crazy. I ain't touched. You want to know something? This town is all wrong about you. You ain't anywhere *near* being the woman you think you are!"

"I never said I was a woman."

"Oh, come off it!"

"I am a rare and unusual creature. Just like you. That's why we are such fast friends. Tea?"

"Black, two sugars," I said with a huff. He got up casually to put the kettle on. "So we're going ahead with this thing?" I asked.

"Haven't I said as much. But I'll need certain assurances first."

"What kind of assurances?"

He looked at me coldly from the stove. "This will be a business, Emma. And so we must be professional. I'll not have my customers turned to parchment to sate your needs. I'll need proof you can stop."

"I can stop."

"I have yet to see that. Therefore, I must subject you to a simple test."

"I said I could stop."

"Then prove it."

"On whom?" He winked at me knowingly. "Ah, hell," I said, "I don't reckon I could stop if I ever started on *her*."

"Precisely," he said sweetly. "If you could dine on Miss Brown without killing her, I'd be convinced you could do the same with anyone."

So there it was. We were staying after all. My war had been won. But the battle was about to begin.

The morning was a liar. More watery dawn than full day. Rainy days can be like that. The view from Hegey's upstairs window was of an alley heaped with rotting garbage and a few tethered mules. Interspersed among the gangs of flies and heaps of steaming mule shit were a few small structures, all with slanting roofs braced by ornately carved corbels. There was care taken with those outhouses, a desire to leave one's mark on the rude wilderness. Even if that mark was scrolls and curlicues on a common crapper. But all that truss and fuss could not change the function or mask the stink behind those closed privy doors. It was a poor philosophy—not even worthy of my mother's worst days—but I saw myself in that moment as one of those tarted-up shit boxes. I felt foolish with my humanity chipping, the change all too telling as to my real nature despite all my fancywork. I heard the door to the room open, felt Hegey enter. "Just thinking of myself like one of them fancy-ass shithouses," I mused to the window, not turning around.

"How incommodious, my dear." I heard the door close. "I suspect you're just nervous about tonight. But come away from there. I have a present for you." Hegey had concluded that for my mission against Miss Brown I would need to be properly camouflaged. I didn't tell him I had arrived at the similar conclusion the night I found Alberta. He had been snipping, stitching, and making ruching for the last eight hours and seemed pleased by his labors, if exhausted. He tossed what looked like a vaguely human-shaped shadow to the bed. "That's the best I can do," he said with a preemptive pout should I dare to find some fault with the garment. It was plain and snug fitting, down to the darts for my breasts and calves. The fabric was soft, dark, with a strange, low nap that ran in conflicting whorls. When it caught the light, it gave a dappled effect.

"It's made of a very rare silk-shot wool velvet, woven for a rather insolvent branch of the Russian aristocracy to imitate—"

"It looks like *fur*."

"Precisely." Hegey smiled as I slipped it on. "It's waterproof, simply *swallows* any ambient light. Notice the slight give in the fabric. Tiny gathers against the weft at the stress points," he said proudly, "removes the need for any type of closure." It fit like a second skin of the purest witching hour. "Although now that I see it," he said, approaching, "a row of tiny black pearl buttons running down the back wouldn't be—"

"It's perfect," I said, waving him away.

"Yes. You look precisely like . . . what you are."

The morning's gloom made good on its threat around ten o'clock that night, beginning as a cold drizzle that ramped up to a real deluge by half past. I waited in the shadows near The Stable. Brown hadn't bothered to rebuild her wooden roof after Hegey had blasted it off. She had opted for a much cheaper covering of waxed canvass that sagged with the accumulated water. Looking from a dim window, I could see her girls had to interrupt their work just so they could poke the ceiling with a broom handle so the tarp wouldn't split and soak them all. Brown had a lock on all the rented woman flesh in Hollywood, and the fact that she hadn't used her profits to better effect made me hate her all the more.

I waited for the last john to leave, pressed up into the darkness of the alley wall. I thought he had passed me when he suddenly doubled back and planted his feet right in front of me. I held my breath as he fumbled with his fly buttons. He was close enough to kiss. The beer in his bladder steamed in the cold as it flecked my ankles, a stray hot stream soaking my shin. I clenched my eyes as he finally shook his member and buttoned up. He hadn't sensed me in the least. But this was not the christening of my camouflage I had imagined. Brown bunked in what had once been The Stable's tack house, a small room whose one window looked out at the shithouses in the alley. Strange how Hegey and ol' Brown could be worlds apart and still share the same view. Her window sash was up a crack, letting in the sour vapors of the early autumn air. Or letting out some corrupted pong concomitant with her private vices. I wasn't sure which.

She was sprawled on a crusty red-velvet throne, tipping the dregs of a bottle of rye into her mouth. I might have once mistaken her digs as high tone had I not done my time with Hegey. But in the weak light of her lamp, her reams of red flounce and stamped tin seemed like what they were: the overwrought trappings of which only the destitute dream. I figured I could have her off while deep in her cups. I curled my fingers beneath her open window but stopped when she spasmed so violently her empty bottle fell from my view. Suddenly, a dull blonde head rose from what must have been Brown's lap. Mercy O'Day, Brown's best earner. Mercy's eyebrows had still not grown back all the way. Her face was flushed and damp, and I watched as she wiped her chin before clawing at the bone of Brown's corset. Brown slapped her away, then grabbed the girl's sullen face and kissed her hard on the mouth.

"That'll do, Mercy," Brown wheezed. "Get ye to bed now. My cock's done crowed."

The girl hoisted herself to her stout legs. She was buck naked. Her breasts and backside jiggled as she began to take her leave. Just as she passed Brown, her mistress whacked her naked arse with a vicious slap. The girl stood there for a moment, fighting what could have been tears. She disappeared from my view as Brown pinched a set of specs to her pug nose and opened a strongbox on her desk. Didn't this bitch ever sleep? How long would I have to wait? The rain had not let up. I was girding myself to bivouac through more of the filthy night when I heard a voice at my flank.

"Capability?" she said. "How'd ye get outdoors so hastily?" Mercy stood beside me, wrapped in a cheap muslin robe that barely hid her ampleness. She stuck a hand-rolled cigarette into her mouth and lit it. The weak light illumined her plain, full face. She took a deep drag, then flicked the smoke into a puddle. "You *do* love me, you wicked thing," she exhaled, flinging her loose bulk into my arms.

A beggar at life's banquet. This is what it meant to be a creature like me—to have no say in the dishes my ultimate host chose to serve me. I had no choice but to feed upon her. I tasted sweat, rough liquor, then Mercy's last memories exploded behind my eyes.

*Green.*
*Green that was the deepest hope of green.*
*Low rolling hills broken only by small, stony walls.*
*Oh, how I had missed this, my heart sang! The wide-open vistas radiant in their verdant fire. I was a girl again, running barefoot and free in the Irish countryside.*
*An unshy sky!*
*Warm grass as soft as feather down!*
*To frolic in a world that spoke only sunshine and wild flowers.*
*"Mercy!" A stab of regret at my dear mother's voice.*
*"Come fer yer kip, now me colly! Supper's nigh!"*

There was a lot to her as I burped down the melancholy of her lost girlhood. And I felt tight as a tick when I'd finished. In the falling rain, the Mercy-shaped ash in my lap pocked into mud and was no more. I rumpled her wet robe into a ball and stuffed it deep into the muck of the alley that had absorbed Mercy along with the rest of the town's refuse. Christ, I had done it again. Hegey had been right. I had failed. I couldn't stop. I turned to Brown's window, trying to stoke my resolve for the test before me. It was dark now in Brown's room. I had to try. My knowledge of scientific theory was patchy at best. But still I knew enough to understand that my glutted state would make it far easier to leave Brown alive and was thus an unfair variable in my experiment of self-control. I wouldn't tell Hegey that. If I succeeded with Brown, the proof would be my own version of events, science be damned. The real variable here, I reasoned, was my own will. And I had enough of *that* to meet Brown naked in the tarry pits of hell and hog-wrestle that bitch in the flames until the Devil himself declared me victor.

Brown snored peacefully in her bed. Small plunks of rainwater dripped from my hair and nose as I eased over the sill of her window to the floor of her room. She chortled in her sleep. I froze. A chime sounded as something glassy careened to the corner of the room. Brown snorted. I had kicked an empty whiskey bottle. I was about to take another step when I noticed another empty bottle set on end at the foot of her bed. Stepping back, I realized the entire perimeter of her bed was lined with rows of empty bottles, stacked delicately to the brim of her mattress like a crude burglar alarm. The bottles, stacked as precariously as they were, would make access to the bed nearly impossible. I suppose I could have stooped and unstacked them. But there was too much concession in that, something too low and menial that rankled me as far as Brown was concerned. She needed to be bested. I was the one with the talent, tainted with the uncanny Beguiler. Not her. I had a sudden hunch that, if true, would make all my caution as useless as tits on a boar.

I kicked the wall of bottles at the foot of her bed. The crash would have jolted the dead. Less so, Capability Brown. The large woman snorted, sucked the drool back to her mottled lips and shouted, "Who's there?" Her eyes had yet to open. But when they did, I froze. "Well, well, well. Who have we here?" she rasped. My guts cocked like the hammer of Da's old flintlock as I waited to see if my hunch had been correct. "A born whore, sure as I breathe. Standing there bold as brass." My gaze stayed pinned to the two malignant slits that peered at me. Slowly Brown's eyes widened as she took in my countenance. I was relieved when she began to weep. My hunch had been right. "Oh, my sweet girl," she croaked as she reached her arms out to me. "I dreamed just now I'd lost ye! The midnight angel herself had spirited you away! But here you are, ye cunny addled mongrel! Come to me, Mercy, my love. Come to momma, then."

# Chapter Seventeen

Miss Brown was very much alive the next morning, evidenced by the heartbroken way she shouted Mercy's name in the backstreets. That forlorn wail had been proof enough for Hegey. That and the lock of her matted orange hair I presented to him the next day.

"Fascinating," Hegey said over our morning tea, the lock of Brown's hair lying like red hot wires on his starched linen. "You actually beguiled Miss Brown?"

"So it would seem." Thankfully, he didn't ask what had become of poor Mercy.

"I only wonder how you will respond when your *belle visage* is continually mistaken for Mercy's whenever Brown spies you."

"You let me worry about that."

"Impossible," he mused, sipping his tea.

"What's impossible?"

"That I could feel anything as tender as pity for that wretched madame. They clearly shared a very special love."

"Heartbreaking, I know."

"And you're quite sure you had nothing to do with Mercy's demise," he said demurely, nibbling his morning toast.

"Nothing at all," I said as I looked him squarely in the eye.

"I can't tell whether you're lying or not, Emma, but still the feat of not killing Brown is impressive." Indeed it was. Was I gaining control of my Beguiler? Or simply being made to think so? He sipped the last swallow of his tea and wiped his lips with a snowy napkin. "Yes," he said, tossing the napkin to the table, "I think that qualifies as proof enough. We shall begin construction on our new bordello today." He excused himself while I sat there relieved but hot with shame. Not only had I lied to my only friend, I had not told him the real reason I hadn't drained her.

Miss Brown had never been a looker. She'd always been short and plain. But she had a vibrancy in her youth. An alluring surliness, even when she'd worked for two pennies a pop in that Portsmouth knocker, servicing sailors under gamey whale-oil lamps. Or perhaps it was her excitement that had made her desirable. The memory I'd purloined while I'd sipped on her had been a special one, after all. Her favorite john was due that night, back from running slaves and black sugar. The one who never slowed or spent before she did. The one the cabin boys feared. The one whose face, though fuller in youth and inflamed by lust, had still been shockingly and shamefully and more than sadly known to me.

Silas Shinnecock. My Da.

True to his word, Hegey opened his bordello, even made efforts to reemploy the girls he'd let go after the Garden was closed. None fancied going backward in social status when they could do the same work on the quiet as shop girls and Hollywood housemaids. He then reached out to what remained of Squirrel Tooth's soiled flock. Some had travelled West, to pastures both anonymous and more manifest. Others hired themselves out as scullery maids in prosperous houses East. The rest, too afraid of repercussions from Brown, refused him. We had no choice but to publicly solicit our special staff as discreetly as possible. He asked me to write up a few flyers offering employment to "domestics of French descent, amenable to a loose interpretation of duties" who "possessed that certain *joie du sang*" that "flouts convention." I told him any poor hussy worth her crotchless bloomers would be lucky to know her letters, let alone be able to decipher the treacle he wanted me to print. My ad was effective and far more to the point:

"Wanted: Maids Of All Work. No References Necessary."

We spent the day nailing up advertisements all over town, steering clear of the two block radius around Brown's Stable. I had sounded confident when I told

Hegey I could handle it when Brown inevitably laid eyes on me again, but I had no idea what would happen.

Our potentially soiled doves showed up in droves the next morning, lining up in the still-dewy road in a silent queue that reeked so badly of better days that regular folks crossed to the other side of the street to avoid them. More than half were Irish fleeing the pangs of the famine. Those I referred contritely to Miss Brown's once I heard their first lilting diphthong. Destitute, drunk, some missing an eye, a limb, most of the rest were missing teeth. Some carried bundles—babies or sick livestock—but all seemed resoundingly of a single stripe: Unmarriable or otherwise unpresentable behind a notions counter or schoolmarm's desk, they had all finally reached the dregs of feminine employment. I lined them up ten at a time for inspection. God, the chords of shared sisterhood that rang from those pitiful eyes! And how that sad music turned even more bitter when the few I beguiled reached for me, crying out names they were convinced I would answer to. These were the next to go. Finally, I whittled it down to seven able-bodied candidates, all with serviceable dispositions and varied if uneven charms. Seven was a lucky number.

Miss Lumbee, Miss Waccamaws, Miss Clapper, Miss Van Guilder, Miss Buckhead, Miss Yellowhammer, and the sisters Creel, who were identical twins and insisted upon being considered as a single candidate. Only Yellowhammer, with her penetrating eyes and bright head wrap, would get my vote for a romp in the sheets had she been so inclined. Hegey gave me my head on the hiring but called me over when I kept Yellowhammer in the lineup.

"Undoubtedly, Miss Yellowhammer is the most comely of the lot," he whispered to me while the ladies stood erect, refusing to speak to one another. "But she is clearly of mixed descent. African and Choctaw, if those delicious cheekbones of hers are any indication."

"Hegey. Come on, now. This is still a free state."

"Not for long if that Little Giant in the Senate gets his confounded way."

"Listen, brother," I said in a stern whisper. "I breakfast on blood, you like boys, and you're squabbling about her complexion? The one place she belongs in this whole cockeyed country is among folks like you and me. She's in or I'm out."

He blanched. "You're right. Of *course* you're right." I began to walk away when Hegey stopped me. "I'm sorry, Emma," he said nervously. "I don't know what I was thinking."

"For once, honey," I said with a sad smile, "you *weren't* thinking."

I called them by their family names to at least give a gloss of respectability to the proceedings. I was offering these poor bitches all the truths of war: horror, boredom, humiliation, possible disfigurement, wasting diseases, and death. And one unique to the profession—the immutable fact that, once they signed up with me, they could never browse for a new set of drawers or head of cabbage in public again. At the very least, I owed it to them to let them know what they were in for. I went looking for chairs so they should be sitting when I sprung the reality of our enterprise on them. Hegey had sent the chairs to the refinishers, and all I could find were a series of low milking stools. So I hunkered down on a stool myself and faced the eight squatting women—all of us in attitudes of childbirth, I realized in that moment. Or on the privy. Any way one cut it, we were bound to be wiping up shit, piss, or blood.

"Some of you might've already caught the scent—some of you not so much. It's true you'd be doing maid's work, plenty of reaching and sweating and clocking time on all fours. But it ain't dirt you'd be chasing. No, ma'am. Fact is, the dirt, I reckon, would be chasin' *you*. Truth is, I ain't offering respectable work at all. This is not a respectable place. And I ain't no respectable female. To sink the spike plainly, I aim to make whores of you. So now you know. Over there is the door." And damn me for a drunkard's daughter but not *one* of those sullen and forsaken females made a move to vacate her perch. "You all recollect me rightly?" I asked. Eight heads nodded in near unison. "I am assuming y'all know what a *whore* is." The nodding again. "You all still want to stay?" Silence this time. That silence was the saddest affirmation of consent I ever ascertained.

"What's our cut?" asked Miss Buckhead, a plain brunette whose square, masculine jaw had obviously wagged over money before.

"Your what?"

"What's the split? Between the house and us?" I had been so addled by the prospect of finding women of a truly sporting nature that I had not given a thought to economics. Eight expectant faces awaited my decree. Perhaps guilt and magnanimity are shadows cast by the same sun. I only know there was more gratitude than charity in what I said next.

"They'll *be* no cut," I said to all their shocked faces. "What you earn, you keep. All of it." Hegey's jaw almost hit the floor, but I ignored him. "You make your own rates," I said. "We'll make our stake on booze and gaming. Sound fair?" These needy women were just lures to my lunches after all. I'd be damned if they would part with a single cent while they aided my convenience.

"You mean minus room and board, of course," Miss Buckhead said with smug resignation.

"No, Miss Buckhead," I said, meeting her gaze. "I meant what I said. If you sweat it, you keep it."

"What the hell do you mean by promising them *all* of it?" Hegey huffed, fluffing his side of the covers that night. I hunkered down next to him, feeling that our relationship had finally rounded the bend to feeling like a real marriage.

"What are you griping about?" I asked. He tugged hard on the sides of his satin night cap. "The real money's in booze and cards."

"That's *not* what you said!" He sat up in bed. "I distinctly remember you telling me that cathouse coin ran downwards!"

"Who cares what I said! These women are at the end of their tether. Are you really going to emulate your father so thoroughly as to snatch the dregs of their livelihoods along with what's left of their dignity?" That did it. He may have pined for his father's respect, but he never wanted to be compared to him. He lay back down and huffed.

"And not a bona fide French tart among them," he shot back.

"We got Dutch," I said, closing my eyes. "Van Guilder's our youngest girl."

"And that's another thing," he said, punching his pillow to fluff it. "We really should call this place the House of Oedipus. For you seem to be toiling under the delusion that most men want to screw their mothers!"

"Now listen up, Hegey," I said, propped up on an elbow. "We both know what this is. You got no mortgage on this place, and the gaming tables and cards you already own. And I know the markup you press on that pig pee you hawk as rye. You sure as shit won't go broke." His eyes flickered as he drew back slightly. I hadn't meant to come off so ornery. I put a hand on the salmon cuff of his dressing gown to soothe him.

"Please, Hegey," I said softly, "if you aim to keep me happy, you'll let me run this *my* way." Real wife-like, I thought, sickened.

"I'll leave you to it," he said testily, looping the ends of his mesh mustache guard over his ears. "You've made your selection, no matter how unfortunately charitable. Perhaps with a little face paint our friends won't seem so dreary."

"Hey! There you go. *You* could show them how."

He chuckled. "I'm sorry I questioned your acumen, Emma." He closed his eyes. "Do whatever you feel is necessary."

"You mean that?"

"If it will draw this rather strident fracas to a close, most certainly." That's when I lowered the boom, the little tidbit I'd been saving all evening.

"I need you to move out," I said. He bolted upright.

"I *beg* your pardon!"

"We can't have no rooster strutting the halls among all these chickens," I said innocently. "What would decent folk think?"

Hegey left at the grim crack of the next day—left with a single neatly packed valise and an umbrella. He had little apartments stashed all over town, like a miser's mad money, and I was a tad surprised he didn't tell me in which one he was holing up. But for all his protestations and hurt pride, I could tell he was happy to get out of there. I christened the place "Lucky's," in deference to Da's second credo. And in the flurry of weeks that followed, efforts began in earnest to turn my joint into a well-heeled alternative to Miss Brown's. The upstairs rooms had to be partitioned, and brass bed frames were bolted to the sturdy floors. I wanted an air of comfort but also efficiency, a clean, tastefully lit establishment that would put its clients at their ease but not remind them too much of the quotidian nature of home. I settled on white washed floors, simple furniture in a similar milky finish, cream and ecru colored bedclothes, and clear glass lamps spiked with lavender oil. On the ground floor, I had Hegey's old candy counter hauled in to serve as a bar, behind which was hung an enormous painting from the botteghe of Ghirlandiao; a massive reclining nymph, with the direct leer of a preacher's daughter, her nipples looked like they should top twin ice cream sundaes. I had gaming tables in the center for faro and stud and even a little brass railing in the corner, behind which a band could spout off without feeling too exposed to the action.

Hegey had become scarce as pork on a Turk's table as Lucky's grew to completion. We had communicated only by letter during those final weeks, delivered by the blacksmith's twenty-year-old apprentice, Jasper Leeds. Young Jasper was a fox-faced lad with a smooth chest and a sensuous gait that would lead even the most menopausal observer to surmise that he had once possessed a tail. I didn't begrudge Hegey his little slap and tickle, if that's what it was. And on matters of paint color and glass size, the sassy little bastard was as reliable as the US mail.

The only thing I procured in person was the box of precious sheepskin condoms I needed to keep my women on the game. Tracking Hegey down myself, I had stood transfixed while he carefully folded each flimsy prophylactic tube, powdering them with cornstarch before loading them in their own box.

"Be sure they rinse them after every," Hegey swallowed queasily, "*use.* And keep them dry. They have to last. Those bloody things cost me a *fortune.*"

"And worth every penny," I said, leaving him with a fleeting kiss. I'd done my research. I knew what sporting women had to contend with when the fun was over. Douches of a one percent solution of lye mixed with sarsaparilla, botched abortions, or worse. Every house has its own cheap recipe to keep their soiled doves off the nest. Not me. If making my johns wear a cap cut into their profit, I made sure my crew knew it was worth the loss.

Finally, opening night was nigh. I moved with the alacrity of plague down the backstreets, carrying my box of precious condoms. In mere hours, my doors would be open, and a few choice throats would mistake me for the lost and the dead. I felt good. The world felt like it would always feel this right. I saw a sprig of chamomile beginning to flower in front of an alley outhouse. Overcome by the beauty of the little flower, I bent to the tiny white petals and thought to myself that I was finally less like these overly ornate privies. I was more like the life that springs undeterred from shit. As I crouched to fondle the defiant petals, the shithouse door flew open, and I was bowled over as if by a myopic buffalo and went ass over teakettle onto the filthy ground with a stinking splash.

"Sorry, ducky," Brown sneered, righting her petticoat. "I didn't spy ye down there among the shite." Scrambling for my box of condoms, I tried to stand but she threw an elbow and sent me flying through the flimsy door of an opposite outhouse. She ripped away the remains of the splintered door and filled the void with her angry bulk. Somehow I managed to retain custody of the condoms. "There, there, me lamb," she said. "I trust the damage ain't permanent." If I thought I could slow her assault by appearing as Mercy, I was sorely mistaken. "I'm learning a few of your secrets, my dear," she said and grinned at my confused face. "And not just the ones about your competitive intentions. *All* of them." My foot had upset a small bucket of lye, and an acrid cloud rose in the close atmosphere. But I didn't cough. I didn't so much as twitch. She raised a boot to kick me, but I caught it with my free hand and shoved her away as I found my feet. I couldn't get past her without too public a fuss, so I faced her in the cramped commode and let her have her head. "I've heard through the bramble ye be havin' a notion to reopen that shameful tea room as a sportin' house," she said. "That true?"

"A *notion*, Miss Brown?" I said, holding her reptilian stare. "It was an infant notion months ago. Weeks ago in it toddled up on its hind legs an actual *idea*. But today? Cock yer ears, my *dear*," I said, mocking her. "You hear that?" In the distance, the cadence of falling hammers, pounding to completion final touches of Lucky's, could be heard. "*That*, Miss Brown, is a full-grown *enterprise*. And there ain't fuck all you can do to stop it."

She broke the tension with a strident cackle. "By the saints, my girl," she said, extending a stubby hand, "seems I was correct as to your natural vocation after all." The shit fumes made my eyes water, but I held her gaze, refusing to acknowledge her gesture. "Aw, take me hand, Emma," she said, forcing her grip into mine. "We workin' girls now, ain't we? Sisters in toil?" She pulled me smoothly to her, her flabby bicep constricting into a formidable lump. "I'd offer ye a hope of heaps o' lucre," she whispered closely, the pressure of her grip not easing, "but 'tis not *money* yer after now, is it?" A chill echoed through my body. I prayed my eyes did not betray my shock. She pursed her thin lips and planted a cold, dry kiss on my cheek before she playfully nibbled at it. The ratty feel of her teeth made me lurch backward, breaking her grip. "A parting word of professional advice, if I may," she sneered. "Best chuck that chest of prize rubbers you got there, and tell yer girls to stick to the bucket and bulb. I never had me a ruttin' buck yet would place a whore's future years above his own mere seconds of bliss."

# CHAPTER EIGHTEEN

The details all defeated, we opened our doors with a near reverence more suited to Sapphic temples than to our genuine intention. The women were all in white, in ensembles that suited their fancy. The sisters Creel in childish night dresses, Miss Lumbee in a ghostly replication of her spinsterly tweeds. From behind the bar, Yellowhammer's eyes glowed beneath her snowy head wrap. Our little world was as pristine as a Christmas card. The only thing that could soil our sisterly bliss was actual patrons. Hours after opening, only one sorry-looking bastard had strolled in. He looked around with a sneer. "What the hell is this supposed to be with all this whitewash?" he said, planting himself at the bar. "The chapel of wayward tarts?" He pointed to a bottle of rye, and Yellowhammer poured him a shot. "What in hell you expect me to do with *that*?" our first customer said, eyeing the shot of whiskey. "I wouldn't take a drink poured by a—"

My slap echoed like a shot in a gulley, snapping his face sideways. "Hey, brother," I said as I bellied up next to him, "you just bought yourself the shortest night of your life. Clear out."

He smiled at Yellowhammer, then rolled his eyes to me. I didn't like his face, hadn't since he strutted in. His chalk stripe suit and hair part said respectable banker, but he'd trimmed his mustache to a narrow stripe above his lipless maw. "What's the matter with you all? Don't you know no decent white man would take a drink poured by a—" I heard a faint rattle of enamel after my next slap. Yellowhammer winced.

"If you're having trouble finding the door," I said with a mirthless chuckle, "it's over *there*."

"I ain't leaving 'till one of you Christian white women pours me a decent drink." I could end this fellow in a flash, but my women had other ideas. They looked from their various stations, silent, leering at the man at the bar.

"Perhaps I could offer some corrective assistance," Miss Lumbee said, approaching us. "I've no little experience in curbing the waywardness of recalcitrant boys." Lumbee had been a school teacher in another life. This was until she'd married one of her older students and was drummed out of town by the scandal. The banker shuddered with pleasure as Lumbee twisted his ear. She gave a knowing nod to the rest of the women. "Now a lady *has* poured you a decent drink, sir," Lumbee said. "What, pray, would base politesse prescribe next?"

The banker's eyes drifted up to Lumbee's with barely contained ecstasy. He reached for his glass, but she slapped it away with the speed of a striking viper.

"No, sir," Miss Clapper said in her Virginia drawl, joining us at the bar. "A gentleman always *thanks* a lady for her efforts." Slowly, the Creels flitted to the bar. Waccamaws abandoned her shuffled cards. And as the women began to gather around him, the effect was of a public park where all breeds of bird have come to peck stray bits of trash. They were like robins and wrens, for their fingers curved in the attitude of birds as they plucked at the banker's tie and lapels. Their tongues and pretty jaws trembled like birds as they taunted him. And I thought he must have felt for all the world like Saint Francis the first time he was flocked. Only Miss Buckhead, dressed all in black, stayed by her post at the door, a stark and luminous crow.

"Look at that happy bastard," Buckhead shouted over to us. "You'll need to start *charging* him for service if his damn grin gets any wider." Lumbee grabbed the banker by the ear again and sent him staggering into the center of the room. His wincing enjoyment was almost too much to bear. All the ladies but Buckhead and Yellowhammer, who stayed behind the bar, formed a circle around him.

"Oh, look!" Miss Clapper twittered. "It's kitty in the middle!"

The circle of women began a rhythmic clapping, the banker's knees buckling in anticipation of what might happen next. With an incredulous smirk, Yellowhammer watched from the bar as the ladies began to push him playfully between themselves.

"*Bad* kitty!"

"*Nasty* kitty!"

"Never no *good* kitty!" They chanted as their pushing became fiercer. If there was cruelty in the game, it was far from obvious on the half-lidded eyes of our sole customer. A schoolyard frivolity rang in the room. Only Yellowhammer did not smile. The game ended only after the banker spasmed suddenly and blushed to the tops of his ears. His hands darted to cover a dark stain that had formed at the fly of his trousers.

"Oh, he *spent!*" Clapper chirped, clapping her hands together in glee. The ladies cackled and guffawed as the banker tried to flee their taunting laughter, but Buckhead stopped him at the door with a steely extension of her arm.

"Where the hell you think you're going, friend?" she said sternly. "You had your fun. Now you owe us two eagles in gold. Or do you want me to take it out of your hide?"

I'll never know what that banker said, if he had been specific about his particular perversion, when he whispered to his friends the next day about his short but thrilling night at Lucky's. All I know is, an hour after supper the next night, our cuspidors began to ring. Customers were bellied up to the bar two deep. The smell of the outdoors began to mingle with the closeness of sitting bodies. Hung heavy upon the air was a haze of cheroot and cigarette smoke as men shook off the chill of early winter and opened themselves to the perfumed arms of our trade. I watched from a seat behind the bar as my women tended to duties, washing glasses, pouring drinks, smiling, shaking a little shoulder at a compliment, a little ass at some lewd suggestion. The Creels had been spotted by an enormous man in a beaver-skin coat. Thickly bearded, he had perched the twins, one on each knee, and bounced them in cadence to the jaunty rhythms the girls produced, one on the pipes, the other beating a Celtic bodhran. I didn't know they played. The music heated up. The mood lightened. Hands clapped. Beer mugs sounded on the wet bar. Waccamaws was pulled from behind the stud table and thrown into a furious reel by two filthy young miners. Van Guilders was propped up on the bar, alternating between girlish giggles and more mature panic while an old man with greasy side whiskers and an almost spherical pot belly ticked her bare feet. He must have been a veteran of the Battle of Detroit or some other 1812 retreat, for he still wore tattered Continental blues over his shabby trousers. A little man with an oiled comb-over, stiff as a churchgoer, whom I recognized as a local alfalfa farmer and Miss Brown regular, rolled his cuffs above his ankles, jumped up on one of the tables, and began an earnest clogging that sent several other men into lusty jigs and Russian barynyas and, with the help of two loaves of long rye, a kind of yeasty variation of the morris dance.

Not one of them looked at me. Not the way I was hoping to be looked at. I only saw the back of the tall drink of water that led Yellowhammer from her post behind the bar. I felt a tap on my shoulder and turned around to see her languidly shifting backside move toward the banister with a departing view of his tailored frockcoat and bowler right behind her. Was that my Boston boy? My sire? Why did I feel an awkward pang of jealousy? The music died. The men went back to their glasses and mugs. The john in the beaver drape flipped me four eagles, and the Creels stowed their instruments behind the bar before they all three ascended to the tattered gods. I went to work the bar and sent Clapper to deal stud, feeling the bottom fall out of the night as the drag of the hours slouched toward another culinary bust. Then they appeared. They strutted into the joint like tango dancers, their wide rib cages barely concealed under their bolero jackets. Three vaqueros up from Juarez, judging from their accents. They wore so much Taxco silver, Buckhead waved them through with hardly a glance. They knew what they wanted and were used to getting it. As they parked their chips in front of Clapper's nervous hands, I saw the panic flood her little bluebell eyes and sent over a round of rye shots that they downed, never flinching, never taking their eyes off the plump, sweating magnolia-scented blonde before them.

"You boys new in town?" Clapper asked sheepishly. But before she could finish the flip of her shuffle, a deeply bronzed hand slapped the deck still. Those same hands then made the universal sign whose meaning lacked all subtlety, needed no translation. From my seat at the bar I saw Clapper pale.

"You," the vaquero said to her. "Now."

He waited. The other two grinned. Clapper looked for all the world like a kitten treed by some thrice-headed hellhound. I saw my chance and moseyed over.

"You gents see anything you like?" I said.

"This one," the head man said, pointing to Miss Clapper, not looking at me. "With the hair like Michoacán honey. We like to make fuck. All three. We pay." He snapped his fingers, and one of his compadres produced a sack of silver so heavy it damn near toppled the table.

"There's fifteen hundred dollars here," Buckhead bloodlessly reported after she finished counting it. That was four years wages for the average tradesman. More money than I hoped to make in our first six months. Damn, there was a lot of coin in Mexican chuck and porterhouse.

"Well, now listen fellas," I said. "My girls don't much relish the idea of being ravished in triplicate, if you get my meaning. So if two of you see any *others* you might fancy . . ."

The headman turned to me, his dark eyes pinched in anger before they suddenly softened under my gaze. I had not realized I had addressed him in Spanish.

"Isobel?" he whispered. I had to leap away from the sweep of his arms as my aspect narrowed into the lithe body of his wife. His compadre caught me by the hips, pulling me toward him lewdly as I suddenly thickened in all the right places.

"Lula?" he rasped lustily. I was tugged from his tight embrace by the third before he pronounced me as "Pinkie." Luckily, there was only a slight physical variance between Lula and Pinkie. But Pinkie, bless her heart, had a liking for peppers and precious little tolerance in digesting them. And as such, the back of my throat burned from her constant bouts of reflux.

I pulled away from the pack and held up a cautioning finger. "Hold on, gents," I said in an odd chorus of desired voices. "There's plenty to go around. Three's my lucky number, after all."

"What're y'all saying?" Clapper whined, a current of relief thinning her confusion. "I didn't know you spoke Spanish, Miss Shinnecock." This was what I had been waiting for. I needed to get them upstairs before Clapper laid on any more questions. And with my mind thumping with the variables of the bedroom calculus before me, I corralled those three beeve pushers to the bottom of the stairs.

"You just watch out for them palmed aces, Clapper," I said in English, lacing my arms around the necks of the men. "I'll take care of these gentlemen." They ran me up the stairs on a sedan of their entwined arms, whisking me swiftly up and ever up to the sound of their jangling conchos and spurs. We burst through Hegey's bedroom door, the men counting loudly to three before propelling me to the bed. I had mere seconds to assess my situation while they fumbled out of their gun belts and clothes, surrounding me. How to describe the sensation! Behind the glamor of what I appeared to be kicked a very real fear. They were naked now, lean and dark, covered in whorls of black hair, all of them vertical except their business ends that now shot perpendicular to their flat bellies. I was the hub of a horny, three-spoked wheel, and hubs must remain central if one has any hope of getting anywhere. "Hold on, now," I said. "You'll all get your flop."

"Isobel, please, my dear. It's been *months.*"

"Lula! Strip it off! Show me your pechos!"

"Pinkie! *Dance*!"

I appeared to be the wife of the headman, a whore to the other, and some unfortunately named showgirl for the third. Pinkie's paramour began to clap a *paso doble*, and I had no choice but to jump on the bed, throwing my arms over my head as I began to stomp rhythmically on the mattress.

"Isobel! Stop that at once! It's not seemly!"

"Ah! Lula! Off! Take it off!"

As they addressed me in turn, I was newly assaulted by a unique feminine demeanor. Warm currents of novel blood, teeth, and muscles jolted through me each time I assumed the individual aspects of the women they mistook me for. It was a supremely disorienting feeling, terrifying in my total loss of control. I felt like a thing seen through the pickets of a fence, a child's rag doll dragged at speed, and each time I felt a glimpse of myself I had a new face, a foreign body. I was destined to be gutted of my stuffing by too rough and indecisive a game of make believe.

"Wait! One at a damn time!" I shouted. But my protest went unheard as their lust raged and my fear surged.

"Hey!" the headman roared, pushing his compadre. "Stop making my wife debase herself!"

"Why'd you stop dancing, Pinkie?" another said, pushing back.

"Get out of here, you two Godless bastards!" the headman thundered. "Can't a married man enjoy his wife in private? Jesus weeps!"

"Jesus didn't pay five hundred to see a pair like Lula's!" his partner said, growing angry.

Brothers in the saddle, sharing bad beans and worse weather for God knows how many womanless months, their inflamed desires made ash of their brotherly bonds. They darted for their respective pistols in a sudden temper I could not slow. The hammers of all three guns were cocked as if with one click. Each man nudged his barrel beneath his neighbor's chin. "Gentlemen! Please!" I shouted, my hands pumping the air to calm them. Then it hit me. What the hell was I doing? Noting the angle of their weapons, I lowered my head and fell to my knees. "Aw, hell," I said, "I never loved a *one* of you anyway!" For one breathless moment, each face fell back to the hurt of boyhood. Then a sound like cannon fire made me flinch as they rouged the walls bloody in the throes of tripartite jealousy. Already I could hear the voices downstairs raised in panic. I had to work fast through the heavy gun smoke and stink of fresh gore. I leapt off the bed and locked the door. There wasn't much left to the backs of their heads. I burrowed deep into the headman's throat. The first kick of his hot berry punch deluged my mind with his memories.

*A nervous madonna.*
*Eyes so deep and holy behind her white veil, it seems a sin to violate her.*
*Why won't the padre speak faster? Why must I fumble with the ring?*
*Antonio, she whispers before we kiss. Be gentle with me tonight.*
*I can hear the rustle of my bride's wedding dress as she struggles in my embrace.*
*The kiss no longer sweet as sugared skulls.*
*Bitter.*
*Why so bitter?*
*This is what it tastes like to be a man in love.*

That triple homicide launched Lucky's books into the black. The lurid taint of the scandal perfumed every sporting book in every horny john's pocket from every trail head and coach route in the country. Lucky's was legendary. Men paid a penny a piece just to finger the bullet holes I left drilled into three of the bedroom's walls. They parted with gold dust, liberty silver, and fancy foreign script just to get a gander at the pink stains on the whitewashed floor my elbow grease, brush, and lye could not fully erase. Everyone wanted to see the whore who had inspired such a passionate triangulation of death. Despite this unforeseen windfall, I still received a note one day from Hegey, heavy linen stock with a gold border emblazoned with one emphatic handwritten word. *Discretion!* it read. But I was feeling too good to be much hobbled by his chastisement. My plan was working. Within the month, even as the weather turned forbidding, the lauded reputation of Lucky's ensured a steady flow of the curious and incautious.

# Chapter Nineteen

I was mistaken for surly redheads, frigid blondes, sisters, mothers, sweethearts of varying comportment and temperament. Unlike with my unfortunate women, none of my johns ever got the chance to have their way with me. One drummer from Stockholm was convinced I was the warbling Swede Jenny Lind and begged me to sing Agathe's act two aria from *Der Freischütz* to the whole rowdy house. My humiliation was complete when he later insisted our time in the bedroom be accompanied by a pound of purified bear grease, an English-style bridle, and a single brandied cherry. Not all the requests of the beguiled were venal. Some just wanted to be touched or cuddled. My favorite of this type was Peppered Pete, a gray-bearded old codger whose sobriquet was in reference to the pebbled nature of his torso. From clavicle to navel, he was festooned with a flaring pattern of roughly healed scars. His memory was so poor, the provenance of his wounds changed with each meeting.

Sometimes they were the still-embedded musket balls left over from his days "catching frolic" with Ethan Allen. Other times, he confessed to having just returned from raiding the Comanche with Coffee Hays's Rangers in the Texas Republic. Either way, he never seemed to remember my name. "Well, hey there, uh . . . oh hell," he'd say, his smile fading in time with his memory.

"Hey, Ol' Pete. It's me!" Without a sharp mind to beguile, I was as in the dark as much as he as to whom I was supposed to be on any given night.

"Don't fret, missy. It'll come back to me," he'd say with a snicker.

"Up we go, old timer," I'd say, guiding him gently up the stairs. We'd sit in Hegey's upholstered chairs, bathed in the muffled voices from below, blank as two bobbing pigeons until he remembered who he'd come for. I was many lost loves to him. His little sister, Annie, who had been born with a harelip and a sunny disposition. His second wife, Morning Dipper, who had been a plump little Nez Percé full-blood who had died in childbirth. Even his old friend Ned Pope with whom he had shared a special intimacy when they were snowed in together one winter in the Rockies. And each time he made his preference clear, I could feel my skin and face and hair slip into the mold of his desire. It was a strange sensation but not totally unpleasant. Not anymore. It was like falling from a great height into a narrow pool of foreign flesh. And yet not foreign. For almost immediately, the thrill of falling resolved itself into a life I felt I had always lived. My mouth had always tasted like this. My smile had always broken this way. My shoulders, whether straight or stooped, felt as familiar as a new day. The sensation was so real, so complete, I had to remind myself it was an intimacy only shared, only seen, by myself and the object of my beguiling.

He was too old and addled for a poke. Just liked my company. For obvious reasons, I always suggested a shave. "Aw, hell! Did I cut you, now, ol' Pete? Let little Annie/Morning Dipper/ol' Ned kiss it and make it all better!"

Not all my beguiling was so simple or benign. Simon Braintree was one of these exceptions. He had perhaps too much intellect to ever suspect the full flower of my condition, but that did not stop him from exploiting it. I didn't want a thing to do with him the night I laid eyes on him. He had a desperate but furtive aspect, with a pale little face that reminded me of a polecat I had once come upon while it was sucking on our hen's eggs. A week after New Year's, I'd seen him waving to me through the window of Lucky's, his small face bundled up against the falling snow in a wide muffler and upturned coat collar. He seemed unsure if he wanted to come in. I watched him stop, stare at me, and then start muttering to himself before moving on. Then he'd stop again and double back to stare at me some more. I had a bad feeling, but finally, I decided to look straight at him. When his eyes made the trek from shock to relief, I knew I had a candidate. It was a slow night, only one deep at Yellowhammer's bar, and so I waited for him to enter, tamping down the mysterious dread I felt as best as I could. His eyes were weak as he approached, no bigger than puny almonds behind the specs he was forced to wear. I could feel him shaking as he stood next to me. Yellowhammer asked him what he would drink. He waved her away. He spread his hands on the bar, breathing in a rabbity kind of way, not looking at me. His shaking was not from the cold. He was winding up the courage to address me. Finally, he let out a sudden sob so loud Yellowhammer shot me a look. I gently backed her off by raising my hand.

"It's a cold night, friend," I said quietly. "Perhaps you'd fancy a toddy or a hot tea?"

He spun his face to me then. His eyes were watery behind his fogged specs. "Is that you, Sarah?" he whispered. "Is that *really* you?" I smiled weakly, not sure what I was getting into. "Sweet Providence! It is!" he said, putting his cold little hand on my arm. His touch made my skin crawl. "Did I leave the cellar door unlocked? How ever did you get out, my dumpling?"

Yellowhammer rolled her eyes and reached under the bar for the hogleg. She leveled the revolver at him, hiding it behind a line of shot glasses.

"Emma, don't," she warned. I gave her a reassuring look and motioned for her to put the gun away.

"*Emma*?" he spat at Yellowhammer, confused. "This is Sarah!"

"That's right, mister. I'm your Sarah," I said.

"You shouldn't be out in your fragile condition, Sarah," he said with a lifeless smile. "You could crack. Or break entirely. We must get you home." He looked around the empty barroom floor, smiling again when he spotted the door under the stairs. "This way, my dove," he said, taking me by the elbow. He led me not upstairs, not to the springy stage of all my masquerades, but to the saloon's cellar. This was new. I was used to being mistook for the misbegotten, but how was Lucky's "home" to him? Was this a novel progression of my beguiling? Or an effect of his own distraction? The last thing I saw before I closed the cellar door behind me was Yellowhammer's hard and disapproving gaze. The stone walls were thickly webbed with spider floss, and as he struck a lucifer, a section of the filthy webs ignited. In the sudden flare, I saw the crooked steps leading downward, the tops of the dusty beer barrels below.

"Haste," he said. "We must make haste." The lucifer spent, we were plunged into sudden darkness. I could feel the cellar floor with my feet, a crate of bottles at my hip. He lit another, found a lamp, and soon the neglected gloom was leavened by a faint, creeping light. He was surprisingly strong and set me on a barrel by my shoulders, like he was putting a child's doll in a highchair. Sitting on a barrel opposite me, his agitation seemed to wane. He unwound his muffler. Then unbuttoned his coat. Sarah, wherever she was, whomever she had been, was beginning to congeal in me. She was bigger boned than me, fuller in the wrists and ankles. Palms rough, knuckles large, my hands were forced together tightly against my belly in what must have been a practice of hers at times of her husband's stress. How many had I lost? Three children? Four? All those small miseries, the roundness failing, the painful tearing away, and only this loose empty belly of mine left to defend. "We will count the wheat this year a loss. But the barley might yet weather the frost. I have done some calculations and—" He stopped.

"What is it, Simon?" came from me as if we had travelled over a thousand fretful mornings together. "What about the barley?"

He stiffened. "Who *are* you?" he said, narrowing his eyes.

"Simon?"

"Stop calling me that! Who are you?" he said harshly as my heart began to race. "Where is my Sarah? Where have you taken her?" A flurry of panic ran the length of my spine. I stayed perfectly still.

"Simon," I said again. I knew the voice was hers. I could see its tone register in his eyes.

"This isn't possible," he said, lowering his head to his chest. "You *cannot* be her."

"Why, Simon?"

"Because she's—"

"Here," I said, placing a hand on his hair.

"*Dead!*" he shouted. "She froze! The cellar was locked!"

"No. Look at me, dear," his Sarah said.

He tossed his head away from me, faint whimpers whitening his lips. "This is some trick. Some mischief."

"Look at me, Simon," I said. The stridency in my voice was false, even to me. I knew she had never shared a raised word with her husband. I cupped his face, pressing his spectacles off the bridge of his nose. His eyes flared once before he squeezed them shut.

"No," he whimpered. "I mustn't. I *mustn't.*"

"Simon. Look at me. It's Sarah. *Your* Sarah. If you want me. *How* do you want me, Simon?" My question seemed to rouse him. His face relaxed in my grip but still refused to regard me. "How do you want me, Simon? Tell me."

"As I found you," he whispered. "As you were that morning." A cold rigor threatened the marrow of my bones, and I knew his desire. I felt the last chill one ever feels begin at my toes, stealing wretchedly up my body.

"Like *this*?" Sarah asked, sickened. My touch was suddenly ice upon his cheek. He kissed my fingertips with fevered lips.

"Yes," he moaned.

"Still? And silent? And *cold*?" These were the last words I spoke before the final march of rigor mortis drew my hands to my sides and stopped my tongue.

"*Yes.*"

My eyes clouded like milk left too long in its bucket. My vision tunneled to pinpoints before it blinked into darkness. I moved neither forward or back. I hung there in the void, a cold bather in the abyss.

There was no comfort in the rumor of me, no solace in the resonance of once having been. For not even my death was mine. My comfort came only because I knew, even in the terror of my counterfeit demise, that I was spared feeling what he was doing to my rigid body. I cannot think there was any pleasure in it for him. My clothes had to be torn from my stiff limbs by degrees. My hips were rusted gates, my knees prized apart by force and odd ardor. It took all my Beguiler's will to finally force my jaws open. When my teeth found his flesh, the disgust was welling sour in my throat. The first taste of him flooded the blackness behind my eyes with what seemed fathoms of the same. Some things cannot be unseen. And what Simon Braintree learned about himself that stark winter morning haunted the last dreadful moments of his life. Just as I fear it will always haunt me.

Coming back from the cellar, newly thawed, almost stupid with repulsion, the last person I wanted to see was Da. Could my night get any blacker? But there he was, hunched at the bar, his shoulders cupped around the mouth of his glass like a mother bird protecting her chick from the wind. Happily he hadn't seen me. I caught Yellowhammer's eye and waved her over.

"How long he been here?" I asked.

"A spell. He says he's looking for Cora. That you?" It was a logical question, given how she had been witness to several johns mistaking me for other women.

"Give him a bottle and get him out of here."

"He comes in here all the time, looking for you."

"He's not looking for me."

"Who then?"

Honesty seemed the only thing I could offer her. "My Momma," I said shamefully. "He's looking for his wife."

"Listen, girl," she said sternly. "We all know you white folks is crazy. That don't give me no never mind. That's *your* business. I just don't want all that crazy coming up on *me*. But that's your pa, girl. And no way can I be party to breaking that poor old man's heart again."

"It's complicated."

"That's what family is, girl."

"Yellowhammer, please. He can't see me. Give him a bottle and get him gone."

"He's drunk damn near a barrel already."

"*Please!*" She read it all in my eyes.

"All right, honey. Don't fret." I watched from the cellar door as Yellowhammer pulled a stoppered bottle to the bar and placed it in front of the old man. His withered hands stroked the amber curves reverently. "Here you go, old timer. On the house. Get on home now. Your wife's waiting."

"Cora? Is she? Is she waiting?" Yellowhammer took his head gently in her two hands, effectively blinkering him as she shot a look my way.

"You're married to Alice, Mr. Shinnecock. Remember? Ol' Squirrel Tooth Alice."

"Alice?"

"Yes, sir. It's your daughter Emma who owns this place."

"Emma? Emma's here?" he said excitedly, trying to break free of Yellowhammer's grip. "Why will she never see me? Why can't I see my own daughter?"

Yellowhammer shot me a look so cold it rivaled my bout with Simon. I couldn't look anymore. I disappeared back to the cellar, leaving Yellowhammer to mercifully wrestle my Da out the door. I would owe her for that one.

# Chapter Twenty

Come spring, an unseasonal bout of clement weather brought out the hardness in men. Dynamite setters from the railheads east. Beeve pushers up from Texas. Coke miners who would never wash clean, working men with rinds as thick as aged cheese. All took advantage of the unseasonable thaw to see if the rumors about me were true. I'd been beguiling too long and too consistently by then for men's tongues to stay still.

"*Tabernac!*" thundered a mountain-sized trapper from the Saint Lawrence River one evening. "*Je veux que le putain célèbre madame!*"

He had pushed past Buckhead at the door when she had tried to stop him, had made short work of both Clapper and Lumbee, and had one of the Creels dangling a foot off the floor from his massive neck before I moseyed to his side.

"Easy there, *mon vieux,*" I purred in his native tongue. "You've found her."

"You?" he said incredulously, his mop of black curly hair dangling over his confused eyes. "I don't recognize you. The rumor was you bewitch men with your blue eyes. But look at me," he said, turning around for all the room to see. The Creel girl let loose from his broad shoulders and dropped to the floor. "I see nothing!" The room was silent. All eyes were on us as my mind churned. Had my beguiling reached its limit? I could assume his language, but why my transformation stopped there terrified as much as embarrassed me in front of all those expectant faces. Thinking quickly, I decided to have some fun with him and perhaps undermine the rumors about me as well.

"Hold on there, buddy," I said, stepping close to him. "The magic don't work unless you play along."

"Magic how?"

"Don't you believe in magic?" I heard a few titters from the crowd watching us. "Hey, folks, this big timberbuck don't believe in magic!" The crowd's continued laughter seemed to anger him. "Take it easy, now. We're just fooling with you. But you know the rules, right?"

"What rules?" he said gruffly.

"Magic rules! See, I can't be nothing to you unless you been something to someone else." That tore it. The crowd roared. I was speaking the gospel truth, but the crowd heard it as the joke I had intended.

"That don't make sense!"

"Okay, real simple now. You got a wife? A sweetheart, maybe?" He shook his huge head. "How about your mother. You love your mother, boy?"

He thought for a moment, then shook his head again. "I never love!" he said, folding his arms over his huge chest. The crowd hissed and booed at his response.

"Well, there's your problem, son. I'm Emma May Shinnecock, the *looove* witch," I said, wiggling my fingers in his big, dumb face. "Didn't they tell you that? Sorry you came all this way, but to a loveless son-of-a-bitch like you, I can't be nothing but myself." He eyed me from near the summit of all six foot six of him and wordlessly decided I was still worth the effort.

"Fine. We still make fucking." He scooped me into his massive arms and began to lope with me toward the stairs. This was an unfortunate turn. I had gotten sloppy, been too cocky. I wrestled myself from his ursine embrace with a stiff kick to both his kneecaps and dropped to the floor.

"Hold on now, don't get all handsy on me," I said, straightening my skirt. "You don't know the price. A poke with some one as famous as me will cost you, brother."

"How much?"

"Two grand," I said without a hitch.

"*No* rented cooz is worth that kind of coin," he said.

"You sure about that, friend?" I had him. I had him because he had come too far, been buffeted by too much bluster *not* to be had. I felt the small tingle of a thrill. How long had it been since I had been wanted, even for an hour, for who I actually was? He reached for his stake in the pocket of his checkerboard shirt. "Hey," I said, stopping his hand. "What say we make this interesting. You a betting man?"

The way he said *bien sûr* sounded titillating.

"I'll flip you for it," I said.

"And if you lose?"

"Name it."

"All."

"All what?"

"All your stock," he said. "A free tumble with each." He then looked languidly, with lustful rumination, at the faces of each of my women. It was clear from their staring eyes this was the one stretch of our conversation they understood. I felt poorly about how things were progressing. No one had the right to bet with another's labor. I heard the crinkle of paper being passed between the men behind me. Those bastards were making book, though who held the shortest odds I didn't know. Pride and being desired had gotten the better of me.

"You sure you got enough spunk, brother?" I said, eyeing the crotch of his wool britches. "Hard to tell in them silly trousers you're wearing." This got me another laugh but did nothing to dent the will of the towering man before me. He stared at me with a handsome smugness. "Lumbee," I said, not taking my eyes from him. "Fetch me one of them eagles from the kitty."

"We'll use one of mine," he said, producing a quarter eagle gold piece from the waist of his britches. "Care to check it?" he asked with a wicked grin.

"I trust you, stranger. Call it." The only sound in the room was the tiny peal of his thumbnail on the edge of that spinning liberty head. It caught the light like a single drop of Zeus's burnished lust upon Danaë. I thought of Da and his credo of luck being as good as labor if one had will enough to love. "Luck and love," I mumbled. "Luck and love."

"Heads," he said. I willed the better part of me into that spinning coin. Tails it was. The room only knew who had won when the big man frowned. Cheers rose up from the majority of onlookers. I guess I had been the local favorite. "Best of three?" he grinned.

"If you reckon you can afford it, stranger. Cuz I know I can." He looked at me sternly before his big face cracked with a smile. He wrinkled his nose and shook his head. His bravado took wing like the geese of his homeland.

"Ma chere!" he said as he slapped his fat bankroll into my palm.

"Not me you owe it to," I said, handing it back. "It's theirs." I motioned with my head to my scattered women. "And pay it out peaceful, hear? *With* your regrets."

March's familiar lion came, a toothy wind laced with ice and the promise of instant death, that kept the streets clear of traffic. The freezing temperatures brought a lethargy, a languor to our mornings that made working-class royalty of us all as we could rightly refuse to leave the warmth of our beds until the slant of the sun pierced our windows and warmed the air just enough to stop our breath from fogging. Then, from the hot defenses of our individual quilts, a game of round robin would ensue—voices raised in the cold, calling for volunteers to brave the icy hardwood and light the kitchen stove. Negotiations—barter in favors or goods—passed through the halls as Lumbee would agree to get the coffee going if Buckhead let her work the door for the early shift. The Creels would agree to light both the kitchen and main room stoves if they could be allowed to service only their beaver-coated regular and then entertain with just their musical instruments for the remainder of the evening.

This morning, the sun didn't bring the day; the windows stayed dim against the rattling cold. After the morning's negotiations had concluded, I listened to them creak down the steps, heard the skillet sizzle and the tin report of the cups and plates as they ate and gossiped. They never asked me to join them. It was an unspoken bond between us, a swap of unanswered questions. I never much inquired what had brought them to my door. They never queried what kept me from their table.

I lit the downstairs lamps around five in the evening, but it could have been nigh on midnight for the steadfast dark outside our windows. The wind moaned through the chinks and under shut sills with the cold breath of the grave. I hollered out that they all could queen it up for the night, stay snug, or tend to themselves. The night was promising to be a real bust, and I figured whatever poor and motherless trade the cold delivered to me I could handle on my own.

He hammered the old heartstrings the moment I saw him hunched outside the door. Just a luckless boy. He wrestled with the door for a bit, trying the knob, convinced that it indeed turned yet stymied by why it refused his admission.

"Push," I mouthed through the glass.

"Sorry?"

"You got to push it, son," I said aloud.

The door finally gave and delivered him, stumbling, into the empty saloon. He was precious—a five-foot paean to the prosaic, stamping his small feet to clear the ice flakes from his boots. He hung up his coat neatly, then moved only as smoothly as his line-dried suit would allow, crinkling as he walked with the tentative sound of squirrel feet on new frost. His face: forgettable. His hair and eye color: unintelligible. I figured him for some ditchwater rube, the middle son of a family with no middle. Lucky's had come to him as a rumor, then a hope. Or he had just turned eighteen and his pa had slipped him a few bits and told him to go be a man. Whatever his story, he was a ringer for a first-timer. I approached him as if he were a new-broke colt, placing my hand on his shoulder gently but firmly. He turned with a jerk so sudden it gave me a start. Then he plucked his cap off his head and swallowed hard and half-bowed and mumbled, "Pardon me, ma'am" and "Sorry, ma'am" and would have rambled on in that way if I hadn't guided him to the bar.

"What say I front you a drink, son? What's your pleasure?"

"Oh, I d-d-don't imbibe no spirits, ma'am."

"Let's get something warm in you at least."

"Nothing, ma'am. Thank you. Where is everyone?"

"I don't strike your fancy?"

"Y-yes, you do. Most s-satisfactorily," he said. It was by no means a raving review of my charms, but it would have to do. I was not concerned that I had not beguiled him. I was peckish as hell. And he was easy pickings.

"Then what say we head on up," I said sweetly. He gave me a stiff nod as I took him by the elbow and led him up the stairs. As we ascended, it wasn't lust that filled his staring eyes. More like a stark determination. He just wanted to get this over with. "Listen," I whispered, taking his cold hand in mine once we reached my bedroom door. "You don't have to say nothing. There's no shame in what you come for." He looked up at me and smiled, blushing slightly. My senses were so piqued with hunger I could see the dark striations in his irises. They reminded me of the gills under the caps of certain large mushrooms. And just like that, he suddenly became as unworthy of concern as any forest fungus. I led him into my room. He stood in the center of it, the grandness of his surroundings reducing him even further. I moved a step closer. He breathed loudly. The room was filled with the thrum of his racing heart. I could smell the sweetness of his breath begin to sour.

"What's it going to cost me?" he wanted to know.

How could I answer him? The price would have been too dear, even for a mogul. "That's all right," I said, pulling him to the bed like a child's wagon behind me. "I'm running a special tonight for relapsed drunks and virgins." I sat him on my satin coverlet and slipped the straps from my chemise. His eyes wandered from me as he studied the egg-and-dart molding, which seemed to have all the fascination I was trying to incite. I whistled once and that did it. His attention snapped to my exposed breasts. Once he got a load of my girls, up came old Lazarus. The force of his arousal was so sudden, it brought him to his feet. "Can't do much just standing there, son. What say you loosen a few buttons." It was like getting a three-day corpse into the sack. Five whole minutes was eaten up just getting his pants over his shoes.

"I never take my cleats off when I get into bed," he explained. "F-farm emergencies." He only removed his clodhoppers and socks when I gently insisted. When I had him in the altogether, I had to heft him onto the bed, pull back the covers, tuck him in. When I slipped in beside him, he slunk back to the edge like I was covered with privy slime.

"You might hurt my feelings you keep shying away like that."

"Sorry, ma'am, er, miss." The dawning of my sex, with its warm and irrefutable proof, seemed almost too much for him to bear. His jaw tensed. A matrix of sweat broke out upon his upper lip.

"Emma," I prompted sweetly.

"Miss Emma . . ."

"It's all right. Just try to relax." He had maneuvered himself to his back, his spine rigid as his member. The boy was a perfect T square. I was about to straddle him when his face scrunched up. I backed off him completely when he gave a strangled whimper. And then the poor thing began to cry. No one with a heart could have had a violent thought against such weeping. "Aw. C'mon, now," I said. "You know, maybe this wasn't such a good idea." I placed a motherly hand on his rigid knee. But his wails didn't cease. "Let me help you get yer drawers on. Shoes first, right?" And my hand hovered above him, holding a muddy boot.

"*Harlot!*" he shouted suddenly. I dropped his boot, startled. The word was pronounced with such sudden force, I thought it was coming from the next room. "Daughter of Babylon, face thy punishment, for thine inequities are legion in the sight of the Lord!" he raved. Just my luck, I thought, regaining my composure. These religious nutbirds were propagating like lice all over small towns like ours. He sprang up suddenly on his rickety hind legs, eyes wild, lips foaming like Jeremiah. But his little general was as adamant as ever. Before I could scramble to the floor, he unfurled like a spring and was upon me, pinning me to the bed in a flash. He spread my knees with a furious knock of his own, spittle raining down on me in foul drops. "For some offenders, the lash. But for thee, oh unwholesome handmaiden of Sodom, the cudgel! Doest thou feel the burden of mine cudgel?" I felt it all right. I struggled as hard as I could against his grip. But with his sinewy arms and thighs, cast hard as rope from constant labor, he had me beat. He began to laugh, a horrible disembodied laugh, and his eyes rolled back in his scrawny head, showing all white and awful. His hips began to rock in an angry pummel. He was hitting foul balls all over the place, ramming me in the thigh, belly, and hips. This was far from the easy pickings I had imagined, and I shuddered when I thought of any of my women fumbling through this horror on a nightly basis. Suddenly, his arms slipped, just a fraction, but enough for my hand to become free for an instant. I swiped blind, caught the side of his face with my fingernails. The blood began to peep, and that's all I needed. I flipped him savagely to his back and buried my bared teeth into his throat, forcing his guttural indictments up the octaves until he was screaming like a girl. Time shuddered to a delicious stop. The hot berry flowed down my open throat, filling me with a new and exquisite rage. Fury stoked the oceans of red behind my eyes. My ears thrummed greedily with the slowing bass of his heart. And there, in the corner of my mind, amid all the deep red satisfaction, I saw little Emma. Knees skinned. Nose freckled from the sun. *You better quit,* she cautioned. *Better leave off 'fore ya do something bad, ya hear? Better quit! Better quit!* But I couldn't. Wouldn't. I felt another's hands on me. Strong hands.

"*Damn*, Emma! You're going to kill him!" Yellowhammer yanked me off the bloody screaming mess beneath me. I spun to my feet and raised my hand to strike her.

"No, honey!" she shouted as she caught my furious blow. Her grip was tense but soothing on my fist. "Listen, now, Emma. No!" A familiar voice, I thought as I came back to my senses. A voice I wanted to like me. My breathing began to steady as I recognized her. "Easy, now, baby. Leave off, now," she said. "Let the boy get some breath." Yellowhammer held me as the terrified sticky mess sat up, frantic. He scrambled about the room, picking up a sock, his shirt, his worn britches with their lolling fly. I couldn't help but notice he was still at attention. Yellowhammer wasted no time dropping the boy to the ground with the simple extension of her arm. "Where you think *you* going?" He hit the deck like a sack of feed. She reached for a towel near the wash basin and tossed it to me. "Put some pressure on his neck 'fore he bleed out." I did like I was told as Yellowhammer began to collect the rest of the boy's clothing. "We got to get him cleaned up and out of here before anyone else shows up."

She pulled on his trousers while he whined about how his shoes must come first. She whipped his shirt over his shoulders and slapped him quiet. He growled, baring his teeth. "Now you listen, here," she spat in his miserable face, "you best think *twice* 'fore you haul your Bible-thumping ass to no whorehouse again!"

"But this sister of Salome tried to *kill* me!"

"No, mister. She merely defended herself. And if I hear you say any different, I'll chase you down and snap your neck like a barnyard hen. Now get!" She chucked a pitcher full of water over him, his wounded throat running to streaks of pink, and told him to leave by the back stairs. When he was gone, she turned to me. I was balled up on the bed, matted with the boy's gore, the sheets tangled and sticking to my belly and thighs. We heard a knock. I recognized Lumbee's concerned voice. Yellowhammer was calm but firm in her explanation, shoving the empty pitcher through the crack in the door, requesting hot water and a clean towel. We waited in silence until we heard Lumbee's knock again. The closed door in her face was all the thanks Lumbee got when she brought what had been requested. Yellowhammer still said nothing while she poured the steaming water into the basin. She dipped the towel and rung it. "Oh, Emma," she said quietly. "This ain't no kind of life." As soon as the warm towel touched my skin, the tears came. I hoped she would not be burdened by my distress. I already owed her more than I could pay. But I was weary of such hoping. Weary of all my lies. I was relieved she had caught me. That she was finally seeing me as I truly was.

She held me tight, buttressing up the pieces in me that had began to spill. I couldn't live like this, not with women I had come to love and trust. I felt filthy and broken, but more, I felt sick at the lie of me, left bereft of solace by the ultimate loneliness the lie had engendered. There was a chorus of voices in my veins, liquid galleries stacked with broken and mocking souls, none of whom I would have chosen to know if I'd had the choice. I needed to confess. I needed to tell someone about me other than Hegey. I needed a friend. But Yellowhammer would have none of that. "Hush, now," she whispered. "I don't want to know none of your business. I already know too much for my own welfare." The calamity had been my own doing, my stupid greed and pride.

"Oh, Lucy," I said, using for the first time Yellowhammer's Christian name. "I broke my rule. My *one* rule and I broke it."

"I hear you, honey," she said with a dampened smile. "I promised myself I'd never give two hot shits about no white woman. And now I got my ass in the thickets, thanks to you."

Two nights later, Van Guilder fled, eloping with her Continental Johnny. From my bedroom window, I saw her clumsy escape, watching in moonlit silence as she slowly negotiated down from the top story, clinging to a rope of twisted bedsheets like a frightened kitten while her aged suitor huffed whitely in the cold. I didn't wave good-bye as he bundled her into his sleigh and whisked her into the dark. I told myself that to have acknowledged what she was doing would have tarnished the moment for her, might have subdued the questionable luster on what was clearly her life's last portion of romance and adventure. But the real thing I refused to acknowledge was not her departure.

The morning after Van Guilder's retreat, all my working women stood quietly in a line before me. They were all dressed for travel, with totes and tussy-mussies they could only recently afford. No one spoke at first. They just stood there, waiting for me to begin. But all I said was, "I reckon you all noticed this morning that Miss Van Guilder has left us." Miss Clapper politely feigned surprise. Buckhead spat. But still they said nothing. "From the look of all those fancy flub-dubs you all are wearing," I continued, "you're fixing to do the same."

"You understand we have been grateful for the employment," Waccamaws said finally. Her cadence was formal, refined. Was she once a teacher like Miss Lumbee? I was ashamed I had never asked. "And your treatment of us has been more than satisfactory."

"Downright sisterly," Clapper offered before Lumbee silenced her with her eyes. The Creels stayed quiet, plaiting together hanks of one another's hair until their heads drew closer and closer.

"Perhaps it is a feminine attribute that we can dismiss the evidence of our senses," Lumbee began stiffly. "But there is an increasing trepidation to the general atmosphere here. A trepidation that exceeds the pall inherent in our duties. At least to our minds."

"You mean me?" I swallowed with a dry throat.

"The blood," the Creels said in spiritual tandem.

"Yes, the blood," Lumbee said. "The gunshots, the names they mistake you by. But mostly the men."

"The *men*?" I asked.

"The way they come in, Emma," Lumbee said coolly. "So full of masculine vigor. And yet, particularly under your ministrations, they leave, how shall I put it? Unwholesomely diminished."

"Oh, hell! Let's just call it out," Buckhead said. "Some of your johns leave here looking like they been mauled by a damn bear!"

"Or harshly chastised with a bull whip!" Lumbee added.

"Li'l ol' Peppered Pete leaves here looking like you done shaved him with a dull spoon!" Miss Clapper offered.

"Sooner or later, folks other than us are gonna notice that. When that happens, this place ain't going to be no kind of safe. Not for women like us," Buckhead continued. I just stared at her. "You lied to us, Emma Shinnecock," she said with genuine gall. That hurt. But I refused to offer a defense.

"I was as loyal to this place as the day is long," Waccamaws cried. "I would have mopped up *buckets* of blood. Patched a *hundred* bullet holes. But you never bothered to be forthcoming with us."

"You called us friends," one Creel sister said.

"Made us feel like sisters," the other chimed. "What kind of sister doesn't have the decency to be honest with us about her real purpose?" She swallowed a sob in her throat and angrily wiped at her eyes.

"I still don't know what's wrong with you," Buckhead said. "I don't know what horse pill of a grudge you got against those sorry bastards in pants who lay with you. I can say plainly, each one of us has thought more'n once of tanning a man black and blue. Why didn't you let us in on it? Why didn't you let us help you? Gentler sex. Hell, you show me a woman who ever got a thing worth keeping by being gentle about it, and I'll show you some sorry fool deserving of her cage."

"We were *different,* damn you," one of the Creels said. She blushed after realizing she had cursed. With their heads still braided together, her sister had some trouble landing a comforting kiss on her embarrassed sister's cheek.

"Everyone of us would have covered for you until doomsday if you'd only told us the truth," the Creels said in spooky tandem. "But you *used* us, Emma. And we *all* have been used enough." I could have come clean right there. I could have grabbed a barrel tap off the bar and delivered a mortal blow to myself and proved the impossibility of my provenance right in front of them. But I didn't. I couldn't. Somehow letting them believe I was some mad, man-hating bully, selfish in my revenge, was easier than admitting the truth. What could I say? Hand them more lies about myself? They were finally standing up for themselves. I was proud of them. Even if their resolute postures broke my heart.

"I'm sorry. I never meant to hurt any of you." That was all I could muster.

"That's it?" Buckhead said with a snort. "That's all you got? Even now, right now, one honest word from you would be enough to get us all back upstairs and on your side."

I looked into the wet faces of all the women beseeching me. I was like a child riding a carousel, passing, turn after turn, the brass ring of their love and trust. But I would not reach for it. I said nothing.

"Well," Buckhead said as she hefted her carpetbag to her side. "I guess that's the shooting match. Ladies?"

I was feverish with shame as I watched them caravan silently into the cold away from me. Everything they had said was true. There had been a slow gold in their companionship, and I had squandered it all. It took real courage to follow their hearts and brave a world bent on swallowing them whole. I would miss them deeply. I was saddest to see Yellowhammer go. I tried to convince her that she could stay behind the bar, and we could run the place as a straight watering hole. No gambling. No women. I reasoned she would be safe with me. We could be prosperous together, look out for one another. By that time, the Honey War had been won and our tiny burg, crude as it was, was still firmly behind a slave-free border.

She had simply looked at me and asked, "What makes you think it's *me* who ain't free?"

# GLORYLAND

# Chapter Twenty-One

After the women went away, my heart went out of Lucky's. I could not undo the damage I had done. But perhaps I could change. Perhaps I could become good. But first I would settle for a good cry and a good long jaw on the only other substance that made me glad I still drew breath. So when I went to Hegey's to tell him the news of my folding the house, my mind was really on the deep recesses of his candy stash, the shelves stacked with French confectionery in boxes as pretty as a rich man's coffin. He was of course dismayed, at first, about my decision. The place had been a success after all. Other girls could be found. Who could possibly justify pulling up the blanket of such a fiscally fat picnic?

"You don't hate me?" I said, coming wet from my bath, a box of his best Debauve & Gallais half-finished in my hand.

"For what? Denying me my most solvent enterprise to date? Don't be impertinent." He gave me a washed out smile and sighed. "Besides, Emma, imagine my solitude if *I* rejected you as well." There was a new austerity to Hegey's apartments, a restraint manifest primarily in the absence of pricks from every decorative surface. Was Hegey wrestling with the same admonishing angels as I? The walls were gray and plum. The furniture fumed oak, ponderous and conspicuously masculine. The bath had simply been that, a porcelain tub. White, not cream. Shaving implements in full view. And was that common bay rum I smelled still lingering about the wash basin?

"*Depeche-toi, ma petite chou,*" Hegey said, tossing me a towel. "I haven't all morning."

"What the hell happened here?" I asked. "Where's all your fancy gewgaws?"

"A long and sobering story that will have to wait for another time. I'm late for church." He could have hit me with an axe handle. Church and Hegey went together like sorbet and shit.

"The hell you say," I said, running the lush towel over my bare legs. Hegey stared at the wall, stiff as a cadet avoiding my nakedness, until he snatched the towel from me before I could drop it in the puddles on the floor. "Since when do you drag your sorry ass to church?"

"It's become prudent of late," he said bitterly. "There is no mention of God on our currency, Emma, but I've been warned His name is quite plainly there. They've beaten us," he said with a sad smile. "The zealots. The hypocrites. What choice do we have but to play along?"

I couldn't believe it. Once our uniqueness had been our bond. Now it angered me that it would be our shame. If staying in Hollywood meant yoking his natural proclivities, how could I do any different? "What congregation?" I asked.

"The only one I could tolerate, I fear. The sermons tend to be a bit bellicose, but the parson's face and figure more than make up for that." There was only one place he could have meant: Five Wounds and that handsome towheaded snake preacher. The prospect of church suddenly seemed less dire.

"Hope you don't mind a date," I said, rifling through his more somber dresses.

"Mind? My dear, I was counting on it."

The Five Wounds had moved to new digs yet again. It was situated now unapologetically on the main street, white as a knuckle bone through a nasty gash, squatting defiantly between the stone Unitarian and the subdued but still quaint Lutheran. It was a great barn of a place with high, rough-hewed beams and lancet windows pierced with only clear glass between the mullions. Clean white light flooded a gallery paneled entirely with untreated knotty pine. It might have been folksy, familiar, but the scale was too huge, too robust in breadth. And so the effect was humble and somehow contradictory—a log house cathedral. The pews were the only thing that seemed scaled to the human, their backs even tuned to the curve of the average spine. Was my father's craft the culprit? No carved crosses. No prayer books. All of one's faculties were meant to be dominated by the church's only animate and arguably decorative feature. Him.

The preacher had gotten himself even more handsome, if that were possible. I figured by this point he was somewhere past twenty, near my age in looks if not years. Broad-shouldered, tapered waist, high cheekbones anchored by a firm, no-bullshit jaw. Ice-blue eyes. A flaxen cowlick that danced to the jig of his invective. He was too pretty for my taste, I told myself. I'd been in the company of all kinds of gentlemen, and I knew lookers like him needed extra pillows for their swelled heads. So why was I fixated on his hands? Hands are important. And his knew a thing or two: large but with long square fingers, competent, intuitive, the kind you wouldn't mind having linger all over you if you had a decade to spare. Okay, I'll give him that. He might be worth a tumble. But a preacher husband? Because, let's face it. That's what I was thinking. What would be better cover? What could whitewash my checkered past any better than a strapping, empty bucket of a preacher?

Hegey winked when he saw the preacher return my steady gaze. "As promised. An Adonis that could recite dry goods receipts and still captivate." We sat in the back of the church, like the two penitents we were, hoping to call as little attention to ourselves as possible.

"Mathew 21:12," the preacher said with his rich bottomland drawl. He railed on about Jesus and the money changers, lingering over upturned tables and the upsetting of a dove vendor's chair. And if his words were void of spiritual instruction to me, his boyish confidence was not. There was possibility here, yes. But only because I liked the odds of him. Aces always beat a full house, and bedding down one man at the end of his day would be far easier than wrangling six in a night. But who was I fooling? In my soiled state I was, of course, beneath contempt and, hence, well below marital consideration. I was most likely only allowed in the church because I shared a little history with Mary Magdalene. The sight of the scrubbed necks of several of my ex-regulars only highlighted what I figured to be the congregation's line on sin. And this was that sins of an animal nature, of dumb passion, of the male member, in other words, required no special compensation. But a willful sin, a serpentine sin, a *female* sin, that would clear the pews in all directions. This much was made clear by the crowd who filed past me without so much as a glance. Hegey took my arm and laced me into the shuffling crowd. The preacher's gaze had lingered on me during his sermon only as a test of his own purity. I was only the devil he had looked in the eye and resisted. With my head down, I did not see the hand that extended to arrest my exit.

"Why, Miss O'Day! I thought I saw you among the flock. My, but you have been scarce of late! Did you enjoy the service?"

It was the preacher, close enough where I could smell the pine soap on his skin. What had he just called me? Surely, he hadn't mistaken me for a dead whore. Hell, I was ten times the looker as that dishwater sow. Was this my beguiler's plan? No future. No redemption. Just a hot lunch between sermons near the pulpit? Why was my hunger for him well south of my belly? And here I was, all dolled up to the nines and—oh, hell, what did it matter how he saw me, I reasoned soberly. What was more important? My feminine pride or my reputation? His beguilement was proof enough that he was well within my reach. Hegey merely gawked. Should I confess to being Mercy? I decided to play it safe.

"Actually, it's Shinnecock," I said, extending my hand. "Emma May."

"Eben. Lightfoot," he said blinking. "I must beg your pardon, Miss Shinnecock. You so thoroughly resemble a girl I once knew about town."

"I hope to my advantage, Preacher."

"To your most favorable advantage, I can assure you." That riled me.

"Mercy O'Day?" I said, smiling devilishly. "I remember her." His unintended insult would not go unpunished. "Wasn't she in Miss Brown's employ a time? Why Preacher Lightfoot, what a sly and surprising fox you are." The reddening of his skin did not compliment his pale hair.

"No, I meant I had seen her engaged—"

"Engaged? Why the mind reels! I can only image what *in*!"

"Please, you misapprehend—"

"And here I thought preachers were beyond such common temptations."

"We are. I *am*. It's just—"

"I suppose I can't blame you. Didn't the Lord have a similar penchant for loose female company?"

"Miss O'Day used to see me from time to time. Regarding spiritual matters."

"Wasn't she Catholic?" I said.

"The Lord recognizes all who accept him."

"My, how unexpectedly *modern* of you," I said. "We must surely meet again and discuss your other progressive ideas." I took his hand and gazed wantonly into his eyes. Hegey coughed and took my arm.

"Lovely service, Reverend," he said, pulling me away. "But I fear Emma must away. She is not quite herself today."

"Oh," he said sweetly. "Perhaps I can inquire about your health at a later date."

"I'd be *very* disappointed if you didn't," I said, waving good-bye to him.

Hegey wasted no time in giving me both barrels when we entered his apartment. "What in the hell was that all about?" he thundered. "The preacher? You've decided to ensnare the preacher? After all the hours I've spent so miserably erect on those pews."

"Don't give me that. You have the same designs on him as I do."

"True, but at least in *his* eyes *mine* are far more virtuous," he said, filling a kettle.

"Who said my intentions weren't virtuous?"

"Emma, please. Not even you would reduce the sanctity of matrimony to a warm feed bag."

"And why the hell not? Don't you think I know what a hot, steaming fraud marriage is? More'n half the johns that darkened my door had rings on their fingers. And their wives weren't any different when they looked the other way. It's a contract. Just a goddamn horse swap. And if all I've got to do is rustle his dinner, fluff his pillows, and make his cock crow twice a week to get my share, I only have one question. Where the hell do I sign?"

"Honestly? You'd willingly puppet yourself about in the unfortunately freckled skin of Mercy O'Day? For a lifetime? That's too mercenary even for you."

"A girl's gotta eat."

"Oh, but the domestic limitations, the constant scrutiny. How will you manage it?" He set two leaf-thin cups on a silver charger and began pouring the hot kettle water into a waiting pot, before he poured it out and liberally soiled it with Earl Grey.

"Some of the worst accidents happen in the home, Hegey. Don't you know that?" He couldn't help but share my wicked smile.

"Why can't things stay the way they were?" he said, swatting me with the tea cozy.

"Oh, Hegey. If you knew half the horrors I'd endured just to get this far. Can't you afford me just this small happiness?"

"Happiness? Is that what we're calling it?"

"Convenience, then. But that's no different than what you're after."

"Well, if you really think you can do no better," he said, swirling the pot.

"I thought you liked him."

"I like looking at him. I like looking at this Haviland," he said, holding up his cup. "That hardly infers my desire to wed it."

"Naw. He's big, handsome, and dumb as a bag of hammers. He's perfect."

"Reminds me of someone I once knew," he said, spiking his tea with a squirt of lemon. "You know I still have that first penny you gave me."

"Do you? Then you realize you still owe me a sweet." He sipped from his cup, his eyes peering at me over the rim. He dipped his fingers into his trousers and came up with the small copper coin.

"If you take that penny, I owe you nothing," he said. I snatched the penny from the table and pocketed it.

"I'll take the penny *and* the preacher," I said and grinned.

"Fine. I'll concede the point. But you must do me a favor. Work the counter at the emporium for me."

"What about Lucky's?"

"Well, since you no longer have an interest in it," he said with a casual wave of his hand.

"Hegey?"

"All right. I just think it prudent Lucky's remain closed."

"What happened? And don't make this about me."

"Think of the worst thing imaginable then double it," he said miserably. I did the math but still could not resist gibing at him.

"Is that why you're having to go to church?" I said with a grin. "Paying the piper for getting your hand stuck in the proverbial till?"

"Stop it!" And he stood up like an indignant lawyer on a losing case.

I chuckled. "What happened? You two going at it hammer and tongs over the smith's bellows when some inconsiderate sot needed his mule shod?"

"You are the most infuriating child I ever had the misfortune to call friend."

"Playing hide-the-pickle over the cracker barrel?"

"*Enough!* Nothing actually happened. Although I must admit, I was deliciously close to the gates of Elysium."

"Who was it?"

"Who almost caught us? Why your favorite fellow brothel keeper, Miss Brown. Sauntered into my notions counter after hours one night for a few new corset stays. I would think with her ponderous girth she would purchase the things in bulk."

"And ol' Brown promised to keep mum just as long *you* vowed to refrain from the liquor business."

"Voila."

"I'm going to get that bitch if it kills me," I said, pulling him to me. "And we both know *that* can't happen."

# Chapter Twenty-Two

Common sense demanded that a team of two horses could only pull effectively if harnessed in the same direction. But I couldn't let Hegey down. Not until I, myself, was profitably hitched. So I split my allotment of effective hours, weekdays in consummate boredom behind the counter of the emporium, weekends, dishwater demure, forcing a grateful smile to my lips when Eben tipped his hat to me in the street or locked eyes with mine from the pulpit. It was a poor plan. No proper lady worth her starch would have bought a ten-penny nail off the likes of me. Within a week, Hegey was forced to auction off the contents of his store. He made a bundle, but the thought of all his fancy loot lining the nests of folks who sneered at him in the street proved too much for him to bear. He plowed his profits into cheap hardware and canvass overalls and reopened his temple of "fertile bramble for the soul" under a sign that simply read "Cheap Goods." The transition was so painful for him, he took to sipping his opium tea during working hours. This was what the town had been waiting for. Disheveled, diminished, the town flocked to his doors just to gloat over how far he'd fallen. Between consoling Hegey in the evenings and wooing Eben, while still making it appear as if Eben was doing the wooing, I was more tired than a three-legged mule at plowing time. Finally, the first of Eben's many courting gifts was delivered to my doorstep. Hegey assured me, as my mother's Thornwell once had, that proper young men required such stale ceremonies to announce the propriety of their affections. But it seemed a powerful waste of resources, especially since he could have had me for the asking.

His first gift was a spray of winter paper-whites, delivered to me in a long, waxy box. They smelled of the breath of a child who had sucked too long on a sweet, and Hegey took them from me as soon as I opened them and dumped them resolutely in the garbage.

"How charming," he said. "Must have been fresh out of daises and crabgrass."

"What's the note say?" I asked, noticing a sealed card in his hand.

"To help speed the days—affectionately E. Lightfoot." Hegey grinned with mock affection.

"Christ, I'd lob off half a tit if speed *were* on that boy's mind," I said, tossing his note in the stove fire.

My nights were awful. To stay fed, I walled up the entrance to the back room of Hegey's "Cheap Goods" store and turned it into the shabby ghost of a sporting house. I risked winning the preacher's hand in doing so. My new endeavor, even without a sign above the door, was an open secret in the town. But among my dubious blessings was Eben's refusal to listen to common gossip. Especially about his precious Mercy. What had once been the enchanting backroom of Hegey's old emporium was now a stuffy, windowless box only the most desperate would frequent. Perhaps that was why Brown never bothered us. She didn't need to aid what fate was doing so effectively without her. Working solo, I sussed the need of making quaint my offered vices. I dispensed with the card tables and reduced games of chance to what my limited dexterity could manage. High-card draw, three-card monte. Dice with stud's rules. I could hoist bottles and have five cups of bones going at once. My luck was no drunkard's friend. But I curbed the chill of my patron's defeat with a few free shots to make sure there were no hard feelings. I kept a weather eye out for Da. I had a shotgun loaded with rock salt hidden at my knee if ever he should wander up to my bar. But he never came. Either Alice was keeping him on a short tether or my last horrible refusal had taken him out of the game all together. Either way, I missed him.

If a customer took a shine to me, I always had the ladies' changing room. Outfitted with but a single sagging bed, I'd answer to whatever name they'd call me, recite the secrets their need had fed me, and drain them dry. It was lonely work. Repetitive and graceless. Without even the satisfaction afforded animals that shared my condition. I wondered how the thrill, the intrepid lust of my remembered night with my Boston boy, had resulted in this stale security of mine. Who was the real victim? Those I swallowed? Or what was swallowing me?

The Tuesday after his first gift, Eben came with a box of chocolates, albeit a sampler size of Hegey's third-best Belgian pralines, with another brief flirty note.

"My, you're looking fresh, Miss Shinnecock," he said. If he'd only known why. "Won't you read it?" He shifted his weight between feet while I slipped a nail beneath the flap and read.

*Alas, only Tuesday—E.L.*

"Aw, Eben," I cooed, hoping his eagerness would deafen the weariness in my voice. "Is it Tuesday already? My, how the week is flying."

Why was I bothering with this boy? Was it really just convenience like I'd told Hegey? Or did I have hope? Hope that maybe life, in all its red trickery, might still afford me what every empty-headed girl thought she so intimately desired. A single companion. A simple home. Anywhere away from all my nightly darkness and death.

One night, I had plans for supper at the backroom behind Hegey's store. I was reticent to keep the engagement as the john bore such a striking resemblance to Da. A wiry bo'sun's mate from Blackpool with a faded blue star tattooed on his ear that meant he had weathered the Cape, he was covered in other such crude stigmas, including swallows on his breasts and a pig and a cock on the tops of his feet to keep him from drowning. He was coy as I let him into the backroom, casting furtive glances about the empty bar. I remembered our initial flirtation the night before, a name he had called me and how I had answered, my jaw suddenly dropping aitches as I twisted through my cockney concession to his heart's desire. I was so eager to get it over with I decided to let him attempt to have me up against the closed door. A two-penny upright like a common Whitechapel whore would not be an insult to him. And I needed him docile.

"Ow, don't be shy, poppet. Old Jenny don't care 'ow ya treat 'er," I said, pulling him to me. "Jus' git good an close, right? We'll 'ave it off proper." He blushed, his grin hidden behind his weathered fingers.

"Only, now I don't fancy Jenny no more," he said as he saw my confusion. "That's right, ducky. I've 'erd them rumors about you. How you can satisfy the devilish whim of any poor bloke who pays. So now, I want *'er*." The wicked will believe anything. Even the truth. I cursed his fickle heart as I felt the Beguiler dissolve his cockney strumpet into a neutral paste from which he would mold his next desire. He raised his sleeve and showed me what was tattooed to his forearm. It was crude work, sun-faded and splotchy. The tattoo looked only vaguely female. Did he want me beguiled in mossy carved oak, a ship's frozen figurehead, where he could root his spunk in a clever split of wood? No. I looked closer at the picture on his arm. Was it even possible I could change into *that?* There was wonder in his eyes. Only Simon Braintree had changed their desired image of me so drastically. I paused as I waited for how the Beguiler would respond. The faint sounds of the street faded. The atmosphere felt close with a wet and briny chill. As I was still assessing the feasibility of his desire, a brackish flush of seawater flooded my throat. I coughed and spat it out, my heart racing. I dropped to my knees and realized I could no longer pull my legs apart. My ankles seemed to fuse. A fissure of slimy cold ran up my thighs sealing them together. Sea water rose in shivering rivulets off my skin like sweat. What had felt like my feet now thinned to a flat splay of unruly webbing. To my horror, pearly scales ruptured my skin, proliferating like flat diamonds up what was once my legs. Unable to stand, I flopped to the floor. He looked with inflamed eyes at me floundering there.

"There ye be, me love," he said, wetting his lips. "A right fish out of water. And ripe for the taking."

I cowered, covering my bare breasts with my slimy arms. I was a shameful freak. A hideous myth. He walked slowly toward me, the salted soles of his deck boots booming toward me with each step. I tried to scamper toward the door, but the ballast of my gaudy fishtail hobbled my retreat. He straddled me as his rooty fingers fumbled with his belt. Desperate to avoid him, I forced an undulating kick from my tail. There was shock on his face as I suddenly drifted off the floor. I felt a delicious power only the ocean fathoms knew. My arms seemed to pull through some liquid resistance as I somersaulted in drafts that had once only buoyed men's voices. I rose still further and wove myself around the ceiling before diving downward in a slow coil around his waist. He laughed like a child, reaching out his hands for me as I glided past. I made circle after circle around him, just outside his grasp.

But then the logic of his illogical desire thickened the air in his lungs. For could he really breathe what supported me so effortlessly? His eyes strained in their sockets. His chest bucked for air. He flailed his arms in panic, trying to stir a current that might raise him to the surface. But the weightlessness of his delusion was reserved only for me. His mouth gaped wide, his eyes pleading as they followed me around the room. And I was forced to oblige him, just as he had forced me. Had this lad never listened during the doldrums to the seasoned sea dogs when they warned of creatures like me? Had he never learned what we have done to unfortunate seamen since Ulysses? I coiled gently around him, my tail circling his legs, my arms anchoring his arms until his eyes went sightless and wide. Sinking my teeth to his drowned throat, he spouted red on a harpooner's horizon. His blood curled like smoke on the lie of the air as I swallowed all of him.

Moments later, I was breathless. Sated. And surprised to find there had been no sea. I sat cradling his ash on a sawdust floor that had been mussed as if a couple had waltzed upon it till morning.

# Chapter Twenty-Three

Looking up that dawn, the chill of the new day hard on the sweat that covered me, I turned to see a lone figure near the front of the church across the street. Only one man would have roused this early. Only one had a sermon to practice to his empty pews. Completely ignorant as to how I might have explained my presence there, I raised my hand to greet him as people do when they see someone they know. Eben looked at me and shuddered. I lowered my arm, ashamed. I could tell from his lack of recognition that he had not been beguiled. Perhaps it was the distance between us that allowed him to see me as I was. Who I really was. A stranger that wished him harm. I scurried from his sight. But I could not shake the distaste I had seen in his eyes. I could not unsee that. Not even when those same eyes would later behold me with what he mistook for love.

Later that same morning, a Wednesday, I received a brown-wrapped parcel containing a thin bolt of tape lace. A clever gift, I thought, bespeaking of domestic but still carnal desire as such lace, popular at that time for valences and fire screens, was also a favorite for trimming camisoles and ladies' drawers. The card? My favorite of the lot: *Why I hate Wednesday. E.*

"What *exactly* about the concept of discretion so completely eludes you, Emma?" Hegey bellowed when I tossed him the parcel Eben had just delivered. "Have you seen the ghastly ring you've left in the tub? Looks like you've performed some ungodly pagan sacrifice to Poseidon. What the hell were you up to last night?"

"Oh, Hegey," I moaned through my smile. "You wouldn't believe me if I told you."

But Thursday did not disappoint. I met the delivery boy before his knuckles hit the door. I was surprised to see a reedy, dyspeptic-looking youth, Eben nowhere to be seen. I snatched the shoe-box-sized parcel from him, flipping him a two-cent piece, and ran to the hearth to gloat above my loot. I was beginning to enjoy this. I caught my breath when I opened it. It was an exquisite rococo silver-backed comb, brush, and mirror set, a surpassing rival to my mother's. The silver was chased to resemble rippling water supporting a few gaily strewn orchids. It still smelled faintly of lilac talc.

"Not one of yours?" I grinned to Hegey, holding up the mirror as he passed. He snatched it from my hand, not dignifying my query, and ran his fingers over the fine chasing, searching for a master's mark. The blood seemed to drain from his face. Then he cleared his throat and handed the mirror back to me. The glass had only the faintest clouding near its round edges.

"*Ancien Régime*, Maître Thomas Germain, Paris," he said in a clogged whisper. "Cheeky bastard has sent you a bloody museum piece."

"Pricey?"

"Prerevolution silver? When most of the stuff was melted down to make Commune pisspots? Not to mention that Monsieur Germain never made toilette articles for any but the queen and her intimates? I must say, the boy is beginning to interest me."

"Damn."

"Damn indeed, my dear."

Moments later, after Hegey had departed for his bath, I found the faithful card, slipped to the floor, face down.

*Let silver now rejoice in what mine eyes have long enjoyed*
*and so suckle the infants of both our souls*
*on Beauty's ambrosia, twin employed. E.*

I wandered into the bathroom. Hegey lingered in the scented water, his belly rising above the lapping milky bathwater like an island of meringue.

"Hey, who said this?" I asked showing him the card.

"What do you mean, who said it? It has an attribution right there in that spare, somewhat pretentious single initial."

"You think Eben made this up?"

"It's hardly Shakespeare, my dear—or Marlowe for that matter. Only Burbage on a binge would forgive such a clunky couplet."

I rose early on Friday and brushed my hair in the cold light of the dawn, pulling the silver-backed bristles through my curls as well as I could, walking slowly, deliberately, to the door and back, counting steps, making deals with Fate. Now the messenger will arrive. Brush one, step two. Now. It was an instructional on greed, I told myself. Just like a preacher to toy with me like this. The delivery boy woke up ill or had absconded with my treasure himself. The world outside had ended. *Yer a fool to care,* called from the branches of my old climbing tree. There was a knock on the door. My heart tucked up in my throat, fingers fumbling on the knob.

"What you got?" I demanded.

"Right here, ma'am." His teeth chattered, fingers stiff as he handed it to me.

A letter. A card really. The same kind as had accompanied the week's loot.

"This it?"

"Yes'um."

"You sure? You ain't holding out on me?"

He shivered. I tossed him a coin and I closed the door. The week's exchange had had the desired effect, had brought my excitement to sap. I tore into the card.

*Be ready at noon. E.*

Later that Friday morning, he had me jerking around my toilet like a puppet on his strings. Oh, there was a girlish glee in surrendering to this ruse. I kicked up a squall of face powder and pancake, drowned my gums with a lordly swig of *rince bouche*. I even chalked on a little tooth powder and ran it around my pearlies with a finger. I warmed up just a dollop of bear grease to give my curls a little luster and burnt a feather and inhaled the fumes to make my eyes shine. I enjoyed the panic, knowing, I'm sure somewhere in my mind, that my ministrations were of no practical benefit. Eben would still see me as he wished. I changed my drawers five times, laced and relaced my corset a dozen more, aiming for the perfect silhouette. Hegey tsked disgustedly at my giddy tempest, but when I had finally decided on a black skirt and bodice with a flaming red underskirt, he could no longer contain his sartorial indignation.

"You look like a Quaker whore," he said imperiously. "Take those mourning weeds off at once. And if your intention is to attract the amorous ire of some rutting buffalo, by all means proceed with that rather strident petticoat."

He dressed me in an ensemble of lavender watered silk with gracefully embroidered tiny pink roses. He insisted on three underskirts, each a darker shade of leafy green than the next, and a lavender-and-green parasol.

"It ain't raining," I said.

"There is a substantial lack of precipitation, I grant you. But you've been freckling rather alarmingly of late." Eben's ardor. Mercy's freckled complexion. At least the excitement was mine.

"See how this pale lilac offsets your raven curls?"

"Don't you mean Mercy's dirty blond?"

"So the effect will be somewhat subdued. Emma, why are you frowning?"

Why was I frowning? "I've never been clucked over by a man before, Hegey."

"No, my dear. That's not quite it." He didn't need to say anymore. I knew what was happening to me. My surest path to misery was to fall for a man who could never see me as I am.

I walked the floor for fifteen minutes, taking only the tiny breaths the clinch of my corset would allow. At two minutes to noon, I heard the sound of tinkling bells. A sound sprinkled sugar might make if you were feeling as gooey inside as I was. I looked out of the apartment window and there, in the distance, came the powdery plumes of hoof-kicked snow, then a charger with a braided mane stuck all over with holly and berries. The horse had a white body with legs black up to the shoulders and haunches. The sleek animal looked like it was wearing stockings. The leather reins were festooned with dozens of giggling silver bells. I smiled as I recognized Eben, bundled up in a beaver coat, presiding over a beautiful oaken sleigh. Sleigh and suitor, horse and bells and berries, along with my own excitement, conspired to create a kind of choir of delights, like voices raised at a party, all bursting with good news. I couldn't wait. I ran out to meet him.

The front of the sleigh was fashioned like a ship, the wood of the bow fitted as gracefully as a girl's chignon. I only knew one man capable of such work. And I could never lay eyes on him again.

"My Da make this?" I asked with a hitch in my voice.

"Good afternoon, Miss Shinnecock," Eben said, dipping his hatless head. I noticed he had pummeled his cowlick into submission, a near pound of pomade and perhaps a prayer employed in the task. His eyes were bright, the skin of his face tight and smooth in the cold. I smiled back as I watched him step from the sleigh to help me into my seat beside him.

"Oooh, such service." I giggled. "You'll spoil me."

"Impossible," he said, regaining his seat. He opened a buffalo robe and placed it fur-down over our knees and made a clicking sound, and we were off in a flash. The icy air stung our eyes and rushed our noses and throats and made a kind of rabbity, shallow breathing necessary. But it was clean and clear and light and oh, so beautiful—the low hills and sparse bushes and trees all dusted with a monochrome of white.

"To answer your question, yes. Your father did make this sleigh. And our new church."

"Sounds like he's as capable as Christ," I said lightly. He gave me an amused look. I saw his teeth, the crinkle of his eyes.

"Maybe better," he said, facing forward. "I always figured carpentry was a kind of sideline for the Lord."

"Yeah. I reckon He'd have Da beat when it comes to souls and sacrifice."

"Souls and sacrifice? Another sideline, I fear."

"Really? So what would have been His main line?"

"Forgiveness."

And to frame the comment, he snapped the reins and sent us sailing like a shot into the airy distance.

Moments later, he brought the horse down to a walk, checking the beast's flank to make sure it wasn't in too much of a lather. I hunkered down under the buffalo robe just as he turned down a path overhung with the bare branches of frosty elms. We slid in silence for a while. And I noticed our silences were as full as our moments of conversation. I thought that must mean something.

"That's a funny kind of horse," I said a with a yawn. "Looks like he got stuck in a pit full of ink."

"Or had stepped into the underworld and found it not to his liking. That's why I call him Persephone."

"Persephone? He ain't no mare."

"No. But he don't know the difference. And I like the name."

"Funny kind of preacher you are, giving a horse a pagan name."

"I must say, I do so love the Irish lilt to your voice, Miss Shinnecock. I always had your father pegged as a Yorkshire man." His comment hit me like a gentle calamity. I was feeling so comfortable with him, I had forgotten there was no *me* sitting beside him. Only *her.* I was merely milk to Mercy's cream. Perhaps no one sees us as we truly are. We are all just reflections of our beholder's desires once deep feelings begin to root. So why did I feel so uneasy when he reminded me he was beguiled? He was supposed to be a convenience. Nothing more. Was Eben beginning to feel like home to me? Was I churlish at sharing that home with a third party? Or was it something darker?

On our way back to town, he stirred Persephone to a fast trot. It was a pleasant pace, but I needed speed and cold to rouse me back to the happiness I'd been feeling.

"This thing go any faster?"

He grinned at me and handed me the reins as naturally as if he had been doing it all our lives.

"Git, Persephone! Git now!" I hollered over the laughing of the bells. The wind turned hard on our faces, and I saw him squint against it. But never did he ask me to slow. He only asked for the reins back once Persephone began to blow.

"You always been God-y?" I asked him as Persephone caught his breath.

"*God-y*?"

"You know. Churchy?"

"Naw. I was saved by the Lord with a quick blow to the head." He smiled as he watched me work around his comment in my mind. "I was raised in a bayou. Know what that is?"

"A swamp, ain't it?"

"Swamp's a word them that don't know the beauty might use. My kin were Huguenots who waited out the idolatry of the Catholics in France and then came to the New World to wait out the American Revolution. I had no real religion as a boy. My faith was in the gospel of the night frogs and hawk owls. All I ever knew was rough country. We had a Bible. Big pork belly of a thing, but I don't remember it ever being cracked. My *maman* read me all the Greek myths in French. Papa taught me to pray only before meals. Didn't wear a pair of store-bought shoes until I was fifteen.

"One night I'm out in the bayou, hunting up night crawlers for the next day's fishing, when I lost my footing and fell into a nest of cottonmouths. I must have been bitten by a whole mess of the babies. Babies are what you have to watch out for. Poison is thick in their little fangs. I figured I had a good ten or fifteen minutes of life left when something struck me, hard, right on the side of the head. Everything went black.

"They told me when I woke up I was ranting in tongues, babbling on some kind of nonsense. Seems the fellow that had struck me was doing a little night fishing of his own and knew if he could get me unconscious, my heart might slow and the poison might not circulate so quick. I reckoned that's why he hit me. All I know is he laid me low just long enough to suck that serpent venom out of me."

"Who was it that struck you?"

"Ain't you guessed? For seven nights, I had dreams of a stranger in a white robe holding snakes in his mouth and no harm suffered. I read the Bible clean through while my strength seeped back. My folks were glad of my recovery but didn't want any part of my God talk. So I rooted around and found a little chapel a few miles out of the bottomland. I was baptized that first night and received my evangel sleeping in a cotton cradle. I was twelve years old. I lit out the next morning and have never gone back." He pulled gently on the reins as the dreary sight of the frozen town came into view. "What about you?" he asked. "I'd so love to hear about your girlhood in Ireland."

I had Mercy's memories but no heart to tell them.

"Oh, I reckon I was raised as rough as you. Wild as a wolf pup till Momma passed. Da never saw me the same after that. Too many ghosts."

"Surely, he did not abandon you."

"No. But sometimes things get in the way."

"Family is the greatest boon life has to offer. And when it is denied us, it is only natural to seek its like, any way we can."

We glided down the main street of town, among the afternoon traffic. And when their gazes happened to catch my face beside one of their respectable brethren, my how they froze. Lips buttoned up so quick you'd think they were full of gold. The old leaned into one another to whisper. A few young men shouted, "whore" or "harlot." But Eben stared straight ahead, his blue eyes almost translucent in the white light reflected up off the snow. They could not have been seeing Mercy. Only Eben could see me like that. But Mercy had not been the only whore in town. I don't know what I expected—that he might halt our progress and produce some kind of arm, a sword or pistol, and defend the pitted honor

I shared with Mercy. But he said nothing until he said good evening. I made to leave him, feeling the wrinkle in my day, when he suddenly grabbed my arm.

"Never take to heart the words of the ignorant, Emma. You can't blame them when they only see the surface of things." Then he told me how splendid a day it had been and how much he looked forward to another much like it, reminding me to go to church next Sunday, and he snapped the reins and was off.

I refused to open the back room that night, feigning exhaustion when Hegey tried to question me about my outing. He caught my mood, steeped a pot of chamomile, and brought the service to bed.

"You're falling for him, Emma," he said casually, with a chiding glint in his eye.

"The hell you say. A hog don't fall for its own slop." I took the cup of tea he offered me but refused to look in his eyes.

"When did self-deception become another facet of your folksy wisdom?"

"You callin' me liar just because I enjoy being treated like a lady?"

"The heart is the most complicated organ in the human body, Emma," he said gently. "And I have always treated you like a lady."

"I know what I'm doing."

"You haven't the faintest inkling as to what you are doing." He cleared our cups and slipped under the covers with me. "Don't misunderstand me, my dear. I'd give everything I own to be in your pretty button boots."

"Even if I was falling for him," I said as he blew out the lamp, "and I ain't saying I am, what would be the use? It's not *me* he's courting."

"Then perhaps it won't be *your* heart he breaks," he said quietly as he blew out the lamp.

# Chapter Twenty-Four

That Sunday in church, Eben spoke about stones and glass houses, and I felt all but pelted by the flinty snickers of the congregation each time the adulteress was mentioned. His tone was calm, patient—a father explaining a common error to a child. Then things got strange. I was not the only Jacob squaring off against a burly host of heaven.

He pulled up a stool from behind his pulpit, a prop I had yet to see him employ, and shifting to center stage, he sat upon it and ran his long, heavy fingers through his hair. "But I'll tell you, friends," he said with a beer-with-his-brother tone that brought the whole congregation to the edges of their pews, "death by stoning is a tedious business. It takes real commitment. Not to mention accuracy. Chucking all them rocks at a frightened moving target until you get a lucky hit and wing or kneecap your luckless victim. Wouldn't do today. Not in our modern age. No, friends. If we had a mind to dispatch such a fallen woman, we would use one of these." He reached behind his back and pulled out the biggest pistol I had ever seen. "Yes, friends. This would mete out justice for us. Four and a half pounds and fifteen inches of steel and brass, percussion-capped, black-powdered, smooth-bored vengeance. *Look* at that. A real killer of the misbegotten if ever there was one." He raised the pistol. Some would remember him pointing it at the congregation. A few would swear he had sighted me with it. But he didn't. There was no malice in his movement. He held up the pistol in harmless profile before he lowered it to his other hand, where he seemed lost in it, stroking the barrel lightly.

"Think of all the innovation, the craftsmanship, the failure and the faith embodied in the design and construction of this single agent of destruction. All the art and will, the hours, months, years, even, of concentrated acumen required to manifest this simple engine, whose only conceivable function is the ceasing of warm-blooded life. Story goes that Captain Walker, the much feted namesake of this weapon, asked Sam Colt to make him a firearm that could dispatch a war horse at full gallop. Quite a request. This pistol was Sam's answer. Now I can't help but wonder what might have occurred if Captain Walker, or you or I for that matter, had asked a *different* question. What if he had asked how can we *love* better? Can you imagine it? Build me a more perfect love, Sam. Make for me a gun barrel meshed with synchronized chambers so we can heal more effectively.

Construct for me a trigger that when pulled lets us better *forgive* one another. What if all that talent and time had been funneled into the simple equation of how can we be more like the Lord? More perfect in our faith? What would happen if each man and woman in this room pooled his or her talent and bent it mightily to such a function?" The church was quiet. I heard the shifting of petticoats that mimicked the dry rustle of birds outside the church's windows. "Well, I reckon it's pretty clear. We'd be struck dumb," he said. A relieved titter broke the silence. "I'll grant you that's a difficult question. But I believe I can answer it. For, ladies and gentlemen of the congregation, none other than your preacher has found a better use for his judgment." He stood up. "'But when I became a man,'" he recited, "'I put childish things away.'" His eyes sought Mercy, found me. "'For now I see through a glass, darkly . . .'"

Hegey leaned toward me. "Oh my God, he's going to do it."

"Hush up!" I said, slapping his knee. Eben stopped. His eyes did not leave mine. Heads turned around, to see the object of his sudden fascination. The heat rose up in me, prickled the shell of my ears. All those eyes. All that heat.

"No," he said. "Not *darkly*. Clearly. Lucidly. Honesty. Beautifully. Emma . . ."

He had come down from the dais, but I had not noticed it. It seemed he had always been there in the aisle beside me. The congregation sensed something momentous, a kind of eclipse, slowly progressing. "Mercy," he said, reaching out his hand. My heart stumbled, but I could not look away. "*Have* mercy, Emma," he corrected himself as I stood, "and be the idol of my affection, be my long companion and marry me." I heard a sudden intake of breath from deep in the small crowd, the palpable anticipation coming to bear on my answer. Hegey folded his arms over his chest. My brain had regressed to the desires of my girlhood. The prince was coming out of my bedtime pages. It was huge and passionate and reckless and dangerous and romantic and stupid as hell, but I was caught up in it, slipping over the falls of the moment, and I threw my arms around the preacher and cried *"yes!"*

Hegey insisted he would plan our wedding. It was painful denying him what was clearly a fantasy of his own. But Eben had been gently adamant. Our vows would be simple and private. Hegey attended only to fulfill the legal requirement of a witness. We had no flowers. No music. We did not employ the aisle for theatrical effect. I was not given away. We were married in an empty church lit only by throbbing candlelight, scented only by the delicious anticipation on our respective breath. Eben officiated in whispers, with vows he asked and I answered, spoken so tenderly and with such profound intent I was thrilled in the least church-like way. The kiss that bound us together was our first. It would have gladly been my last.

"My God," Hegey said breathlessly when I hugged him after the ceremony, "that was sublime. Be happy, Mrs. Lightfoot. Please, be happy."

I began to get the picture of my unique brand of marital bliss the first night we spent alone together. The preacher lived in a modest frame house on the same acreage as the church, its furnishings best described as early monastic. He had a table for eating and composing his sermons, a chair for sitting while attending both tasks. A small larder, mostly beans and flour and salt. A tin safe for meat. A chest for clothes. A small iron bed with a straw mattress to spend his unconscious hours between sermons. He had one window of fatted paper. Not even glass. A hearth with logs and kindling stacked and ready for the match. There was a water pump out back near the stable where Persephone slept in what seemed relatively the same comfort as his master. A small chicken coop with about a dozen contented hens and an exhausted rooster. I denied Hegey all connubial gifts except his blessing. My only trousseau was my mother's tooth and her unopened letter that I gripped nervously while Eben took the fifteen required seconds to show me my new home.

He requisitioned a busted chair from the barn and balanced his well-formed bulk on this while he offered me the "good" chair and a bowl of beans for supper. We ate in silence, which I figured must be a preacher's way, he using all his faculties in giving constant thanks between bites. When we finished, I offered to wash the bowls, but he said he'd tend to it. When he came back, his hands still wet, I watched him stack the bowls on top of the larder. We had lost the day, and so I watched him light his only lamp. Then he sat back down and asked me if I wouldn't mind getting him the Bible and a heap of papers, the pen, and ink he kept in a box in his clothes chest. I was so thrilled to be of some use I practically jumped at the chance. I brought him his things and then sat next to him. He pinched a pair of spectacles to the bridge of his nose, an accoutrement I had never seen him wear before. He dipped his pen and began scratching away.

"Nice cheaters," I said. He paused in midstroke, looking up.

"Pardon?"

"Your specs. Right handsome."

"Thank you." And back he went to whatever he was writing. The lamp threw long shadows on the raw floor. The wind picked up outside. I must have shivered, but before I could say a word as to my comfort, he was up, a match struck on the seat of his britches. The hearth was already beginning to blaze when he was back in his seat in a smooth, almost uninterrupted ellipse of thought.

He must have written for an hour. And that entire time, not a single complete sentence was shared between us. It was our wedding night after all. I found myself in a constant state of anticipation that any second he would drop the bizarre pretense of monkish silence and look up, maybe laugh, suggest a game—a little liturgical slap and tickle?—before ravishing me on his single bed. Would I have the heart to sip from him our first night?

That was the only conundrum I foresaw when I thought of the hot hours that spread before us. At precisely nine o'clock—I knew because I had seen the unmistakable right angle on his pocket piece—he snapped the watch closed and stood up.

"Well, then, my dear. Good night." He collected his papers, stashed them back in their box, and made to head out the door.

"Hold on, now," I said, smiling, because I thought this must finally be the start of our socially sanctified love games. "Where you headed?"

"To bed."

"But the bed's over *here*."

"Emma. That's for you. I'll sleep in the barn until I can make other arrangements."

I felt a little light-headed. "Other arrangements? What are you talking about? This is our wedding night. We're married."

"Yes. And I hope you pass a pleasant night."

"But we're *married*." I must have thought there was some charm in the word, a two-syllable aphrodisiac that would get his embers stoked for an evening of perfectly legal debauchery. But he just stared at me, deaf to my explanation.

"Oh, Emma. Oh, my dear. I thought you knew. I'm a man of the cloth."

"Yeah. Now let's see what we can do about gettin' you out of said cloths." I moved toward him. He recoiled. "What in high hell is going on?"

"Please, Emma. That's not like you."

"What am I not getting here?"

"I've taken vows, Emma. Sacred vows."

"Yeah, at twelve years old you took vows to a conveniently placed swamp hobo, a bunch of snake babies, and a week's worth of dreamy Jesuses."

"And I take those vows very seriously. It has nothing to do with you, Emma, or your past," he said, lifting my face with a gentle finger. "You are as clean and desirable to me as any woman I have ever seen." He dropped his finger. My hope fell with it. "I have never known a woman in the carnal sense," he said. "I never will. The Lord never had children. He was content being the Son and so a father to all. The church is very clear on that."

"To *Catholics*. It's only clear about that to Catholics. And even that was more about the Pope's fear of who would inherit papal land. Every other denomination, those vicars breed like bunnies." And here he chuckled, to his credit and my frustration. For with his eyes lit up like that and his pretty teeth flashing, he was all the more desirable.

"It's no use, Emma."

"Then why in the name of high heaven did you marry me?" He didn't have to answer. His silence screamed what had been alluded to all along. He had done it for me. To give poor, plump Mercy O'Day new traction on her road to righteousness.

"I don't want to be forgiven, Eben. I want my husband."

"I will be a husband to you. In all ways but that."

"But that's the best part!"

"Are you sure?" I had run out of aces. His face softened and he came toward me. I thought of flinching, just to get him back for his earlier recoil. But I couldn't. I wanted him. In the worst way, I wanted to melt right into him.

"Would it ease your mind to know I am sorely tested?" he said, placing a gentle hand on my face again and letting it fall to my neck before pulling it away right above my breast. "That every fiber of my being yearns to know the secrets of your flesh and golden hair?"

"That's supposed to ease my mind?"

"If ever a woman deserved to know perfect love, it is you Emma May Shinnecock."

"*Lightfoot*, mister."

"I truly am sorry."

"Not as sorry as me."

He smiled a sad smile. And I tried to smile a happy one, a dismissive one, one that could set things right between us. But I was heartbroken. This had not been in my plan.

"Well, go on. Get your beauty sleep, husband."

"Good night, wife."

"Yeah." And I watched him turn and leave the little house. I ran to the open door and saw him, reduced to shadow, without a lamp, without a moon, enter the dark and silent barn.

That first night was a hard one. Lying on that straw mattress, I kept having visions of my family's barn and the dark stranger the last time I'd lain on straw. I thought of Alberta and the dusky bliss I had known with her. I had seen the dirty face of God those nights. Now His celestial visage was squeaky clean. And I was dry as a bone.

# Chapter Twenty-Five

I woke up to the smell of fresh coffee and frying side pork. "You gonna do all the cooking too?" I asked, blinking the daylight into my eyes. He handed me a steaming tin cup after I shook the sleep from my hair. Of course, his coffee was excellent.

"I've been alone so long it just comes naturally. But if you're so inclined . . ."

"I can't cook a lick."

"I could teach you."

"I'd hate to crab your routine."

He smiled, his eyes shifting to serious. "I'm sorry, Emma. About last night."

"What part?"

"My intentions. I should have been honest with you from the start. It was unfair of me to assume you would share my calling."

"Well, your coffee makes up for it," I said sarcastically.

"You like trout? I thought I might stuff a few with rosemary and wild onions for supper."

I couldn't take it. I had to know. "What exactly do you want from me?"

He smiled and got up to get my breakfast. "I understand your disappointment. I hope in time you will realize there is far more to a marriage than . . . the *other*. All I want for you, Emma, is to be happy."

"Doing what?" He brought me a plate of eggs and crisp pork. How he knew how I liked them I just chalked up to more of my bad luck.

"Whatever pleases you. Take Persephone out for long rides. You can even go back to your employment with Mr. Hegemore. I have no rule against my wife working in town." Such an attitude was damn near revolutionary. I should have been happy. I was getting everything I thought I had wanted. But nothing I needed.

"What do *you* do all day?"

"Between chores, I think. I commune. Write."

"Mind if I commune with you?"

"Emma . . ."

"I mean help you. Around the spread. Listen to your sermons."

"You don't have to do that."

"What else am I gonna do?"

"You like fishing?"

We stood in the cold spring melt of the running creek, his britches rolled to the knee, my skirts hitched in what

I shamefully hoped was my best advantage. We'd freed a couple of cane poles from the marshes along the bank, equipped them with twine and hook and bait, and I watched as our two distinct angling techniques began to diverge. Mine was simple, the dunk-and-wait approach of my girlhood. But the preacher, who seemed to have a practiced hand at all things, had a far more lyrical approach. He whipped his pole and string around like some professor of music teasing a charge of distant brass from the critters beneath the water. Even if he didn't catch a thing, just to watch him flail around with such purpose, such passion and fluidity, was worth the freezing feet and ankles.

"I thought you bottomland boys only knew how to cajole *catfish* to the table."

"True. I'm still pretty new to this trout fishing." And as if on cue, he got a strike, and the pole bent as the panicked fish tried to escape.

"Jerk him back!" I hollered, dropping my pole into the shallow water. "Get that hook good and in him!"

"He really wants to run!"

"Well, hold him! Hold him!" I hitched up my skirts farther as I waded into the deeper running water then followed his taught line hand over hand until I came to where it twanged like a guitar string. I gripped hard on his line and gave a yank. Oh, the glorious leviathan that broke the surface, kicking rainbows and freezing droplets all about my face and neck. "He's a beaut! A real beaut!" I slipped my fingers under its slippery gill and wrestled the fish to the bank.

"Look at that! Supper for a whole damn army!"

"Hey!" he shouted and threw his arms around me. I hugged him back and felt the hard muscle of his back through his damp shirt. He nuzzled his face in the lee of my throat and there was the softness of his lips, a tickle of his eyelash on my neck. Dizzy tingles raced over my scalp and slipped down to the pit of my belly. I thought surely the Beguiler would trip my teeth into his jugular. But it didn't. The lay of my peculiar sexual land became very clear in that moment. This was as close as I would get to any kind of intimacy, a stolen moment like this, fleeting, fumbling, but nothing more. We would need to go fishing more often.

Attendance at the church picked up the Sunday after our wedding but then dropped off markedly when folks realized we would not be preempting the usual sermon for the airing of our more intimate laundry. It seemed the whole congregation had known our marriage would never be consummated. They had waited for some outburst from me, some public hee-hawing over my marital frustration. I never gave them the satisfaction. I just sat there in the front row of the church for two Sundays running with a stiff smile on my face, faking the same ecclesiastical calmness as they. The only one I confided in was Hegey, and he was as astounded as I.

"So he won't lay a finger on you?"

"Sure a finger. A hug. A handshake. But nothing south of the finish line, if you get my meaning."

"Astounding. And he's not Catholic?"

"I don't think denomination has anything to do with it."

"And he does all the cooking?"

"And cleaning, too, if I'd let him. Says he just wants me to be happy."

"Astounding. How are you feeding?"

"I'm not," I said wearily.

"What about those domestic accidents you mentioned."

"Damn bachelor shaves himself."

"There's always the backroom."

"That's just it. He'd let me work. But I just can't do it. Somehow it feels like I'd be betraying him if I got up to my old tricks."

"Emma, this is serious."

"I'm all right. I'm just not running tip-top."

"Have you thought of pressing things?" He put down his teacup and stood up.

"I don't follow."

"Well, if we look at your situation as a kind of race, a foot race perhaps, what would qualify as 'winning' per se, is quite clear. That being actual—"

"I get it."

"But what about the *rest* of the race? What about all the things that lead up to a win? Things that don't quite go over the line yet retain more than a hint of victory?"

"You mean foolin' around?"

"His vow is to chastity, remember. Not stimulated interest. Not arousal. I would imagine there is plenty of leeway between breaking his vow and merely bending it. In that case, a silver medal might be as good as gold."

Hegey had a point. Eben hadn't made one vow. He'd made two. It was time to see who was tougher. The Lord or me.

# Chapter Twenty-Six

I'd like to say I burnt that pie on purpose. That the smoke of incinerated apple was all part of a plan. That I had flung open the front door to let the fumes out of the room. And that the seasonably cold night air that flooded the room had made me shiver and had motivated Eben's arms around me. But I'm just a shit cook. I'd baked that pie to assuage just a little bit of the guilt I was feeling for being treated like a five-star boarder in my own house. And I'd simply forgotten all about the pastry in the oven.

He had made another delicious meal. Pork chops braised in wild thyme and shallots with sorrel pudding and steamed collards and watercress. We had just sat down to eat when the smoke from the oven billowed over our heads. He went to put out the fire. I'd run for the door. And before I knew it, he had his arms around my shoulders, the meal all but forgotten. To regain his composure, he insisted we finish our meal on the front porch, bundled up in blankets, the plates on our knees.

We laughed between bites in the clear night air. Even dropped our forks at the same time to pick up the pork bones with our fingers so we could shamelessly gnaw at the last delicious morsels of meat. I hadn't properly fed in weeks, and yet the Beguiler was strangely quiet on that score. My senses had not dimmed. If anything, they were more acute than ever. When the meal was finished, he sat back in his porch chair and opened his blanket. I took this as an invitation to curl up on his lap like a kitten. He closed his blanket around us. And that was that. There we were on a spring evening, in one another's arms, immune to the floral ethers that nature herself sends forth to cue the myriad reproductions that keep the planet varied and interesting. I needed to take a more direct approach. His wrists were snug upon my shoulders, his hands like the paws of a lion. I took one absently in mine and began to stroke his long fingers until I heard a purr of pleasure. To cover so mammalian a reaction, he began to prattle on about the chicken coop and how we needed to expand it and get the pallets ready for the spring chicks that would be here any day now. I drew the pad of one of his fingers down the slope of my face until it teased the edge of my lips. He didn't break stride with his prattle until I guided his finger into my mouth. I closed my lips around it and his voice continued, husky now, but still soldiering forth. My tongue began to tease the tip, the nail, the firm knuckle. His voice faltered, fell for an instant, like a trapeze artist defiant of gravity and then reminded suddenly of its laws. I did the same with several other of his fingers until I reached his thumb. And there a gentle raking by my teeth released a sound distinctly less feline, an unmistakable moan.

"Emma. What are you doing?" he whispered.

"Am I doing anything? I was just listening."

"Oh."

"Something wrong?"

"No. Nothing. I . . ."

"Yes, Eben?"

That did it. Call the creature by his name, sister, and he appears. He turned me around and plunged his lips onto mine. When I braided my tongue into the mix, I felt his initial shock and then the wave of pleasure that quelled it. He crushed me to him and kissed me long and deeply. Over and over. Then his face began to work down my neck and my hands went hunting, my fingers skittering like stones over the buttons of his britches. He was up in a flash, hightailing it to the yard. I heard the squeak of the pump handle, a flurry of muttered prayer. When he came back he looked like he'd just wet himself. I laughed because he looked so handsome, so young and foolish, with a huge wet stain in his lap, but also to show him that it was a laughing matter. No harm had been done, the tight threads of his precious vow had not been unraveled.

"I'm so sorry, Eben," I said innocently. "I must have gotten carried away."

"Yes. Well. No . . . um. No harm. Actually, it was… no harm." He headed toward his tuffet of hay in the barn then he stopped. "Good night, my dear."

"'Night, Eben." He emerged from the shadows after a mere few moments. He had his britches in his hand, the red of his long johns a becoming dusty rose color in the moonlight.

"Would you mind, possibly? Could you please set these by the fire to . . . you know, dry?"

"'Course, Eben." I stretched theatrically, thrusting my breasts to greater advantage. He didn't blink.

"Good night," he said huskily.

"'Night, now."

My heat was up. I felt good—lazy, tingly, as I brought myself to bed. I undressed slowly. And in my heightened state of sensitivity the cotton had a touch almost human as my garments slipped off my shoulders and thighs onto the floor. I stretched out under the covers and thought of my husband laying there on the cold straw of the barn. He must have been as confused as a baby squirrel in a hawk's nest with an adamant hunk of hickory poking through his drawers. Too terrified to touch it, too worked up to ignore it. What delicious torture he must be enduring. So, out of solidarity, I chose to leave myself unattended as well and just lay there, letting my body simmer.

Eben's kiss had given me all the encouragement I needed to continue with my flirtatious enticements. It was a relief to realize I had married more man than monk. I would spend the morning hours, while he communed, cooking up in my head all kinds of near misses and casual come-ons, anything I could apply in the afternoons while we worked side by side, tending our spread.

I'd nuzzle up behind him while his mouth was full of nails, or take a Sunday stroll of kisses around a conveniently placed bruise. I even once decided to feed the chickens topless, and with my skirts in one hand and the feed tin in the other he had no choice but scoop me up in his hands if he wanted to preserve my modesty.

As the nights turned warmer, I convinced him to set up his cot on the porch out of the heat of the barn. I made sure he was laid out under our one obscured window of fatted paper. After night fall, when I knew he was hunkered down but not quite asleep, I'd light the one lamp we owned and position it so my shadow was in crisp relief upon the surface of the greased paper. I'd hum some kind of foolishness, something Arabian sounding or equally exotic, and begin to undress right there in the low light, making sure to favor the silhouette of my profile as much as possible. I could hear him squirming on his cot as he watched me.

"The light bothering you, Eben?"

"The light . . . no. It's a . . . well it's rather a . . . no."

We never lost interest in one another. But it wasn't all folksy burlesque. Running a farm was like having quadruplets, all of whom had rickets, croup, and bottom rash all at once. Work was never done. Once we got a piece of fence mended, out went the latch to the chicken coop. Once the hogs were fed, damned if one of them didn't come down with fever. Plant for barley, here came wheat weather. Plant both, here came the hoppers and crows. But it was lovely work—good, rewarding work— that was only especially hard on me as I had not properly fed in what felt like ages. But I prevailed, toiling next to the man I cared for. And I thought then I knew the reason why. Love. My love for Eben was what sustained me. Funny how one's delusions can shatter so suddenly.

One morning, with the dawn came dread. I had reached the limit of not feeding. Love be damned. I woke up that morning, weak and feverish, needing a shot of hot berry punch in the worst way. The tips of my teeth itched. My throat was parched. Why the Beguiler had let me go without so long, I didn't know. All I can say is that it was a blessing I didn't know then the Beguiler's dark plan for me. It was as if the breaking sun had lost it's voice, had ceased its comforting hymns that for weeks had been happy prophets of the coming day. Bed felt treacherous. Lingering there in the cold sheets was a sickening augur of another restless night.

*I'll give you bad dreams.*

There was only one way to stop them.

I was up before the cock crowed, out on the porch, then off the steps, not bothering to dress, standing on the combed path that led to our front door, feeling lost and restless and helpless against the rising fear in my belly. I wondered how quickly I could make it into town. Was there a sick child, an old woman lodged in some dark corner who, even in the daylight, would not begrudge a visit from my Midnight Angel? Before I could clear my mind and set a course, Eben appeared from the barn.

"Emma? Are you quite well?" I ran my fingers through my tangled hair, tried to smile.

"Just a tad off my feed," I said.

"You look flushed. I have an elderberry tonic—"

He reached out to touch me. I knew if he did, I could not trust myself. At even the ghost of his fingers on my face, the fire would rage up in me and I would glut myself upon him, in full if uncomprehending view of the chickens. I slapped his hand away. I did not realize such a simple movement could be so loud. The hurt, the shock in his eyes, was worse than my sudden fantasy of his open throat.

"Eben!" I said breathlessly, too conflicted to cry. "I'm . . . *shit!*"

I turned away. The last thing I wanted was to be stared at. The last thing we needed was for him to be so near me.

"Your hair, Emma, has it gotten darker?" I had never prolonged my beguiling for so long before. Was it slipping? Something had to be done. But not now. Now I needed to be alone.

"Do I have to explain it to you preacher boy?" I said pointedly. "Don't you know *anything* about what we women go through every month?" He blushed, then lowered his gaze, stepping back as if the condition to which I had alluded was somehow communicable.

"Sorry. Of course," he said, holding his hands up. My bill had finally come due. But I would not pay it. I would not feed. I would be true to Eben. I would be good. And if such a denial of my nature would be my undoing, then that was the price I would pay.

"Please, my love," I said, looking at him as steadily as I could. "Spend the day away from me."

"But why?" he asked. "I understand your condition. I can be respectful of—"

"*No*!" I said louder than intended. "You must leave. Just for today. Pass tonight by the river, in the church. Anywhere away from me. Just until tomorrow morning."

"But why so long?"

"Eben! Please!" I raced into the barn, grabbed his bed roll from the floor, and thrust it toward him. "Go! Now! Just until tomorrow!" He cuddled the bedroll to his chest, his eyes still bleary with sleep as he turned and shambled toward the rising sun. He didn't protest. He didn't question me further. I think I never loved him more than in the moment I watched him go.

With Eben safe, I marched back into the house. Closed the storm shutters. Locked the door. I made the cabin as dark as possible. To an unaltered soul it might have appeared that I shared the suspicion that sunlight agitated illness. But I could only beat the Beguiler if I denied it my attention. I could only beat it in the darkness. I hunched in a corner, shivering, sweating, pummeling the need in me as if it was a fever. That night, the minutes passed like hours. Since it could not goad me by stripping the outside world into nothingness, it began with my body. It hobbled any distracting thought I might summon by reducing everything under my skin into painful aches. Armies of weakness marched through my veins. Every muscle twanged and twitched, but I would not move. I don't know how many hours passed like that. My body must have finally given out. I don't know if I slept or not. And here was the cleverness of my host. Its cruelty. For if I slept, I dreamed I was awake. Or perhaps I was awake in the utter darkness of a dream. After what felt like centuries languishing in the void, I heard her name.

*Cora?*

My mother's name was fragmented in the dark around me, dissipating suddenly with force but no sound. Had I heard it? I moved to stand and collapsed back to the floor. Every joint and muscle in my body sang. With my last effort, I willed myself to my feet. I was drenched in sweat. My temples throbbed.

"Cora!"

There it was again. Her name. Was I still dreaming? But I had *heard* my mother's name. Clearly. Shouted as if from my own front yard. The floor heaved as I limped to the door.

"Cora! Cora! Come to me, now!"

I fought to stay upright, clambering for the door latch. Throwing it open I saw Da, frail and ghostly in the moonlight, down on his knees, mouth open to the night.

"Cora! There ye be!" At the mere sight of my father, the Beguiler seized me with all its unrelenting hunger.

"Silas!" I hissed, running to him with my mother's ponderous thighs. "Stop this foolishness at once!" I slapped him hard across his sharp face. He fell to the dirt, coughing, grinning. I clamped my hand over Da's mouth and shook him. "Listen to me, you stupid, selfish man. People are trying for their rest now. They are abed!"

"Yes, Cora, my duck," he said wretchedly. He was warm in my grip, warm and all too willing. It was not my mother's burly grip that kept him still. It was her rage. My mother's murderous and jealous rage. In the moonlight, in the light cast from inside me by my brimming hunger, my Da was nothing. A poor blighted creature late only for my jaws.

"I know why you brought us here, Silas," I seethed, pulling him toward me. The wiry hairs of his ears tickled my lips. "You were following that trollop. That whore Miss Brown!"

"Not true, Cora. Not true! 'Twas mere happenstance, I swear."

"Liar!" I backhanded him hard to the dirt. "I saw you! Saw you with these eyes. You've been conspiring all along. You brought little Emma and me to these foul wastes just so you could plant your filth in that Irish cow!" Spitefully, she raised my hands above her head. "Admit it! Confess!"

"Capey Brown, deliver me!" he cried.

The blow that knocked me to the ground barely let his words register. My eyes stung. My nose clogged with blood. There she was standing over me, the offending shovel in her hot, mottled hand.

Capability Brown.

She showed her yellow teeth, then brought the flat of her shovel down upon my skull with a savage swing. I felt my frail dome crack as thick liquid filled my ears.

"Nice form, *Cora*," she purred. "About time someone tanned this poor sinner." My eyes saw only distorted shadows.

"Please, Cora!" Da whimpered. "I had naught choice in the doing. Miss Brown promised me!"

"Shut it, Silas," Brown spat, kneeling to me. I could feel my nose begin to knit, the break in my skull start slowly to fuse as I struggled to turn to her. She was quick. Rabbit quick for a woman of her size, and my arms were pulled behind me before I could stop her. She tied my wrists together smartly with a hank of sharp twine. "There, now, my girl. That should keep you quiet while we finish our business." She drew a knife from her waist and held it to my face. "I believe you have something that could well oblige me." She tore the front of my nightgown with her free hand and scooped out my breast. "Did you think you'd fooled me, Emma? Did you think me *bewitched* that night you serviced me so sweetly?" She looked down at the play of moonlight on the edge of her knife. "Let's say I've suspected what you really are for some time. I was nay but convinced until I had the pleasure of your handsome stranger. You remember the lad. The one who sent you to heaven in your Da's barn while your mother's body burned to ash? My, how that boy likes his gab. Almost as much as his gash. He told me all about ye after a certain bit of persuading.

But when I heard that brawny preacher describe his pretty new wife one day in town, something rankled me. Wheat-colored hair? Ample breast and bum? And an oh-so-charming Irish lilt? My, how the clouds did part. That was not my Emma he was hitched to. Nay. That was my Mercy." I strained upon my bonds, but they would not budge. "I had naught left to do but wait. Wait until you were weak. Until you were ready." I noticed Da had managed to pull himself onto all fours. "Now, truth be told," she continued, "yer charmin' stranger did offer to turn me like he done you. But I never fancied sausage over cabbage. Besides, why shouldn't *I* finish what *you* started?" She grabbed the torn front of my gown and pulled me roughly to her. Reaching for my breast, she brandished the knife at my nipple. I gnashed my teeth, the edge of my incisor tearing her wrist. She slapped me wetly across the face. "We'll have none of that now," she growled. I winced as the blade sliced into my flesh. My blood flowed blackly in the moonlight. She shoved my bleeding breast into her tarnished maw and sucked. I squirmed and bucked. But nothing would quiet the rush of guilty ecstasy that exploded through me. I knew what she was seeing behind those tiny wrinkled eyelids of hers.

Everything. All my girlhood, all my bright vistas, all my hopes and heartbreaks and dreads. My critters and creeks and reliable tree trunks. Everything that made me whole and recognizable to myself, flowing down her sour throat in liquid gurgles. She broke the suction finally with a loud pop and a thick salty spray.

"Sweet Jesus!" She laughed, wiping her mouth with the back of her hand. "If that don't kick like a bonny balled mule! I'm obliged to ye, Emma. Or shall I call ye *sire*?"

"What about me, Capey?" Da wheezed. "You got what ye come for. What about what you promised? About us being together?"

"Oh, Silas," she said wearily, gently placing her hands on either side of his thin face. "Ye always were a *dreamer.*" She snapped his neck with a casual twist. I could not contain a small shriek when I saw his lifeless body flop to the ground.

"You bitch!" I screamed. "You barren bastard *bitch!*"

She clamped a huge hand over my mouth. "Hush, now, my lamb," she cooed. "I'm only settlin' accounts to right. Ye took my Mercy. I take yer Da. Now we're both in the black."

# Chapter Twenty-Seven

Eben found me the next morning, sitting on the ground where he had left me. I had washed the gore of the previous night from my body and face. But he could sense there was something very wrong with me. I couldn't tell him what it was. That I had watched Brown feast on Da, no more than a few mouthfuls in his whole pitiful frame. She'd left his husk by my face. I had tried not to breathe lest my breath disturb his papery likeness. But I could do nothing to stop the late night wind. He twinkled whitely on the breeze, the dusty motes of his body circling in clumped swirls like midnight bees breaking toward their hive.

"Emma?" Eben's voice was soft. I looked up. His eyes were puffy from lack sleep. There were bits of grass in his hair. Oh, God. Did I miss my Da. If only his skinny shell had lasted near me just a little bit longer. The horror of the night could not make my smile convincing.

"Eben, go back! Don't look at me!" I cried, breaking into a deep sob.

"Oh, Emma, my love. My little love," he said, drawing me into his arms. When my weeping had passed, he held my chin as I looked into his eyes. No anger. No fear in those eyes. Only sadness and a desperate need to understand.

"Jesus, Eben," I croaked. "Why don't you just—"

"What my love?"

"Why don't you just call me Mercy?"

"Because you are *not* Mercy, my love. You never have been." This brought on a new round of weeping from me. For even though everything felt wrong in my world, that small kindness gave me hope. "Can you forgive me, Emma? Can you ever forgive my blindness?"

We held each other close, neither of us speaking. Was he really seeing me for who I was? What I was?

"Oh no, Eben. It's you who must forgive me."

He led me to bed and tucked me in. Placing a gentle hand on my face, he asked if I'd like him to stay with me for a while. "We don't need to speak of forgiveness until later," he said with a slight chill to his voice. "Rest."

"No."

"What?"

"Now," I said, sitting up. "I want to speak of it *now*."

"All right."

He smoothed my hair, looping a loose strand behind my ear, a movement I have always found soothing, and said, "Your behavior yesterday, when you sent me away. It was so harsh. So unlike you. Of course you're contending with a monthly condition and I should be more sensitive to that. But it was almost as if you were—"

"What? Possessed?"

"It sounds silly when you say it."

"Maybe not as silly as you think. There is something not quite right with me, Eben. A sickness."

"A sickness of the soul?" he asked.

"No. Of the blood."

"Do you need a doctor? Do you need to be bled? Leeches?"

"No. no. Those leeches got nothing on me."

His confusion and sweetness were what did it, what got me talking, telling my whole story as I watched his boyish eyes.

"And you believe this to be true?" he asked when I had finished.

"Look at me, Eben. Look at my body. My hair. My voice. I'm not the woman you thought you married. I'm just some wicked thing that tried to trap you. Tried to beguile you so I could feed." I looked up. He was smiling.

"Then why didn't you? Why didn't you feed? What stopped you?"

"I don't know. Timing. Opportunity."

"I don't believe you," he said softly. "Love, Emma. Love stopped you. Maybe I did once covet the likeness of another woman. And maybe you did once have dark designs. But you didn't go through with them. And I'm looking at you, now, Emma May Shinnecock. With your raven hair and gray eyes. More in love with you than ever." Oh, it was true! So very true! My Beguiler had been bested. He was finally seeing me. All of me. The realness of me.

"Damn, you preachers ramble on so." I laced my fingers behind his neck and pulled him in for a deep embrace.

Only that's not how it happened. Not entirely.

Eben found me the next morning spry, chipper, and as convincingly plump and flaxen-haired as Mercy. I'd watched him trek into our yard, still sleepy from his night away. He shook his bed roll and smiled at me. The chickens scattered noisily as he approached.

"Feeling better?" he asked as he stopped to peck my cheek.

"What do think?" I said, smiling.

"I think to answer that truthfully might imperil my vows," he said with a wink.

There was no evidence of the previous night's carnage. In truth, Brown had been too giddy with her newly beguiling state to even think of topping up on my Da. Her ignorance had been my windfall. I'd spent the long hours of the night eyeing my father's corpse, weighing my options. If I drank from him, I would risk my mind bleeding with my girlhood memories.

*Da's wiry arms reeling toward me as he laughed, teaching me to box.*

*Da's flat voice blissfully bellowing out one of his bawdy sea shanties.*

*Da's words. Da's fractured wisdom.*

*Da's love.*

But not feeding on him meant a life of misery. I could not be killed. But my weakness was so great I feared it would inevitably lead me to being caught. Caught by Eben when he finally saw me as the wretched thing I was and took away the love that had never really been mine. I had become, finally, a practical creature.

Near dawn, I had finally decided if I wanted Eben, I had to be Mercy. I could hear what Hegey might have said as I peeled my lips from my teeth, hovering over Da's dead throat: *Love was never meant for creatures like us.*

The blood of a dead man doesn't sing in your veins like the blood of the living. It's like a parry in a knife fight giving you just enough strength to redouble your attack but little more. When Eben found me that morning, I may have looked the same to him. Seemed my old playful self. But that was a ruse. I needed to feed in the worst way and would soon lose all patience with our little love games. I had become that morning more predator than partner to him. The day after Brown's visit was sheer drudgery. My and Eben's flirting, which had once been a harbinger of our growing affection, was now pure tedium. Coy splashes over the water trough, suggestive rolls of my rump as I trudged through the mud of the hog's sty, lingering dips of décolletage as I stopped to collect a few stray eggs, were all executed with such exaggerated seduction I feared Eben might deduce the contempt in my displays. But he only bit his lips to slow his grin. I was simply doing as I was told, as the Beguiler in me prompted.

It was after midnight when I entered the barn where Eben was sleeping. Persephone whinnied. I could smell the musk of the animal's panic as I unlatched the gate of his stable. His teeth were bared, his eyes white to the predator shadowing him in the dark. He bolted from the barn as soon as he could, tossing his head as he fled. I looked down to Eben, curled on his tuft of hay. What a prize fool I had been. You never name your chuck, and you sure as shit don't fall in love with it. I was as still as the blackness around me, tense, primed to any movement of his waking. I stepped over him slowly, gaging my weight to perfect silence as I straddled him and lowered myself to the even rise and fall of his sleeping belly. He murmured Mercy's name. Hearing it no longer cut me. We were both guilty of our private deceptions.

"Yes, my love," I whispered to his hot ear. "'Tis me. Hush now. Dream." He did not need to open his eyes to be sure of my nakedness. His hands were enough. I had waited too long to take what I'd hoped he might offer. I could have sipped from him and left it at that, but predators crush their prey. And to crush mine meant first crushing his sacred vow. He gave a small cry as I slipped him inside me. Our movements were slow and tidal. His lids stayed closed as his eyes rolled beneath them. With just the soft blade of the tip of my tongue the flesh of his throat gave, opened like a tiny mouth receiving a lover's kiss. His mind was a gallery hung with but a single likeness as I drank from him.

*Mercy seated behind a dirty pane of glass, lifting a mug of beer to her small lips.*

*Mercy among men. Mercy shy. Mercy laughing.*

*Mercy bent over a basket of fallen linen in the street, clawing at the sheets now soiled as passersby stepped absently upon them. My hand, his hands, helping now, handing her something soft, the fire in the flit of her eyes, the sparks I caught at the casual brush of her hand.*

Oh, to have been coveted like that! Why was it not *me*? Why didn't the most unconscious actions of *my* day inspire his devotion? In my confusion and jealousy and desire I gave no thought to slowing our bodies. Until it was too late.

"*Mercy!*"

I put a shaking hand on his chest as his body quieted. His eyes opened as I swallowed my tears. What had I done?

"Eben, I—" I rolled off him, shielding my nakedness with my elbows and knees.

"Emma? What is it?"

"Can you forgive me?"

"Forgive what?"

"Oh, God, Eben. Can you ever forgive me?" He came to me and wrapped his arms around me. When he drew my eyes to his there was no condemnation there. No fear. Just a touch of sadness at what had passed.

"The vow was mine to break, my dear," he said quietly. Now it was my turn to lift his face to mine.

"Tell me, preacher boy," I said, looking into his weary eyes. "Would it help if I let you call me Mercy?"

# Chapter Twenty-Eight

After that night, the fire between us dimmed. The promise of a desired thing is never as bright once you attain it. He was still dutiful and respectful. Even affectionate. But I was always Mercy to him in private. Only Emma in public. The Beguiler had won. I was finally that thing I thought would always elude me. I was respectable.

My acceptance among our flock owed more to the town's economic growth than to Christian charity. As Eben's old congregation became prosperous, they traded their old brimstone and doomsdays for the more fiscal starch of the Presbyterians and Lutherans. And The Five Wounds found itself treading the economic backwaters among the immigrant poor. Before long, I had no history among our fellow worshippers. I learned to bake without burning. Roast, stew, poach, sew, churn, shear, card, spin, and catch babies. Our new congregation survived by barter, by brotherhood, sisterhood, personhood in the true sense. Providing for those who had lost a crop or kin or who needed a leg up, a firm shoulder, or a soft bed.

Hegey's emporium was now closed—boarded up and abandoned, taking on that sick appearance buildings assume that can no longer claim a purpose. I was saddened to see it so. Saddened further, perhaps, to feel an odd kinship to it. For my life had indeed lost most of its primitive luster. I was flourishing but only in a way that I can describe as inwardly. Not being able to trust my aspect in Eben's eyes, I was even distrustful of mirrors. But still, when I took the brief moment to gaze into them, I thought I saw a flicker of the girl I once was. I refused church with Eben, preferring my time alone. A new peace had found me. I spent hours among the chickens, sitting still until I could reach out and hold one, smelling deeply of the sweet corn upon its feathery shoulders. Persephone trusted me now, and to curry him, to run a hand over his hot flanks, was a sensuous delight. Something was coming. I knew not what. I would find myself singing, absently, to someone who was not there. I wanted to share this new, strange peace. But to tell Eben of it scared me, frankly. I didn't want to open old wounds in my heart. So I sought out what was left of my past.

Hegey had sold his interests in common mercantile, leaving him free to never conflate his livelihood with actual labor. I finally tracked him down in his Atèlier de Dessous, his lady's underwear shop, holding forth on the myriad advantages of his newly imported stayless corset. He pinched the unmentionable between two sets of even fatter fingers (his love life must have taken another header) when I mentioned how the damn thing looked like two sling shots sewed together. I smiled. He looked stern, then promptly shouted, "Show's over ladies. Please come back later. Something dire has just come up." The women scattered, perhaps used to these sudden dismissals. When the store was empty, he locked the door and looked at me. "Well, if it isn't Jean d'Arc."

"Hey, Hegey. You're looking prosperous."

"You mean corpulent. And I wish I could return the comment. What in the world do you have on?" He twirled me around with the tip of one finger as if my ensemble was constructed of cow turds and twine.

"Good enough for chores."

"Mending and milking, is it? Listen to you. You're like something out of a Danish pastoral. You've aged, Emma."

"I'm all right."

"Do you still drink civilized tea or only coffee boiled over an open fire?"

Moments later, we were seated familiarly, if somewhat distantly, around his silver tea service. He had changed his walls to a paper of flocked arabesques in a deep hunter green. His mahogany furniture was upholstered in burgundy and gold. He said nothing. I looked down at my tea. I had yet to take a sip of it and knew it had grown cold.

"Would you believe me if I told you I was happy, Hegey?" He sipped his tea and wiped his pursed lips with the edge of his serviette.

"I would believe you were reconciled. Much like myself."

"Fair enough."

I told him the simple stories of my past few months, the small community we were building, the church socials, the births and barn raisings, the unglamorous daily routine that saw me from one sun rise to another. He suddenly slipped his cup onto his saucer with a pert clink.

"It pains me to see you like this, Emma. I'm sorry if I offend, but I must be honest."

"I found peace, Hegey."

"Yes, but for how long?"

"I can't be like I was." I didn't tell him that the Beguiler was less demanding in me now. That my diet was rustic and almost indistinguishable from my brethren. I didn't tell him much of anything and that pained me. I was feeling oddly beholden to something deeper, something apart from our old alliance that I would not name.

"You can't even be as you are, Emma. Not in his eyes. Are you really prepared for a lifetime of such deceit?"

"I'm not deceiving him. Not about what matters."

"Perhaps."

"Love will see me through," I said quietly.

"Ah, so we've finally come to *that* have we?" he said, leaning back in his chair. There was a sudden chill between us. I finally had the thing that he had longed for most in life. He could not look at me.

"You once told me to be happy, Hegey. You remember my wedding day?"

He smiled coldly as he looked at his empty teacup. "I never intended the price of your happiness to be this dear."

"I shouldn't have come," I said, unable to bear the thought of having to leave him.

"Perhaps not." The room grew cold, suffocating in its finery. I stood up.

"Don't end up like me, Emma," he said, not looking my way. Then he took my hand. His was clammy and pale. There were tears in his eyes. "The only thing worth a proper shit in this world is the capacity for passion. Deny that and you might as well . . ." He began to sob. I bent down and kissed his bald head.

"Bless you," I whispered. I could have sworn I felt him cringe.

# Chapter Twenty-Nine

It was after a potluck in the front room of our own small house, straddling the splatter of my upchucked supper, that I learned the real reason for my newly found peace. I was pregnant. I had become a kind of curiosity cabinet of ailments before I was sure of my fragile condition. Each time one presented, be it dizziness, weakness, curiously glutted breasts, I was recommended to an expert in our group. Women are connoisseurs of misery, and as I had no fever, no rusty puncture, had not ingested turned milk, or nibbled any unusual mushrooms, I was remanded to the care of the only woman among us expert in diagnosing my condition.

Mrs. O'Malley had spent every moment since her wedding night in some phase of reproduction. It was said she could smell a pregnancy like a sailor could scent grass twenty miles from shore. And after cleaning my sick from my chin, she turned her freckled pug nose upon me and smiled.

"Best come with me, my dove," she said in her quiet brogue. "Addy?" And a little replica of herself, down to the yolk-orange hair and tired green eyes, followed her mother into our bedroom. "How long you been spilling yer slops?" Mrs. O'Malley asked as she guided me to the bed, laying me out like a suit of Sunday best.

"Only a few times. Today's been the worst."

"And our bloody caller? He come this month?" she asked, lifting my skirt to my chin.

"I don't reckon so."

"Ye still feelin' the flutters?"

"A mite."

"Addy," Mrs. O'Malley said, and her daughter came dutifully to her mother's whispering lips. She listened before she dug into the deep pockets of her immaculate pinafore, surfacing with a vaguely man-shaped root and a penknife. The little girl then began to whittle the tan bark from the root until a moist, fibrous flesh appeared. She sliced a small hunk of the root and handed it to her mother, who gave it a tender squeeze before placing it on my tongue. It kicked like fire for a minute then settled to an earthy spice that slowly began to settle my stomach. "Wild ginger, my dove. Have ye right soon enough. Loosen ye drawers." I wasn't sure if it was a statement or a request, and I moved my hands to my pantaloons just as I felt the older woman's deft fingers upon the buttons. Her swift hands slipped the garment to the crook of my knees.

"Spread ye shanks a tick, my dove. That's it." Then like a scout checking the direction of the wind, she licked two fingers before plunging them swiftly inside me. She slipped the fingers free then held them to her nose, her brow furrowing. "Curious," she said. I felt a pull of fear that O'Malley ignored. "Addy?" And her mother slipped her wet fingers under the girl's tiny nose. "Remember what I told ye? About rust and turning cream? Ye scent that?" The little girl nodded. Out of Mrs. O'Malley's twelve offspring, Addy must have been chosen to carry on the knowledge. "How far along you reckon she be?"

"Three maybe four months, Ma."

"Ye've no cramps? No blood on yer sheets?" O'Malley asked me. I shook my head as I felt another kick of panic. "And her not showin' and just now spillin' her slops. How you reckon that?" she inquired of her daughter. Addy stroked her tiny chin while she thought.

"A weak placenta?" the girl ventured.

"She'd hardly look so fresh," her mother said.

"Breach?"

Mrs. O'Malley chuckled. "She'd be round as a harvest moon had her babe but proper feet. Think, my dear." Her daughter twirled her tongue inside her mouth as she mused.

"A late quickening?"

"Perhaps," her mother said with a thoughtful frown. "Rare. But not unknown."

"Should I be worried, Mrs. O'Malley?" I asked finally, trying to stay serene. She laid a warm hand to the side of my face and smiled her weary smile.

"Tsk, my dove," she whispered to me. "Life is worry enough. Babies take care of themselves. I knew a lass from Derry who passed her seventh child without ever knowing she was on the nest. She was stirring her family's pot when she had a pain, and thinking she had a bit of wind to pass, hunkered down by the embers and out popped Sarah Joy McKinney, her third daughter. She just looked down at the wee thing, squirming there all pink and perfect as you please, and said, 'Well, at least you ain't late for supper.' She was always plump as a butter barrel, mind, and could have hidden the sins of the world under her skirts. But as long as you feel well, all will be well." She patted my knee as she stood up and wiped her hand on a rag. "D' ye care to know the sex of the little darlin'?"

"You can smell that?"

"Sussed the plumbing of all twelve of my own with nary a miss."

"No. I want it to be a surprise."

"Suit ye'self." And she bent over me and kissed me warmly on the forehead. "Addy, hand the new ma her ginger root."

A child. Finally, I had a secret that I could share. I lay there on the bed after they left, my fingers laced over my belly, staring at the ceiling. How would Providence mix the paint for this new one growing in me? Would it be dark like me or fair like its father? Or would it be of a decidedly different nature? Surprisingly, I felt no trepidation when I thought on the little one's nature. *Mrs. O'Malley, I have beaten the Beguiler*, I thought to myself.

I'd given lease to a being that had no choice but to love me as I truly was.

I was happy at supper, flirting during the washing up, and Eben hadn't the faintest clue as to the why for. Night came. The lamp got lit. I was so excited with my news and had thought all evening about just how to break it. As Eben got down on his knees to pray, I wondered if he was still right with the Lord. Were his prayers for forgiveness for him breaking his vow or for my happy transgression and the real family I was bringing him? When we were finally in bed, I asked if he wanted a little Rollo. This was code for my reading from one of Jacob Abbot's several books dedicated to the "cultivation of amiable and gentle qualities of the heart." His lead character, Rollo, was an anthropomorphized vision of "youthful folly" prone to all types of juvenile shenanigans, which lead to some simple yet instructional moral. A genial rascal without real paste, I suppose. But Eben loved him. And I loved reading aloud to him. He would prop his flaxen head on the pillow of my chest and holler, "Watch out, Rollo!" or "Dang that little dickens," every time something that might pass for plot floated through the monotone of my voice. I was rambling on about little Rollo hoeing beans, when I realized Eben wasn't really listening. He hadn't uttered a sound through the sludge of the whole first chapter, and I figured he must have dropped off, when I felt something hard on my thigh. The connubial knock that cannot go unanswered. Now I've always been one to encourage healthy habits, and as I was edging my beef to better advantage, I found myself suddenly saying, "Easy with that plantin' stick there, mister. Don't want to make a one-eyed beggar of ol' junior 'fore his time." Out it came. Just like that. All that burnishing of my lovely news and out it pops, common as hell. But the message was not lost on Eben.

"What did you say?" he said, sitting up.

"Jus' go easy."

"You on the nest, Emma? Is that what Mrs. O'Malley told you today?"

"Well, yeah, I reckon—"

"You said *his*."

"What?"

"Just now you called junior *he*. Is it a boy?"

"I haven't got the foggiest."

"But you said *he*."

"Right. And you say *He* every time you refer to the Almighty. How you think you're going to feel when judgment comes and *She* has to hike up her cloudy skirts to heave your sinful ass up to heaven?"

And out came a whoop from Eben that rattled the paper in the window like a snare drum. "Oh, Emma," he said. "I'm so happy. I was afeared I might have fallen from the Lord's favor. But this . . . He wouldn't allow all this if I had."

"Don't you figure you and me deserve just a little of the credit?" He laughed and hugged me hard again. Then stopped.

"I hurt you?"

"I ain't glass, preacher boy."

"What do you need? Water? You hungry?"

"Just a little rest. Take it easy, now."

"Are you happy, Emma? Is it what you want?" Find me a frontier husband worth his sack who would tender the same query to his pregnant wife, and I'd have sold my tits for saddlebags right then.

"You make a better husband than you ever did a preacher, Eben, you don't mind my sayin'."

"That mean yes?"

"What do you think? Now you gonna finish what you started?" I said, tossing Rollo to the floor. "Or I gotta school ya all over again?"

# CHAPTER THIRTY

My pregnancy, at least after the sickness passed, was a wonderful racket. All the purpose of being alive with none of life's heavy lifting. I was finally starting to show and spent those early months laid up like I was harboring the heir to the Hanover reign. Hot grub and drink for the asking. A whole body rubdown before bed. Eben played two-handed speculation with me, using sixteen-penny nails for chips, until I thought the cards would crumble from overuse. And when we got bored of that, he read aloud from the Bible, doing the voices of the saints and prophets with a self-effacing aplomb that had me grinning like a kiddie at a Punch-and-Judy show. The ladies of our congregation called it my "confinement," which, to me, was just a fancy word for goofing off. But to the mothers of our church, it was a necessary caution until one was sure the mother had actually "caught." To a woman, they had received the news of their respective pregnancies with the same mortal dread of a young man conscripted to war. I pretended to share their fears, but deep inside I was blossoming. What was beating in the red murk of me heralded nothing less than my own redemption.

Eben made plans for an expansion of our house, staying up nights drawing schematics that blew out a whole exterior wall and allowed for a little nursery with a real glass window. Then we started coming up with names. Humphrey was prone to flab and wouldn't share his blocks. Priscilla would turn her nose up at every odd smell and worry over the whiteness of her bloomers. Ezekiel would never shut up and Hanna was just asking to have her moniker plugged into every nasty rhyme a school yard could cultivate. But *Caroline*, that was sweet. Not too prim. Caroline sounded like soothing bells. And for a boy? Caleb. Little Bible-y maybe, but honest and handsome and considerate and tough without being a bully. A good honest, quiet boy with a touch of melancholy that spoke of hidden depths who would still share his marbles.

And so it was settled. A "proper" woman would have begun her confinement the day she couldn't button her ball gown. But among us "rustics," it was only when I was as big as a blue-ribboned sow that I was deemed well enough to receive callers. And on came a parade of quiet smiles and happy nods behind flotillas of casseroles and brown breads and puddings. We received all our gifts and well wishes with humble gratitude. But the real fun came when we were finally left alone. We eyed the table full of food, then glanced at our bed. Our mutual glee was unbridled. Sitting nude on the bed with all our tasty loot spread out around us, we fed each other like lusty Greeks, reclining near a roaring fire. Huckleberry preserves slathered over buckshot stew. Trout salad sandwiches on rye with caramel sauce. Fried chicken dipped in late-season honey. Heaven. One morning, I felt so good I damn near bounded out of bed, tugged on a pair of Eben's old canvas britches before he was even awake, and started auguring saw holes in our back wall. I was waddling behind my big belly, still barefoot among all the wood chips and dust that was collecting on our cabin floor, when Eben woke up, hair spiky from sleep.

"What are you doing, Emma?"

"What's it look like? Don't tell me you plan on knocking out this back wall all on your lonesome."

"Mr. O'Malley was planning on coming by this afternoon."

"Well, there'll still be plenty to do." I poked the saw into the first of the four holes I'd drilled and starting moving the blade back and forth. "Ain't you got some cookin' to do?"

"I was aiming to roast those root vegetables."

"I thought you was making soup?"

"Roasting first makes the broth all the sweeter."

"Then get to it. You're crabbin' me." He grinned as he laid back, watching me. "Git up, now," I said, going back to my sawing. "I'm eatin' for two. One might accommodate your foolishness. But two won't wait."

"It's looking like I'm going to need some regular work when the baby comes," he said, yawning, moving to the stove.

"Hell, I got that all figured. You will offer proper instruction to husbands whose wives are expecting. A four-week course. I'll just hire you out like a plow mule." He laughed. "You could teach a class in men's cooking. Washing up. Foot rubbing. Back scratching. Not to mention your *other* blossoming skills," I winked with a smile.

"I'm serious, Emma. We can rely on barter for most of our needs. But the baby will need proper schooling, clothes. A business he or she could inherit." His Sunday collections yielded pitiful little. So, Eben had worked every possible angle he could to foot our bills, denying Hegey his magnanimity when he had insisted on helping us. He'd loaned out Persephone during planting season. Then himself. Then he'd taken to doing odd jobs in town at a penny a pop, coming home so tuckered I could barely get him into bed come evening.

"You have something in mind?" I asked.

"Actually, I do. I've been approached by certain individuals in town who think I might make a pretty fair marshal."

"Marshal? What do you know about the law?"

"I know about fairness, Emma."

"Then keep preaching."

"They're serious."

"Yeah, they're serious. No other fool would take the job."

"Be that as it may, it's a real job. With a real salary."

"I don't know if I'd like to be married to the law. Preacher was bad enough. Of course they'd expect you to tote."

"I could hardly expect to command the required respect of my office without a gun, Emma."

"Who's gonna do all the cooking and washing up?"

He smiled. "I need to do right by you and the baby, and this is on the table," he said. "They want my answer soon."

"How soon?

"Tomorrow, soon."

"Hells bells, Eben. Sounds like you already made up your mind. You even know how to shoot straight?"

"I was hoping *you* might school me on that."

Not long after Eben had begun his shooting lessons, I was in town to purchase two strong four-by-fours that would pillar the header of the back wall I had finally busted out. I was on my way to the lumber yard, Persephone hitched up to a dray wagon we had borrowed from the O'Malleys, when I noticed Hegey's old emporium was under new management. I'd seen little of Hegey in the last several months. Promises to come to afternoon tea had been broken by both of us, our written regrets similar in tone in that they both implied preoccupations with lives that were no longer dependent upon one another. I missed him. I felt pretty bad about not having reached out to him more regularly. So, with this troubling portent of his financial fortunes, I thought it time I saw him again. I found him behind the counter of his lady's underwear shop, putting the last of his sadly unsold stock in a great cedar shipping chest. I could only see his stooping back as I approached. Without tuning to face me, he stood up and said, "Emma?"

When he turned, there were tears in his eyes. He had lost some weight. His face looked wan and troubled and that, along with the crisp gray silk suit he was wearing, made him look more handsome and distinguished than I had ever seen him before. I noticed he had a black arm band circling his upper arm. He came around the counter and embraced me, his body trembling with emotion.

"My, God," he said when he broke our hug. "What a serendipitous surprise. I was just on my way to call on you."

"What the hell happened, Hegey?" With his empty shelves and mourning band, there was a dual intention to my question.

"Oh, where to begin?" he said, wiping his eyes. "My parents, those twin bastions of neglect, have died. I received a letter from their solicitor last week." He tried a brave grin but let out a sudden sob.

"Oh, Hegey," I said, taking his limp hand. "I am so very sorry."

"I am too, if you can believe it. Their passing has conjured in me the most curious emotions imaginable. Is it possible to be both furious and heartbroken at once?"

"Are you heading home for the funeral?"

He smiled weakly as he nodded. "That among other things. But, please. I can't speak here. Not in front of all this woefully *dead* stock."

His apartment was as barren as his shop. Only his green walls remained as testament to his exquisite taste. We sat at the same table that had been privy to so many of our past changes and schemes. He did not offer tea. There was no tea to offer. Everything around us was packed and labeled in expectation of his departure.

"You look well, Emma," he said, smiling. "I heard you were expecting."

"I feel pretty good," I said, wishing I could say something else. Anything else. There was too much to say to one another. Too much lost ground to cover for either of us to know where to begin.

"Yes, well," he said, stretching out a leg so he could reach into his pocket. "Before I forget, I have something for you. For the baby, really." He placed a pretty little silver rattle on the table. I took it.

"Oh, Hegey. It's beautiful."

"In aspect, yes. It's a rather quality piece. It was mine. Or so I've been told. I don't remember ever playing with it. Perhaps your child will gain some small pleasure from it."

"I'm sure the baby will love it," I said, curling my fingers around its cold, shiny form. "It doesn't look like you're coming back, Hegey." He took a deep breath as he looked at the crates that populated the empty room.

"I suppose a funeral is as good a reason as any to admit defeat in one's past enterprises. They only reason I stayed in Hollywood was you."

"Hegey—"

He raised his hand to gently silence me. "I don't say that as prelude toward any regret on your part. We've known one another too long and too well for that. Truly. You've grown up to be *precisely* the woman I'd always hoped you'd be." Now there were tears in my eyes. I grabbed his hand and held it tightly.

"I'm gonna miss you, Mr. Hegemore." He clenched his eyes shut against his tears as he forced a formal smile to his lips.

"Yes. I believe you will. But don't." He gripped my hand tighter as he spoke. "Try to remember me even a fraction as fondly as I will surely, wistfully, and most lovingly remember you, my dear."

It was a funny, happy kind of sadness I felt on my ride home with my small stack of lumber. Saying goodbye to Hegey felt like the natural end to our wonderful and curious association. I had been privy to so many unnatural ends that my sadness was really stoked by the realization that the warm and sometimes filial feelings I had for Hegey were never expressed to my real Da at his ending. Forgiveness is not something you suddenly come upon. It is built, timber by timber, brick by brick, like a new room in an old a home. Especially the brand of forgiveness you erect for yourself. The clean, piney scent of the wood in my wagon smelled fresh. And so imbued with hope, I arrived home to continue Eben's shooting lessons.

# Chapter Thirty-One

Eben made good behind that badge. With his height, build, and cool demeanor, he was a natural for public service. A typical day was throwing reason on any number of domestic disputes: widows angry at wagons driving too fast past their town houses, shop owners wanting the streets cleared of local toughs, a stolen harness, a lost cat. He only pulled his piece once in his first three months behind his tin star, and then he only had to wave it around a little to bring the fracas to a close.

Some drifter had wandered into a miner's supply store and tried to make off with a pair of canvas britches and a pickaxe. And when he was kindly reminded by the owner that it was customary to pay before departing with store merchandise, the drifter, hopped up on hemp or hooch, pulled out a knife, a real Arkansas toothpick. It was only lucky chance Eben had been walking by the store that day at precisely the moment the drifter was acting like Ivanhoe with his cutlery. Eben had sauntered in, stood his ground, and palmed his Walker as calm as a seasoned slinger. My lessons had paid off. Even a doper knew the special language of Mr. Sam Colt. The merchandise was calmly if shakily folded, dusted, and returned to its shelves. The offender was escorted past the mouth of our main street. Eben made the front page of our little ditchwater rag. But that wasn't his only reward. The proprietor of the shop where this aborted depredation occurred was none other than Gentleman Abe Rose, the famous work pant manufacturer.

Né Abraham Rosenthal, the son of a woman's wear manufacturer, young Abe was struggling to make a name for himself on the legitimate New York stage, when his father had come to him in a lather. He explained to his son that there had been a dire mistake on a recent order, and instead of receiving several bolts of French tulle from Provence, he had been delivered a whole mess of heavy indigo-dyed canvas from Nîmes. When I heard Mr. Rose tell this story some time later, it was in tones of pure vaudeville:

> *"Oy!" his father had moaned. "We're ruined! What self-respecting lady will flounce about Broadway in a shirtwaist of heavy blue canvas?" But young Abraham had been undaunted.*
>
> *"What the heck is de-nim?" the boy had queried, looking at the words printed on the crates of useless fabric.*

> *"That's 'de Nîmes,'" his father had corrected, never too distracted to edify his wayward son.*
> *"Denim," young Abe had mused. "Gee, pop, I bet that stuff would sure make swell trousers. You know, for folks who never want 'em to wear out."*

Rose's father saw no other option but to take his son's advice, and with shears that had once allowed for corsets' curves and cupping darts, he cut straight-legged trousers with bulky triple-stitched pockets and button flys. He called his new trousers *Rose's Everlasts, The Last Pair Of Pants Your Knees Will Ever Need!* The pants were a flop east of the Hudson. But once they branched out past the Ohio River, clear skies. They made a fortune selling them to coal miners, doubled it when copper boomed farther west. Abe married. After his father died, he cashed in his stake in the family business and settled for a quiet but comfortable life on the plains. Of course most of Mr. Rose's story was not really his own. The real hero of that story was living a prosperous life in the Nob Hill section of San Francisco. But the story's attribution did not matter. The Roses were warm and lively people. Even if their glory was borrowed.

I didn't recognize the messenger who brought our invitation to the Rose's house. I was ten months gone by this time, an unusually long pregnancy, I was informed, and considered gauche company by the calling card crowd. But the Roses were different. Children were a blessing. Life was life. And they wanted to thank Eben personally for his gallant interference with a little seven-course get together. I knew the particulars of dinner party etiquette only in theory. This was proper. This was class. It was me who was skittish as hell at the prospect of attending.

Eben forked over seven whole dollars for a special evening frock that would complement my battleship measurements. In the end, you could have launched me with a magnum of champagne. I looked like a ship of the line under grape-colored sail, but Eben was speechless. I was finally safe, respectable, mere moments from being able to claim, without caveat, my hearth as a real and venerable home. Eben wanted to splurge for one of those new hired drays that were doing such a thorough job of paving the streets with yet more fertilizer, but I couldn't cotton to the idea of my bulk arriving in so heavy a wagon. I was feeling too jittery to sit, and it was a velvety smooth evening, so I insisted upon walking to our soiree.

The Roses lived where the new sidewalks began. And what was once a hushed walk in scrub grass and beetle shells became clotted with the sounds of our footfalls on the hard gray crust of poured stone.

"Let's *race*, Eben," I said, grinning. "I bet you a slug from one of my titties I can whoop your ass!"

"Promise me you won't curse tonight, Emma." He smoothed his pomaded head and straightened the red rose pinned to his lapel. He looked so handsome; how could I refuse him?

"Whatever you say, poppa."

The homes here were massive and vacant. The gaudy offspring of a new kind of con man that had recently come to Hollywood known politely as real estate speculators. Gothic lightening rods perched on blown glass orbs threatened the quiet night sky. Fussy wrap-around porches that could have accommodated the footprint of my girlhood home sprawled empty, festooned with fret-worked swings and silent rockers. Eben stopped in front of a lilac and lime green-colored beast, all knotted gingerbread and corniced curly-cues. He checked a card in his hand and squinted at a shiny brass plate etched with numbers.

"This is it."

"You still happy about the baby, Eben?" I asked.

"What?'

"You still *love* me?" Suddenly, all I wanted were his warm hands roaming every inch of my acreage. He kissed me back with a bit of practiced tongue. But the front door hushed open then, and we shifted into stage smiles, recoiling slightly at the sight of a new face.

"Now that's what I like to see," Miriam Rose said with such geniality I slipped effortlessly into her embrace. "A husband still hungry for his wife. Emma! Eben!"

Abe Rose stood behind his wife. Shortish, bearded, loving eyes tinged with as much sharpness as sadness. He wore a loose silk cravat and a pressed waistcoat of expensive fabric with worn house slippers on his wide feet. "You both look enchanting," he said, pumping Eben's hand. I could smell wood polish and cooking smells in the foyer. The house was clean but not neat. It was hard to separate the Roses from their surroundings. The animal and the environment were of such a piece, were so well suited, that the one seemed a seamless continuation of the other. Their interior pulsed with a warm amber glow that seeped slightly into the faintly yellowed smile of our hostess.

"Before we eat, seems you two must pass muster," Miriam said. Lined up on the carpeted stairs, leaning shyly on the polished banister, were three children, dark as their parents, all possessed of the same bright, slightly sad eyes.

"Come on, general," Abe called to the oldest. "Inspection." The three children filed down the stairs toward us. I could smell the bathwater still on their plump bodies, the slight smell of rinsed borax on their nightgowns. They walked in mock procession, trying not to smile, little arms folded behind their backs. Eben straightened up and saluted as the oldest boy stood at attention in front of him. The child gave a nervous glance to his father, who smiled and motioned with the fingers of one hand. The boy then reached into the pocket of his night shirt and pulled out a wrinkled paper ribbon that had been pasted to a crude five-pointed star cut from the lid of a biscuit tin. Pounded into the still visible colors of the tin were the words "For Conspicuous Valor." He motioned for Eben to lean over. His brother, the next in line, solemnly handed the older boy a diaper pin whose hasp was shaped like a maniacally smiling duck. Tongue through his teeth, he pinned the medal to Eben's chest and then kissed him on both cheeks.

"My, my, general," Eben said with a misty grin. "Looks like my official star's headed for the sock drawer." Miriam Rose beamed. The youngest, a girl who had been studying me during the whole ceremony, suddenly broke ranks and put her tiny hand on my belly.

"Like me, Momma?" she asked, turning to her mother, the heat of her small hand stealing through the berry velvet of my frock.

"That's right, Ruthie. You were tucked into Momma just like that once."

"So what's the verdict, Washington?" Mr. Rose asked, smiling.

"They'll do," the oldest boy said soberly. And Mr. Rose clapped his hands, and the children squealed and ran to their father, hugging him all at once in a gaggle of vibrating curls. Then they affectionately ravaged their mother. Finally bowing to us, they took the stairs two at a time to make their exit.

"Half an hour of Robin Hood, Noah," Mr. Rose called up the emptying flight. "And no *Struwwelpeter* tonight, Jonah. I don't want to be having to hide the scissors again in the morning."

"They're beautiful," I said to Mrs. Rose after they had gone.

"Aw," Mrs. Rose said almost dismissively, "they're just happy. I hope we didn't embarrass you, Eben." I swear Eben was wiping an eye as he shook his head.

The place was furnished with a proliferation of styles: Grecian, Gothic, Moorish, all in scuffed pearwood, the tables nicked, the cushions creased. On the good Persian was a toy elephant and a plate still smeared with jam. Mrs. Rose picked up the plate as we passed, carrying it almost like a part of her evening ensemble as she asked us about drinks.

"Mrs. Rose—," I began.

"Miriam."

"*Miriam.* I don't know what's with me today. I've been as jumpy as a toad tacked to a hot rock," and I saw her eyes crease as she smiled at me. "You happen to have a few drops of valerian about?"

"Babies are a blessing, but they can bring the jitters some nights. I have just the thing."

"You need a calming tonic, Eben," Mr. Rose said. "Or can I tempt you with something more bracing?"

We ate on a massive trestle-style table suited more for sword fighting Saxons than our plates of sautéed veal with petits pois. Our chairs were huge, with crowns of ornate carving, upholstered with leopard skins that were beginning to wear in places. I saw Mrs. Rose remove a few stray predator hairs between bites with a practiced ease. The meal progressed, as good meals should, through hearty fits of laughter and gripping conversation.

"I understand, Mrs. Lightfoot, that you knew the gentleman who built the store I currently inhabit," Mr. Rose said, eating his peas off his knife while his wife playfully hit him.

"Yes, Mr. Hegemore was a real friend to me when I first came to town."

"Oh, that shop must have been a *wonder* in its day," Mrs. Rose enthused. "It was such a shame to tear out all that beautiful Moorish fretwork!"

"He must have been quite a character," Mr. Rose said sweetly, seeing the smile fade from my face as I thought of Hegey on our last day together.

"He was wonderful," I said, swallowing hard.

"I'm sure you miss him very much."

The fruit and cheese were served with little cordials of syrupy port. The talk split between two camps, Mr. Rose complimenting Eben on his cool head and good timing and the need for more conspicuous law enforcement, while his wife admired the feel of my frock and guessed incorrectly how far along I was.

"*Ten* months? Mrs. Rose said with raised eyebrows. "You poor thing!"

"Best ten months of my life," I said, my mouth full of grapes.

"What part of Ireland are you from, Emma?" she asked. I almost choked on my mouthful of fruit. Was the beguiling throwing its glamor in concert with Eben's delusion? Why would it do that? But before I could suss this new development, I heard myself answering.

"Skibbereen," I said. Clearly she did not know the place any more than I did.

"You're carrying low," Mrs. Rose said, over her husband's loud and easy laughter. "It was that way with

Ruthie, and I thought sure we were headed for a trio of all boys."

I smiled. "Oh, I'd love a little girl, but Eben here—"

"Men and their boys. Unavoidable, I'm afraid. Either way it will have such lovely blonde hair."

"You ever think of public office, Eben?" Mr. Rose said. "A man like you could make a real difference in a burg like this. With the repeal of the Missouri Compromise, we need as many enlightened people as possible in the country right now."

"I certainly believe all men are born free," Eben said quietly, "and we are late in unfettering the black man toward what our founding documents guarantee as already his."

"Did you hear that, Miriam?" Rose said, slapping Eben on the back. "Is he not a man and a brother?"

"Oh, Eben," Mrs. Rose chided playfully, "don't even *mention* the passing of the Fugitive Slave Act unless you like the idea of staying up all night. I could set up a cot by the fire for you!" She laughed.

"Well it's damned unfair! These damned Southern pharaohs, chasing down a new batch of Israelites!"

"How about a little chamomile in the front parlor, Emma? Leave these men folk to their mutual admiration?"

"And deny me the charms of this town's greatest beauty?" Mr. Rose said, smiling at me. If he was seeing me as Mercy, that last bit was twenty-four-carat horseshit. "Not on your life. I have a proposition for you too, Mrs. Lightfoot."

"I thought you meant *me*, Abe. I'm crestfallen." Mrs. Rose laughed.

"I always mean you my dear. But hear me out, Emma." Mr. Rose finished his port. "I don't know if you've heard tell of my history in the theatre."

"One year as the *shlemiel* in the Yiddish playhouse and suddenly he's Edwin Booth."

"I trod the boards with style, you must admit."

"*You* admit it."

"Anyway. I was thinking, after your baby of course, of starting a little troupe of players. Not much at first. Some light comedy. The odd drama. But you would make a divine Juliette, my dear. Or Cordelia. Even a Lady Macbeth if we can get these sticks-in-the-mud who pass for society out here to relish a little good old murder and intrigue. You'd make a striking brunette. What do you say?"

I had never felt my ease among folks like this before. Even if they did not see me as I was. They were so easy with their knowledge of current events. The air seemed spiked with some heady gas, the room so beautiful and lived-in cheerful. I gripped Eben's hand, and I could tell he was feeling the same way.

"I don't know, Mr. Rose," I said. "I was kinda hopin' after tonight you might be willing to *adopt* me." Peals of heartfelt laughter. "You could give Eben here visiting rights, if you've a mind." More tender guffaws.

"Then as my newly adopted daughter, I'm afraid it's my patriarchal duty to insist you hearken to the muse."

I belched. Eben looked pained as he stared down to his empty plate.

"Mazel tov!" the Roses shouted together, raising their glasses.

My laughter agitated a slight pinch in my gut. I wasn't used to such rich food, all that lovely sweet wine. I stood up with a jerk. Miriam Rose read my sudden move.

"Oh yes, I remember that," Mrs. Rose said with a wink. "The ever sounding call of the water siren. Down the hall, first door on the left." I dropped my napkin onto the seat of my chair and nodded, smiling. I could hear their voices rise again as I retreated from the room. "She's darling, Eben. Just a *dear*."

Why *not*? I thought as I waddled down the warmly lit hall. Why *not* tread the boards? Eben could graduate to municipal judge, and we could set up in a big house like this. Have a whole heap of kids running around. Fill up on this banquet of real *living*. We could bring the O'Malleys up with us. Eben could get them jobs. We could keep things as they are, only better, wider. Move the whole operation uptown.

The convenience was housed in its own room, twice the size of Hegey's. Bar soap still fragrant in its wrapper with a girlie picture on it. Towels draped over warm tubes by the bath. And what was this, coming out of the wall above the tub? Some kind of metal sunflower all pricked through with tiny holes. One of those new standing douches. Hegey would have spit green if he'd seen it. I fumbled under my carriage for the two loops of satin that would lift my ponderous skirt above the bowl of the commode. I could hear the rise of disembodied laughter from down the hall. The chime of forks on good china. Civilized. I noticed a figure through the obscured glass of the window in the water closet. Some one was standing in the alley, across from the Roses, loitering in my purview. A dark unwavering shadow I did not need particulars to recognize. My handsome stranger. The author of all my misery was watching me. Not watching. *Aware* of me. I felt a sudden cramp and winced as it passed. When I looked back through the window, he was gone. I began to sweat. It was hard to catch my breath. Oh no. Oh *God,* no. Not now. Don't come now, baby whomever-you-might-be. Don't come *now.*

A knock on the door.

My head snapped around to the sound. "You all right in there, Emma? You need anything?" came Miriam's voice through the wood. I dipped a hand between my legs. It came out clean. No blood.

"I'm fine, Miriam," I shouted. "All that lovely food, I'm just not—" I was suddenly wracked with a gassy wave of pain so severe that it bent me in two. It was as if I were trying to pass a dry stool but clearly through the wrong orifice.

"You sure, dear? Shall I fetch a doctor?"

I felt feverish, then cold. My heart began to race as I reached between my legs and gripped what was blocking me. A bolus gave at the slight pressure of my fingers. I pulled it into the gaslight.

"Emma? Dear? Can you see your way to unlatching the door?"

I looked at what I held with sickening horror. A tiny translucent hand. Or what was left of a hand. The miniature nails were perfect, the fine empty-veined wrist rounding into tiny denuded bone. Bloodless. Had I been feeding on my *own* poor child? Sipping from its quickening body only enough to sustain me as it grew into this final unthinkable feast? Had this been the Beguilers plan all along? The nausea came up quickly. A garish slosh of bright peas and veal chunks spattered upon the white tile. My head drew back. The sound that issued from it was not a wail produced by a creature with lungs. It was the sound of collision between inanimate things, between sheets of twisted metal or of planets themselves when their orbits become fatally interlinked.

"*Emma!* Eben! Abe! Come quickly!" I heard feet frantically pumping down the hall. The lock rattled. Fists pounded on the door. "Emma? *Emma!*" The shriek of splintering wood.

And all went white.

# CHAPTER THIRTY-TWO

The light was as knives when I finally came to, the memories of the previous evening pelting me like stones.

"I wanna die. Just let me die."

The room in which I found myself was not familiar. The smell there was not of home. I was on a simple brass bed, a wash-worn quilt beneath me. A loveless shack of plank walls and floor. A single lamp illumined a simple wooden cross tacked to the wall. As my eyes adjusted to the gloom, I saw him standing over me. Smelled him as I had smelled him that night in the barn. I tried to turn away from the lamp light, shunt my mind from the horrible flurry of images that inhabited it.

*The animal fear in Miriam's eyes as my lunging jaws shortened her scream.*

*Abe Rose's eyes, dead and staring, that could not blink away the blood flecked upon them.*

*And Eben—merciful was the darkness that accompanied his last moments. But still the crackling in my ears, the terrible splintering of bone that echoed there.*

I sat up to meet my stranger's gaze as he lowered himself next to me on the bed. I could feel his breathing as I knew he could feel mine. He tried to lay his hand on my face, then pulled it back when I shied away. I had questions to which I already knew the answers. But still a waning part of my mind insisted on articulating them.

*What did you do to me?*

*Only what you let me do.*

*I did not ask for this.*

*Neither did I. I told you I could only give you bad dreams.* We spoke without moving our lips.

"The baby," I whispered aloud. Bitterness still at the back of my tongue. "You told me I would never feed on the innocent."

"I lied," my stranger said softly. I wanted to cry, but weeping seemed useless. "It can be a cruel condition we share, Emma," he said softly. "But such cruelty will only last as long as you let it. You must embrace it. As I have. Let your history go. It will be of no use to you now."

"Just tell me how to end it," I demanded, turning away from him.

"You won't want that an hour from now."

"There has to be a way." Something in my voice made him recoil.

"Why do you ask me how you can end it? Why aren't you asking how you can *live* with it? Because that's what we share, Emma. Life."

"This isn't life," I spat. "My husband is *dead.* My baby is *dead.* I did that. Me. Just so I could—"

"Everything preys, Emma. Everything that burns or flows or kills or grows snatches what it needs from something else. Even the moon, that shyest of all thieves, steals its pale fire from the sun. The sun steals moisture from the waters of the earth. And the grasses and creatures that require that water don't parse it out by virtue of some democratic contract. They take it as they can. Laws rob your freedom. Morality robs your instinct. Love convinces you that you are somehow incomplete and then steals your deepest sense of yourself. Each thing's a thief. And this life, this *living* that you think has been denied you, is really nothing more than your stubborn reticence to accept the innate and necessary larceny that all living things share." He sat back on the bed with that self-contented look on his face men get whenever they think they have lowered the boom on the poor logic of some female. I couldn't believe I had ever seen a future in his eyes. Perhaps only women ultimately understand that you can never take the world on its own terms.

"I know that play, stranger," I said.

"What?" He looked stricken. Caught.

"*Timon of Athens*? William Shakespeare? You just gave a faulty summary of its best monologue, but I got the gist. My momma didn't raise a fool. Now can we get back to my original query, or do you just want to blow arrogant some more?"

"Would you believe me if I told you I was there in that tavern when Will first wrote it? That I had been the one to tell him not to finish it?"

"Have most women through the ages gone all dewy when you told them that?" He crossed his arms over his chest. "Are you going to help me? Or I gotta make you?" He shifted closer to me as he uncrossed his arms. His face was mere inches from mine, yet his gaze came from a remarkable distance. I dived deep into his mind, swimming among thousands of gossamer memories there until I lighted on one I knew would hurt him the most. I was suddenly a young girl, no more than fifteen. My hearty limbs thinned to childish branches of flesh. My face bled to a youthful innocence, my hair long and flaxen.

"Gwen?" The pained desire in his eyes was the deep cut I'd hoped for.

"We can do this all day," I said, willing myself back to my natural aspect. "Tell me."

"Don't you see, Emma," he said slyly. "We could be anyone and everyone to one another."

"I've never much cared for masquerade parties."

"Did you love your husband?"

"More than anything," I said with a dry throat.

"So you could never see a life with me?" He looked back at me with Eben's boyish face. But I knew the edges of it, the conceit and falseness of it. And I felt more sadness than desire.

"Eben was a *man,*" I whispered. I could see my answer cut him deep. Even creatures like us could still be hurt in the ways that mattered. He took a deep breath and sighed.

"It's a precious boon you'd be throwing away. Even wolves have their packs. Do you really long to walk this world alone?"

"I don't long to walk this world at all."

"You say that now, but in time—"

"If all you can offer me is darkness, I'll take it. But only in the grave." He leaned back on the bed and peered at me.

"What if I refused to tell you how to end it?"

"Then you will become even less of the friend you pretend to be." He looked away. "Why am I here, stranger? To torture you with Gwen's girlish face?" He glanced at me as if he was about to speak. He stopped himself. "Or did you bring me here for what you hoped I could do for you."

"It's a funny thing about Beguilers like us, Emma. We can only end one another."

"How?"

"By eating the heart of the one who made you. It's my heart that binds us, Emma. If you were to steal my heart and consume it, you would still live but cease to be a Beguiler. And I would simply cease to be." He unbuttoned his shirt. His chest was firm, heaving only slightly as he spoke. "I had the chance once. It took me over a hundred years to find Gwen again. In the summer of 1779. On the banks of the Hudson, just outside of Tarrytown. I remember the hood of her crimson cloak that shadowed her face in the moonlight. Her bare breast was a luminous porcelain under my touch." He took my hand and placed it gently on his exposed chest. I curled my fingers into his flesh, my nails making tiny furrows in his skin. "But I couldn't do it, Emma. I loved life too much. Her life. And the life I saw through my Beguiler's eyes."

My fingers stalled.

"You can't stop what has happened *because* of you any more than you can change what has happened *to* you," he said. "Our condition is not so different from anyone else's. Not in the vast scope of creation. It takes courage to continue, no matter what your circumstance. Do you have the courage?" He pushed my hand tighter against his chest, yearning in his eyes. "Can you do it? Can you do what I couldn't?"

With my palm pressed so heavily upon him, I could feel the steady kick of his heartbeat. My happiest months inhabited by little Caleb or Caroline had been accompanied by the hope of feeling such a pulse. I remembered waking up in the dark hours after midnight just to burrow into Eben's arms and feel his steady heart upon me as he slept. And for how many nights before Eben had I lain next to Hegey, soothed by his faint snoring? None of us are the authors of our bindings. Only the pages within them.

"The greatest myth about us, Emma, is that we are creatures of death. That we are dead ourselves and glut ourselves upon it. But nothing could be farther from the truth." I curled my fingers into a fist as I lowered my hand. Was he relieved? Disappointed? He never said. I got up off his bed and went to the door.

"Thank you for telling me," I said as I opened it.

"Why do you thank me? You won't get another chance." He looked small in the weak light of his lamp.

"You never know. It's a big world, stranger. And we have nothing but time."

"Wait," he said as I was about to leave. "I have something of yours." He fumbled in a drawer near his bed and took something out of it. He waited with his head down as I crossed to him. He handed me a folded leaf of paper. I recognized it immediately. It was a page torn from my mother's diary, a diary I thought I had lost in the fire that had consumed the last of her.

"Don't ask me how I came by this," he said. "A pleasant mystery is rare in this world. Almost as rare as you."

# Chapter Thirty-Three

I waited until I had walked a full mile from his shack before I read it. Under a gibbous moon, with darkness lush upon me, did I finally consent to look at it with my predator's eyes:

"April, quarter moon, 1827— 'A journey of a thousand miles begins with a single step' is a limp adage so singularly remedial in its assertion, so blandly married to the obvious as to defy comment," I read aloud under the brightly starred sky. "It is also wrong. It pays tribute, as most such ill-worn tropes do, to only the physical. Real journeys, the ones worth the trouble, do not begin with steps. They do not require the agencies of knees and breeze. They ferment in the stillness of the guts, are distilled in dark restive states, where the present in all its consuming continuity has become an enemy, and only a flutter of the will, a release of a self-blown wind, can get the mill turning." I smiled to myself as my mother's words washed over me. "Journeys begin in anger. In regret. In fear. And in hope. We do not walk a real journey. It, at first, walks us. And only after that, after being firmly rooted and yet resolutely traveled, can we even really imagine that first thirsty step. Only one thing in this world can save you, Emma. And it cannot even begin to do so until you completely abandon all interest in what happens to you."

I decided then I would let fate have its way with me. But first, I would sneak back into town. I had to assess the damage I had done with my own eyes. I had to know if in my frenzy I had killed *all* the Roses. I was sickened by what I had done to the parents. But I wasn't sure how I would cope with having harmed their children.

I walked to town as the moon became small in the still-dark sky. The air was cold, the main street deserted of residents. But not objects. Three toe-pincher pine coffins reposed on sawhorses in front of the Roses' store, the corpses' decay slowed by the midnight chill. Votives in red glass flickered on their sealed lids. Three meant I had left the children alive. Small mercy. At least I had left enough of their parents that they could be properly mourned. What had I done? Nothing I would not do again. My real punishment was knowing that. And how fleeting that knowledge was. Standing there in the cold, glutted with the blood of my unborn child, I could feel those three boxes were becoming just boxes. I had to fight to remember their faces, the way they smiled, the way their hands and voices had touched me. The Beguiler had no use for such things. It pushed me mercilessly into the now and now again.

The gun cocked so loudly I jumped.

"Stay where you are Mrs. Lightfoot," a quavering voice said from the shadows. "I would be obliged if your hands remained where I could see them." I raised my hands and turned slowly. He was only a boy, his face still swollen from crying, his small hands shaking on the grip of the Colt he leveled at my head. Eben's Colt. That gun was a friend to me. It was well practiced at pretending. I had seen its deathly purpose denied twice now. First when Eben had used it as an awkward prop when he proposed to the woman I wasn't. And again, now, in the hands of the boy. He was no more a killer than I was Mercy O'Day.

"Noah, is it?" I asked, stepping slowly toward him. "Noah *Rose*?"

"Stay where you are!" He renewed his grip on the gun, but his stance, much like the intent in his eyes, was unsteady. I saw him then as a mother might see her own son. He was not a creature breaking into his maturity by the nearness of violence. Not a man at all. He was a child with his shirt buttoned badly and his boots untied.

"How long you been laying for me, Noah?"

"Pardon?"

"How long you been waiting by these coffins, son?"

"Four nights." Had it been four nights since the dinner? It seemed like only a few hours had passed. How long had I slept on my stranger's cot while the town had awoken to my horrors? And why four days to digest my feed? It had never taken as long before. My nourishment had never been so precious and terrible before. I could not think on it. Before me was another child. Would I entangle him as roughly as I had my own?

"Where are your brother and sister? Are they safe?"

"Safe!" he cried. "You didn't keep my parents safe!" His tears shook him so harshly the barrel of the gun began to dip. "Did you *see* what you *did* to them, the pieces you left so mangled and bloody we didn't know what belonged to *who*?" He wiped his eyes with the back of the hand that held the gun. But I had no heart to step to him. "My family's faith demands they be shrouded and in the ground by now. But there they are, in *boxes*, as if on display! I should have sung the *kaddish* over them! But I've been singing it alone for the past three mornings!"

"I'm sorry, Noah. It was never my intention to cause them harm."

"How can you say that, Mrs. Lightfoot!" he said, aiming at me again. "My father taught me there is *no* action without a *clear* intent!"

"It's different with me."

"How!"

"Use that Colt and find out." I was so close to him I could smell the sweet copper scent of his sweat. He hesitated. But I saw no other way to ease my selfish guilt.

"Go on. Get your feet under you and cup your hand under the—" His shot split the night. Taking with it a fair section of my temple and the top of my ear. My vision went black in that eye before sparking suddenly back to light. His eyes went wide as he watched.

"*Dybbuk!*" he screamed in horror. The coolness on my bleeding bone faded to warmth as I felt the wound knit.

"Noah, please. I never would have hurt them if I had a choice. I loved your parents."

"Stay away!"

"Or I would have loved them had I—" My progress toward him was arrested in violent jerks as he shot into my shoulder, chest, and belly. He was still dry-firing the pistol when my hand fell gently upon the hot barrel. I twisted it from his grip and cast it aside. He fell weeping into my arms. How I envied his agony. His tears seared me worse than any one of his shots. I had been a fool to remove my hand from my stranger's chest. He had seduced me after all with his talk of life. I only hoped I would not be too late. Slowly, by degrees, by ragged hiccups, Noah's rage faded. I tilted his face to mine and brushed the running tears away. "Only I can end this," I whispered. "Only *me*, Noah. Won't you let me end this?"

Shots in the dead of night had awoken the town. I gave the boy a quick kiss and sprinted into the dark. Why had I hesitated when my hand had been upon the stranger's chest? A creature like me did not deserve to exist. If guilt and the gallows were my fate, so be it.

I would find my stranger and come upon him with all the wrath I deserved. I would rip his beating heart from his still warm chest and swallow it whole. And when the change came upon me, when I receded back to a thing that could feel the crushing weight of all of its wet transgressions, I would not wait for the jailer or the hangman to speed me toward oblivion. I would perform the justice myself. Douse myself with lamp oil, and answer my mother's last desperate beacon with one of my own.

The door to the stranger's cabin was open when I arrived, swinging eerily on its leather hinges. I smelled death the moment I entered. There had been a struggle. The lamp glass was in pieces on the floor. A crude chair lay on its side. On the bed was a body. He had been crudely opened from the base of his throat to the top of his pelvis. His killer had been a poor surgeon, for I could see the slashes where the knife had failed purchase, the jagged edges of his rib cage, where his chest had finally been cracked by some blunt object. His heart was missing. My mind reeled as I fumbled with the base of the lamp. Once lit, I examined the damage more thoroughly, ending my inspection upon his untouched face. It was not the face of my Boston boy. My handsome stranger. This face was old, with a large hooked nose and lined cheeks that ended in a receding chin. But even without its caul of beguiling glamour, I knew it was him. There was no mistake. And I knew who had taken his heart, for upon the wall above his bed was written, in blood, his killer's jeering challenge: *Your Move, Ducky,* it read. Brown had beat me to it. But why? She matched me in strength, excelled me in cunning. If her desire was my undoing, why had she not tracked me down and carved out *my* heart? The heart of my sire was useless to her without my cooperation. Was she tempting me to perform the grisly surgery upon myself? Or just lording it over me that she had something that made me vulnerable? Was she a monster or just still a bitter matron? What was her game?

*Beguilers can only end one another.*

Unsure of her motive, only one thing was clear. She was daring me to follow her. I felt I had no choice but to oblige her. Smashing the lamp to the floor, I waited until the flaming oil licked the edges of the stained quilt on the bed. Then I ran into the night.

# Stirs The Gravy

# Chapter Thirty-Four

Come sunrise, I had run as far as I could. It was the time of year when the moon didn't set, not even during the day, and there was a fat chalk moon on the horizon, the smoke from my stranger's cabin a faint wisp, polluting the pale light. After running at a predator's speed all night, I stopped to tend to my wounds. My bullet holes had waited to knit until I could dig out the slugs with my fingers. The pain was an unexpected pleasure as I burrowed into my congealed blood to remove them. I realized then that pain could be an anchor of my old life, slowing my drift into the thoughtless waters of the Beguiler. Healing in the warming sun, I had time to assess my lot. My time for mourning must be over, I cautioned myself. My thoughts must now be honed toward a single purpose—finding Brown. But where would she go? Where *could* she go where her beguiling would be most effective? Where were the valleys thickest with remorse? Where were the loved one's mourned, where men had lost everything? California. The western gold fields. Where the sky was darkest now.

The arrow shattered my shoulder blade and pierced the crown of my lung while I was washing off the rind of several days travel in a shallow rapid of what I assumed to be the fork of the Platte and Missouri Rivers. The native boy on the riverbank who had shot the arrow was not brother to his companion, although they called one another brother. They were maternal cousins bound by blood and bad luck into the same clan. They had discussed the wisdom of bringing hurt to a bad spirit the way fifteen-year-old boys would, with boastful whispers and fearful shushing, oblivious to the fact that I could hear their nervous scheming. I had heard them tussling, hard slaps and an even harder push that sent one of them to the ground. The tougher one, the one who had done the pushing, had snatched an arrow from his quiver and notched it into his bow. "Go home to your auntie's tit if you're going to whine like a shit-assed baby," he had said. "You're messing up my aim." I had heard his knuckles rustle against the flight feathers as he caressed the arrow through his fingers.

"But that's a Two Face," the other boy pleaded. "It has eyes in the back of its head, and it will see you and chew your strength like green lodge skin."

The aiming boy had just hissed at him and let his arrow loose. The twang of his bow string had reached my ears at the same instant I felt his arrow sear into my back. I lurched forward slightly at the impact then stood up, dripping wet, my back still to them.

"Hoka-hey!" the boy who had shot me shouted. "I have struck it! Go home, white bitch, and tell your relatives of my perfect aim!"

"What are you talking about? You have angered it," the other boy said as he began turning in circles, mumbling prayers to himself.

"Stop that! That's no demon. It's a stupid white woman pissing in our river." They were speaking Lakota in the Oglala dialect, addressing me in a brazen masculine tense that would have made their mothers hot with shame if I had been anything but a hateful bather.

"Hey, white dog," the one who had shot the arrow said, "if you do not have the good sense to die, at least give back my arrow."

"Stop talking to it! You will anger it further."

"Oh, go bind your balls! That's a good arrow!" I could have listened to the bravado of their bickering all day. But I needed that arrow out of me, and I could not reach it alone.

"Are you in the habit of asking for your arrows back after they fail?" I asked, feeling the exertion of the glottal stops and nasal plosives required when addressing them in their native tongue. They stiffened when I faced them, and I saw for the first time how young they were.

"That is no stupid white woman."

"Why is she not dying?"

"How does she know the People's language?"

"We mean no more harm," the shooter said with considerably less bravado. "Go haunt the Hard Heads up river, and leave us in peace." I lowered my head, peering at them from under my brow, and stood to my full height.

"See? I told you you would anger it."

"Do you know other prayers of protection?" the shooter asked the other nervously.

"Only against owls."

"No good."

"No." As much as I enjoyed watching them squirm, I could feel the deep tissues of my back buck against the flinty tip of the arrow.

"I thought you wanted your arrow back," I said with a frown. "You boys want to help a lady out?" I turned, offering them the shaft sticking out of me. "Or do you want me to start thinking poorly of the mothers that raised you?"

They were both thin as crickets, with broad faces and fierce eyes. But they were well shaped and proportioned. Long legs, broad if shallow chests. I thought they could both be lookers if they packed on a little meat. They stood at the bank, gaping down at me. The one who had shot me had a clump of what looked like dried mud on his head, a flurry of black feathers fanned over his skull like a rustic showgirl. The other was painted with chalky red earth on his arms and legs, black bands circling his biceps, forearms, thighs and shins. Their hair was long, free of plaits, shining in the sunlight. The fan-headed shooter approached me cautiously before he grasped the shaft and tugged. It gave with a release of sour air as it slipped from my lung. They muttered low prayers as they watched the wound knit, one going so far as to poke his finger into the closing wound, only to wrestle it out again as my healing bone nibbled at it.

"I *told* you it was a bad spirit." I was a little woozy from the cold water and slipped on a mossy stone as I tried to clear the bank.

"Seriously, fellas," I croaked. "Help a lady out?"

A real demon would not ask for their aid, and it was a demonstration of their charity to reach out a hand to me. I could feel them shudder as our hands touched. They dropped their grip on me just as soon as I gained footing with them.

"What are we going to do with her?" the shooter asked his cousin.

"Nothing. Leave it. She *stinks*." They pinched their noses with theatrical disgust. But they did it in a pretty novel way. They didn't use their thumb and forefingers the way a white man would. They shoved the knuckles of their first two fingers into their nostrils. That was when I noticed it. The pinkie and ring finger of both their right hands were missing. This was no coincidence. They had not suffered the same misfortune. Those fingers had been cut off, leaving only the thumb, fore and middle fingers, the bow string fingers. These two rude skinny little shits were members of a secret warrior society, I would later learn. And although they had yet to win any war honors, they were still baby brawlers. I wish I had known that before I did what I did next.

"Go back into your bath, white she-dog," the one with the black bands said. "We don't want any trouble from you." They turned like two kids whose stickball game had been a washout and began to walk away. If they were loath to offer me hospitality, perhaps they could give me some information.

"Hey, gents!" I shouted. "You seen another white she-dog skulking around here?" Assuming Brown had beguiled them, I had no idea how further to describe her.

"No," feather top spat. "Just an ugly one with hair like crow wings," he said, referring to me.

"And ugly eyes like rain water," his cousin added. Why was I not beguiling them? Why were they seeing me as I actually was? Could the same be true of Brown if they might see her? This possibility made me interested in their company. Two Beguilers can still beguile one another, can still hide from each other. I didn't know the country. They did. I would need to win their favor if I was to find her. I started toward them. The one with the feather tiara dropped me to the dirt with what looked like a mere blur of his leg.

"Back to your river!" he shouted, pointing. I could feel grit blow into my teeth as I hit the earth. Not a promising start. I was weak from not feeding. I could understand them, but I could not best them. All I needed was a little hot berry punch, and I could school these two full-breed bastards in proper etiquette. I spat and squared my stance. The boys looked intrigued when I raised my fists.

"You want to *fight* she-dog? You want to stir the gravy?" the banded one said, the muscles tensing on his skinny thighs as he readied himself. "Let's go."

They crouched down like wrestlers with open hands. All I needed was first blood, one lucky hit, and I'd be home free. But these two were cagey, eyes alert to my every move. They circled me, peppering high yips back and forth. One would yip, I'd turn only to find the other had advanced. Another yip. I'd startle. One would feint, the other would sweep out a leg and try to trip me. They'd been play fighting like this since they could walk and were masters of the game. A leg darted out, caught my ankle. I stumbled, rolled, righted. Feather top made a leap for my hip. I lunged away as he tucked into a ball, slipping past me, righting back into the shape of a boy. I churned my fists as we circled one another. They regarded this affectation with curiosity. How could one grip with a fist full of one's own fingers? I saw a look flash between them that spoke volumes of strategy. They spread out to the boundaries of my periphery, forcing me to turn my head rapidly, as if at some lethal lawn tennis match. Yip. Yip. Then old black band made his move. He came in low, sprung from his haunches, his fingers and his face flying toward me just as I turned to see him. He never imagined what my tossed elbow could do to his proud nose. It exploded in a burst of red. And that was my cue. I leapt upon him, my mouth capping the flow in the middle of his face as his feet and fists began to rain on me with equal fury. Feather top was stunned. He'd never seen an enemy suck another's nose before. This was unholy. Angered, he whooped as he had been taught to do if he should ever be so lucky to honor his people with the shedding of his own pulp. He drew his knife. I saw it flash at the edge of my eye. Then I felt it sear into my back, stopping as it nicked my ribs. I howled. My power surged. I swung wildly, my hand lashing out in a furious backhand that caught the knife-wielding brave on the cheek that dropped him to the ground. A spray of red spittle misted my vision as my screams kept coming. The brave with the bloody nose gripped his face and rolled away from me as I flailed around, desperate to remove the blade from my back. I threw out a flurry of ragged pantomime all of which should have been obvious as to its meaning. Or so I thought. But the brave with the bloody nose just stared. "Git this fuckin' knife *outta* me, son, 'fore I tear your head off!" I shouted in English. My meaning would have been clear in any language, and he reached his hand slowly behind me, almost a waltzer's embrace, and gripped the handle of his knife and pulled. It stayed fast. I howled and threw myself on top of him. When I rolled free of him, the knife was in his grip. I didn't want to kill them. I was damned impressed by their paste. Feather-top was coming around; the bloody boy helped the woozy one to his feet. The woozy one ran a hand through the rumpled feathers on his head. One was crushed, and I heard him suck his teeth in disappointment before plucking it out. I could have broken his jaw. But that wasn't problematic. His bent little black feather, that was what put a crimp in his afternoon. Then they both crouched on their haunches, working wedges into their tribal cosmologies that would make room for my mysterious resilience. They began to speak below ear shot, in the wowed tones of boys who had just gotten past a bouncer at a gaming house. They floated a few ideas, shot them down either themselves or from the quick reaction of the other. All the while their sparkling black eyes were on me, assessing, heads nodding.

Finally, the banded one stood up. "Okay, white dog," he said, "we have decided. This other she-dog you seek, she is like you?"

"She is," I said.

"My cousin says he has seen this other dog-woman traveling toward the People's summer camp a few twilights ago. You have power because you refuse to die. This is unusual in white dogs, so it is of use to us. But if you swallow your fingers in your hand again and try to strike us, we will put our knife *back* into you and hang you from the tree at the center of the world and leave you there to howl in torment until not even the pity of Wakan Tanka will free you." He said all this on a single focused breath, his young eyes burning into mine without a trace of fear. Then he turned and jerked his head to the setting sun. I would be allowed to follow them.

# Chapter Thirty-Five

The clan of the Drunken Bear, the extended family to which these two boys belonged, was at the ass end of the Lakota Nation, the poor relations of a people who themselves had nothing and measured their wealth by what they could consistently give away. The clan's name was less dissipated than it sounds. One can be drunk with spirit, or birdsong, or flower scent. But neither does it imply favor. Hence, theirs was a predisposition that placed their clan just shy of the wide and ruminative shell of Wakan Tanka's ear. It was a clan of predominantly holy women: seers, healers, spirit talkers, ghost walkers, and *winkdahs*, or sacred people who housed both sexes in their souls. (Hegey would have been revered among them. And the thought of that made me a little misty eyed.) The clan leaders were sisters, the mothers of the two boys respectively, who had both lost their husbands on the same day during a pony-stealing raid against the Hard Heads. Losing one clan chief was problematic. But two in a single night was primo shit luck. And it was a trend that was to continue, no matter what supplications and personal denials the clan made. Run a few hundred buffalo over an embankment, you could bet your balls some brave of warring age was going over too. Try to scrape together a little hair just to save face at the winter camp? Sure as shit two of your best deer stalkers were going to lose more than their scalps. Freak rock slides. Sudden blinding snow storms. Even a herd of stampeding antelope had picked off three family heads at one tumultuous go. By the time I came along, only my two escorts could call themselves warriors among their clan.

Now, men aren't necessary. Except for procreation. And even a full-tilt *winkdah* will oblige seeding an empty womb in a pinch. But the Nation had its traditions, one of these being the great summer gathering where all the clans got together and gossiped and ate and tried to marry off their young women. Blue-balled braves, relieved to look at females they were not somehow related to, played their elk-medicine flutes for all they were worth in hopes of cracking those deer skin skirts after their fathers received horses in exchange for them. But the young men couldn't show up empty-handed. They needed some kind of gift. And here it was late spring, and the Drunken Bears didn't have an extra pony or hunk of hair to spare. That was the plan when they decided to lead me back to their camp. They would help me track Brown if I would be this summer's prize.

A few held their noses as I trotted into camp. But that was about the size of the impact I made. I passed a gaggle of toddlers, some running around naked on short little legs, others asleep or in distress. One child was screaming, his eyes and nose thick with wet. A thing that looked like a comb with a head was tossed to him. It was a skinned trout carcass, its face still staring blankly above the white branches of bone. The child immediately stuck the glistening fish head in his mouth. Fish eyes were the closest they came to candy. I was led up to a central lodge where the banded brave stopped and pushed me to my knees.

"Auntie," he called, "we have found a good gift to bring to the summer gathering. An unusual white woman of power." A handsome but stern-looking woman appeared at the lodge flap. She was short, like most of the women, wide-hipped in a golden deerskin dress that smelled faintly of cook smoke. Her face was round and dark as a chestnut moon, with a crease between her eyes so deep it could reach out and hold you viselike, between the brow folds.

"This *it*?" she asked angrily, looking fleetingly down at me. "This thing is our summer gift?" She sucked her teeth disapprovingly.

"But Shouting Bull, she is one that can refuse to die," he said earnestly.

"Bah! She is a dusty white woman in a men's clothes. Why do you bring such filth here? Where are the ponies you said you'd steal?"

"She has power. She cannot be hurt when she stirs the gravy. I have seen it."

"A white woman isn't worth a raccoon's pecker."

"But she can really stir the gravy, Auntie," Black Band said.

"You fought her, this *thing*?"

"She made the blood run out of my nose," Feather Head said, tilting his head back to display his crusty nostrils.

She shot a look over to me. "Is this true, Gravy?" I was so stunned by her ire I could only stare mutely back.

"Answer her!" Feather Head said, elbowing me in the ribs.

"She speaks the People's language," his cousin added. Shouting Bull looked at me expectantly.

"It is true," I said quietly, terrified I might flub the feminine tenses as I spoke to her. "I did not mean to harm them. And they showed only honor when they fought me. They have promised to help me find one I seek. And I have agreed to help them any way I can." If she was impressed by my lexical prowess, she did not show it.

"If you can teach her to steal horses, she can stay," she said sternly. "But wash her first. She stinks." She eyed me again, sucking her teeth. "You've brought water to the river, nephew. The last thing this clan needs is another belly to fill."

Their camp was set up on the northwestern bend of the river where they had found me. When I reached its bank, the banded boy pushed me in. I sputtered to the surface, only to find Feather Head laughing. They made mock stern scrubbing motions at me. I splashed the cold water on my face and hair, rubbing as briskly as I could, when I was hit in the head with a chunk of some waxy substance. I looked up to the bank to see a tall figure who had joined the boys. I cleared my eyes of water and got my first look at Comes At Dawn. The person looking down at me was not a he or a she. With laughing brown eyes, a hard, narrow jaw, and tied, painted hair that shined with bear grease, I knew that this person was different, special. Both sexes roomed in that soul. A *winkdah.* In a pristine dress of brain-tanned deer hide decorated with elk teeth, Comes At Dawn pointed to the bobbing brick that hit me and smiled, baring teeth that were nearly all black. Making a vague rubbing motion with raised shoulders Comes At Dawn looked as one might when finding the cuteness of something almost too much to bear. I took the chunk in my hands. It was slick in the water. I sniffed it. It smelled strongly of sage and rosemary, with a faint kick of barbecue. It didn't lather much but it felt good on my skin. Comes at Dawn whispered something to the boys then smiled at me before gliding away on the soft soles of ankle high moccasins.

"That's right, Gravy," the banded boy called out, laughing. "Get all that stink off of you."

"Hey," I shouted back. "What do I call the two of you? Doodle one and two will get mighty confusing."

Names are not mere baggage to the People. They're more like porters, beginning as one thing at birth but then changing, helping to carry the ripening gist of a person as they are formed by individual deeds. The brave with the black bands was known as He Alone They Sing Over, whom I came to know merely as Sing. And the cousin with the feather crown was called Stares The Night. The real nuance there was stares *down* the night, the implication being his countenance was so formidable even the night was subject to his unblinking intimidation. But that's not how the rest of his band understood it. His name could also suggest a fairly pronounced paranoia, like when he was only seven and thought he'd heard enemy moccasins in the night and had stayed up till dawn staring, weak and bleary, at an empty horizon and six perfectly safe ponies. Sing's name came from a chanting cure that had relieved him of a severe fever when he was still an infant and so his moniker, like his cousin's, was just itching for an exciting and less lullaby-like enhancement. My name had stuck, this Stirs The Gravy business. After Shouting Bull had referred to me as such, there was nothing I could do about it. Stirring the gravy was the People's slang for bloody infighting. Once the arrows and lances fail, the next level of offense is to engage the enemy by hand—clubs, knives, bodies. It sounds like a fairly rugged appellation until you realize the cleverness of planting it on a woman. Then the domestic angle rears up, and the name devolves into a pretty corny in-joke. Names were like that among the People. You could earn one, cleanly, proudly, consciously. Or you could just step into one, like I did.

My early days among the People were soft and precious like the burnished gold from my girlhood. Untarnished by my mother's lessons or her rude dinner bell, they ambled into green forests where the deer stood still as sentinels or rippled into creeks where the trout hovered as speckled shadows in the bracing cold. The boys and I avoided the open grass where the real herds of horned bounty grazed. We had no horses, so had no real wealth, and the vast plains were closed to us. I learned the most about my new hosts when I fed on them at night. I'd duck through the flaps of my boys' lodge, into the smoky dark where their hearth fires burned low, and watch them sleep. Standing next to them, as silent as death, I'd flavor their dreams with flute song or brave exploits before I'd sink to my knees and sip from them. I was gentle and sparing with my feeding and had to visit many lodges to stay useful to them. Women curled in pairs, a babe on a pap between them. I never touched the children. I'd only breathe deep the sweet milk from a babes's sleeping lips, the grass on the soles of its mother's feet, and I learned about the arc of their day as I drank from only their mothers. After I was sated I just lay there, taking in their rich surroundings. How well did they tan hides or butcher? Were they skilled at sewing, quilling, and gossiping? All was clear in the things they made. The most informative of these were the winter counts, deer hides covered in pictographs that documented the events of an entire year. It was from these, from various lodges, that I learned of the band's chronic hardships. There was only one lodge into which I had yet to venture, the lodge of the person in the dress who had thrown me my first chunk of rough soap, Comes At Dawn.

When I finally mustered the courage to venture into it one late spring night, I found the lodge a gallery of dangling curiosities, a native doppelgänger of Hegey's emporium. From the ribs of the teepee hung every kind of drying herb imaginable, all tethered in tight bundles. There were parfleches for holding dried meat strewn about the place, the geometric designs on the rawhide polychromed in soft pinks and ochres. Combed buffalo robes lined the floor, and in the center of Dawn's lodge, just now beginning to simmer, was what looked like a pale leather pouch suspended from its circular lip by a small scaffold of stripped sticks. I could see a tracery of fine, deflated veins on the belly of the pouch, a desiccated reminder of its original use as a buffalo's bladder before it became a cooking pot. Dawn slept beneath a buffalo robe, neat braids laid out on top of the hide. Upon this robe were drawings similar to those of the winter counts I'd seen. Dawn's draftsmanship was prodigious. I recognized Sing from his black bands, Stares The Night from his fan of feathers, both boys painted blue, dots running from their eyes as they sat over two bundled bodies that shrouded their two recently dead fathers. Skimming over several other figures, I noticed a rendering of myself, waist deep in the concentric circles that represented the river where the boys had found me. Black squiggles for my hair, red bull's-eyes on pie tins for my naked breasts. Behind the river was a jagged rendering of a ridge I had not noticed when I was in the water. It was beautifully done, treeless, with gray and purple shading giving depth to the small ravines. And upon the ridge, in a crude but still fluid attitude of running was a squat figure with what looked like buckle boots on its feet. In one hand it held what looked like a valise. But its most discernible feature was its flaming red hair. A sudden chill rattled me as I recognized Brown. I placed my tongue on Dawn's throat. The *winkdah* tasted as clean as I'd hoped, but I could hardly focus on my meal as the image of the running figure kept wavering behind my eyes. Was it possible? Had Brown really been there the day I was shot with the arrow? The People did not measure time as I did, so when had her appearance been recorded? Was it a month before my coming? Or did the drawing depict something that had yet to occur? I was roused from my reverie by the pinch of a thumb and forefinger on my tongue.

"There you are," Comes At Dawn said, blinking awake. "I was wondering when you'd get around to me." Releasing my tongue, Dawn felt the spot where I had been feeding, and the flap of skin sealed beneath the *winkdah's* touch. "I've been waiting for you for a long time, Gravy. Or should I call you Em-*ma,*" Dawn said, grinning. "What did you see? When you tasted me. What did you see in your mind?"

"How did you know—"

"Never mind. What did you see?" I sat back on my haunches, blinking. What had I seen? Dawn stared at me calmly, waiting for me to speak.

"Stars," I said finally. "I saw a night sky filled with stars. But no horizon. It was as if I was drifting in an ocean of stars."

"A great water of stars, yes," Dawn said, smiling. "I often dream of stars." I was confused. The Beguiler did not show one's dreams. It showed where one had *been*. I was about to ask about this when Dawn changed the subject. "But tell me, Gravy. You have no knife on the tip of your tongue. How do you do it?"

"I really don't know," I said. "It's kind of a new development. When I first became like I am, it was—"

"Messy, yes." Dawn sat up, yawned, then crouched at the simmering buffalo bladder and used a pair of bone tongs to place a hot rock into it. "I swear I'd give a testicle for one of your people's iron cooking pots. Takes forever to get these things to boil." A few more glowing rocks from the fire were stirred into the bladder. "I must say, I am grateful you feed like a mosquito spirit," Dawn said, frowning. "Getting blood off this buffalo robe would have been a real chore." I was reminded so much of Hegey at that moment I almost kissed Dawn. I drew near the fire. "You've already eaten," Dawn said, still stirring. "Will you find me rude if I have my breakfast now?" I shook my head. Dawn speared a chunk of meat with a beaded skewer and ate it. "You know what I think, Gravy? I think you are not a spirit at all. I think you are just a white woman. With a sick spirit inside her."

"That drawing on your robe, the one running on the ridge . . ."

"The red demon." Dawn winked.

"When . . . *why* did you draw that?"

"Some things I see. And then I draw them. Some things I draw. And then I see them." I watched as Dawn's tongue ferreted out a ribbon of meat, then waited as the meat was pulverized by the rapid chewing of black front teeth. "You, for instance. I drew you before I saw you."

"But that figure . . ."

"Tell me why she is important, Gravy. This red-haired woman." Dawn listened through my whole story, offering no more than a few grunts and the odd nod. When I was finished, the *winkdah* sat back. "Do you wonder why you cannot charm us like you do the whites? Why we can see you as you are? It is because one can only believe a lie when one is afraid, and we are not afraid. We are made round by Wakan Tanka, and fear cannot come into a circle. But one day we will be afraid. After you take all our buffalo just for their skins and tongues, the circle will form tiny edges. When you take all the good earth for yourselves and leave us the badlands, those edges will get sharper. When you lie to us and gives us bad blankets full of fever and bad water boiled down till it stings, the edges will be almost complete. Then you might charm us. But never all of us, the Nation's hoop will be buried. It may even be lost for a time. But it will never be broken."

"Knowing that doesn't make you angry?"

"It is the way of things. As long as the roots are not severed, the tree at the center of the world will blossom again.

"You, too, are filled with a lie you did not choose," Dawn continued. "So you are afraid. You get your power from stealing, as do all who profit from lies. But this is also the way of things. You think you want to rub out this red-haired woman because there is justice in it. This is a lie. You want what she carries. You think if you consume it you will be as you were. This is another lie, but you will still believe it. What happened to your baby, how it faded into you like water on earth, this I think has given you most of your power. Often such pain will give one power. But I do not approve of it. It is too difficult for the mother." Dawn stared at me, then leaned forward and brushed at the tears now streaming from my eyes. "Remember, Gravy. Many women have lost many babies. More than there are stars in the night. But few have gained power from it. I would not be in such a hurry to lose this power you have so painfully earned. Also, I do not approve of the eating of human hearts. But I am not a white person."

# Chapter Thirty-Six

I left Dawn's lodge well after the break of morning, my head swimming with all I had been told. Yes, the *winkdah* had informed me, I would meet this red demon near the summer camp. But I would meet something much more important first. My quest would be expensive in the lives of others both loved and not loved. But if I was still in a hurry to open the gates to all the misery before me, I first had to help bring the boys wealth, something that would insure them honor at the gathering. This, they said, would not be easy. Stealing an enemy's horses never is.

I decided I would try my first horse raid alone, but I didn't know where to begin. The boys might be hurt by my not including them, but I couldn't risk their safety or them crabbing me. I figured, like the People, the enemies of the People would pitch near the water. And I had miles and miles of flowing river to follow. So I headed south. I could make better time at night. The night's heart was soft for the predator. Colors narrowed. Scents demured. I was fleet during those hours, dusk until dawn, flying through shallow creek beds that flashed like quicksilver when broken in the moonlight, over black rocks and gray grass, my pupils wide as twin stove pipes, my nostrils sucking up the vaporous ramblings of hundreds of now dead or sleeping creatures. The wolves howled their strangled variations from blinds of cloaked trees. I travelled for two nights like that.

On the third day: spoor. Human. Quarter mile down stream. Head up. *Yes. There it is.* The savory scent of people. Three, maybe a fourth. Not People. Enemies.

I came upon them at a sandy bend of a river, keeping my cover behind a few smooth boulders. They wore their hair shaved at the sides, dyed deer tail roaches laced into the little tufts that ran from the crown to the napes or their necks. Hard Heads. I recognized them from the memories of the boys when I had fed. They were powerfully built and scarred, coup stripes running like a gunslinger's notches around every inch of their tensely muscled real estate. They were chewing hanks of pemmican, speaking the only way natives speak when returning or heading out on a raid: with gestures. This was good luck. Sign language was universal among natives. What were they saying?

*Hobble pretty one.*

*Leave rest until nightfall.*

*Here tonight?*

*No.*

*Ride tonight. Rest now.*

Hobble? Ride? I'd be damned if those boys didn't have ponies. And they weren't waiting around to get them home. A little nap and they'd be off. I snuck upwind of them, away from the river. I could smell them now, the horses, a dozen, maybe more, tossing and snorting behind a corral of greenbreak. This was my chance. Wait for the braves to knock off and then make my move. Only there was a problem. Natives don't sleep during the day, not while on the game. They ease up on the reins, slow to a trot. But they stay as alert as blind sailors in a whorehouse. And those three days at top speed had drained my gut. I needed a good feed.

They lay like dead men on the ground, arms crossed over their chests, faces stiff under closed eyes. I needed to separate them. Get one alone and get him done. Then the other two would be easy. If they had been white soldiers, I might have been able to snap a twig, show a little tit, and get close enough for the kill. But not these boys. They'd taken vows before this raid, had purified themselves in stifling sweat lodges, scourged themselves with sage branches, emptied their minds of every impure thought they'd ever had or hoped to have. That's how they knew they could not fail. They were afraid of only one thing. A poor death. But I had fed enough on the People to know that their fears were as universal as their sign language.

Only one thing would rile them up. The daylight hoot of an owl. A sunlit hoot meant death was on his way. My boys had taught me that. If I could produce such a hoot, I might set them on edge enough to have a real shot at them. I knew my performance had to be perfect. These men had logged enough time in the forest to know the real thing when they heard it, and no self-respecting harbinger of a shitty undoing would hoot from five feet six inches off the ground. I needed more height. I saw a copse of prairie pine not far from where I was standing. Only problem was, scrub pines drop needles year round. Needles made a natural cushion, would dampen the sound of even a heavy footstep. But not when dry and not when they were reporting back to native cochleae set like hair triggers for the slightest seismic disturbance. I had to *float*. I had to *hover*. If I was going to pull this off, I had to make like the Lord and pray those needles would be as forgiving as water.

Toe, ball.

Slowly bend the arch.

Heel.

Repeat.

Like my tits were full of nitro.

By the time I finally made it to the base of the trees, the sun was already becoming amber. I wrapped my arms around the first trunk I found. My childhood crush came flooding back. I tensed my arms, felt my bulk shift upward, legs wrapped around the hard trunk. The old language. Up. And up some more. Oh, the rough embrace of bark. How long had it been? Up. *There it is.*

*Nice little flurry with that last effort.* Why had I ever left the trees? Such reliable husbands.

Window-pane eyes on my heated skin.

White hair tousled on a crude pillow.

Eben.

*Shit. Don't think of him now!*

*You'll fall.*

I willed my mind numb. My balance stuck.

I could see the ponies from up there. All paints. Tan and browns, a few spotted grays. Pretty as windup toys. The braves were hidden by the bushes. But I knew they were there. Ears cocked for the avian death-lie I would feed them. I gripped hard with my knees and cupped my hands; my lips embraced the opening between my thumbs. *Think of an owl's thin windpipe, how short a journey, how little the distance.* Just a breath. A whisper. One tone. Then the lower third. I blew into my cupped hands.

*Ooo*-eee.

Not bad. Again for good luck.

*Ooo*-eee.

Now, wait. The ponies rustled. One of the men was roused. Then another. Enemy hands slashed the air with frightened signs.

*Owl.*

*Day.*

Bad *pejúta.*

*Was it a trick? Check it out,* one gestured.

The elected man approaches my exact tree in seconds. After two weak hoots, his powers of triangulation are that deft. Jesus. It is almost a shame to have to splatter equipment as good as his. I wait until he moves just beneath me. I look down and see the glittering tines of his red-dyed roach rippling slightly with each breath. I drop, landing squarely on his shoulders. He falls with no more than a muffled grunt. I have less than a second to do my job before his buddies will have skull crackers on the downswing. I quickly rifle his belt, finding his knife. He is still struggling when I insert the knife in his throat. My mouth hones in on the red stream. I suck. Colors slam into my eyes. I squint past the memories he offers me, focusing only on the power he gives. Joy and heat and giddy peals of strength coil like carriage springs in my joints. He goes proud, quiet, never throwing fear. I hear a rush of air behind me, the only betrayal of his friends' attack. I toss an elbow blindly and hear bone squeal. I turn. But I don't have time to study the place where his lower jaw once hung. The third one is upon me and lands a wet-sounding smack to my shoulder. My arm sags, the fingers going suddenly numb. I shrug hard, slamming my dislocated arm back into its socket. My adversary's eyes go wide. No terror. No denial. More light. We are fighting in the shade. All his trained eyes need is more light. He howls, ramping up his battle anger. I don't see his second swing. But the Beguiler in me does. I stop his war club in sickening midstroke. My hand leaps from the bloodied ball of his weapon to grip his wrist. He tries to sweep a leg. I sidestep behind him, still holding his wrist, and hear his shoulder snap as he hits the ground. That is the only time he even grunted. I give a hard kick to the base of his skull and was surprised his roach stays attached. That was it. It was over. Seven seconds? An even ten? I waited for my breath to steady as I scanned their fallen bodies for movement. Theirs was the sleep of the just. I blinked a slip of blood from one eye. Then I fell to my knees and fed.

Covered in gore, I was a terror to the corralled ponies. They bucked and reared, kicking one another, spooking by degrees until by chance one kicked at the gate of stacked branches. Pieces of pine flew, the main branches tumbled, and the ponies were free, frantic, pulling short before trees, confused, yearning for an open stretch to *run*. I took off after them, throwing my speeding body at any hoofed and panicked blur I could. I gripped a rough tangle of mane and managed to throw a leg over a small mottled gray. It reared and I was back on the ground. But I didn't need their borrowed speed. I had enough of my own. I raced out ahead of them, chucking turf on all fours, wide open on the plain now, pumping past the blond, whipping mane of the lead stallion by only half a foot. I couldn't get the edge on him. Fear had sent him into a frothing gallop. And so I barreled my weight into him, dropping him in a sinewy tangle of hot hooves and eye whites. The others pulled up short and screamed. They reeled back, feinted, snorted. The lead stallion was back on his feet and reared, his front hooves windmilling so close to my face I smelled the stir of fresh grass in the air. The hooves rained down. I dodged. He reared again, drilling a shrill whinny through his bared teeth. His hooves churned the earth. I veered again, leaping to my feet, and raised my hands to the lead horse, attempting to calm him.

There was a bond, an understanding, between humans and horses that had taken eons to forge. But in my enlivened state I was not part of that bond. I was just another four-legged predator to them. I needed to prove I was still human, that there was still a refrain of trust between us. Closing my eyes, I took a deep breath, summoning whatever anthropomorphic calm I could when the lead stallion slammed into me like a loosed dray wagon. I inhaled a whole face-full of dirt, puked pink soil, rolled, and was back on my feet. *Stay down*, my head sang. *Stay the hell down.* On all fours. They knew men. But they *respected* wolves. I dropped to a crouch, my lips peeling from my teeth, my fingers twisted into angry claws. The fierce roar that tore my throat rattled even me. The lead stallion backed away. It tossed its head and galloped back to the group, kicking its rear hooves behind it. I howled for all I was worth, beating the ground through my flying haunches and my hands in a full-out dog run. The group startled at this frantic thing scurrying before them as I chased around the shying herd in a wide arc, cutting off their escape, beginning to cut them into shape. I narrowed the arc as I saw them begin to bunch. I darted forward. They edged back in mass. I ran around the now grouped herd, paying out little warning growls as I did, solidifying the invisible boundary between us.

Finally, they calmed. A few disgruntled snorts. Then they began to lower their heads and graze. I could hear their barrels blow as their massive hearts began to ease. And I pushed back to the soles of my feet, tuckered to hell. Catching my breath, I walked back to the bodies of the men I'd killed, praying the ponies would stay grouped. Caked in blood, the bodies had begun to pull flies. Their mommas wouldn't recognize them. Perhaps their gods would. I picked up the knife I'd used to bleed the first one. The tip was black with dirt. These boys didn't have much hair to begin with, and I wondered if the People made an exception when they took trophies from this particular tribe. Then it hit me. Those roaches, those dyed deer-tail headdresses they sported, were meant to be *taken*, cocky even in death. I sliced the three roaches free from their heads, stripped them of their belts, and headed back to the herd.

The blond stallion for sure. Maybe that mottled gray. And the multicolored piebald seemed pretty chatty. These three I marked as the leaders. I held up my hands, made kissing noises. I was just another two-legged rider now. I laid a hand on the blond one's velvet, stroked it. I ran my hands all down its lathered neck, past the barrel to the haunch. It tipped up its back hoof to meet my hand as soon as it felt pressure on its knee. There was an agreement here. An equine memory spanning all the way back to the Andalusians of the conquistadores. So I had trophies. I had horses. Now the hard part.

Ponies aren't quarrelsome creatures. Not once they trust you. They ride shotgun in the periphery of men, right along with dogs. Maybe that's why the People's name for horse was *sunkawakan*, which literally translates as "sacred dog." At any rate, I had little trouble getting them moving once I mounted the blond stallion. Show one their leader's rear end and they all move right along in an elephant walk to doomsday. I was maybe ten miles shy of the People's camp when it dawned on me that I'd been nursing this whole parade along at an almost grandmotherly pace. What the hell had I been thinking? These magnificent beasts were built for speed, after all. What good was a long and tangled mane if you couldn't feel it whipping you in the face at a full-throttled gallop? I shot both my heels back hard and shouted, "Haa." He took off like a shot, shattering all limits of Newtonian inertia.

It is a poor magic that reveals its magnificence too soon, what was once *one* thing then suddenly another, with no build, no snare, no showmanship. But that was the crude wonder of my gallop—to be rolling leisurely atop a horse's shifting gait and then suddenly jarred into blur, filled in an instant with a chorus of bad weather. The Beguiler shouted its good news then: reckless joy was the only profundity worth getting up for! It was the old Epicurean yarn my mother cautioned me against. But that didn't stop me from thinking my speed wasn't big enough, wasn't grand enough. Any mammal worth its incisors would have known not to make like some high-speed Lady Godiva and let go of the mane and stretch out her arms and tilt back her head. But not me. Once my stallion felt me let go of its mane, our connection was broken, and my horse stopped abruptly. And *whoops*, there I went, ass over tits, tumbling in the air to land in a blistering bone-shrieking, turf-feeding tumble. I felt all twelve of half my ribs spear the closest organs on impact. Several cartilage-paved sockets shattered like dropped teacups. Bowels compressed, then burst. Gobbets of my own shit geysered my face. The squeeze box of my cervical spine wheezed out a final dirge for the lost use of my lower extremities, and I'm pretty sure my pelvis and nose were shattered. The horses pulled up short, only mildly irritated the fun was over. I didn't know how much of me was functional, ambulatory, or just ready for the fertilizer heap. I *did* know every inch of me sang with a hot finale of pain. Flopped there in a heap of splintered bone and blood, looking up at that ever changing bowl of sky, I did the only reasonable thing I could. I laughed. My shoulder bones knitted with a pinch, the heads of my upper arms reinserting into the sockets with a feeling like branding irons jammed into my armpits.

*Ahhhhhhaaahahah!*

Hilarious.

All of me began to roil and burp and realign and shimmy. Suddenly, my whole body was a whiskey circle worth of pains all trying to outdo one another over a barrel of hundred proof hurt. When it quieted down to a mild agony, I did a quick inventory. I was all there. Getting up was another matter. I took a breath and spat out the blood that had pooled in my mouth, before planting my palms and feet on the grass. I pushed my ass into the air like a newborn foal until I was balanced on my legs. My blond stallion nuzzled me with his wet velvet, and I took the hint. No time to be a quitter. I hooked one leg over his back and hauled myself astride him. The world did look richer, clearer, fresher, a little slower. Blondie reared, whinnied, wanted to keep hauling. No, I told him. I reckoned we'd walk a spell. The sun was short on the horizon, just a few fingers from setting when I held my hand up to it. How would the boys take the new found wealth I had brought them? Would they be grateful? Or resentful? A young man's pride is as touchy as a house-proud spinster. The slightest thing out of place could send them reeling. Maybe I should not tell them I had stolen them. Maybe I should just leave them someplace where they could find them. But where was the honor in merely finding one's bounty? They were not prospectors or bank managers. The honor was stolen, and I had no idea how I could give it back.

We were there.

This was the camp.

Where the camp should've been. Only it wasn't. Yep. That was the sound the river made. That's the bend in the bank I remembered. But the place was deserted, a carnival site after a marshal's citation. I saw the divots left in the turf from the lodge poles, the burnt rocks in rings around black piles of cold ash. Footprints of all sorts. And a few hanks of dyed deer tail. Roaches.

Enemy roaches.

*Shit on me.* While I was out gallivanting, the camp had been attacked. I didn't need the keen eyes of the Beguiler to decipher the recent carnage. At the western rim of the camp, someone had stacked the bodies. But what had happened? I closed my eyes and heard with the sharp ears of the Beguiler the events of the past few hours. Ghost cries of the first enemy sighting, eaten up by the whoops of war. The children screaming, the mother's defending arms cracking under the enemies' blows. The chaos. The scattering, the skirmishes, a hundred heat trails of horror and silence. I couldn't believe what I sensed. Who the hell would butcher a camp of old women and widows and two brave young boys?

"They weren't butchered, Gravy." Comes At Dawn was ragged but still looked regal, emerging from the smoke of the *winkdah's* lodge. "They were taken in atonement." When? How had those roach-headed bastards telegraphed what I had done so quickly? I'd left none alive. Comes At Dawn looked over with no joy at my stolen ponies now nibbling at the blood soaked grass. "You were supposed to steal the enemy's *thunder.* Not slaughter the riders." Dawn slapped the roaches and belts I offered to the ground.

"You think they would have handed over those ponies with a few harsh words?" I said.

"What honor is there in stealing from those that cannot defend themselves against a creature like you? Because you are stronger and faster, your responsibility is heavier." Spoken as if I were a just a brainless bully with much of myself yet to travel. "I'd hoped since you knew our language and many of our customs you would understand that as well." Dawn began to shuffle rhythmically, chanting softly with the movement.

"But women and children," I said, clearing my throat. "How could they do such a thing?"

Dawn stopped suddenly and turned to me with a ferocious look. "They couldn't! When I was young, no person of *any* Nation could have done such a thing! When I was young, you stole your enemies honor by touching them with the coup stick, not stealing their lives! Now our young men are bewitched by the white man's power, their bigger horses and louder guns, and they begin to forget who they are!"

"But how?" I wanted to know "How could they have attacked so fast?"

"How? *How?* Always *how* with you, white woman." It was Dawn's worst insult. And it stung. The *winkdah* tossed something at my feet. It landed with a slight flutter. My mother's letter, wet now, singed from before. But still whole.

"I hope there is wisdom in those talking leaves. Because my words to you are like mist on rock." Dawn turned away.

"Was everyone . . . *lost*?"

"Lost? No. All will find their way home on the good red road. But other than me, only Sing and Stares The Night are alive."

"What will they do now?"

"The only thing they can. Finish what you started. Ride against the men who did this."

"And die a glorious death? There're only two of them."

"Allow them at least *that* bit of happiness."

"But it's my cock-up. Let *me* fix it."

Dawn's smile was humorless.

"Oh, Gravy," they said, softening. "How can your people be masters of *anything*? You're like young turkeys in a rain storm, mouths open for more and still more until you drown. I will tell the boys the ponies were a gift from the Spirit. Now go and find another horizon." Comes At Dawn turned and began to walk to the banks of the river.

Following like a puppy, I said, "I want to *help*. I still want to—"

Dawn turned to me and said, "I sometimes wonder what it would be like to play my flute with the wind I pass through my bottom. But I know such noises would never be confused with music."

# Chapter Thirty-Seven

If there had been more of us, we would have built scaffolds and buried the bodies from the camp in the sky; they had been brave and fought like warriors and deserved such an honor. But in the end, there were too many of them. Dawn sewed Shouting Bull and her sister in a single buffalo-skin robe and buried them near the others while Sings and Stares The Night sang death songs for four solid days. On the last day, the boy's voices were as thin as blades of grass, whispering out their sorrow as they dragged more bodies to their final grave.

The political philosophy of the "consent of the governed," enshrined as it may be in our Constitution, is far more evident in the affairs of the People. If the People grow weary of their chief, they can simply remove him from stewardship by laughing at him. If a wife grows weary of her husband, she can simply divorce him by removing his effects from her lodge. And if a holy person and his two young wards deem the actions of an over zealous, blood-guzzling white dog like me too stridently ignorant, they can simply banish her by resolutely denying her presence. I might have helped dig the graves, but my efforts were the actions of my disembodied hands. Neither Sings or Stares The Night would even acknowledge me as I toiled beside them. Shamed in my abandonment, I finally repaired myself to a clandestine vantage point from where I spent my hours tending to the horses that Dawn had made me hide until the "Spirit" deemed it the right time to reveal them. The horses might have been ill-gotten, the unwitting impetus of a suicidal blood feud, but they were still money in the People's bank. When the time of mourning was over, Comes At Dawn led the boys to where I had left the ponies. Stares The Night bonded with my blond stallion, sticking wild radishes in its lips. Sing fancied the mottled gray. I had to watch them on my belly, hidden in the tall grass, tamping down my shame and hurt and longing to be with them with every breath. My guess was they were going to ride out the next day and start tracking their attackers in the morning, when the dew refreshed the scent. Dawn helped the boys construct a squat, dome-shaped enclosure of willow branches covered in buffalo hide that would serve as a kind of purification chamber, a sweat lodge, where the boys would spend the evening cleansing their souls for the "good death" that surely awaited them. While the boys were thus occupied, Comes At Dawn, whose deft fingers up to that point had only fashioned the latest in indigenous couture, made arrows, running the shafts of fresh willow reeds through a hole drilled in a small hard rock. Holding the shafts over the fire, Dawn waited to hear a faint hiss from the warming sap of the reed, then pulled the shaft though the stone. Then back over the fire. Over and over until the shaft was as hard and dry and straight as my path to hell.

I may have denied them the honor of stealing their own ponies, but it was clear, to me at least, that I still owed them. I could not simply seek "another horizon," as Dawn had instructed me. I needed to get back into their fight. And I thought I knew the way to do it. One could never fully pass as one of the People unless you were born to their ways, but I was too full of what I thought was my indispensable physical prowess to allow that fact to influence me. The People could speak to animals, could hear the spirits of animals. Perhaps there was a way I could get them to listen to me.

I prowled the darkness outside the glow of their fire for hours, looking for some suitable skin in which to cloak myself. But all I could come up with was a medium sized coyote. The few hot sips of blood I took from the animal refreshed like only a dipper-full of water. I managed to skin the thing and wiggle the wet pelt over my head and shoulders like a kind of fanged and furred cape. But it was like sticking a pachyderm into a pair of lacy drawers. And as it was warm night, the sticky pelt was already beginning to shrink as I walked back to the perimeter of their camp. I could feel the stinking rawhide squeezing my skull and shoulders, forcing me into the shape of a question mark, riding up awfully as it compressed the tops of my thighs, cutting off circulation, making walking about as easy as a geisha running a footrace. I knew those boys knew the difference between a wolf (brother) and a coyote (joker). I knew that, if they got a good look at me, all they'd see was a crooked trickster. I figured I'd do better in the shadows, away from the direct light of their fire. In silhouette I could just be a little wolf, a little wolf bent as a busted horseshoe with aching tits.

I waited until they settled for the night. Needing to get their attention, I tilted my head back as far as I could. I placed my hands around my mouth to amplify the sound. And I hooted. *Shit.* What the hell was wrong with me? It was that damn shrinking skin suit cutting off my air and raising my voice to a feathered peep. I knew the bit about daylight owls signifying death. But nighttime owls? Maybe that was good news. Wrong. I saw the boys startle awake before they hid their eyes and mumbled prayers. Comes At Dawn remained supine, a slight smile on the *winkdah's* sleeping face. The boys finally lowered their hands and looked around, panic gathering. Owls, *anytime*, obviously only meant one thing. Finally, the boys looked to Comes At Dawn. Afraid to wake them, all their hopes of the morrow's good fight seemed dashed. I couldn't take it.

"*Not* an owl," I stage-whispered sheepishly. "I'm not no owl." If my lame explanation didn't tip them, my pitiful grammar would.

"Who's there?"

They were really on high alert now. I tried a ghostly voice.

"*N-n-not an aahhhh-wwwwuuuulll!*"

I sounded like a touched yodeler. They reached for their bows.

"Is that you, Gravy? Come out and fight!" I tried to howl wolf-like, but with the ever tightening pelt all I could manage was a strangled yelp. They had their bow strings drawn, aiming at me when I looked up at them.

"Guys. *Shit*. Stop! I'm not . . . I wasn't supposed to be an *owl*."

I stood up awkwardly into the light, twisted pretzel-wise by my ridiculous getup, my voice now pinched to an anguished falsetto. They lowered their bows.

"Gravy!"

"Sorry, guys. I jus' . . . *shit*."

Sing frowned. Stares The Night spat. Then I pitched forward, falling spectacularly on my face.

They cut me out of my furred cocoon. Why, I can't imagine. They sat back on their haunches staring at me with blank faces, a native hanging court.

"I see you got the horses," I said.

The boys' faces furrowed with angry disbelief.

"Gravy, I asked you to leave us," Dawn spat, now sitting up.

"*This* is the spirit that gifted the horses?" Sings said.

"Is this true, Comes At Dawn?" Stares The Night wanted to know. If Dawn could have killed me with a look, it would have happened then.

"Don't blame Dawn, boys. This is not Dawn's doing. It is mine. My dishonor." I should have left it at that. But I didn't. "It just seems like a waste, you two going off to your deaths," I said. That opened the floodgates of singed masculine pride.

"*What?*"

"How do you know we will be killed?"

"How *dare* you?"

"How could you . . ." Blah, blah, blah. There I went again. Not knowing when to shut up.

"*Hey!*" I shouted. They were suddenly silent. "I'm terrible at this. Probably best if I just keep my mouth shut and let you two tootle along to whatever you got comin'. But I *can't*."

Sing stood up defiantly. "We are the sons of chiefs!"

"We have vowed our *lives* to protect our People!" said Stares The Night, brandishing his bow.

"Yeah. And neither of you could hit the side of a barn at two paces."

"Shut your white lying mouth," Stares The Night shouted. "I hit you, didn't I?"

"At high noon with my back to you." I hated the way he winced as I said it. "Listen to me, you won't have odds like that against these guys. I just want to make it plain. Clear and simple. You will be facing seasoned braves. They will not be gentle with you." I watched them consider this, their heads jerking right and left like proud roosters. "I've taken your honor, so I owe you my life," I said, softening. "Isn't that how it works?" The two boys' repulsion was countered by a glimmer of pride before Stares The Night suddenly flicked his thumb nail against his front teeth. It was the most dismissive gesture one could make in their world. I let that sting all the way down before I spoke again. "All right. Fair enough," I said as graciously as I could. "Before I go, let me ask you just one simple question. Is your pride really worth risking never seeing the eyes of your unborn children?"

That did it. Honor in defense of the People was deep in their race. But propagation of that race was deeper. It was crooked poker, but I was desperate. They looked at one another. Then at me.

"The horses," Stares The Night mumbled.

"What?" I asked, excited by the turn in the conversation.

"*You* can watch the horses."

If minding the ponies was the best I could do, there it was. At least I was joining a real war party. A warrior knows he can lose a mount in the melee, and instead of losing his advantage, he brings a spare. And who watches over these spares? Usually some peewee still pissing his leggings, seven or eight at the outside, just happy to be part of the team. This was to be my role.

# Chapter Thirty-Eight

The next morning, to honor my low status, they gave me a feather. Not a full-blown trophy like a golden eagle feather. More of a token, a thanks-for-showing-up medal: a floppy prairie chicken feather. They were very specific as to how that feather was to be worn. Earn coup and I can wear my feather how I pleased. But spend the battle sidestepping road apples away from the ruckus, and I had to wear it according to Hoyle. And what was the traditional fashion of said feather? Strapped to one's forehead. Riding out that morning, the two boys were slick as hell, looking finer than town dandies in their body paint and hair pipe chokers and breast plates. I looked like a damn baby quail. Leaving Dawn back at the camp, I trailed behind them, wondering if the tradition was apocryphal, if they were just trying to get back at me for being such an all-fired horse's ass. More than a few times, I caught them looking over their shoulders, snickering at me behind their hands. I just set my jaw and took it on the chin, holding the reins of the spare ponies like I had a grand reason to be there.

We came up on our enemies after only an hour's ride, circling around to make sure we were downwind, and hobbled the ponies behind a copse of scrub oaks. There were seven men, heads shaved clean, roaches flying. They were older than the one's I'd dispatched. Harder, like I expected, with upper bodies that looked like they lifted anvils for fun. Their war clubs were still caked with dried gore. Tresses of hair hung like fringe down the outer seams of their leggings. Scalp trophies. I caught the scent of one of them and recognized it immediately. Shouting Bull.

"There is honor in taking the hair of these dogs," Sing whispered. "Let me have first blood." He mumbled something over his knife.

"*A-ho,*" his young companion nodded firmly.

"When do we go?"

"This afternoon," Stares The Night said. I bit my tongue. A day raid was a bad move. Best wait until suppertime, right before they bunked, then swoop in and stomp. But what was I going to say? I was little shit feather top. I didn't have speaking rights, let alone their ears for any council.

Then we mounted and rode with the ponies about a mile out from their wind. My boys had a lot of prepping to do. They had to dust their bodies with earth, remove all their fancy gear, offer smoking sage leaves to the four directions, and get through about a hymnal's worth of purification songs. It's a common misapprehension that natives fight in their full regalia. They don't. That'd be like a farm wife killing hogs in her wedding dress. You *leave* wearing your best. And hopefully come home wearing it. But the dance? That happened, weather allowing, in just a breechclout and moccasins, hair plaited tightly and twisted on top of the head like an old spinster's bun. Not one of the illustrations in Hegey's history book had got it right. Real native tussles looked more like a mounted version of a naked riot than something you'd pin to a schoolhouse wall.

They were a half hour into their prebattle toilette when the wind changed. They were both so deep in their fluty gratitude they didn't notice the change. But I did. I could smell it. A bad scent on a good breeze. Even the horses began to toss. We'd been spotted and were being flanked.

Ten seconds later, I heard the low grass surrounding us brush the malice of our enemies' approaching bodies.

A second later, I could feel the grass vibrate from each silent footfall. I sussed the barely perceptible complaint of palm sweat pushed over the polished handles of their war clubs. I felt like a geyser about to blow. I had to suck my lips into my face just to stop myself from shouting a warning to my little braves.

Five seconds later, the enemy separated, following seven different trajectories, the farthest traveling fastest, the closest moving more slowly. All conspired to form a circle around us at precisely the same moment.

"You hear that?" Sing asked suddenly.

But it was too late. I felt a wrinkle in the atmosphere, a slight intake of the ambient air.

Then they attacked.

Stares The Night was the first to stand, and he dipped to Sing, guiding him to his feet. They didn't have time for their bows, and their faces showed that first seed of surprise that sprouts into mature terror.

They reached for their knives.

Stares The Night moved forward, knife held like a fiddler's bow, and sidestepped a furious swipe from one of his attackers.

Sing crouched and swung out a foot but was caught by the arms of his foe. Twisted, he spun to the ground and spit pink.

The ponies shifted uneasily. I itched to enter the fray.

Stares The Night was smacked to the ground, his jaw making the wrong sound as he fell.

I winced for him but kept a tight hold on the reins, watching.

The enemy were laughing at them now. These are mere boys, the sneers of their attackers said. Not worth dirtying their weapons for. Sings was kicked sharply in the gut. Stares took a quick foot to the side of his head. The kicks of their enemies began to rain in furious cadence upon them as the boys balled up on the ground.

I couldn't stand it. I sprang.

Eight pounds of pressure. That's all it took to break a man's arm. The same weight as a healthy newborn.

Eight pounds not nursed or coddled but repurposed, directed and slammed onto the honeycomb of living bone. I started with their fighting arms. I attacked them in a cascade of anger, seven separate hits just shy of their shoulders, dealt out in a fanned blur. I heard the heads of their humeri snap. They tossed their weapons into their healthy hands, with no pomp, no pause. The boys were back on their feet, scowling at me.

*I am humiliating them. I am hurting them.*

If I couldn't fight the battle for them, I could take the punishment meant for them. I stepped into the middle of the fray and screamed. The fight to this point had been performed in respectful silence, the only sound the report of thrown and received blows. So the scream had its effect. The enemies paused. I saw they recognized me. I was the one they had heard sung about, the Little Bad Weather, as they called me, that stole their brothers' thunder and hacksawed through a handful of their best. Their weapons were not too good for me. It was like being caught under an open spigot of canon balls. My sternum, kidneys, and clavicles all wailed in a wet, crunching dirge.

"*Now, boys! Get them now!*" I shouted under the shield of my arms.

Had they even heard me? Was my gift of a diversion lost in the licking of their wounds? I rolled as best I could, a fouled gyroscope spinning off into shaky orbit. Then, one of the enemy's eyes went cold as I saw the tip of Sing's knife sink into the man's stomach. Another fell after Stares The Night slammed his blade to the hilt into his throat. Sing threw his knife, and it hit its mark in the back of a third. My diversion had a dividend. *That's* my boys! Odds almost even, I swept out a leg and dropped a fourth enemy right in front of Sing, damn near serving the son of a bitch on silver. After what seemed like ages, Stares The Night leapt on top of him, beating the fallen man's bad arm until he was forced to roll near Sing, who sank consecutive knife jabs into the enemy's chest. Sing, drenched in red, his eyes spiraling high in the galleries of bloodlust, now exhibited his last bit of stupid grace. He charged the enemy, knife gripped tight. He paid no mind to what his foe held in his hand. The force of the enemy's club lifted the boy off his feet, his face a slop of glistening tissues and puked teeth. Sing died before he even hit the ground. The enemy paused for a victory whoop over his first kill. That pause was all I needed. I was the mother bear. The great maternal imperative. I knew who these boys were to me now. I was reduced to a gnashing head on top of four pulverized limbs, but love, yes *love*, trumped all that fancy native culture, all that stultifying masculine bullshit about pride and honor. I flailed my useless legs under Sing's killer and dropped him. My teeth tore into his throat. I lashed out a bad leg and dropped another and sank my face into his shoulder. My enemy dead, I watched while Stares The Night, with a kind of dreamlike nonchalance, stabbed his knife into the belly of the last man standing. Stares The Night tensed his thin arms and opened his enemy, pubes to throat.

It took us a minute to realize it was over. Stares The Night was still alert, jumping to the ready, left, now right. It took me more than a minute to sit up. I was waiting for my fingers to regain their feeling when I saw Sing's fallen body. There was little left of Sing's face. But I recognized his slender chest. Those now still, cricket-thin legs. Stares The Night rubbed his jaw, then made a sudden movement from beneath the mandible, and I heard it snap back into place. His face was bloodied, but he could walk. He could still blink. And he was blinking then. Blinking as he sunk to his knees by the body of his fallen brother. Blinking harder as he slipped his arms beneath Sing's body and lifted all that wet and limp mess to his chest.

In a fairly nice restaurant, a chop house, some place where the grub was actually more expensive than the booze, when I'd left nothing but a little gristle, usually a boy came around and asked if he could take my plate. If he was good at his job, his voice was low, calm, formal. A tone I wouldn't mind more folks using before they took something of mine. That was how Stares The Night queried me.

"May I take your ears?"

He didn't mean my ears. He meant the enemies' ears. He knew he hadn't dropped all seven, but still he was respectful of my efforts.

"Sure, kid. Be my guest."

He sliced them from the periphery of the enemies' dead faces, even the ones I had damaged in my race to lay them down. I was strangely comforted by how he managed to perform this task with such stark elegance. I watched, winded, as he strung them on a strip of leather he had cut from an enemy belt before slipping the wrinkled ears over this head. They smeared splotches of red upon his chest, all fourteen of them. I wondered why the ears. Was it because they were the instrument of our ambush and must be separately vanquished? Dawn would not have approved of laureling oneself with such grisly trophies. The old never approve of modern ways. But I did. The People were never savages. The coming of the whites had made the *times* savage. In future wars, our soldiers might indulge in similar horrors, the fevered ones, the ones who made the change under fire. And the bookish and the privileged will call them savage for it too, never understanding the delicacy of the exchange. The scalps of the Drunken Bear clan still dangled from the dead men's legs, some as soft as down, not yet the true black they would have become. Others were confident in their hue and sheen. Still others were shot with gray. Stares The Night cut them from the leggings of the dead enemies and laid the hair over Sing's body. They would all go home together.

Sing's body, with the hanks of hair, was sewn into a buffalo robe, with songs and a strange kind of fake weeping. The counterfeit nature of the crying was important. The strained formality was what the spirits understood. Then Stares The Night hoisted the bundle over the back of one of our ponies. The last thing he did was make sure all of the faces of the enemy were facing the sky. He took care in this, using the side of his thumb to clear the gore from their closed eyes. He could not speed them home, but he could show them the way. They too had fought bravely. He said nothing to me during all these actions, performing them with a ritual precision. Before we mounted, he bent down and scooped up a handful of soil from the ground that had witnessed so much. He spat in it and then smeared my shoulders with the mud.

"You are ugly, Gravy," he said. "You cannot help this. The Great Mystery creates all things in shapes that reflect their real natures. But you are brave. And you have honored our brother. You should be happy in this." He was somber as a judge when he spoke. He held one of the ponies for me and waited for me to mount it. "Come on," he said over his shoulder as he kicked his horse into a trot. "There is still time to make the summer gathering. Comes At Dawn will be waiting for us."

But I wasn't happy. I knew Sing would still be alive if I had acted earlier. But I had kept my word to Comes At Dawn. Perhaps something deeper than life had been respected. And Stares The Night now had more to share with the other bands of the People than my miserable carcass.

We buried Sing in the sky at the center of the world. An igneous hill somewhere above a shoulder of sweet grass in the vast center of the plains. I walked seven hundred feet to the peak of the hill with a ripe corpse on my back and every ounce of my regret. Stares The Night painted himself blue, broke out the rattles and the feathers, and walked ahead of me, wailing, fake crying, real crying, while the sky thickened above us with clouds that darkened to the color of dirty metal. The scaffolds near the top of the hill were ancient, weathered gray and tempered hard by rain and cold. Rawhide shields painted with the personal heralds of long dead warriors slalomed in the rising wind. Sing would have company. Two bundles were already up there on scaffolds of their own. These bundles resembled people as much as certain clouds do human faces, by general mass, by suggestion. But they were already more mineral than bone. Then Stares The Night took out four long leather bands, holding up each band to one of the four cardinal points until the compass was served. These bands were tied around Sing's throat, shoulders, waist and knees. We placed the body on its scaffold.

"He was He Alone They Sing Over!" Stares The Night shouted, choking, spitting, righting his throat as he cleared it of his own tears. "But You will welcome him as Stands His Ground! Now he is Yours, Great Mystery! *Welcome him!*"

Then we headed back to the horses just as the rain began to come down.

# Chapter Thirty-Nine

The horses slowed by instinct as we came into the huge summer camp. And it was the change in their cadence that made me look up from my bleak thoughts. It was a massive spread: nearly fifty clan circles, each bunked concentrically with its neighbor, forming a huge spiral of tents along the bank of a river. Willow, dogwood, high fragrant grass everywhere. Paradise. More men this time, shirtless, clean and lean, their hair and faces shining from the care taken with them in the hours between hunts. One brave sat wincing while another plucked stray hairs from the first's chin with trade tweezers. Others stepped over the grass, knees high like ponies themselves, pacing our progress as they looked over our small group of horses. They sucked their teeth or nodded their approval. Other's spat or sneered. Some gave me the stink eye, unmistakable even as I rode my horse behind Stares The Night's as was the custom with women. I was audacious, something unspecified but still intolerable. Deer and buffalo skins were staked to the ground, being scraped clean by sullen women with bone scrapers. Two young women were sawing a deer skin over a log, turning the brain-tanned hide into a cloth that would rival the finest velvet. Trade pots boiled; men sat smoking, regarding themselves in trade mirrors while the women labored. And for all the mystery and complicated custom, the bright colors and exotic fierceness, it was all really just a pageantry of housekeeping.

The last lodge at the center of the camp was the largest. Its skin was painted a blue that muddled past a murky green before resolving itself to a dusky yellow as the color descended. All this color was shot through with tongues of jagged black lines, all emanating from flat bottomed clouds. The lines were meant to represent a dark kind of lightning. I'd been taught the language of color among the People, and black was the color of the west, of introspection. And so this lightning had brought more than fire from the sky. It had brought insight, some transformation worthy of public display to the irrepressibly handsome man standing at the opening to this lodge, waiting for us. I was about to meet the chief.

A Lightning That Teaches Cold Meat To Stand was a war chief in a time of forced peace. Tall by the standards of the People, his body was broad and lean and riddled with the scars of his exploits, a spray of healed bullet wounds on his chest—ochre constellations in a russet sky. I recognized an unusual embodiment of the feminine in his features. His brow was heavy but shadowed large, liquid eyes. His nose was narrow above his full lips. He wore his long black hair loose, and it cascaded over his broad shoulders. He stared at me as I approached him. He fanned something long dormant in me. I had perhaps three seconds to luxuriate in the possibilities in his eyes before he aimed a Colt Walker at me and fired four rounds (an auspicious number) into my chest, duly unseating me from the back of my mount. The black powder created a showman-like fog as the hot slugs seared through me. Even in my short decent to the dirt, I was reconciled to the snares of this stranger's beauty. I heard him shuffle to me. Stares The Night had joined him and another man I could not see. The shots had ripped clear through me, and the beautiful man crouched down to my wounds, peering at the large points of daylight that were furiously knitting closed in my chest. He nodded approvingly without a smile as I sat up. A Lightning, as I would come to know the beautiful man, lowered his hand to mine. He pulled me to my feet, pirouetted me front to back, examining the entrance and exit wounds that were testament to his only seeming interest in me, and grunted.

"So the rumors about you are true," he said.

The entire camp suddenly exploded with raucous laughter. The men yipped. The children brayed. The women, covering their mouths with a single hand, let out a furious tremolo. But the sudden communal joy was not for me. It was for my utility. It was the gleeful approbation shown by one farmer to another when he sees his neighbor has brought home a sack of blight resistant seed or a new steel plowhead.

"Come," he said, slapping Stares The Night heartily on the back and pushing me toward the flaps of his lodge. "We must smoke on this new weapon you have brought me, cousin." Stares The Night nodded respectfully and followed us inside.

We were not alone in A Lightning's lodge. It was only after we were seated around the chief's fire, reposed on the hair pipe backrests that surrounded it, that I got a good look at that third person. It was Comes At Dawn, who gave me a polite nod and took a pert toke off the pipe we were all passing. Was this chief the "important thing" Dawn had predicted I would meet all those moons ago?

Stares The Night, stiff as a preacher, started things off by launching into a long-winded oratory about the paucity of his gift, how only a few pitiful horses could be procured for the chief's honor, and even those were of only a middling quality. But A Lightning seemed to take no interest in this sweeping apology. His eyes never left me. Not once until finally, midsentence, A Lightning extended a finger toward my breasts and asked me to show him. I shot a look at Comes At Dawn who formed a hand into the shape of a gun. It was not lust. It was cosmetics. The chief wanted to see how a creature like me healed. I pulled down the neck of my shirt. Two of the four bullet wounds were still visible, faint pink puckers, slightly raised but sealed. A Lightning touched them gently, the tips of his fingers brushing the newly healed skin. Chills ran the length of my body as I struggled to keep a poker face. His face creased slightly into a boy's puzzlement. Then his dark eyes came to mine. I can't be sure what my eyes betrayed at that point, but I sure as shit would not have minded him fondling a little more of me.

"You have any *other* holes?" he asked.

"Just the usual ones," I blurted out. Comes At Dawn glared at me. Stares the Night lowered his head and blushed. It was as if a prairie dog had asked the chief to bed. I lowered my gaze when I saw his expression harden. But he didn't worry the point; he just waved me off and then turned his talk to Comes At Dawn.

"How is this possible?" he said. "She's just a pretty white woman." I lighted on his use of "pretty" and shot a look to Stares The Night. The boy smiled slightly, shaking his head. Had I finally won his respect? Comes At Dawn said nothing but took a turn sucking on the stem of the pipe.

"Has she the power to give this medicine?" the chief wanted to know. Comes At Dawn paled slightly and coughed.

"Hers it not a power appropriate for the People to take for themselves."

"But she is *was'ichu* and yet has the power of spirit. I just saw it. Why would Great Mystery not honor one of the People with this medicine?"

"But He *has,*" Comes At Dawn said foxily, shifting to the formal tense and shooting a brief glance to me.

"She is among us, is she not? Can you say we are lessened because our arms do not end in the muzzles of our rifles? That we are cursed because our legs are not hoofed and fleet as our ponies? These things have been sent to us for our use. Just as she has. We *have* been endowed with the power of spirit. And this particular power I want to give to you. For a white woman, she's not bad looking, as you've seen. I think she may bring you luck." Did Comes At Dawn just give me away? Was I just reduced to some old trade pot? It didn't matter. I was finally at the summer camp, finally that much closer to Brown. A Lightning grunted, then killed the pipe with one long drag.

"She can sleep near the door," he said. The chief and I were not going to glow in an aura of domestic bliss. Even the camp dogs slept closer to the central fire. My status was the equivalent of a flintlock kept over a fireplace. The truth was, A Lightning already had three wives, all sisters, shy as doves and just as lovely, who kept the lodge neat as a pin and his belly full. But even with the contented look on all three of his wives' faces, he was still somehow childless. I hoped that wasn't one of the reasons why he took me. That night while his three other wives slept, he kept me up late, plying me with a barrage of questions.

"*Parlez-vous français?*" he asked me. I was surprised he spoke French. I knew enough from my run-in with the big logger from Lucky's to converse with him. But I told him no. My peculiar condition was strange enough, and I wanted to seem as familiar to him as possible. Reverting back to formal Lakota, he wanted to know everything. He had heard of the Great Water, as he called the sea, and wanted to know if I had come from the other side of it. I told him I had been born here, on the Great Turtle Island, as the People called North America. But my father had come across the sea.

"Was he a North man?" he said. He was referring to the Vikings who had allegedly braved the Atlantic in open long boats centuries ago. There were legends among the Mandan people of full-bloods born with auburn hair and over seven feet tall. "They came here many, many seasons ago and mixed with our cousins from the east. But your hair is not red like theirs." He was remarkably well informed, I thought. Then I chastised myself, as my mother would have, for such a colonizing judgment. I told him that there was a small country across the Great Water that prided itself on its ability to make vessels that could travel to any edge where the sun sank. I told him this place was called England, that my father had come from such a place and had been one of these "gliders on the long waters."

"He lost his power then," A Lightning surmised after I told him of my father's drinking. "He should have never built his lodge on dry land. Missing the Great Water, your father made a vessel of himself and drowned what he had lost with the bottle. I have seen it before among the whites."

Interesting theory, I conceded. But I reckoned Da was just fundamentally weak.

"A weak man could never have had a daughter such as you."

About my mother's suicide, he understood. She was *wakan* and so had decided "to make a house of herself and open all her doors."

He liked the stories of my girlhood, the climbing of trees, hunting with my father, the long walks along the creek. When I came to my change into the Beguiler, which I had to translate as "that which charms as it lies," his only question was about the handsome stranger.

"Do you think, perhaps, that you lay down with a trickster spirit? Maybe Coyote himself? I have heard he can steal the penises of unworthy men and make lonely women give birth to rocks."

I just let that one lie.

As to my madam days at Lucky's, he had no judgment. "Women of power can do as they please," he said as if such a summation was obvious.

But his real fascination was not with my history. It was with me, with what I could do. He had heard the stories of how I had stolen the ponies and made the sound of the day owl and destroyed the enemy. He also knew about our recent revenge raid on the enemy and how I had fought with just my mouth.

"Comes at Dawn says you swallow a person's soul along with the blood you take from them. Is that true? Are you truly a Two Face as Stares The Night once thought you were?"

"I have many faces," I said quietly. He touched my chin and raised my face to his, searching my eyes.

"You have only one face to me, Gravy." I was so struck by this I could not help my eyes from welling up. His brow furrowed for a moment, his eyes curious, before he let my face go and, yawning loudly, burrowed under his buffalo robe.

"You will be precious to me," he said before he closed his eyes in sleep. In his lodge, the air mixed with the sweetness of wood smoke and the slow breathing of his wives, I wondered if I had finally come home. What did he mean by precious? Would I ever feel I was one of them? Or was I destined to be just another useful thing? I closed the lodge flap, buttoning it with the slender lengths of bone reserved for that purpose, and laid my head down on my gamey robe. I cried myself to sleep that night and woke up early the next morning, my cheeks stiff with the dried salt of my tears.

# Chapter Forty

Like the falconer princes of old, I was prized for my unerring talent to bring death. For the next several weeks, A Lightning had me tearing ass around the prairie, bringing down bucks, running down rabbits. We even went for a buffalo hunt, him mounted, me on all fours. I would launch myself at the slower cows, clinging to their necks with my arms and legs, struggling through their densely tangled fur until my teeth found an artery. I'd squeeze my knees together as I bit, twisting my pelvis slightly to guide the animal to the ground. We'd tumble, both us females, elbows and haunches, onto the ground made hard only by our velocity. It was messy, not as graceful as I would have liked. But A Lightning seemed to enjoy the spectacle, and it did save on arrows. It felt good to be seen for who I truly was and be able to do what I truly could without secrecy or shame. But that seemed to be the extent of my joy. If A Lightning even casually returned my fondness for him, he did not show it. Because of that fondness, I starved myself. I couldn't bring myself to feed on him and his wives as they slept. And it was impossible to leave the chief's tent at night as he kept sentries outside after sunset. Buffalo blood came the closest to closing my nutrition gap. Better than rabbit and just a few pegs up from deer, it still was not my libation of choice.

A Lightning was sensitive to my needs, as all good hunters are with their working pets. After I had just brought down a cow and was enjoying a fountain created by the animal's slowing heart, A Lightning waited patiently, his knife idling by his side.

"You're beginning to slow, Gravy," he said with concern. "And your aim was slightly off." I nodded, swallowing the last of my gore. "You have the wrong the food," he said. "Like a dog forced to eat grass when the winter is high. Is this true?"

"Hot berry punch ain't that easy to come by," I said, looking directly at him.

"You drank power from our enemies before you came here. Now we have a truce with them. This is good for the People and bad for you." He looked to the horizon. I could feel him thinking. He came to me and wiped the cow's blood from my lips with his thumb. "This is not a becoming way for a woman such as you to replenish herself. We must do something about that." A woman such as me. How long had it been since a man had honored all of me, had approved and perhaps desired me without the necessary camouflage? I was not looking to be completed by a man. I was looking to be complimented—as night compliments day by their equal yet individual agencies of the hours. The revelation gave me hope. But nothing more.

The raid wasn't going to involve the whole tribe. We weren't going to war; we weren't declaring open season on the white man. We were just trying to get me back to speed. That's why we decided on a small strip of prairie where an overland mail coach made its dash through open territory. The People's territory. It was on the eve of our raid that A Lightning told me about his name. I had taken it upon myself to fashion my hair as practically as possible, loading it with generous scoops of bear grease to manage the curls and then splitting it into two hanks and plaiting these tight enough to shed water. But that night A Lightning asked me to take the braids apart. It was the first time he had asked me to do something that had no practical utility, and I was hopeful if confused as to his intent. I'd been like a favorite pet or weapon to him for so long, I hardly knew what to think.

"I like the ripples in the black when the braids are loosened," he said, touching me with only his eyes. "Like waves on night water. A bit like black lightning."

Unlike me, the language of the People had not come upon him all at once. He was born among another tribe, a woodland clan from the East whose beadwork was round with the shapes of flowers. They were a small band and had fallen to conversion by a group of well-provisioned French Jesuits after a particularly bad winter had left most of his tribe starving. His parents had been killed by Canadian trappers and as a child had been taken to a rustic log church on the banks of the Saint Lawrence River, run by the Jesuits. He refused to speak his real name for fear the whites might steal it, so the priests called him Joseph. They made him wash with lye soap. Fed him cheese. Forced his feet into hard-soled shoes through which he could no longer feel the earth. When they tried to cut his hair, he finally resisted and bloodied the priests' upturned noses. He sat on benches less accommodating than the ground, listening to talk read from a big black book. But this boy, who was not really Joseph, did not believe their stories. He knew the real reason their Jesus had died. They had tied him to the center of two straight lines, and everybody knew all power was in the circle. They tried other Biblical stories on him, all translated for his benefit. There was the one about a chief asked by his god to kill his own son, and when the chief had readied his knife to do it, the god changed his mind at the last minute and told the chief it was a test of his devotion to him. But the boy who was not Joseph just laughed. What a poor god you whites must have he told them. Great Mystery would never show His power like that. Then there was the one about the god who told another chief to build a massive canoe and to fill it with all the animals he could find. A Big Water was coming, and only those in the canoe would survive. But the boy had stopped the priest right there. Had their god really been so foolish as to put the wolves with the rabbits? Did their white god really know so little about the natures of his own creations? The priests were at their wits' end. No catechism or forced prayer drove from the boy's mind what he knew to be true about the world. As beautiful as this native boy was, as naturally confident and intelligent as he was, such excessive pride could only be his undoing. But, as Jesuits, they understood the power of knowledge to convey a point. So the priests had gone outside the Bible, had gone to romantic literature to make the boy appreciate the danger of his pride. I would have loved to have heard the priest's exposition of Mary Shelly's *Frankenstein*. I was pretty sure that was the work to which A Lightning was alluding. How had it sounded to such young ears accustomed already to wonder and miracles? The tale had bored him. Only the lightning was of interest to him. The lightning that had taught the cold meat to stand. That was what the boy remembered. The boy had heard no cautionary tale. He heard what lightning could do. And he knew the priests did not have this power, would *never* have this power. They had tried to make it seem bad. But the boy who was not Joseph knew it was good. Everything in nature, even death, had its purpose. Realizing they had nothing more to teach him, he left. He stole a loaf of bread and headed west. Eventually, he met Comes At Dawn who became Merlin to his Arthur. The rest was still unfolding.

"So hold on," I said after he had finished. "If you understood the story to be about the wonder of nature having more power than the pride of a white man, why didn't you tell the priests that?" A Lightning laughed and looked at my slyly.

"One does not try to teach a dog to speak the language of the People. A dog's nature is to bark or growl or whimper. But still that is enough language for the animal to be a good companion to a man." I smiled at his explanation. He smiled back. A rare occasion, his smiling. Grown warriors believe excessive smiling makes a man look touched and so avoid it in public. But here, in the warm dark of his lodge, I guess he felt free to do as he pleased. He said nothing more. Just stared. But the air between us began to warm, to hum as if strummed by the tiniest thumbs of intent. I could not read his gaze. He had made a career of being unreadable. Was I so beneath him? A fascinating creature but still only of interest as a weapon? Finally, I could take it no longer.

"I know I am ugly to the People."

"Why do you say that?"

"Stares The Night told me on many occasions of my ugliness. I am built backwards. My top is too full and my bottom too light."

"Stares The Night was raised by old women and taught to see as an old woman. You are not of great ugliness."

"Just *passing* ugliness, then?"

He didn't answer. He simply moved toward me and placed a warm hand on my breast. This should have been a shocking liberty on his part. But the thrill that coursed through me that moment confounded my surprise.

"Your top is softer than I supposed. I thought you would be hard here."

"Nope. Pretty damn soft, truth be told."

His hand moved down my belly to the swell of my hip. "Here there is an argument. A softness and a hardness." It was the nicest damn quarrel I was ever party to. "Tell me, Gravy. We have spent many days together. Many times you could have taken my life like a curious child crushes a worm. But you have done everything I have asked you. I have thought about this for many nights."

"And what have you figured out?"

"When a man is the head of his people, women want him because the head must go before all things. But you are the hands and legs and heart as well. So by staying with me, it is not my power you desire. You have enough of your own. You crave something else, perhaps."

"You're getting warm."

"But all that is left is what you see before you." His dark eyes sparkled in the wavering firelight. I smiled. "Curious," he said softly. And it *was* curious for a man in A Lightning's position to be wanted not for what he could provide or protect one from but merely for himself. And the clarity broke. We were alike in that need. We fit then, even though we had yet to say as much. "You see me, I think, like a colt fresh from his mother," he said. In answer, I pulled my shirt over my head. My hair fell freely, parting gracefully away from my breasts. I could smell the heat rise in him. I laid on my back and looked up into his eyes as I draped my arms around his neck. He was brave enough to be dazzled.

The People understand the value of silence. It is said their babies are born into it. So what we made, a slow walk of discovery that was thighs and hips and other places, happened in quiet, in the half-light of a dying fire, throwing shadows larger than our entwined bodies. What was the use of all this time he took? Was it fear? Perhaps at first. But by the time he reached the holy of holies, my whole body was ringing. And I responded in concert with his movements. I was awake. Truly aware. Every breath, every touch, every subtle change in rhythm was augmented with the knowledge that, for the first time, I was loving with no other motive but love. I didn't wait for him to cross the threshold. I pushed. And when we were finally over it we did away with silence.

We awoke in one another's arms, in a darkness that was a rumor of first light. His other wives were already preparing breakfast. Had they heard us in the night? What had they thought? Had they been jealous? Relieved? I would never know.

We had a mail coach to take.

Later that morning, still in his lodge, I raked my fingers through my hair and plaited it tight to my head. He tied his hair in a war knot at the top of his skull. He checked his quiver, the string of his bow. I motioned to his Colt Walker hanging from the lodge poles in a quilled holster. One did not speak before battle. He shook his head no. Then he made sign for spooked, then horse, then the sign that made it a negative. No guns. He didn't want to spook the horses.

# Chapter Forty-One

The sun was just coming up, the cook fires just beginning to smoke. We slipped onto the backs of our horses, his a huge buttermilk roan, mine the little mottled gray Sing had once favored. With muted clicks, we kicked our horses and headed for the open plain. We knew the only route the coach would take, a long, open stretch of grass that skirted the base of the purple foothills, a bit north of our usual hunting grounds. We hobbled the horses, and A Lightning crouched down to read the bend in the grass. It was faint, but he could just make out two continuous indentations swallowed by distance. I pressed my nose to one of the tracks. Iron. A faint tang of horse shit. The coach had been through here all right. The question was, when would another come? I burrowed my fingers into the soil near the tracks. Now came the sorting. The weak vibrations of beetles, of earthworms, all manner of blind and moving things. The cribs of field mice, the tenements of prairie dogs, all these distractions had to be ignored if I was to get an accurate reading. I reached out further with the antenna of my submerged fingers, and now came the tickle in the palate, at the base of the throat, the perfume of larger warm-blooded life somewhere stirring, unaware, but there. A herd of something fleet. Deer? Pronghorn? Further, the bass beats of grazing buffalo. And there at the tip of my reach, tingling just past my feeling, well over the horizon, a low but adamant thunder. Something big approaching, something rolling. How far? Twenty miles? More? At a top ground speed of fifteen miles per, I figured we had a good hour to kill. And kill it we did. We positively murdered that son-of-a-bitch. If you've never made love on the open prairie, in early autumn when the grass is still warm from the morning sun and the air is cool enough to accommodate a good sweat, where wild chamomile winks and birds flutter and dive in a sky as blue and wide as a first cleansing breath; if you've never held your lover as he flows and ebbs above you like the rippling tides of all the waters of the world and you find yourself burrowed deep in a moment so rich and long with happiness you'd think you'd burst, I suggest you drop these words right now and try it. Just stop reading and get yourself a lover and patch of ground, a parcel of sky, get yourself the *day* and do it.

I promise you'll understand the mystery of your birth.

Languishing there in the warm sun afterward, I mused to myself. Why did people complicate life? Life was simple. *Find what you like to do and then do the shit out of it*. What was so all-fired hard about that? I took a quick reading from the ground. The coach was maybe ten minutes away. If I looked hard, I could see its cloud of rouged dust kick up over the horizon. We hopped to our feet, flopped back into our clothes, set our war faces.

*You take shotgun?* he signed.

*If you take the driver.*

*You calm the horses?*

*So long as you can make your way into the coach.*

*Then I guess we're set.*

*I reckon we are.*

Still tingling from your lover's heat and now an exchange like that? Sex and death. Did it get any better than that?

There was no cover. Not out on the open prairie. So we would be in sight when the coach approached. The trick was to pace ourselves slow enough so we would eventually wind up on either side of them. We had no war party, no feathers or paint that would give away our intention. Just a chief and his white demon woman in her men's trousers out for an equestrian jaunt in the early autumn morning in the middle of nowhere. Still intoxicated from our recent intimacy, it never dawned on us we might be targets ourselves.

The first bullet whizzed past my cheek like a hornet on fire. Crack shot, Sharps rifle, I figured. I turned back and saw A Lightning had dipped below his horse's neck, still at a decent run, arrow notched in his bow. I kicked my horse into a dead broke gallop, circled wide, and headed right for the coach. I drew their fire while A Lightning sighted his target. The fat son-of-a-bitch riding shotgun drew a bead on me, a huge dribbling gob of chaw in his gums. His first shot caught me in the neck. A pink mist exploded in my periphery as hot chunks of me took to the wind. A Lightning got off his shot and down went the shooter with a stick in his chest and heaven in his heart. The driver pulled up hard on the reins. He yelled something behind him. The coach began to circle, and as it did, a man in government blues peeked out from beneath the leather curtains and began firing. Colt Army issue, percussion cap. Bastard would only get six shots before the whole confounded tango of reloading, priming, and greasing took him out of the game. He concentrated his fire on A Lightning, sussing rightly that only the native was armed. He got off two shots before A Lightning plunked two arrows into the window mullions, driving the shooter back into the dark of the coach. I could hear feminine screaming coming from the coach, then a man's voice raised patronizingly, convinced it was calming. I paced back, pulling hard on my pony's mane to slow him. I wanted to get a look into that coach. Bad idea. The shooter's bullet hit me square in the chest with enough force to knock me off my seat. I landed hard on stiff legs, a searing pain shooting up my shins. Both ankles were shattered. A Lightning meanwhile had fallen in behind the coach, using its back boot for cover as he launched another few arrows that glanced off the speeding stage. I figured he wasn't trying to hit anything, just keeping the shooter inside until I could get back into the action. I got up on my knees as I dug deep into my chest, wiggling my fingers around for the bullet. I eased past the hard rungs of my ribs, trailing the hot flow of my berry punch until my fingers brushed the ball off my beating heart. The bullet was lodged just shy of the muscle, deep in the left arch of the vena cava. A kill shot if ever there was one. I knew that if I didn't get that slug out, even with my prodigious capacity for recovery, I ran the risk of bleeding out before I could knit. Blood is slippery. Hot blood is as good as axel grease, and it was a fine trick to pinch that slug out of me blind. By the time I'd done it, the coach and my man were a blur on the horizon. I didn't have time to track down my horse. My only option was to four-foot it after them as fast as I could.

By the time I got there, the coach was spilled on its side, the driver dead with three of A Lightning's arrows in a tight grouping in his chest. A Lightning's horse was dead, two shots to the neck, and there was my man, crouched behind his dead mount, his fingers unfurled before his face, counting shots like a schoolkid.

*How many?* I signed as I approached.

*He has one left.*

*You all right?*

*I will miss my horse.*

*Zing!* went the last shot, and up went a red chunk of horse flesh.

*Now or never*, I motioned.

Together we rushed the fallen coach, knives out, blood-spangled and hearts racing. Never could I remember being so in love. I caught the soldier with his grease kit still in his hands. My peeled teeth were so close to his throat I could smell the dank wool of his collar. But something arrested my strike. A sudden icy jolt in my solar plexus. He'd had no opportunity to reach for a blade. And in the brief time when such things are reasoned, I realized it was not the sting of a knife's tip I felt edging its way inside me, up to my heart. It was something dull, something with a pulse of its own, closing slowly around my vulnerable organ. His hand. He had thrust his hand inside my chest. Even the thought of renewing my attack resulted in the slightest constriction of his grip upon my most precarious pump, and I was powerless to move.

"Easy now, me bonny colly," he purred in a dreadfully familiar brogue. "Ye wouldn't want me to foul me aim, now." He did me the dubious courtesy of moving slightly aside so I could sight down the barrel of his gun. He had a dead bead on A Lightning.

"Don't bother," I whispered. "You're out."

"Am I now? Maybe you should teach your man to count." The soldier raised an eyebrow for my miserable benefit, and I beheld with regret the transition of his brown eyes to a malignant green. His straight brown locks had shuddered into ginger-hued coils that seemed to writhe at his collar. And as the very earth fell away from the small feet of my happiness, his ruddy complexion faded, and the cancerous blotches of Brown's unmistakable freckles bloomed as her beguiling ebbed. "Ye've been well occupied I see, Emma," she chuckled. I had no breath to scream, less still to shout a warning. For through the shattered window of the stagecoach, I watched as A Lightning approached at speed with nothing to impede his progress but the deafening cock of Brown's Colt. I could do nothing as she fired her pistol. Through the black smoke of the shot I could see A Lightening no longer stood upon my horizon. With a sudden fury, I flung myself backward with enough force to send me crashing through the opposite side of the coach, feeling Brown's fingers graze my racing heart as it slipped from her grip. The air rang with her cackles as I flopped to the dirt. I jammed both hands on either side of the wound beneath my rib cage, willing it to heal faster, as she pulled her plump self from the coach's open window. She was wounded. One of her kneecaps had torn through her trousers and was leaning on the top of her shin like the open top of a beer stein. "I believe you have your good-byes left to utter, my duck," she cooed as she looked at A Lightning writhing but a few feet from me. "At least to the man he once was." She limped past my periphery as I rolled to my belly and crawled to him. There was no time to mourn the failure of our quest, to weigh the wisdom of pursuing her. I crawled to his side, cradling his head as I held his face to mine. His breathing was quick and raspy, a look of utter childlike wonder in his eyes. I clamped my face to his chest and sucked at his wound.

The slug came hard upon my teeth, tasting bitter of bad chemistry. I spat it out and pressed upon his wound. He opened his eyes weakly.

"Gravy . . ."

"Shut up. We ain't done."

"Leave it, my heart."

"Shut up! Shut up! Don't you *dare* quit me! I said we ain't *over*." I raised a finger to my throat and dragged a deep gash into my flesh.

"No, Gravy," he moaned as I forced his face to my wound.

"Drink it," I whispered, my eyes flooding. His head struggled in my grip, my blood smearing his tightly closed lips and cheeks. I pushed his face back into what was flowing from me. "*Suck*, goddamn you!" My grip upon him was firm. His will to live battled his last hope of a good death. His lips parted in the desperate junction between us as he finally made a weak sucking sound, his eyes clenched in anguish. I saw in my mind what he was seeing in his. He was alone on a high bluff, his body straight and immaculate, as his long black hair bellowed in the warm wind. The image of him began to grow small as he struggled to push me away. I held him tightly. His new strength surged as he drank deeper and deeper of me. Life had its hooks in him now. He squinted against the quick and confusing images of my past. "Suck! *Suck!*" I felt my darkness enter him. And with me all the complications and poor choices of my loving him so recklessly, so selfishly. He broke our bond and heaved a huge breath. The wound on his chest was already beginning to pucker.

"Gravy?" he said, blinking into the air. My answer was a hard kiss on his lips. I didn't have much time. He needed more than what I could spare if his fatal wound was to heal completely. I limped to the tipped coach, woozy, praying there was still someone inside it left alive. Under a stout traveling chest I heard a faint moan. Crushed beneath it was the body of a young woman. I fumbled the chest away from her.

"Thank, God!" she wheezed. "Oh, thank sweet Providence!" She was a pretty little thing, blonde and delicate, buttoned to the neck in her best traveling suit of pink serge. Her legs were shattered below the knees, flailing loose at wrong angles as I bent to pick her up. "What are you doing?" she rasped. "Don't move me!" Her eyes were wild as I dragged her screaming from the coach and set her down near A Lightening's face.

"*Stop!* Please stop," she said breathing hard.

"Gravy, no."

"Hush, now. You're weak. You need to feed. We both do." The girl's panic calmed as she looked into A Lightning's eyes.

"Poppa?" she said through the blur of her tears. It was a huge and hateful miracle that he had beguiled her so quickly. Her passing was soft as he drank from her throat. But what would soften the regret that stole into me? I sipped from her birdlike wrist, hoping my longing for him would somehow edify me more than what I swallowed from her. When he was finished, he was curious as to the emptiness of the clothes crumpled on the earth beside him. He lifted up her still buttoned blouse and watched as the motes of dried bone and flesh left the sleeves, catching the sun like pollen.

"I saw square lodges, tall ones," he said, "painted every color, hundreds of them on many hills, all looking upon a large calm water." San Francisco? I wondered. "Why do I see these things?"

"Hush. It will ebb," I lied to him.

I was surprised to see how little damage had been sustained by the coach. The horses had broken free of their traces as soon as the coach had floundered, but there was still a baron's worth of bounty to be had. The luggage rack had spilled its contents, and three trunks had burst open upon the ground, scattering white petticoats and skirts like strange flowers. Where were Capability Brown's personal effects? The first chest held no real secrets, the usual equipage, cotton, and cheap lace. But the other two were conspicuous in the qualities of their fabrics. Acids greens in watered silk, angry carmine-colored velvet. Three bottles of Irish mash had miraculously survived the tumult. That was Brown's luck, all right. I felt the trunk's cedar ribs until I found a small recessed notch. Pressing upon it I heard a slight click. The false floor lifted easily and beneath it was the strong box I remembered. Where was the key?

"Feel around those clothes, there," I said to A Lightning. "See if you can find a small brass key."

"What do you need a key for, Gravy?" he asked, taking the metal box from me. He wedged the tip of his finger beneath the clasp and tore it from its lock. I winked at him and looked inside. One photograph, a plump young woman staring back at me, washed out in the natural light of the studio. Bonds, stock certificates, and deposit slips, all issued from the Bank of San Francisco. A canvas pouch containing perhaps five pounds of gold dust. No heart. Where had she stashed it? A Lightning picked up the photograph I dropped to the ground and was looking at it severely.

"Mercy," he said in awkward English

"You don't need to fuss with that." But he held it away from my grasp.

"You shared a face with her once."

"What?"

"You moved inside her skin once. In the eyes of another."

"Give me that," I said, reaching for the picture. He would not let it go. He would not take his gaze from the pale, broken eyes in the photograph.

"What does it mean? Have you opened all my doors so that others can enter me now, too?"

I gently took the photograph from him and crumpled it in my fist as I pulled his face to mine. "Look at me. Look at my eyes. These are the only doors that are open now." His look told me he was willing to walk through them.

# Chapter Forty-Two

A good raid deserves, *requires* even, a good gift. A Lightning and I gripped the traces and pulled the coach to camp. Size matters to the People. Almost as much as bald novelty. This hollow behemoth, rippling with gold leaf and sprung with straps of useful thick leather terrified as much as it delighted. Many had never seen such a conveyance before, could not understand its function. Even after I explained it to them, many could still not comprehend why one would rather sit in the dark than walk or ride in the sunshine. None of the braves would enter the empty coach. They knew a stomach when they saw one. So only the foolish and the wise, the giggling girls and saggy old women, would dare sit upon its tucked leather seats and peer out through its broken windows. The trunks were opened like troughs, their contents available to whomever took a fancy to them. And as this was all booty from an alien world, it was not uncommon for the braves to favor the ladies corsets and crinolines, while the woman seemed content fighting over the shaving brushes and mugs. A few grandmothers unfurled the folded trousers they found, sniffed the wool, wrinkling their noses. Then they bit off the tin fly buttons and shredded the rest for kindling. Everything was appropriated. Nearly everything repurposed. Boot soles made better knife grips or kettle patches. The arms of blouses were torn off and used as leggings. Bonnets carried water. The coach itself suffered the most from their scavenging. For a people with such an affinity for the circle, they had surprising contempt for the wheel. These were the first to go, the spokes smashed and burned, the iron rims cut up and refashioned into knife blades, hand axes, and arrowheads. I was watching the carnage when a small boy, six or seven, handed me what was left of a cardboard sign. Much of it had been torn and discarded, leaving only a few lines in English. He seemed frantic to know what the scratches, as he called them, meant. I reckoned it was the coach rules, posted on the inside of the cabin that listed correct overland etiquette. All I could make out were the words "no rough language" and "should you be compelled to expectorate, please spit *with* the wind." The last part he made me repeat. First in English and then in his own tongue. He seemed moved by the words, swaying slightly as I repeated them. Was there music there? A piper in print leading him off to a new identity? Would he now want to be called Spits With The Wind?

By evening, all that was left were odd bits of hardware, harness rings, door handles, turnbuckles—decorations left for the children. The luggage rails were busted up and made into tongs and fire pokers. Everything was used. And everyone seemed happy. Everyone but Comes At Dawn, who had sensed the change in A Lightning almost immediately upon our return. I could see suspicion in the twist of the *winkdah's* mouth and the way they stayed apart from the excited throng. That evening, A Lightning and I were called to Dawn's lodge. It was a formal request.

"I know that you love the People, my chief," Dawn's voice was clipped and officious. I was ignored. "You have led us through hard winters, famine, bounty, war. Sometimes an even more difficult peace. All with conviction and wisdom. You are truly one of us, even though you were born into different ways. But tell me, chief, how can you lead the lives of others when you no longer share the same heart as the People?" A Lightning made a move to speak but was silenced by Comes At Dawn. Power should always defer to wisdom. "You need not protest. I can sense the change that has come upon you. I know misfortune found you out there. Even though the wound has left no scar." Dawn, imperious, finally looked at me with cold eyes. "Look at him. Look at what you have made him." A Lightning gripped my hand.

"I allowed it to happen. I am responsible," he said quietly.

"You are *dead*, my son," Dawn said with quiet rage. "Your wound should have been mortal. Your death, if not honorable, was at least your own. Now you are stuck on a distant shore. A shadow to those who would follow you." Dawn addressed me without looking at me. "And I know why you did it, Gravy. I have sensed the love growing between you.

"So perhaps your making our chief like you was not done in wickedness. But strength and cunning do not lead the People. Truth and honor do." Dawn then spoke to A Lightening, "How can you speak truth to them and hold a fundamental lie in your heart?"

"What if I told them?" A Lightning asked respectfully.

"What? What would you tell them? That you are now a creature like Gravy? A stranger under the skin? How many would follow you then?"

A Lightning was silent. Then he spoke. "Why is my power any different from the man who dreams of elks and then can romance any woman of his choosing? Or the man who dreams of buffalo falling like rain from the sky? Are the People deceived when he comes home with much meat?"

"This is not the same."

"Why?"

"Because your *spirit* has changed. Is that not the price of your power, Gravy? Are we to be at constant war just to appease the hunger you now both share?"

I moved to speak. A Lightning shot up a silencing hand. "We don't *have* to go to war to feed. We can—"

"What? Attack the white men's wagons in secret? Feast on them like foxes among rabbits in the night? How long will that last until they send others like this foolish white woman to kill us all?"

"Hear me, my friend," A Lightning said quietly, looking into their eyes. "The whites are coming anyway. It is not the change in me that brings them. But perhaps it can slow them." It was respect that made Comes At Dawn look down.

"Hawks cannot lead doves, my chief."

"Hawks," A Lightning said standing, "are not men. Or do you believe I am no longer even a man?" We watched him go, waiting in conflicted silence until neither Dawn nor I heard his quiet steps.

In the summer of '55, Col. George Tilman Wright was sent from the capital to clean up a messy skirmish in the Pacific Northwest that had been begun against the Yakama and included the Battle of Seattle the following January. And so for a good long stretch we had a steady stream of fresh recruits, still dizzy from breathing the sage-tinted expanses. Yes, they were mother's sons. But they were also soldiers and we took them quickly, always at night, squinting against the stream of their first loves and youthful follies that flooded our brains. At first, A Lightning was disturbed by the images he drank from his victims.

"Why do they call me white women's names? Why do they all approach me with such tenderness? It is not honorable among warriors."

"You get used to it."

"We have legends of blood-drinkers among the People," he said. "But they are shy and filthy things that must hide their hunger in shadow. Your Beguiler is uniquely American, I think."

"How so?" I asked.

"You whites are skilled in appearing to be things you are not. Generous when you are greedy. Just when you are corrupt. I remember my father wore a treaty medal around his neck until he died. He got a gold medallion around his neck, and the whites got our best hunting grounds and mastery of all our waterways."

"Isn't power just power? Doesn't its strength depend on how you use it? You told Dawn you could slow the whites."

"But I am just one man. I think I would share this power with the People if it were not such a poor gift." I had no answer to this. But not all of his observations were so honest or dire.

"What is corn pone and side pork, and why do I have a sudden taste for it?" he'd muse. One Sunday night after a good feed on some Boston reserves, he was compelled to yodel a long stream of gibberish, unfathomably distasteful to his ears. I hadn't the heart to tell him the words had been English, the song he'd howled with such gusto had been "Yankee Doodle." As the moons passed, the lives we took began to blur. The myriad souls we ingested lost their separate narratives until the memories we swallowed were indistinguishable. Fours years passed like this until a protean A. Lincoln, once Whig now Republican, decided to resupply a federal fort off the coast of the Carolinas. And our gravy train began to slow. All fresh meat was told to muster for duty in the newly formed Union Army. It took nearly a year to drain those western territories of its able-bodied men. But there were still the overland coaches.

The People prospered, even in winter. Between the two of us, we were always able to scare up a few bucks or buffalo. We even led a few raids against the People of Little Black Eagle, who had the bad taste to muscle in on our hunting grounds, holding back when the knives came out and allowing the other braves a chance to prove their mettle. Stares The Night distinguished himself quite nicely at a few of these raids, taking the most hair, rounding home with the most ponies. Before long, he had two wives, six kids, honor, trophies, and his humanity firmly intact.

Through all our nights of rough living and even more strident lovemaking, A Lightning and I were everything to one another. Our happiness, like our secret, was as reliable as the rising sun. There were rumors among the People about us. There are always rumors about prominent people. What lead to A Lightning's undoing was not started by gossip. It did not begin with a threat of foreign armies because of anything we did together. What kicked it off simply wandered into camp one day on its own two weary feet.

# Chapter Forty-Three

Henry Road was a scrofulous shit shack that housed a Bernini altarpiece. An ever-soused compendium of soured tobacco and noxious booze with a near maternal devotion to vice. But for all his spectacular shortcomings, he possessed a talent for painting, for sketching, for *seeing*, that with even a modicum of discipline would have made him the American Masaccio.

Born into the filthy tenements of lower Manhattan around the same time as me, Road painted pictures on the curb of his ghetto the same way other kids soft-shoed for pennies. He once made a gouache study of the local rabbi's daughter with such pulsing detail he had to spend a full eight hours in jail before he could convince the constabulary that those perfect pelvic shadows and lovingly rendered areolas were mere flights of gynecological fancy. He never had respect for his talent. At twelve, he turned to oils only so he could take brain-pummeling nips from his jar of turpentine.

At seventeen he was accepted to the École des Beaux-Arts off two wrinkled life studies and a nude he'd pasted to the bottom of an old cigar box. He supplemented his meager school stipend by running a prostitution ring that featured both male and female life models. And when that was broken up, after his architectural drawing instructor threatened to go to the prefects (he complained Road's prices were scandalous), Henry stayed flush stealing jars of turpentine from the supply shack, flavoring it with rose petals and red pepper. He sold it to his fellow students for seventeen francs a shot, calling it "Bonaparte's Revenge." He took third at his first salon. A second at his second. And seemed primed for a first when he was suddenly forced to leave France after two shop girls from the Marais and one underage Bois de Boulogne chestnut vendor all filed paternity suits in the same week. Back in the United States, broke, disillusioned, and with little hope for patronage, he spotted an ad in the *Brooklyn Daily Eagle* seeking "individuals of artistic bent, unencumbered by familial obligations, with a thirst for adventure and a penchant toward the rustic accommodations of the virgin frontier." He reported to a six-floor walkup on Flatbush, a government front for the Department of the Interior. He smoked his last butt while his induction officer perused his portfolio with barely cloistered awe.

He was assigned two decommissioned cavalry geldings, ten bolts of heavy-gauge canvas, a cord's worth of stretcher bars, and enough tubes of pigment to paint the whole Seven Nations. And, most precious of all, four beer barrels of double-distilled turpentine. He traded a gallon of the solvent for a year's worth of cheroots to a barge pilot who ferried him over the Missouri before heading West. His government instructions were sufficiently nebulous to make him feel like he could do whatever the hell he wanted:

> *Go forth and render the savage in all his natural nobility, concentrating on those likenesses that are at once the most indicative of the race and instructive as to their countenance and customs. Upon completion of portraits return said commissions either by steamer, coach or any other reliable overland conveyance to the offices of the Department of the Interior, Bureau of Indian Affairs, Washington, District of Columbia.*

He had a drunkard's luck, suffering a single bout of dyspepsia and a stubbed toe after six full months on the open plains. The natives loved him. When they were dubious as to his intentions, he plied them with tobacco, wowing them with what he could conjure on the whiteness of gessoed canvas in just three short hours. He was pumping out several masterpieces a month, not the stiff quasi-classical tripe that had dripped from George Catlin's brush decades previous. These were the People as they saw themselves—flawed, feral, robust, spiritual, romantic, average.

But I still didn't like to him. Not that first day.

He was singing an altered version of "Oh! Suzanna" when he first stumbled into our summer camp. It was a hot day, and he was on foot, leading his two horses, both packed so poorly I could see them favoring their downhill hooves just to stay upright. Road was sweaty, his collar open at the neck, a loop of white heart trade beads around his throat. (A parting love gift from some silly native's daughter, months gone with his child?) His hair was long and greasy. His brown eyes sparked with a kind of devilish fire. And maybe there was a ghost of roguish charm in the make of his face, if it hadn't been blanketed with his sour thatch of beard. It was strange seeing a white man stroll among the People with such shambling confidence. The fact that he was not dressed in military blues must have been the reason that he solicited more curiosity than outright hostility. He would have food and a place to pass the night, if he chose. The People are naturally generous to strangers. But I saw him as an invader. As he spotted me and slowed his gait to address me, my plan was to hear his business and quietly kill him later that evening.

"What rhymes with 'runt,' my buxom princess of the plains?" were his first words to me. The fierce look on my face just made him grin. He paused, rubbed his eyes, and looked at me again. "Well, I'll be dipped in sheep shit and fried in my own piss. I haven't seen a pair of blue eyes over a warm cunny in a coon's age."

"Whatever you're hawking, brother, we ain't buyin'," I said in English, hoping my frank rebuttal would send him on his way. But Road was not thwarted. He clasped his hands together and looked skyward in a stagey swoon.

"And it *talks*!" he said theatrically. "Sweet Jesus! I haven't heard real Yankee speak since the last time I wiped my ass with the *New York Herald*."

He placed a grimy hand on my shoulder as if we were old drinking buddies and chuckled. "With your dark skin, I just naturally assumed you were some half-breed." I sloughed his hand from my shoulder and watched it burrow into the whiskers on his neck. "You speak English like you were born to it. Please tell me you ain't some kind of captive among these fine folks." He was calling attention to himself now; a few braves and their children stepped toward him, followed, per protocol, by their shy wives. He dropped his attention from me and faced the gathering crowd. "Henry Road, folks!" he shouted, raising his showman's hands above his head. "Epicurean of the rustic and the exotic, interpreter of beauty and truth in linseed and *vivid* color! I'm here to make you *famous!*" It didn't matter that the People could not understand a word he said. He could still feel the proverbial pennies fall into his pockets as they buzzed toward his carnival barker's honey.

Four of Stares The Night's own children were among the crowd that swarmed Road, and he delivered, knitting fake beards out of buffalo's tails and stringing them over the children's tiny ears, much to the amusement of their parents.

"I say we end his sorry ass tonight," I said, frowning at the giddy children later that day. A Lightning looked at me, amused, not able to take my suggestion seriously.

"I must avoid his eyes for fear I might beguile him," he laughed. "It would be like feasting on a dung pit."

"I don't like the way he looks at me."

A Lightning grinned.

"He has teeth in his stare, true," he said. "But eyes cannot eat."

I couldn't name the flavor of fear I sensed in Road that day. Beneath his braggadocio, something fateful lingered. I wondered if I should share my concern with Comes At Dawn, the only one of the tribe who had not left their lodge to look at him. Road didn't take out the pigments right away. His first week in camp, he was everyone's favorite uncle, a welcomed scamp who trolled the campfires conveniently at mealtimes, dipping a finger here, accepting a morsel there, familiarizing himself with faces, outwardly getting what he called "the lay of the land." He knew a few words of the People's tongue, which he charmingly mangled whenever in conversation. His real mode of communication was the universal hand gestures of the Plains, and of these he favored two. First was the gesture for "beautiful" that seemed to apply to everything from the splay of a maiden's cheekbones to whatever was simmering in that evening's pot. His second favorite gesture was "more," and I reckon between the two, the butter-up and the payoff, he had about as much language as any competent freeloader required.

One morning, he set out a sampling of his finished canvasses. He lined them up on the bank of the river where the morning sun would kick off the water and show them to their best advantage. Road looked nervous as he watched the People look at his work. He peered at them, his head lowered, chewing absently on a callus on his thumb. Beautiful things, I thought begrudgingly, strolling past them with the rest of the tribe. Vibrant, immediate, where you really felt the weather and the subject's place in it. But the People had a very different relationship with the rendered image than whites did. Women usually preferred geometric patterns on the things they decorate. Men seemed to favor stylized pictographs for recording their prowess in battles or personal visions on their shields or winter counts. Such images describe the spiritual accuracy of things, not their surfaces. The men filed past the paintings, bunched in their separate warrior societies, puffing, grunting, clicking their teeth at what they saw. The women followed them, their reactions similar to their men if less loud. What their reactions meant I could not know. Road was sweating when I glanced over to him. Only one painting solicited a response that was clear in any language. The People had a habit of laughing behind their hands. It was a mannered, almost spinsterish quirk that affected men as well as the women. Show them something funny, and up went those hands and they'd tee-hee it to death. I noticed one portrait getting this particular treatment in spades. It was a big one, half life-sized, all slurried over in creamy ambers and oranges, an obviously proud chief in profile, the top of his head exploding in a dazzling array of feathery fireworks.

"I don't get the joke," I said to A Lightning when he came to join me.

"You don't see it? It's the pose. He's made him half a man."

"So why aren't you laughing?" I asked him while he looked intently at Road's paintings.

"I've seen paintings like this before at the mission when I was a boy. The tortured saints with their insides spilling open and their faces still so full of peace." He stood close to the painting of the chief and raised a hand to touch it before he stopped himself and looked at me. "The world is changing, Gravy. And if we do not at least try to change with it, we will be left behind."

# Chapter Forty-Four

Henry Road was undaunted by the spotty reception to his work. The next day, he set up his easel by the creek, his pigments and oils hidden beneath a filthy cloth. He'd strapped a huge grass-stuffed bag to his ass complete with a rawhide tail, another strip of rawhide cut sharp was strapped to his face like an enormous beak. I watched him humming to himself in his ridiculous getup, the sun rising higher as he stood there, idling, a buffoon without a court. It was midmorning before the camp roused from the blows of the previous night's revelries. Children rubbed their crusty eyes. But when they saw Road, hallelujah! Out came the circus, and the kiddies lit out after him like their little heads were on fire. Amid his braying and teetering, his pratfalls, both in the dirt and the river, he still managed to produce a worthy cartoon of the laughing children. Still wet and hamming it up for them, he began to paint in earnest, perfectly rendering their gleeful faces and protruding tummies in what seemed like mere seconds. When Comes At Dawn approached him, furious, imperious in a fine buckskin frock, it was for the first time.

"What are you doing there, you filthy man?" Comes At Dawn shouted, trying to shoo Road away from his work. "Not the children! You cannot steal the children."

"*Steal* them?" Road struggled with Dawn's syntax before waving me over to translate. "What the hell is this old fool squawking about?" he asked me.

"Comes At Dawn wants you to leave."

"Leave? Naw. I'm pretty sure he didn't say anything about leaving. You kids want me to leave?" The children scowled before mobbing the artist with their wet bodies.

"Say, princess, what's your percentage in all this," he asked, peeling a set of little arms from his neck before lowering the child to the ground. "Why haven't you and I hit it off?" I looked at him with cold eyes "Hey, fine by me, sister. We don't have to be friends. Just ask that fellow in the buckskin skirt if he wouldn't mind me painting him." Dawn looked at me. "Go on. Ask him."

"We want you to leave us alone," I said in English.

"We? You speaking for the *chief* now, honey? I thought you were just fucking him." I would have slapped his cocky face if he hadn't gently draped his raw hide beak over the closest child's nose. "Because unless I hear that from the head man's lips," he said, still smiling at the child, "I'll assume you're just here offering to translate. Right?"

"He says he wants to paint you," I said to Comes At Dawn through clenched teeth. The old native made a rooster-ish show of outrage, yammering on about the affront, how I, who had no soul to steal, would make much more fitting prey for the snares of Road's cunning. Road ignored it all, just sauntered up and placed his hand on the jaw of the flustered old sachem.

"Look at you Dawn, ol' girl," Road whispered approvingly. "Why would you tease your trade mirror with such a face when I could capture your pulchritude for eternity?" Even without my translation of his silky seduction, Dawn blushed. The old Indian looked at me expectantly. "I'll tell you what," Road said, addressing me. "If he doesn't like what he sees, if I fail to render that redskin as a rough-hewn Narcissus, I'll leave today. Deal?"

Comes At Dawn stood in a small clearing, as demure as the belle of the ball. Road had constructed a swag of blank canvass for Dawn to stand under, the fabric defusing the light and sharpening the shadows of Dawn's nose and jaw. Road's canvas was round, stitched to a bent-willow hoop, a clever concession to the People's affinity for circles. In preparation for the portrait, three extra feet of hair had been hoof-glued to the tips of the *winkdah's* already cascading locks so they touched the ground. Gripped in long fingers was Dawn's best eagle feather fan. The People clicked their tongues approvingly. But when Road set up his canvas and commenced with his undercoats and varnishes, the People fell silent. Perhaps it was seeing the completed portraits, the flat images consigned to an unlucky rectangle that had stymied their appreciation before. But observing the process, looking from the quickening lines and colors to the breathing person that fed them, was another matter. The white man was not conjuring, had not torn the air and entered the spirit world and brought the image back as they had assumed. He built it. Slowly, carefully, lovingly. The way they built their lodges, clothes, weapons, and meals. They sincerely thought only good people could make beautiful things. One by one the People sauntered over to Dawn's finished portrait. Road studied their stares and slack mouths as he cleaned his brushes in silence. The men sniffed it and winced from the sharp stink of the oils. But nothing could hide their approving grunts as they looked from Dawn in the flesh to the mirror that was not a mirror that had held Dawn's likeness. The women all raised a low tremolo, that guttural keening that meant they had witnessed a truth. Among the People, it was the consent of the women that mattered.

Then Dawn strode to the portrait. Standing stiffly before it, thin lips drawn into the frown of the critic, Dawn took a sudden deep breath, blinking rapidly. The *winkdah* began to mutter a soprano prayer and then slowly flapped the feathered fan while turning four times in a circle. Dawn was still standing before the painting even after the light was lost. The children had taken Road by the hand and guided him back to their families' fires, leaving a few of their ranks to sleep by the portrait's feet. They drummed songs that featured Road's name, offered him first dip into the communal stew. They gladly took the tobacco he offered them. Some even dared draughts from the foul-smelling flask he offered. They thought he was sharing with them his power as the paints and the burning water he drank smelled the same. All this I watched from the shadows, powerless to heal the circle they so innocently opened for the painter.

"Have you fed on Road, Gravy?" Lightning asked me one day, wiping the last of some widow's hope from his lips and cheeks. We were on our favorite high bluff surrounded by a few twisted dogwoods.

"*Road*? Why would I do that?" I asked, fluttering my fingers through the ash left by his meal. "You think we're running out of white men?"

"No. There will always be white men."

"Would you be jealous if I had?" I smirked, glancing at him.

"I refuse to answer that. But I would still have to kill him." He grinned as I laughed and kissed him. "I just wondered if you had. Perhaps you'd seen behind his eyes."

"What's all this about?"

"Do you think he has power?"

"Road? He has cunning. Craft."

"But do think he has *sight*?"

"He sure rendered Dawn like he does." I could feel him thinking, drifting deeper into something, away from me. I leaned my head on his shoulder.

"Hey, what does all that matter?" I said. "He'll get a belly full of us soon enough and pack up and be on his way."

"Perhaps that is best."

"Sooner the better," I said. He draped his arm around me as the sun shimmered on the horizon. The air turned cold.

"He has asked to paint me," he said without looking at me. I sat up.

"What? When?"

"Soon."

"What did you say?"

"He has painted Comes At Dawn as if he has seen inside him."

"Is that what you want? What if you don't like what you see?"

"Perhaps it would be good to fear something again, Gravy."

I turned his face toward mine.

"You told Dawn you chose this. You chose to be like we are now. Didn't that take courage? Doesn't that still take courage?"

"That is a woman's courage," he said with a wry smile.

I slapped him playfully. "The hell you say!" I reached for him and kissed him deeply. There was a slight hesitation at the root of his tongue. He pulled away, gently.

"I don't have your words, Gravy. I can't name what I have inside. I can only tell you what I have in here is mine," he said, putting his hand on his head. Then he put his hand on his chest. "Not ours."

There were no crowds to watch Road paint A Lightning. No converts. He posed for Road's picture in the low mist of the morning, alone. The significance was not lost on the artist, who wore no silly tails this time. Only I was allowed to watch, and then only under the pretext of translation, should Road's poor grammar need clarifying. Dressed up in his full war regalia, it was painful to see A Lightning. His bonnet of seventy war-won feathers fluttered almost pitifully in the light breeze. The quill work that ran down his shoulders, the hair pipe breastplate on his chest, the fringes of enemy tresses that lined his leggings had all had voices once. Now they were silent. He shivered in the morning cold, standing proud, with no conflict on the horizon other than his own. A few braves, refusing to look at the painting, made the keening sounds of women, ribbing him from behind lodges. I turned and hissed.

"Leave them, Gravy," A Lightning said. "Soon enough they will see their chief as he is."

When Road broke for a rest, A Lightning remained standing. This was the hardest time of all. The time when he would not even look into my eyes. He clutched his coup stick, head down, a groom in a borrowed suit, a conflicted creature whose rough beguiling magic trumped that of every talisman he wore. As his image brimmed to the surface of Road's canvas, the People walked in single file before it and said nothing. Something had gone wrong. Or too honestly right.

But A Lightning smiled when he saw it. Never before had he seen the *all* of him spit back so thoroughly. Despite his heroic pose, the exotic ruffles of his dress,

A Lightning was depicted only as a man—raw, simple, caught somehow in midturn, in the single action of being. In his eyes was a new quarrel between what he was and what he had become. And this feature seemed to please him the most.

"It is as I hoped," he said to Road, placing a hand on the artist's shoulder after the People had filed away from it.

"Is it? Well, *trahit sua quemque voluptas*," the artist mumbled weakly. He was quoting Virgil. *Each one is drawn by his own delight.* Road was not soothed by his Latin quotation. He knew it was his best work, but with the portrait's public shunning, he was at a loss as to his standing among the tribe. "You know, Chief," Road said, "I read somewhere Charles IV put Goya on a royal stipend for depicting his king with such candor. But I'm starting to wonder where my next meal's coming from."

"Don't worry, Road," A Lightning said. "You won't go hungry. But not because I am any more pleased with what you have painted than the People. I do not recognize the human being on that cloth any more than they do." Road tensed and lifted his head to speak. But A Lightning silenced him with a smile. "That is good, Mr. Road. For you have shown me how far I need to travel back to myself."

# Chapter Forty-Five

I smelled Stares The Night before I saw him stumble into camp. There was a promise of early snow on the cool autumn wind, and upon its back was the scent of Stare's wound. His particular musk of pride and stamina that had once delighted my nostrils, now stank of dirty metal and shame. Whatever misfortune he had endured was not the work of some rival tribe. His silhouette wavered on the horizon as he approached, his image severed by a trick of the afternoon's light that only reassembled when he fell to the ground hundreds of yards from me. I ran to him. He was hot with fever, his breathing shallow. In one hand, he clenched a dun-colored envelope closed with a US Army wax seal. In the other, his severed left ear. His horse was gone. I draped his arms around my neck as I lifted him from the ground and jogged him to Comes At Dawn's lodge as fast as I could. The People were in turns shocked and outraged to see what had become of one of their fiercest warriors.

"Long knives," some shouted. "White men," others whispered as they congregated around the entrance to Dawn's lodge. Dawn, unsurprisingly, was ready for him when I laid Stares The Night down on a buffalo robe. The air of their lodge was already spiced with medicinal herbs and boiling sinew. Eyes closed, Dawn felt the young man's head.

"Get rid of that filth," Dawn said, not looking at me, referring to the letter Stares carried, not the severed ear. I pulled the letter from Stares' hand and called for Road. He dipped his head into the lodge.

"What the hell happened?" he said.

"Read this," I said, handing him the bloodstained letter.

"Jesus Christ. The US Army? Don't you want to read it first?"

"I think I already know what's in it."

Road fumbled with the letter as he took it. "Is there anything I can—"

"Go!" I shouted, and he hastily retreated. "Where's A Lightning?" I asked Dawn. I hadn't seen him since the previous day when he had finally torn himself from his portrait.

"He's on his own path now," Dawn said. "I must hurry if Stares is to heal properly." I noticed Stare's ear was in a tea-like fluid, the clotted bits of its severed edge sloughing as it soaked. Dawn held the end of the sinew he had been boiling to the fire, drying it to a hard needle point. "He will be fine," Dawn said, shooting me a severe look. "Go and tell the clan chiefs to build a council lodge. We will have much to decide this evening."

Four braves were sent out in four directions to chop down forty-four trees to be shaped into the lodgepoles of what would become the council lodge, wherein the future of the tribe would be discussed. As I watched them ride away, I noticed Road near his two horses, furiously strapping his rolled canvasses and paints to their pack saddles.

"Where are you off to?" I asked.

"It's over, sister," he said tersely, tying a hard knot in the leather strap that held his chest of brushes and paints. "Read that damn letter and tell me different." He nodded to the open letter on the ground.

*In Field,*
*Western Terr., N.W.*

*Sept. 21st, 1862*

*Col. G. Tilman Wright*
*CO, 23rd Light Infantry Division, Special Mounted attndt.*
*United States Army, retired*
*Active, Army of the Confederacy, J. Davis presiding.*

*Greetings Sachem:*

*Having encountered of late a member trueborn to your faction I took it upon general inquiry to ascertain said individual's actionable intent. He communicated through a rough show of gestures that his sole intention had been the hunt. His only desire was to procure one or more hoofed and/or fleet animals of a nutritive nature. These animals I intuited to be deer, as he was quite fluent with gestures consistent with what could easily be digital simulacrums of the intended quarry's distinguishing antlers. But the genus of his pursuit could only be hazarded as he was quite adamant as to a splay of fingers above his head. This gesture, with its eight simulated points put several of our company in mind of the distinguishing rack of a buck or stag and therefore we felt quite confident in ruling out your man's intention of dispatching a buffalo or perhaps a moose. (As the gesture for the one would have been simply two hooked fingers at the crown of the head. And as for the moose—this I assume would have required the addition of some clever pantomime redolent of the creature's characteristic hump, accompanied, for greater clarity, by a reproduction of its congested bellow.) And since none of these gestures and or sounds were forthcoming, deer it was! But I was not fooled by his ruse of merely hunting for sustenance.*

*I informed your man of the many losses my division had suffered while bivouacked not far from his village. He denied any knowledge as to these unlawful depredations but made his contempt for members of my regiment quite clear. I informed him that his attitude, though admirably brave, still designated him a hostile. As you most certainly know, it is the stated policy of the Army to remove from present lands all parties and their immediate associates who harbor such mortal animosity against the standing if transient Federal Gov't. When his attitude but little improved, we felt obliged, in the spirit of necessity and as a general reprimand, to deny your agent of his horse. And to further our immutable if regrettable intent to employ military force if the option of relocation is denied, I felt a respectful obligation to part your man from the integrity of his left ear. This was done with such expedient solemnity that I am proud to report that he made but a single masculine grunt that could in no way be construed as an allusion to any pusillanimity or laxity of resolve in his character.*

*In summation:*

*I implore you to review this missive with all due gravity. I will be attending to your present location posthaste, where your compliance or defiance will serve as my answer. In the spirit of humanity, as much as it can extend to you and your kind, please know that I command several armed troops, mounted and infantry, with an accrued force of over three hundred. I tell you this only in regards to the security of your women and children as I can unreservedly assure your resolute destruction should you refuse to comply.*

*But if you resist relocation, as it is our sovereign right to impose upon you, please abide in the knowledge that you would have both my respect and my heartfelt condolences should this unfortunate decision be yours.*

*G. Tilman Wright*
*Col., Confederate States of America, acting US Army, reserved.*

"This Col. Wright character has clearly flown free of his rigging," I said, looking up from the letter.

"And yet never was there a more concise declaration that the party's over. Relocation or death," he chuckled. "Not much choice in that."

"So you're just gonna light out of here?"

"Come with me."

"I'm going to pretend you didn't just say that."

"Three hundred US Army regulars are on their way here right now. Hell, even your dreamy chief had enough sense to clear out while he could." The accusation against A Lightning made me angry. Worried and angry. I could feel him in my mind. Smell his body when I took a deep breath. But, like Brown, I could not find him.

"You're a coward, Road."

"A coward wouldn't hazard the chance I'm about to take," he said, grinning coldly.

I laughed. Was he seriously considering making the trek back East on his lonesome? "Every war chief in every tribe of the whole Seven Nations knows the army's on the move. You really think they'll roll out the welcome rug now for a white man like you? You'll never make it off these high plains alive."

He swallowed hard and stared at me. "Then my initial invitation still stands. Come with me."

"And guard your sorry ass for fifteen hundred miles?" I said, stepping close to his face. "I don't slaughter the innocent. Or ain't you been paying attention."

Now it was his turn to laugh at me. "Well, brave little Gravy actually *believes* the People have welcomed her into their sacred little hoop," he said. "What if the People vote to relocate?"

"Not all of them will."

"You really think you can take on a whole battalion with a handful of angry braves?"

"If we have to."

"But that's just it, princess. Even if by some miracle you succeed, you'll never be one of them. You take from these people their exotic luster and rustic concepts of honor and humanity because you have none of your own. You're just a tough little bitch with delusions of belonging. Trust me. I'm the same creature, in my fashion."

"You're wrong, Road," I said evenly. "And you'll die alone out there just as wrong."

I walked away from Road without another word, leaving him to stew about his dubious choices of escape. I figured he would suss the wisdom of his odds and delay placing his bet until he knew who had won. If the People chose to stay and fight, he would simply ingratiate himself to whomever was left. If the army was triumphant, he'd have an armed escort back to civilization and new subjects to paint. But my options were not as obvious as my alliances. Road's words rang inconveniently true as I headed back to Dawn's lodge to check on Stares The Night. I would kill for the People, but would I follow them to the badlands? Would I share their shame and heartbreak if they decided not to fight? How could I when I knew only one of them returned my heart? And he was somewhere beyond me now, perhaps as lost in his own depths as I.

Stares The Night was sleeping when I made it back to Dawn's lodge. His wound was open to the air, his ear beautifully sewn back to its function at the side of his head. I marveled at the tiny stitches that circled the base of the ear near the skull. With flesh-colored deer sinew as thread, the damage was barely noticeable.

"How you get them stitches so tiny?" I said as a way to avoid what I had really come to ask. Dawn grinned at me and held up a tiny shaft of hooked metal. It was a trade needle used for fine leather work.

"This is the most precious object I own."

"But a white man made this," I said holding the hairlike curl of nickel in the palm of my hand.

"And a red man gave your Constitution the lodgepoles on which you hang the best parts of your self-government. It's a poor exchange as this needle has proven its worth many times, while your Great Fathers in the East have yet to do the same. But one day they might." I handed back the needle. I could hear the preparations for the tribal council outside the walls of the lodge. The *tock* of the lodgepoles as they hit the ground, the encouraging chants of the People as they stretched the skin of eight regular lodges over these poles. Children laughing. Camp dogs barking. An oddly quotidian chorus to welcome the coming apocalypse. "What other chitchat should we make, Gravy? Shall I tell you that the men will speak in the council lodge for hours, because that's what men do when they are afraid? That the women will listen quietly before they give their final verdict to leave with the soldiers because they are less afraid and more practical than the men? Perhaps I should tell you that the wide world is shaped like a child's ball and hangs among the stars like a chokecherry without a stem. That the toy world spins and the moon does not. That we are new to this earth and will not grow as old as other beings have before us. Or perhaps you would like to know where your chief has gone." I looked up. Dawn's eyes were kind and expectant.

"Does he love me?" I blurted out. Dawn smiled.

"Ah, now you have asked me a question only you can answer."

"I can feel him. But I cannot see him in my mind."

"He has covered himself from sight like a turtle pulled into his shell. But he will not mind if I show you where he is."

The substance he shared with me looked wrinkled and angry. It might have been a part of a cactus once or an animal's dried organ. It smelled dusty with a trace of something that had once been green. "This medicine is very powerful. It is precious and holy to the People and must never been taken by the whites. It is Great Mystery's special gift to us, and I only share it with you because your heart is loud in its sorrow, and I have a weakness for such a sound." He placed the dried object in his mouth and tipped my hand toward my face so I might do the same. It was bitter beyond belief, resistant to the cadence of my teeth and flow of my spit. I shivered as I swallowed it and immediately wanted to puke it up, but Dawn's hand gently covered my puckered lips.

"The bitterness will pass. Now we wait." Dawn began to chant in a high, keening whine. I could not tell if we sat for hours or mere minutes. The song seemed to make the fire at the center of the lodge grow brighter, the flames freezing in triplicates of themselves for a few seconds before they began to writhe again. The whole lodge seemed to breathe with me, the blackened hide near the smoke hole at the top slowly dissolving until the swirling embers from the fire rose into the night sky above us, becoming stars and pushing the stars that were all dancing before me now.

"You wondered once when you first drank from me why you saw stars," I heard Dawn's voice whisper in my head. "All my fondest memories are of stars and my walks among them." I felt myself rise out of myself, shedding the warmth of Dawn's lodge as I drifted up through the flaps of the smoke hole. I felt the last of the fire's heat as I mingled with the thinning blue smoke from the branches burning beneath me. I was bathed in a delicious coolness that permeated all of me as I beheld a blue sheen that curved over the daylit earth. Above me I saw a celestial river of curling light. I longed for a moment to dive into that current, but thinking of A Lightning would not let me ascend any further. My feeling began to sink as the stars faded from view, and I descended into a blue sky filled with flocks of tiny birds. The birds swam inside me, around me, carrying me down into the cool galleries of the morning. I drifted over the land until I saw a place I recognized, the high bluff of A Lightning's and my favorite hill. He was there beneath me, tiny and crouched, finishing the day's prayers, growing larger and larger as I descended toward him. Finally, I stood behind him. I was hot and sweating, breathing hard as if I had just run for many miles. He turned to me. He was naked to the waist, wearing only a breechclout for ease of movement. He was greased, not for warmth but to slip more easily from an enemy's grasp. And he was painted blue, a crisp, high-summer blue. *I welcome death.* That's what the blue said. He had painted his horse for war, black lightning bolts on its flanks and his own black handprints on the rump. His mouth was stone, but his eyes were happy to see me. I was shot through with such a furious longing for him I thought I might lose my balance. He made a sudden move of his arms to catch me, but I righted and he simply held his ground and stared. Amid the blue of his throat was a small splash of orange and black, spread over his Adam's apple, the wings of a monarch butterfly. Insanely out of season. How had he found it? How had he come upon a creature as rare as himself? His breath fogged in the cold. That was physics. The rest of him was as reposed as if he had just stepped out of an herbed bath. I noticed the otter skin belt then, coiled in his hand. The one he would unfurl on the battlefield, tying one end around himself, the other tied to his lance, driven into the ground till he fell. He was making a one-way trip.

*You riding out?* I signed. He could have nodded. But he made the formal sign for *yes* instead.

*They voted to move camp*, I gestured. *They will not fight.* The People are silent before battle. But I knew that even if I could have spoken, I could not have done so without crying.

I held both my hands to my heart then flung them wide toward him, signaling what I hoped he felt for me. I waited until his blue arms moved slowly to his chest, my eyes welling as he mimicked my gesture.

*There is another way,* I motioned. *A way back for you.* That's when I showed him the knife. *I am your sire. Eating the heart of one's sire reverses the hunger, stops the Beguiler. Take mine and be as you were. Go home.* His look was harsh, and in that condemnation was an intimacy almost more unbearable than any love we had shared.

*You have already given me your heart once*, he motioned. *It is foolish to offer it a second time.*

*Fool, me, yes,* was all I could manage to sign. He looked at me deeply, opening for just a moment a path into his eyes.

*I know why you made me, Gravy,* he signed. *I would have done the same to you.* His gestures made a shushing as he formed his words, an agonizing whisper of his gently flowing hands that made me dizzy as I imagined them upon my own skin one last time. *I have never been loved like this before. I never will be again. We both act from our heart. You know this. You act from where you now stand. But I must act from where I have been. It is only right I do this. Just as loving you has been right. You know this too.*

The tears filled my eyes, threatened to hide his face from my view. I wiped them away clumsily just to get a last look at him. I nodded my head. He smiled. He understood we couldn't touch. He couldn't risk a sudden passion between us.

I will miss his heat.

His moving skin.

His hands at full sail upon me.

The slow set of his closing eyes.

I felt a lightness beginning in him. I watched him mount his pony. He pulled hard on its mane. The animal's narrow head jerked toward the white of the horizon all around him. A Lightning made no sound as his mount kicked into a gallop. He was suddenly a blur ebbing from my sight.

Then he was gone.

# Chapter Forty-Six

The camp dogs were packed for the People's move. Cooking pots and utensils hung among dolls stuffed with sweet grass. Lodges bundled like the closed umbrellas of giants. The whole camp waited for the approach of the soldiers. We had expected them a day ago. Something had delayed them. I finally heard in the distance the music of the approaching army. It reminded me of rain, gentle and trifling, a light trill of fife and distant drum. It was a cold morning. I hadn't slept. I could not sleep without him. All night I had wandered alone, waiting for our enemy. If the song they played had a name, I did not know it. The white man's music meant nothing to the People. Only that they were coming. A few children still chewed their breakfast, smiled, rubbed their wide brown eyes as their mothers tensely held them. Comes At Dawn was ready for them, trussed in a pure white buckskin dress, hair perfumed, greased, and plaited, and looking prettier than ever. The music came closer, traveling farther and faster over the hush of the snow that had fallen in the night.

Stares The Night had slept enough. He didn't bear a trace of his recent trauma when I looked at him. He and his followers had formed a dreamer's society. They all had shared the same vision, and now their eyes and mouths were smeared black as they looked expectantly to the horizon. There were only four of them. Black crow wings were woven into their hair. They had hoped for hawks, for falcons or eagles, any kind of proud raptor would have done. But they had all dreamed of crows. Crows among the dead. They peered from beneath angry brows but could do nothing. The women had voted. They intended to wait for the tribe to leave camp before they followed.

The army came into sight. One boy on the fife. Another boy on the drum. Boys in blue, clear in the morning light, marched over the snow. Then the mounted troops. And up in the soft, cold breeze a blue flag with a single star. Not the flag of the nation. The first flag of the rebellion. The Bonnie Blue. At least the land will not be taken under colors the People have grown to dread.

I didn't bother to look at Road. But I heard him, frantically prying the painting of A Lightning from its stretcher bars. If A Lightning had gone to meet this American army, he wanted no connection to himself. I had thought Road a coward before but never as damningly as then. I watched his eyes, the ones so comfortable with flattery and lies. He finally freed the canvas and quickly rolled it into a tube and stuffed it up under his shirt. He ran his fingers through his greasy hair and waited near his packed horses. He smiled at me. I could not return it.

"Cease march!" shouted a lieutenant, his voice pushing through rough tobacco and no sleep. Only sixty-nine men stopped at full attention. I did the math. *Is it possible?* Did I really *want* it to be possible? No single warrior, not even one as darkly emboldened as A Lightning, could have dispatched 231 soldiers and survived such a prodigious offensive. Roughly 150 men, women, and squirming children faced the exhausted-looking army. Of that number, just over fifty were warriors. The People began to murmur among themselves. Someone had lied about the odds. A few of the braves clenched their bows and let loose with warning yips. The People did not know who had spared them. I was about to shout his praises when I heard a commanding voice say, "Gentlemen, form a staggered line. Sharply now."

The armed men immediately formed two lines, the front row kneeling, as they all raised their cocked rifles to the muttering Indians. Col. Wright emerged from their ranks, attempting to quiet Stares The Night's horse. The pony smelled home and ran Wright in dizzying circles, rearing on his haunches to get a glimpse of Stares. The colonel, exceptionally well seated, clicked his tongue and stiffened the reins, which made the horse swivel his head all the more. "Lieutenant, steady this animal," he said, tensing the improvised reins again. A young blond officer, a large bandage on his neck, obliged. The horse calmed. The colonel dismounted. He was a man of medium height. His chin was rough with two days of growth, with a long mustache still perfectly groomed. He wore no hat, and his hair was wet.

"Good morning," he said. He cleared his throat. The blond lieutenant handed him a dented flask. The colonel raised the flask in salute before he brought it to his lips. "Pardon me." He took a long pull. Road was transfixed. "Yes, good morning," he said, nervously wiping his mouth. "I trust all are assembled and are ready for escort. To whom should I address my instructions?"

The women moved instinctively away from the raised rifles while the braves moved cautiously forward. Several of the children began to whine as their mothers moved them backward. Had their mothers broken their promises of a long trip? Why were they moving this way? I watched as the women and children continued to walk backward before they discreetly turned and began to disappear over the low hills, unseen because of the warriors that hid them. The soldiers flexed their grips on their weapons, waiting for the command to fire. The braves facing them were similarly tense but would not attack, because their women had voted against it. It was a standoff between those who served their betters. Wright was so lost in the maelstrom of his delusion even he did not notice the women and children were leaving.

Road rushed up to him and, beaming, pumped the colonel's hand. "Sweet Jersey Jesus, are you ever a sight for sore eyes. Colonel, is it?" He grabbed the colonel's arm and slapped the eagle on his shoulder strap. "Yes, by Christ! A *colonel.* A real honest to shitting Christ colonel! I'll be dipped in . . . high holy hell if you ain't as welcome as a two-twatted whore!"

The colonel sneered. The lieutenant closed his eyes as if waiting for a blow. There were twitters among the ranks.

"Silence!" the colonel shouted.

"I say something wrong?" Road said.

"Lieutenant, seize this man and hold him for general indecency and blasphemy."

"What the hell?" Road sputtered as he was escorted away.

"Anyone else here present that can converse in English? Anyone?"

I'd love to let Road twist on his own twine, but I coughed and stepped forward.

"I can. Sir."

"Ah. A captive," Wright said, looking into my pale eyes. "We shall add restitution to our blessings. We will take a moment of leave while I converse with this female before we commence with relocation. And Lieutenant, find this woman some proper linen."

I followed Colonel Wright to the council lodge. Who's to say why a light infantry regiment fresh from protecting the government's interests in the West would be in possession of a woman's frock and knickers? But they were. He averted his eyes while I peeled off my buckskins and stepped into my new clothes. There was no point in inciting his ire by not indulging him. Moments later, I was seething, feeling the old chafe and squeeze of pantaloons and corset under a mauve dress damn near a decade out of date. The colonel raised his chin to inspect me. "You're quite right my dear," the colonel declared, misreading my silence. "Your coiffure is now completely incoherent. Lieutenant, wash that repulsive unguent out of her hair and style it accordingly. And fetch me a full flask along with the tub and soap." I don't know how long it had been since I had suffered such "civilized" indignities to my sex. I only know I wanted that damn colonel's balls for billiards as I was dunked, scrubbed with lye and dried with an old horse blanket. I sorely missed the weight of my bear grease and braids. But I said nothing as my hair was piled atop of my head. When the lieutenant tried to pinch my cheeks for color, I had had enough. I slapped his hand away but was denied a confrontation when the colonel only smiled. "That will be all, lieutenant," he said. Finally, I found myself alone with the colonel. He leaned his trim weight on a backrest and pulled out his fresh flask. Taking a nip, he screwed up his nose while he sucked hard through his teeth. "Don't you feel better, my dear?" he said to me in his Virginia drawl. I didn't answer. I was thinking how many steps I could safely steal toward him before my jaws shut him up for good. I decided against attacking him and pulled at the collar of my dress, focusing on my breathing. "I must apologize, my dear, if your garment seems woefully out of step with current fashion."

I stared daggers back at him.

He shifted uncomfortably.

"I see you have adopted the habit of your hosts in not smiling when a consideration has been afforded you," he said. "Our selection is rather limited. But rest assured, you still look comely. You'd look fetching, dare I say, in a horse blanket." I still said nothing. "What comfort can I offer you in compensation?" And here he took another nip, and the old wheels began turning in my mind.

"I'd take a nip from that flask you keep waving around." I needed something to quell my real thirst.

"Spirits? You partake in spirits?"

"Don't looked so shocked, colonel. I sit to piss too."

He laughed. "Sporting!" he said, handing me his flask.

"Not for years," I said with a seductive raise of my eyebrow. He chuckled again.

"You show remarkable resiliency, my dear. How ever did you manage it?"

"Manage what?"

"Life here among the *savages*."

"Here among the savages? Are you and your company really so cavalier about yourselves?" The colonel sussed my comment with a stern look before he slapped his knee and laughed again.

"Savages! You mean *us*! Capitol! I haven't bandied with such a wry creature in ages. Simply edifying, my dear. Would it surprise you to know they are not in possession of souls?"

"Who, the army?"

"No, silly woman! Your hosts. They are completely bereft of any spiritual organ. I don't claim this from any lofty perch of racial superiority. This is an immutable scientific fact."

"And how did you rustle up this idea?" I asked, leaning back.

"Simple. They lack the necessary soul anchors."

"Soul anchors?"

"Yes, the small white condyles of the ventral region that act as a kind of cleat for the proper tethering of so gossamer an organ as one's soul."

"I'll be hog jizzed."

"My surgeon informs me these cleats are easily recognizable with even a cursory knowledge of gross anatomy."

I decided two things then. One, this poor crazy bastard had spent *far* too much time sniffing his saddle. Two, he would be more entertaining squawking out of his opened throat.

I decided to change tack. I had to know.

"Do you mind if we get back to the business at hand? I assume you came here to parley," I said with mock gentility. "You mentioned you were coming in force."

"There is a kind of salvation for these poor heathen creatures, however," he said, oblivious to what I had just said. "At least theoretically."

"Colonel? Your *letter*? What happened to the majority of your force?"

"A soul graft. Radical. Experimental. But *possible,* my surgeon informs me. All that is required is a volunteer of stout Christian conviction who will donate just a trifle of his own soul for seed—"

"Colonel?"

"Yes? Quite." He killed his flask and tossed it aside. "The troops. You are fascinating. A real head for protocol. Always unexpected in women of more obvious charms."

"Where are the three hundred?"

"I'm getting peckish. Should I call the lieutenant? He could bring us a light refreshment."

"Your letter said a force of three hundred."

"Three hundred?" His eyes clouded suddenly. "Yes, of course. Collateral, I'm afraid. Unavoidable." He scrambled for the flask, tipped it to his extended tongue, then chucked it away again.

"I count sixty-nine, Colonel," I said. "Just sixty and nine. Would you say that's a fair assessment of your present force?"

"Quite fair."

"We got just shy of that number in young warriors ready to tussle."

"Do you?"

"What happened?"

"Pardon?"

"To your men. Your army? Where are they?"

"Detained. Indefinitely."

"Dead?"

"If you like."

My heart soared. "How?" I asked, unable to wrestle the smile from my lips.

He told me an "indigenous wraith" was the culprit. A "blue devil" he also called it. His whole description took on a spectral cast, as if he were describing something he had heard from an unreliable but still compelling source. Not something he had seen firsthand with his own unbelieving eyes.

"The *speed* with which he moved . . . the biting, the *tearing* was the most disturbing. I don't recollect him employing his weapons at all. They seemed to have been repurposed. He was restricted by a kind of hirsute umbilicus, I suppose. Just *tethering* him there. Wave after wave I threw upon him. The product of all those mephitic clouds of black powder seemed to have little effect on him. A real demon hot from the pages of Dante."

I was desperate to know and yet couldn't dare to ask. Finally: "What became of him?" I said quietly.

"The letters of condolence I must write. Wherever will I find such copious rivers of ink?" I snapped my fingers. The colonel winced, focused.

"Did he survive?"

"The devil?"

"Yes. I instructed one of my men to flank him and sever his cord, as it were. Simple logic, really. It was clear the tether was creating an entropic vortex. Cut it and the creature would lose its center. Took nearly two hundred men to do it. But finally we prevailed."

"And then?"

"Then? He did what devils do. He disappeared. In a ponderous yet viscous cloud of foul smoke and brimstone."

His deluded answer was the best I could hope for. Lucid truth might have crushed me. Was he still out there? If I sunk my fingers into the earth, could I still somehow *feel* him? I had to let such theories go. A Lightning would want me to do no less. I had the future of the People on my shoulders.

"I was wondering, Colonel. Would you consider a third alternative?"

"To relocation?"

"To butchering."

"No harm will befall them if they calmly comply."

"My concern is for *your* men, sir. What about just leaving the People alone."

"Sorry?" he said, cocking an ear in my direction.

"Leave them alone. Just take your men and ride away."

"Impossible."

"Why?"

"I've given my word. In writing. Surely you've read it. And that poor lad's ear . . . Most unfortunate," he said, righting himself suddenly. "And I am an officer in the United State—rather, the *Confederate* Army."

"It seems to me the bite's been taken out of your argument."

"Are you saying they will *not* comply?"

"I'm saying reconsider. For your own safety."

"My men would have no recourse should they resist. You see, their rifles are already loaded, and they get rather testy if they are not hotly discharged."

"I think we're all done here, Colonel."

"Have I made my position clear?"

"Perfectly."

Stares The Night's face was sullen but still game when he caught my eye as I left the lodge. I noticed he and the other braves had their weapons ready. At their sides I saw a sliver of bow, a quiver strap over a shoulder, a glint from a trade axe. I gave an almost imperceptible jerk of my head. Stares The Night ducked away from his gang and came toward me.

"Lieutenant! Alternate contingency! These creatures have decided against a peaceable relocation. Redress your lines. Prepare for engagement."

Stares The Night was close enough to kiss as he stood next to me. He looked at me with a confused expression. I could feel my lips brush the tiny spurs of the sutures around his wounded ear as I whispered to him. "They'll be slow reloading their rifles after their first volley. Be sure to duck." I saw the front line of the soldiers tense their trigger fingers, their lips blackened as they tore their packets of powder, ready to reload. "Kill 'em," I whispered in my best Lakota. "Kill 'em all!"

"But the women, Gravy," Stares The Night whispered back fiercely. "The *women* decided we should not fight."

"Ain't I a woman?"

# Chapter Forty-Seven

Birch burns with a civilized cologne. There is no hint of wilderness in it as with piñon or apple. While it burns, one cannot help but be reminded of silver tea services and leather easy chairs, ironed newspapers and proper beds. For that reason, it made sense why the colonel would have insisted upon it as his fuel of choice. And a few of these logs were some of the only things left after we had finished with the colonel and his men. There were several ponies left alive. But only one that would suit the shaky equestrian skill of Henry Road. He protested at first, riding an animal with a U.S. brand so brazen upon its rump. But then he quieted. I reckon it was the bodies that had done it, for the boys were not gentle in the taking of their trophies. That, or what he had seen me do.

Feeding had become no more emotionally hazardous to me than breaking bread. I no longer struggled through the memories of the dead I swallowed, and I was completely unaware of the impact my depredations had on the warriors who paused in their atrocities to gawk at me. To see a human being, once so round in his individual features, reduced to something as common as ash must have been terrifying, or at least supremely disorienting. How else could I account for the stunned silence of those around me as I fed? Looking up from the throat of a young corporal, I saw the braves move en masse away from me. A few muttered prayers. Some hissed or even spat at me. Even Road, who had bragged of being immune to anything in nature's extremes, could not look at me. Only Comes At Dawn dared reproach me.

"Stop, Gravy. We will bury the rest with our own dead." Dawn's willingness to bury whites along with his own was all the chastisement I needed to know how far from favor I had fallen. I stood up sheepishly and wiped my mouth, smearing it further with congealed blood and grime. Dawn tore a clean patch from the hem of my skirt and spat in it. Like a mother cleaning the face of her child, the old Indian wiped my face clean and smiled at me.

"I found some of the chief's old clothes," Dawn said, handing me a bundle, "a pair of deerskin leggings and a hair shirt. I have altered them to fit you for your journey. They will suit you better than that frightful rag you're wearing."

So it was good-bye. I swallowed hard as I looked at Dawn's kind face. "Where will you go?"

"North, to the winter camp of the Hunkapapas. We must hurry if we are to catch up to the women and children."

"Let me come. I can help."

"We have hard times ahead of us," Dawn said softly, putting a hand on my shoulder. "But the young men will no longer fight in your shadow. If it is in your heart to help the People, take this white man home. Take *yourself* home."

Those were the last words Comes At Dawn ever said to me. I changed into A Lightning's clothes and saddled my horse, packing it with pemmican and robes. When I was mounted, Stares The Night approached me and patted the velvet of my horse. I wanted to join him on the ground, wrap him in my arms with a deep, motherly hug. At least chuck him on the chin and hope he might return my smile. But he was a man now. And I was what I was. Distance was the most appropriate parting gift I could offer him.

"You have honored us, Gravy," he said solemnly. "You have taught me what was not yours to teach, but I will never forget you." I nodded, choking back my tears, and turned my horse east, motioning for Road to follow.

Road was quiet now over our fire, chewing on venison gristle from the haunches of a deer I had brought down.

"They are a wonderful people," he said. "I can understand why you will miss them." I poked the fire and said nothing. "I couldn't help but notice we are rather lightly provisioned for such a long journey. Will you be joining me at mealtime or—"

"Eat your supper, Mr. Road."

I watched as an uncomfortable revelation, though unconfirmed, pummeled the pink inside his head. He swallowed and quickly changed the subject. "So the painting, my portrait of the chief was—"

"A kind of cartographer's effort, I'd guess you'd say." Even with our breath fogging, the air seemed to chill further. English sounded flat and unmusical to my ears.

"I thought I recognized a similarity between you two. Something in the eyes. You sure you won't have some of this?" He cut a slice from the carcass, holding the meat toward me on the knife. I shook my head.

"Of course. You already . . . *Tell* me, will it hurt? I mean, when you get hungry again? I don't suppose you could alert me to the—"

"You'll be asleep. You won't even know I'm doing it."

"What if I can't sleep?"

"Everybody sleeps, Mr. Road. Eventually." I saw the meat enter his lips, the idea of it beginning to change as his chewing slowed. He tossed what remained in the fire.

"Will I have the morning to look forward to or . . .?"

"Right now we have a long journey ahead of us. You ready to turn in?"

"I hoped we might chat awhile. I seem to be wide awake." I reached into the colonel's saddle bags and tossed him a flask.

"Go easy on that stuff," I said. "It needs to last." He fumbled with the screw cap then quaffed it gratefully.

"You know, Miss Shinnecock, I don't recall if I ever offered my gratitude for your willingness to offer me escort."

"No, you haven't," I said, watching him swallow. "And I ain't offering you escort. I'll provision you because you're here to do the same for me. But I'm headed East for my own reasons."

"And what would those reasons be, if I may inquire?"

"Let's just say I have an itch to scratch in the form of one Miss Brown."

"Is she like you, this Brown character? As formidable as you?"

"You might say that. You could also say she has a nasty habit of taking things that ain't hers."

"I see. So your unfinished business with her is… *terminal* in nature."

"That depends on her. But things could get sticky, yes." He nodded, pursing his lips as he avoided my gaze. "You don't happen to have a square of chocolate handy, do you?" I asked, changing the subject.

"Chocolate?"

"Only other thing I ever get a craving for."

"I usually keep a stash for the kiddies, but I fear I'm fresh out."

"Pity."

I watched his throat pump greedily as he drank. His eyes were watering when he finally faced me. "You don't mind if I speak freely, do you?"

"Say what you need to say."

"It's just, how shall I put this? After seeing you under the full sail of your particular condition, I must admit to never having witnessed an appetite so . . ."

"What?"

"Elevated, I suppose. So pure. Tell me, do soldiers taste different than say—"

"Artists?" He laughed then took another pull from his flask. "Only the flesh is varied, Mr. Road. Blood is . . . what's the word?"

"Common?"

"Ecumenical."

I shot him a look I hoped might calm him. He leaned back on his packed effects, burrowing into the alcohol's warm abstraction. "I remember reading Catlin as a younger man," he said. "His adventures among the natives. I wonder what he would have made of you."

"If you're set on telling my story, make sure you're good and drunk. No one will believe you sober."

"They would if they saw you in action."

"Then they wouldn't have long to look."

He tipped his flask to his tongue, then shook it weakly. "Please tell me you have more of this stashed somewhere."

"I told you to go slow." His voice had lost its panic, but his eyes were alert. He still had questions. My look let him ask them.

"Were you born this way?" he asked.

"No. *Sired*, they call it. When I was younger."

"So you're not as fresh as you seem?"

"Hardly."

"Did you . . . die? In Goethe's story—"

"That's the one thing we *don't* seem to be very good at."

"You know you really should do something with it."

"Like what?"

"Oh, I don't know. Decide if you look better in blue or gray and lead those lucky bastards to certain victory."

"I don't cotton much to the military mind."

"So I've seen. The stage then. Clearly you're a natural at appearing to be what you're not. I'm friends with some rather influential people in New York. Laura Keane would adore you."

The idea seemed familiar. I stirred the fire.

"No, Mr. Road. I have become, as of late, increasingly reconciled to the unique demands of my nature."

"It really would help me, both of us actually, if you kept talking. Right now I feel as wide awake as a cat on a hot griddle."

"I don't know any lullabies."

"Then tell me what it's like to be you. To be *like* you. You have no idea, for a man of my temperament, how fascinating your situation is."

It seemed the only way I would get him to come down was to keep jawing. So I took a deep breath. "My situation? It's really no different in its development than anyone else's. There's a birth. An adolescence. And I'm realizing now, a maturity."

"Birth?"

"Like a baby, when you're new to the change, when you're stupid and constantly disoriented and in the greatest need of nurturing, that's when the beguiling is the strongest. When our food, like a baby, is chosen for us."

"How?"

"By appearing to our prey as the thing they desire the most. It's a difficult stage in the condition. You take your victim gracefully, in a mutual embrace. But you are haunted by your victim's memories. You see what they have lost as though through their own eyes."

"Fascinating," he said with little fascination.

"But that fades as you grow stronger and the Beguiler becomes more resolute." I swallowed hard, thinking of the infant Caleb or Caroline I had once carried. His artist's eyes perhaps saw the depth of my sudden regret. His face softened.

"I was with child once," I said haltingly, hating myself for being so seduced by my sorrow and still tempted by the thought of setting my deepest regret free.

"What happened to it?" he whispered.

"The Beguiler took it," I said as steadily as I could. "It is a fierce opportunist. Relentless in fulfilling its needs. Like the rest of us, I suppose. Only more so."

"It sounds horrible," he whispered. "I am so sorry."

I wiped the tears from my eyes. "That's when you finally mature, Mr. Road," I said, staring into the fire. "When you realize life, in all its desperation to survive, poses one simple question that we are horribly unqualified to answer."

"Which is?"

"Are we all merely passengers on the back of some great and lumbering creature called existence?"

"I don't follow."

"Do we really ever have a choice in things? Are we ever truly responsible for the boons and dire consequences of our deepest natures? If that is true, then all we have is our willingness to either embrace or repel what we got no damn control over." I saw him smile through the dancing flames of our fire.

"In other words," he said, "we live life as much as it lives us."

He nodded off when the sky was still full dark. I dragged him to his tent, then sat by the dying fire. I would not need its light to see by. I removed my mother's letter from my moccasin. Already this tiny missive had survived more miles and mishaps than any proper letter should.

*Emma.*

Had I heard my old name whispered, or was I reading the envelope in my mind? Black, stained, tattered and worn, showing all the age and effects of circumstance I no longer could, it was the last of my history. The last thing I had left to lose. I opened it and removed the folded contents. The words were looped in her severe copperplate.

*The sweetest honey is loathsome in his own deliciousness.*
*And in the taste confounds the appetite.*

I knew the quote, *Romeo and Juliette*. I also knew the quote was not complete, that the friar's admonition to the two impetuous lovers ended with: *Therefore love moderately. Long love doth so.* And my mother was meticulous with her citation. Her omission was as good as an emphasis. I took her final words to me as a truce, an acknowledgement, if not an approbation, of my unbidden extremes. Regardless of my history, had I become a Beguiler or not, I would always have run free in the open grass at risk to my elbows and knees. As a woman in the company of men, both those who paid and those who loved by contract, I would have always hazarded being regarded as someone I was not. And if I had sensed love in my heart, either of the body as with A Lightning or of the mind as with Hegey, I would always have risked revealing the ugliness of myself. My stranger had been right after all. Circumstance can either heighten or hinder us. It is never meant to define us. I thought that was the end of her long-in-coming message to me until I saw a scrawl at the bottom of the page slowly appear from the heat of the fire. Invisible ink. Still reactive after all it had been through.

*You will survive, Emma, because the fire inside you burns brighter than the fire all around you.*

I hugged the letter to me, crushing it against my chest as my tears flowed freely. I missed her more than I ever had before.

"Good-bye, momma," I said to the dancing flames. Then I threw the letter into where she had been, and I, if her last words were true, would never go.

In the moondark, the snow was gray in its endless sheets. My footfalls echoed back to me, close and dull, as if I walked in a closed room. The felted plain curled up to the distant mountains but betrayed no distance, no time. The wolves were silent. If life stirred, it was in burrows, cottoned beneath my feet. Road was whiskey-dream deep when I entered his tent. Even under three buffalo robes and fully dressed, I heard his teeth clink in his sleep from the cold. I stripped quickly and stole beneath his covers. He came to me, boyish, as if I were no more than good weather, a pleasant front come to keep him warm and steady in his dreams. I rolled to my back and pressed his head to my chest, my arms around him as his breath continued its deep rhythm.

A test of what could have been.

What kind of mother would I have made? What kind of tenderness could I ever have taught? Love was the one force that did not require evidence of its effect. Effects could be misleading. The proof of love was only in loving. My tongue opened a rent in Road's throat just south of his jaw. I perfumed my feast this time, feeding him dreams of the French whores he knew as a student. In return, his history stuttered behind my closed eyes, and I was grateful for the distraction, the low burlesque, the high art. He was a man so much more palatable in slumber. Why wasn't I born with such a prodigious talent like his, that even a slothful betrayal of it would not dim its flower? Or was that what it truly means to be a Beguiler?

I snuck out at dawn before he roused and had the bark tea boiling and some partridges already frying when he came out into the morning. Sparks from the fire took to the air in a quarrel of bright and starry bees.

"I had the most startling dream last night," he said, rubbing his swollen face. "I dreamt that—"

"*You* didn't do the dreaming, Mr. Road." His hand shot to his neck reflexively. His smile was tentative, then warm.

"I'll be goddamned," he said, looking at his clean fingers. "And my visions?"

"Free of charge."

"Seems a more than equitable exchange. *And* breakfast? My God, you'll spoil me." Then he saw them. "What the hell are *those* things doing there?"

Our little camp was encircled by a phalanx of eleven buffalo cows. A hoofed herd of steaming fur. Their usual stink was beaten down by the thick mantle of snow they wore, and their breath billowed in the hard air.

"They came after I dropped these birds," I said. "Protecting their calves, I reckon."

"From what?"

"From me. They sense peril, some kind of predator, and they didn't press out their babies last spring just to have them laid down come winter. They'll move along once their calves get a gutful of whatever they can grub."

The cows had no intention of moving. Even when Road approached one, she only walled her eye to white when he sunk his fingers through the crust of snow on the beast's back.

"My God, she's so warm. I can feel her heart. It's racing."

"You're scaring the tar outta her. Come on. These bird's are burning."

"But still she stands there. Is the instinct really so strong?"

"Didn't your momma put up with your nonsense when you were young?" He slowly removed his hand, then warmed it in the hot breath from its nose.

"I must preserve this," he said. "Have you seen my pencils? Would you mind?"

"Me?"

"It would add incredible perspective to the scene."

"You want to render me with a bunch of frightened old cows?"

"Unless you'd be willing to oblige me in another way."

I agreed to let Road paint me because I had nothing to gain or lose. And I was curious what it would feel like to be under his gaze. Would it sting or soothe? And could I still tell the difference? At first he considered a Diana, but the idea of me as huntress was too obvious for the subtleties of his brush. Then Judith, a westernized Judith, but with whose head clutched in my vengeful fingers?

The colonel's? The *chief's*? Then we settled. An odalisque. He walked me through a brief history of the feminine profession, trilling out peppery descriptions of seraglios and imperial harems.

"So you reckon me to be some kind of Arab whore?"

"We'll drop historical pretext and do something like Goya's *La maja desnuda*. Ever seen it? My God, what frankness. And such an incredible piece of ass."

"I think I prefer the whore."

"Done. I'll paint you as an *American* odalisque. Exalted in her allure. Power reclining."

"But you'd still be seeing my hardware, right?"

"To the Greeks nudity connoted kinship with the gods. Or am I too liberal with my flattery? Your fervid natural state will seem your right, your honor. The truth of your skin will glisten like fur, will glow with the same pacific honesty as your eyes."

"I bet *that* line got your clock wound more'n a time or two. Why don't you just say you want to paint a dirty picture?"

He stopped. Squinted. Grinned. "All right. I want to paint a dirty picture."

We traveled at night. Slept in the mornings. Which left only the afternoons for Road's work. This made him ornery at first, as he preferred the less direct light of the early part of the day. I could feel Brown in my quiet moments, more a general sense of her interest in us than direct knowledge of her vicinity, and I was anxious to settle with her. But not that anxious. She was waiting for something. I just wasn't sure what.

Being short of supplies, Road told me he had to make the most of the canvases he had, so I was painted onto the back of his portrait of A Lightning. He stretched the blank side of the painting on a frame of thin lodgepole pine, so the image of the man I had loved stood before me as I posed. Road was a master of manipulating his sitter's mood, and I could only think he did it on purpose. He had several canvases of less familiar likenesses he could have repurposed for my portrait. It was the longing in my eyes, inspired by the image of him, that Road needed to elevate my portrait from pornography to something close to poetry.

Road's pockets were magical things, producing all sorts of inspiring minutiae: a rock with the same concavity as a woman's waist, a thimble's weight of bird's skull, bits of crayon and chalk. He would fumble with one of these items in silence, his mind almost audibly clicking, then he would move my image around on his canvas, first in languid sweeps of his blackening thumbs, finally committing the line with his chalk. Occasionally we'd speak.

"Aren't you cold?" he said.

"Hmmm?"

"Cold? Don't you feel it?" My nipples were aroused, but that was more from his steady scrutiny than the temperature.

"Cold? No. I feel it. I'm just not threatened by it, I guess."

"That sounds marvelous," he said, shivering.

"Comes in handy if you're sitting out here naked as brass in the dead of winter." He chuckled at what he called my "gameness." Then an hour would pass in silence. I could feel the animal of his gaze, something kept pure from his personality. It was a blessed intimacy. Then nothing, just waiting. Then a spark would fire in his brush as he began moving with more purpose.

"The most alluring parts of a woman aren't what you would expect," he said. "They are the paths to those places. The descending dunes of the belly. Precipice of the shoulder. That patch of fair skin at the sides of the eyes."

"Then why is your brush still moving in them slow red circles?"

He raised his gaze from my chest and grinned. "Damn. You caught me."

Then hours of just the scratch of the brush.

"Leonardo always painted his subjects under a white sheet to diffuse the light. Have you read Vasari?"

"Nope."

"He would have loved a sky like this. A glorious winter sky. Only bitch is these washes won't dry. That's all I got today."

I built the fire, cooked the meat I'd caught. He'd hold the portrait away from the hottest part of the flames, just close enough so the portrait would be tacky enough to take the next day's work. When the sun went down, we'd continue our nightly travels. The sky seemed somehow hollow, and in the distance, under the placid stars, we could hear the low concussion of exploding shells as we rode farther east.

"Emma," he said one morning, "when we finally find Brown, when your mission, as it were, is finally complete. Will you kill me? I know we got off on the wrong foot when we first met. And frankly, I have regretted my general conduct toward you." Looking at him, all his bluster and bad manners seemed puddled at his feet. He was nothing more than a shaggily bearded child with mortal terror in his eyes. I answered him as tenderly as I could.

"Well, Mr. Road, I seem to have a bad habit of speeding the demise of only men I have loved," I said. "And while you have many estimable qualities, I figure I don't rightly *like* you well enough to kill you." His relief was palpable.

"I have never been so heartened to be found so frankly low in one's esteem, Miss Shinnecock."

One crisp midmorning, about ten miles west of the Ohio River, we were in a snowy glade of bare birch trees, me reclined on a cold lounge of deadfall, Road bundled in his buffalo robe. His pauses between brush strokes had grown more frequent, and I noticed he had not replenished his brush for several minutes.

"Brother," I said finally, "either your inspiration has stalled or pieces of you are about to break off from this cold." He looked up, startled, shedding whatever halting thoughts had been delaying him.

"What? No. It's finished," he said, dropping his brush and blowing on his fingers. "It's actually been finished for the better part of an hour." I sat up and slipped on my buckskin shirt and leggings and was about to join him in front of the painting when he held up a hand to stop me. "Please, Emma," he said with an embarrassed smile, "I must admit to no little trepidation in your perusal of it." It was interesting how formal he became when he was working.

"Why?"

"It's an intimate thing. Not unlike sex—save the final consummation, if you'll allow me, is ever so much more delayed. And far more devastating if not satisfactory." I stood up and walked slowly toward him. When I was mere inches from the back of the canvas, he stopped me again with a laughing smile. "This last month with you has been the best of my life. You have proved an exceedingly rare and compelling companion. I know you don't think the same of me, and for reasons you've articulated, that is in some ways a welcome relief. But I think the world of you, Miss Emma May Shinnecock, and want more than anything . . ." He grabbed my arm and pulled me around to face the portrait. "Aw, hell, sister. Just say you *like* it!"

"My Lord," I whispered. "Is that supposed to be me?"

"You like it," he said with a relieved smile. I could only nod my head.

He had kept the winter setting with its deep shadows and diffused light. There was only a faint delineation between the shade of my winter-faded skin and the tone of the snow. A stark contrast in the darkness of my hair, where he had found reds and sultry purples in the black of my tresses. My gaze was frank, arresting, with a mystery and a confidence I never felt inside. The blue of my eyes? Surely, I had kept the hunger and wildness from them in walking life. How had he found them? My body seemed reposed, natural in the cold setting. Then how did he capture the predatory tension in my shoulders and thighs? I was beautiful but still somehow forbidding. Was I an animal with pretenses toward the human? Or a mere woman harboring a goddess? Road was delighted.

"You don't recognize yourself?"

"Not at all, brother."

"Then I have succeeded. I was never going for a mere likeness. Beauty is too narrow, and truth too relative."

"So what the hell were you aiming for?"

"The Beguiler."

# Chapter Forty-Eight

At the dogleg of the Ohio we caught a captured stern-wheeler headed to the Union capital so Road could deliver his canvases. (My portrait would never pass muster under the current censors. But I thought some day, when things relaxed a little bit, that dual portrait of the chief and I might fall into a collector's hands and perhaps, under gaslight or sunlight or very sympathetic moonlight, our images would once again mingle and so forever keep us as one.) This rebel vessel had once been christened *Tuscaloosa Tessy,* running cotton and molasses to Southern ports before she had been surrendered at Sharpsburg. Her decks were still sticky with sugared tar and fibers, even though considerable effort had been made to scrub the commerce out of her. And poorly gold-leafed over her previous moniker was her new name, *Mary Todd*. Her lines were neatly coiled and faded tricolor bunting rattled in the cold wind from the lip of her upper deck. She ran Union guns now, single cap-and-shot, the odd barrel of hardtack, and foreign dignitaries who didn't rate first class hospitality with Secretary Seward and the Lincolns. For such people she had but one cabin that could be mistaken for luxurious. It was a scuffed beadboard box with a big bed of pulled brass and a tattered chenille coverlet embroidered with a fuzzy eagle and the words *Union Forever!*

We had emerged from our years of living among the People looking like scat shat from the sphincter of creation. With me in my buckskin and greasy braids, the skipper was reluctant to even give us passage. At the extremis of his Christian charity, he finally offered to billet us in the hold. At which suggestion Road produced a creased and yellowed document, too weather-beaten to be deciphered but, which Road confidently explained, confirmed him as an agent of the U.S. government, and only the ship's best accommodations would do.

"And who's this raggedy-ass half-breed you got with you?" the skipper wanted to know.

"My *mother*," Road said without hesitation. I hid my smile by keeping my head down. "She's been on a mission of charity for the past several years, teaching the western heathens the finer points of digging latrines."

"You mean them reddies don't shit in no holes?"

"Absolutely not," Road said, edging to a conspiratorial tone. "They relieve themselves in their hands, where augurs of the coming day are read, then saved as projectiles to assault any vulgar white men too intrepid with their questioning."

"She gonna chuck a turd at me?"

"Mother dear was once enchanted by their native ways, I'm obliged to say. Luckily, I was able to break her of the habit. I assume this reeking barge is in possession of the proper facilities?"

"We got a bath tub below," the captain said eyeing me. "But that's strictly for—"

"Capital!" Road beamed. "Now I think a scalding bath is in order for mommy dear. Followed by rigid spirits for me."

The bath was a repurposed pig trough in a closet not far from our room, whitewashed with lead paint. I undressed as the tub filled with hot, pink water from the boat's rusting boiler. I could sense movement on the decks above me as I settled into my bath. Men's voices, the weight of their bodies on the boards. I could smell their tobacco, their poor whiskey, all woven through the distant thunder of exploding ordnance miles away. But soaking in it was not as soothing as I'd hoped. I kept thinking of Hegey and the homey decadence of his exquisite chocolates and floral scented baths. His beautiful dressing gowns and ridiculous smoking caps. The conversations we had. The fights. The love. All the changes we made together. I missed him. I hoped wherever he was, he was happy. And the stark contrast between those sweet memories and my spartan accommodations laid me low. But that wasn't all that was nagging me. The stillness of that little water closet was not to my liking. Something wasn't right. My melancholy lifted as I became aware of a sudden disturbance in the atmosphere. A kind of tympanic dampening of sound that buried the movements above me in an aural fog. Only one sound was reaching my ears. The baritone thump of a beating heart that I could not only hear but feel pulsing in a kind of counter rhythm inside me. The sound finally forced my own heartbeat into cadence with it, synchronizing in me a dread and a vague excitement. No purely human heartbeat could have forced mine to follow its rhythm. Was is possible? Was it time? I drew myself from the bath, my senses singing with anticipation, as I pulled my filthy buckskins over my wet body.

A ghostly fog shrouded the empty deck as I crept to the port side of the bow. The Potomac ahead was frozen solid. Crouched on the ice, in worn great coats, shawls over their shoulders and heads, were what looked like the majority of a mobilized Union platoon, all piling wood directly on the hard surface of the river. Peppered for a quarter of a mile were hundreds of glowing cones of light, small kerosene-and-scrap-wood fires, lit there to hurry the melt. For a moment it looked as if the night sky had fallen to earth. That the world had turned upside down. Then I noticed the shattered glass of the wheelhouse. Blood flecked on the fractured panes. I smelled it. Hot berry punch. Still fresh. I walked cautiously toward the steps that led to the wheelhouse.

"Fancy a wee tuck in before we begin, my duck?" There it was. That old grating brogue. Brown leaned casually on the boat's railing. The blood on her lips was black in the moonlight. So it was possible. It was time. Why, then, was I still surprised to see her? My legs begged me to move. But my eyes would not leave her. In my mind was a flurry of feelings. Hatred and sadness. Even a little fear. But all these feelings seemed somehow rusted over. As if too much time had passed. "Go on up for yer kip, darlin'. I'll wait." I swallowed hard. My breathing became shallow.

"Begin what, Miss Brown?"

"What ye come for. What I *called* ye here for," she said with a dry chuckle.

"*Called* me here?"

"Bonny Christ, child. I been calling ye for ages, now. Ain't you heard me?"

"No."

"Damn me, if the beguiler ain't wasted on ye. Don't ye think it a tad...*convenient* we be here together just now? At the same time? On the *same* ruddy boat? Ye think events like that just *happen*, do ye?"

"I don't know."

"Well, then," she said turning to me. "That's what I so dearly love about ye, Emma. How ye go about with yer eyes wide and yer wee thumb stuck in ye mouth. Go on. Get some blood in ye gut. I don't be wantin' no unfair advantage on ye."

"I think I'll pass. I don't much care for the blood of the dead."

"Yer talkin' about yer Da, ain't ye," she said with a tilt of her head. "Sad bit of business that. Perhaps yer right.

Perhaps I did end him a bit prematurely. After all, I did give the poor man my word. And I do so value my word. But as ye know. Ye can't break a promise to dead man. But all the same," she said with a mischievous twinkle in her eye, "*he* ain't dead. Not yet."

"Who?"

"Go on up and find out."

The captain's body was barely recognizable as human when I entered the wheelhouse. Both his hands still gripped the helm, torn from his arms at the wrist. Legs broken and flopped at wrong angles. His throat had been slashed clear down to the top of his chest. But from the wound, red bubbles burst as he took his last labored breaths. Only one of his eyes had the power widen as I dropped my body over him.

When I finished, my muscles sang beneath my skin. Having only sipped on Road durning the months of our crossing, I had forgotten what a deep feed could do. I floated down the wheelhouse stairs and stood squarely, facing Brown, with as much defiance as I could muster.

"There ye be!" Miss Brown laughed. "All topped up and brimming with spunk. Seems a pity to waste all that energy on just chit chat. But that's what we do. We women. Men fight and fuck with no thought of the consequences. While we *negotiate*."

"Not always," I said. "Where's Road?"

"The painter fella? I let him go."

"Why?"

"Because he paid me to do so."

"Paid you? With what?"

"This," she said with grin. She reached down to a tube of rolled canvass that was tied to the top of a valise near her feet. I knew what it was immediately.

"No."

"Ah, yes! I would have spared a *thousand* lives to possess this beauty."

"Give it back!" I reached for the painting. But she caught my hand and held it fast.

"Now, now. None of that," she chortled. She pushed my fist, trying to bend my arm. But I would not budge. "This here is mine. *My* private joy," she grinned. "And what a joy it is, sweet Emma, to see you like that. Layin' there, bold as brass, with nothing to hobble the imagination as to your *real* charms."

"That's as close as you'll ever get to *my* charms, bitch!" I said. She laughed and relaxed her grip, freeing my hand.

"Well, now. Seems I've already had a taste of 'em. *Twice,* I recollect. But you're right. A taste is nay a feast. So here is my offer."

"Give it back! Or I swear to Christ I'll—" She pressed her finger to my lips .

"You ain't heard my offer yet." I snapped open my mouth and gnashed my teeth, barely missing her finger as she yanked it away. "I'll *give* ye the painting," she continued. "I will. But in exchange, you must eat what's in me case."

"No," I said. Brown's eyes flashed with fury.

"Open that case, you stubborn brat! Or I swear I'll shred this painting to bits!" It was all I had of him. All that was left of A Lightning. The thought of him crushed in her mottled paw made weak with fury. But I could do nothing.

"Fine. We both know what's in that case. What's your deal?"

"You eat it. *All* of your sire's heart and go back to being your old obliging self."

"Is that all?" I asked.

"No," she said, her tone slightly softening. "Then you must come away with me."

"*What*?" I chuckled.

"And if I ever get my fill of you, I promise, I'll let you go on your way. No worse off than you were before this whole damned affair began." She couldn't be serious.

"That's *it*? That's your *price*? To make me weak?"

"You were never weak, Emma."

"I could never love you." Her eyes glazed when I said that. Had I actually hurt her?

"*Love* me? Ach, child. Love ain't worth a dead man's pecker," she muttered dismissively. "Just a token. Just a kind glance every now and then. That's all I'd be asking for." Her tone was firm but sincere. And the thought of finally ending this was tempting. Could I trust her?

"Why I gotta eat the heart?" I asked.

"Why? Because I'd need assurances. Because I'm weary of chasin' ye. Just like you're weary. And I can't rightly pull out *your* heart and eat it *and* keep you as a companion.

You follow, ye dizzy sow? Or need I make it plainer?"The sudden irritation in her voice made me blink.

"Then keep it."

"What? You really think I'd let you feed if I wanted anything more than what I'm askin'?"

"Keep the painting. I don't need it."

"Saints be damned, child. Don't you know a stalemate when you see it? Look at us. Both fresh from the feed. Both strong as heaven's own bulls. Where's my advantage in that?"

"I'll risk it. You can follow me until the trumpet sounds. I don't need you. I have memories of the real thing. And what I felt for him, what *we* shared, you could *never* hold in your spotted little hand."

"*Damn* me, if you ain't the most infuriating woman God ever shat into creation!" she spat. "You sayin' you *don't* want it?"

"Not at *that* price."

"You're bluffin.'"

"We're all done here."

"I'll do it!" She tightened her grip on the canvass and cocked her arm to throw it.

"If that were true, Miss Capability Brown, you'd of done it by now. I'll see you in hell." My face showed nothing, but my heart was in my throat when I turned from her. I wanted that painting in the worst way. But I wouldn't be suckered by her again.

Only the faintest sound of what could have been a small bird in flight arrested my steps. I turned to see the tightly rolled canvass arch into the night, flashing brightly in the moonlight, before it skittered soundlessly on the the far edge of the ice.

"You *bitch*!" I hollered as I sprinted over the boat's railing.

"I *knew* you were bluffin'!" Brown shouted as I fell. I landed, then slipped, falling hard onto the ice. I had barely got my feet under me when Brown came crashing down next to me. She scrambled to tackle my legs. But I managed to kick her squarely in the jaw. I heard it crack.

"You should have *shredded* it! Like you threatened!" I laughed over my shoulder. I hunkered low as I found my feet. With my predator's eyes, I could see the canvas in the distance, teetering on the edge of a hole the soldiers had managed to cut through the ice. I began to skate after it when I was brought down hard from behind, falling on my face. My legs went numb as I felt Brown's furious weight shatter my lower back.

"How the bleeding Jesus do ye *tear* a thing with *one* hand?" she slurred, her jaw still healing. I squirmed with all my might beneath the grip of her thighs, twisting my body with the help of the ice until I was facing her. She delivered a blow to my nose so powerful I saw whole galaxies of stars.

"You use your *teeth,* you stupid cow!" I managed to say through the blood cascading down my face. My legs back in service, I managed to deliver a blow to her back with my knee that sent her sprawling like a baby ox. I was back on my feet in an instant, swooshing toward the canvas with all my speed. Soldiers skittered out of my way as if a human cannon ball was flying before them. And there, in my periphery was Brown. Skating expertly now in her little ankle boots over the ice.

"I'm a woman of word, Emma," she shouted as she skated next to me. "You *know* that. Let's just settle this thing like sensible females."

"Go to hell." I doubled my speed as the faces of shocked soldiers blurred past me. But Brown was quick and would no let me get the lead.

"When have I ever broken my word to ye?" she said, her red hair writhing in the wind. "Think on that. Can you honestly say the same?" The canvas was in sight. I sprinted toward it with every ounce of my strength. "*My offer is the best you can ever do!*" she shouted into the frosty air that rushed past my ear. I dropped to my knees and deftly slowed to a stop near the canvas. I snatched it to my chest and stood up just as Brown skidded to a stop next to me. Our heavy breathing fogged thickly as we both leaned on our knees, catching our breaths. "Why are ye so set on stayin' like you are?" she asked breathlessly. "It's never done ye no good. My God, girly. Thanks to your damed beguiler, ye've killed everyone ye've ever loved."

"You've had more than a fair hand in that."

"Not I," she said with a deep breath. "*Never* have I raised a hand against ye that was not fair in the exchange. Think on it." She pulled me up from my slouch over my knees. Patting my back as my breathing slowed. "Poor Eben and your misbegotten babe? I had no hand in that.

The Roses offered you the warmth of their hospitality, and how did you repay them?" I felt a glimmer of shame at her words and looked away.

"At the coach. You tried to kill me."

"I gave you pause. If my intent had been any other, ye'd not be standing here now." Why the hell were we chatting like old friends?

"You killed A Lightning!" I shouted, sloughing her hand off my back.

"Technically, I but shot him. *You* did the killin'. Or killed the only thing in him he cared for. Worst I could have done was give him the noble death he wanted. You denied him even that. 'Twas *you* what hobbled his manhood," she said steadily, "stole his courage and honor as ye hollowed him down to a desperate shell that was fit only for *your* conflicted heart."

"Maybe."

"Sweet saints, child. I'm standing here like Christ, Himself, offering you naught but peace."

"Peace?"

"Passion, then! A chance to spend a few ticks with a creature who understands and accepts you so well there will never be need for explanations. Or regrets."

"I can't," I said softly.

"But *why*?" she pleaded with a break in her voice.

"I don't know anymore," I said, looking up to the starry night sky. "I honestly don't. Maybe its because I've hated you for so long I can't see you any other way."

"Are you so sure about that?" She moved closer to me, tears running down her freckled cheeks. "Listen to me, Emma. Please. I despise love because I've never known love. You could teach me. You are the most wondrous and confounding woman I've ever known," she said, choking back a sob. "You must be with me. You *must.*" There was not a trace of guile in her eyes. It was as if something had opened in her. A long closed door to the innocent child she must have been once. Frail and soft and full of need. And for one strange moment, she was beautiful. "I wasn't always like this," she said, wiping her eyes roughly. "It was never my dream to run poor and ignorant women in no poxy sportin' house. Serving cheap beer to blokes not fit to lace my boots. Never wanted that life. But then the troubles came, and the Orangemen followed. And good Catholic girls like me were badgered and abused by the bushel. When me Da learned I'd been raped by one o' them, he kicked me from his door. Ruined, he said. Tainted. I was naught but twelve, out on the Dublin streets with only my wits to guard me. I've spent my life kicked from pillar to post," she said with a sad smile. "Knowin' only a counterfeit variety of deep feeling while laying on my back. And sweaty men siphoned away all that was good in me. I know it made me rough. And hard. But that's what I needed to be. And then I saw you that day. Ignorant sprout of a girl, flashing her paps for her Da's liquor like she was born to the game. And I was smitten. And I know I was hard on ye. And rough. But I knew you could take it. But then I watched you fall in love. Not once but *twice.* Two good men held your heart. Something you could never offer old Brown.

And jealousy reared up ugly in me. And I got harder. And rougher. But only because I wanted you so dearly."

"What about Mercy?"

"Ach. Mercy was as thick as pig's arse. You know that well enough."

"I never understood what Eben saw in her," I said with a cold smile.

"That's men for ye," she said, smiling back. "Cunt drunk and post thick the lot of them."

"Maybe you're right," I said tucking the painting into the waist of my leggings.

"Now, ye have yer precious painting. Follow me back to the boat and finish your end of the bargain. Let's end this madness for good." She moved to leave. But I grabbed her hand.

"But if I go back to my born self, you'll just kill me."

"Perhaps. In time, maybe. But even if I do, with the miserable life you've led as a Beguiler, wouldn't that be a kindness?"

"You're right. I *am* ignorant." Her eyes clenched in gratitude as she moved closer to me. "And your offer is more than fair, when I think about it. I've been running too long. Seen and lost far too much."

"There's your sense talking now," she said with a relieved smile. "It's a lovely night. Ye fancy a stroll on the ice? Don't think I can run no more." She tried to pull away, but I would not let her go.

"But you, Miss Brown," I said, looking into her wet eyes, "are standing far too close to me." It was only the catch in her breathing that let me know the viper strike of my other hand had broken through her chest. Her heart raged against my stubborn grip. I looked into her eyes. They were smiling.

"You didn't feel that one, did you duck?" She lowered her eyes to my chest. Looking down I could see just the stump of her wrist protruding from between my breasts. She cackled wetly as her fingers fluttered over my beating heart. "That's the trick, isn't it? Always letting your opponent *think* they have the upper hand. What do you propose we do now? Fondle one another's pumps until doomsday?"

"Then you didn't mean it?"

"Stop it, Emma."

"You really don't want me to teach you?"

"Oh, this is beneath ye. You want me to believe the likes of you could ever care for the likes of me? Come off it."

"You want me I prove it?" Before she could answer I pressed my lips to hers. I intended our kiss to be just a little peck. Just enough to distract her. But she reached her free hand behind my head and pressed me closer in the embrace. Her sour tongue slithered like a toad against mine, making the bile rise in my throat. She broke our kiss with a wet pop.

"Ah," she murmured. "I win again." She slowly eased her hand from my chest. Raising her bloody fingers to her lips, she licked them with relish, grinning. "That's *all* I ever wanted. And you've obliged me. Just like I knew you would." She smacked her satisfied lips and swallowed before addressing me again. "So if you won't let me free you, Emma," she said quietly, "perhaps you would do *me* the courtesy." I tore her beating heart from her chest without another moment's hesitation. She fell into my arms, a smile of pure bliss on her dead lips.

I must confess to some sadness at her passing. Maybe it's just that I wanted to believe she was different in the end. But my relief was greater than my regret. I sat down on the ice near her fallen body and pulled the painting from my waist. I needed to see a loving face. Even if it could no longer love me back. The moon was bright, high in the winter sky as I unfurled it. I could only laugh when I saw it. It was Road's painting of Comes At Dawn. "Touche, Miss Brown," I said aloud. I dragged her body to the edge of the hole and pushed it into the freezing water. I didn't bother to watch it sink into the black depths.

Walking back to the boat, I thought about the price of freedom. And I wondered if maybe Brown didn't get the better end of that bargain.

# Chapter Forty-Nine

It was the time of year the People call The Moon When The Ponies' Hair Grows Long. A bit long winded, perhaps, but far more lovely a name than mere February. The Potomac had been breathlessly cold when I'd rinsed Brown's blood from my fists. With any luck, they won't find her body until spring. I kept Dawn's portrait. I couldn't risk returning to Washington. And maybe it was happier with me. Cautioning me, whenever I looked at, against excessive pride. Making sure I appreciated the magic life still had to offer. After all, I was alone now. I could use the company.

The creek of my girlhood was just as cold as the Potomac. But it was a cold I recognized, an ache I could negotiate with an old confidence, an old innocence. Hollywood was no more, just a burned husk consumed in some forgotten fire that blackly testified to the end of all its earthy vices. I had walked west for nearly a month, and now I was finally home. Snow furred the square foundation I watched Da once build. The barn was a mere hill of whitely covered planks. But the ghosts still frolicked here. My girlhood laughter still rode on the wind.

All this travel had cleaned my sire's heart of its grease when I took it from under my shirt to look at it. But it had not lost its purpose. I'd had a thousand miles to decide my next move, entertained twice as many arguments to revert back to my old self or remain as I was. Should I continue a Beguiler and bend my power to a worthy cause? Or should I eat my sire's heart and learn to fear the cold once more? Should I reap the ineffable future in a skin that will stay fresh for all ages? Or catch the seed of some ruddy swain and tell my stories to my own blinking babes? So many possibilities and only two choices. I knew what my mother would do. I was equally convinced of Da's culinary preference.

Sitting in the cold sunshine on the snowy ground that had once been the main room of our cabin, I remembered how Da and I had once bandied over hearts much smaller and less consequential than the one I held. But his old credo still felt true. I was a betting woman, after all. I reached into the top of my buckskin legging and found the penny. The first penny I'd given Hegey, the one that'd gone unspent until now. It had gone green in the traces. But I could still make out the Indian head on one face of it. *How shall I do this? Heads I eat it? Tails I don't? Is that right? Can I live with that?* I had the luck of a drunkard's daughter. But what good was luck when you truly did not know what you might prefer? Hells bells. That was what the flip was for. I set the coin on the nail of my thumb and took a deep breath.

"Call it," I said aloud as I flicked it spinning into the winter air.

It was not my fist that caught it.

The relief that wracked my body was almost hateful in its violence. When I finally willed my head to turn, A Lightning looked as if he'd been waiting for ages. The shoulders of his Union Army great coat were ringed with circles of salt from months of melting snow. The broad brim of his cavalry hat was faded almost a sky blue from too much sun.

"You're late," he said as he looked into my eyes. There was not a trace of weariness in them. "Didn't you hear me calling for you?" If he was just a vision, I did not want it to ripple away. He pulled me toward him slowly, by degrees, somehow sensing that the truth of him was a tenuous thing, a thing that must be revealed with great care.

"You found me," I said as I confirmed his warmth with my hands.

"What else was I going to do with the eternity you've given me?" He chuckled lightly. "Can't say I care much for the condition of your girlhood home."

"No. I hear there is no life in a square."

"Then we," he said, lifting my face to his, "shall live roundly."

# About the Author

Bradford Tatum has worked as an actor and writer in both film and television. He lives in Los Angeles with his wife and daughter. His first novel, *Only the Dead Know Burbank* was published by HarperCollins in 2016, followed by LO (Soft Moon Press) in 2022. *Hot Berry Punch* is his third novel.

Connect with Bradford at BradfordTatum.com.

Milton Keynes UK
Ingram Content Group UK Ltd.
UKHW010817081123
432193UK00005B/269